BEAUTIFUL

Mess

KASEY LANE

sourcebooks
casablanca

This book is for Niko's family and for every person who has ever felt so frightened they couldn't go on. You are not alone; stay alive. #longlivenikø

Chapter 1

A TATTOO SHOP WAS EXACTLY THE KIND OF PLACE Jami Dillon, a certifiable pearl-clutching, sensible-shoe-wearing attorney at law, didn't belong.

Anymore.

Jami stood in front of the building, staring at the flashing neon sign that read "Tatuaggio" in the window, and realized her brother had lost his ever-loving mind. There was no other way to explain the downward spiral Mason had been on since he'd gone crazy for the tattooed, blue-haired, pierced pinup girl Kevan Landry. His epic pitch off course had started with him quitting his job as CEO of one of the biggest entertainment marketing companies on the West Coast, and now Jami was chasing him into a trendy Hawthorne neighborhood tattoo parlor in Portland.

She could deal with a little idiocy due to increased hormones—her brother was only a man, after all—but this was getting ridiculous. Time to put her foot down before it got too out of control, before everything he'd worked so hard for crumbled into nothing. If Jami didn't get involved, he'd end up a pathetic midthirties hipster grasping for his missed youth through heavy-metal concerts, trophy girlfriends, and tattoos. She'd smack some sense into her Ivy League brother and drag him back to reality. If Mason Dillon was anything, he was logical and ambitious. Like Jami. Solid. Dependable. All business.

Jami straightened her light-brown blazer, smoothed her matching skirt, and gathered her courage for the inevitable battle. It wasn't like she disapproved of his new fiancée. No, just the opposite. Jami liked Kevan very much. When you got past her colorful hair and clothes, and all those tattoos, it was easy to see how Mason had fallen in love with the quirky ball of energy. But he'd moved past the deep end and was currently treading water in a sea of crazy. It was one thing to fall for the girl from the other side of the tracks—it was a completely different thing to turn yourself *into* the guy from the wrong side of the tracks.

Which is how she found herself stomping into the quaint ivy-covered brick building with the Italian word for "tattoo" flashing obnoxiously in the window like some tacky, overly obvious, ink-drenched disco ball.

The moment she pushed through the glass door, she was assaulted by the music of her youth. Metallica's "Ride the Lightning" blared from multiple speakers mounted high throughout the open room. The sound almost drowned out the hum of several tattoo machines busy permanently etching color into the skins of their paying victims. The song momentarily stunned her. She froze as images of another lifetime disinterred themselves from the graveyard of her past. A flash of a door slamming. Tears and crying. The screeching of tires and the sickening crunch of metal bending in unnatural ways. Then the heavy, suffocating darkness. And then nothing.

No. Now was not the time for that. Not after all these years.

The tinkling of the bells over the shop door snapped

her back to the present. She took in the scene while a voice called out, "I'll be right with you. Gimme a second."

It had been over five years since she'd heard that deep, playful sound, but she recognized it immediately. The familiar baritone sent unwelcome shivers down her neck that continued down her spine. Her body responded almost instinctually to the low timbre. Her nipples tightened and long-forgotten desire pooled in her belly. Then her stomach clutched and the room tilted. After all this time. He was right here in Portland.

Jackson Paige.

Jami usually had a quick-witted response for about every imaginable situation. Every scenario except the one where she ran into her college fling in a tattoo shop while attempting to save her brother from impending doom. She glanced around the busy shop and pressed her lips together, quickly trying to assess her next move. Stay and continue with her plan to set her brother straight? Or slowly back out of the shop's lobby and run like hell before she opened a new can of worms? Her gut ached as though someone had punched her.

"Hey, Jami," her brother bellowed across the loud open room and waved her over. Like it was normal for them to be hanging out in a place like Tatuaggio. "Come meet Jax." Her huge brother was leaning over a black, vinyl-covered chair angled mostly away from her, except for his face. Tissue paper covered in purple lines was pressed to his otherwise bare back. Behind him sat the still-recognizable form of his tattoo artist, Jackson freaking Paige.

The long, wide hands that had once so skillfully explored her willing body now smoothed the stencil across Mason's shoulder blades. Jackson's toned arms were covered in colorful tattoos that danced as he transferred the stencil to her brother's torso and then pulled it cleanly off. The corded muscles in his forearms flexed like steel cables. His messy dark brown hair was styled loosely in a rockabilly curl up over his forehead, but one rebellious lock fell forward over his eye.

She knew she should turn and walk—or more likely run—away. Get the hell out before he turned around. But maybe she'd get lucky and he wouldn't recognize her. She'd changed a lot since law school. Maybe it wouldn't matter either way, and his big gorgeous brown eyes wouldn't affect her like they used to. Maybe she'd feel nothing, and the hurt from his disappearance would stay buried, compartmentalized and stored away like all the wreckage of her past.

While she stood there debating the million different ways the scene could unfold, the truth was she couldn't look away, couldn't give up one more chance to admire the way the man's body unfurled—like a lazy but lethal predatory cat—as he stood from the stool and turned, an indolent grin painting his full mouth before he even looked up to see the shop's visitor. And the way his smile froze and his eyes widened as they met hers. It would have been almost comical and she would have laughed—if the adrenaline in her body hadn't picked that exact moment to dump into her bloodstream and increase her pulse to triple its normal rate.

And right away, there it was: the electric connection that sparked the second their eyes met. It zipped down her spine and through her limbs. A real, tangible current that felt both sharp and heavy at the same time, making her feel lighter and needy.

Despite his obvious shock, she had to give Jackson credit for how quickly he schooled his features. He would have made an excellent lawyer. Fleetingly, his eyes widened and his scruffy but irritatingly angular jaw dropped. Then a sexy smirk spread across his lips. Pausing for a second before crumpling the stencil, he tossed it into the trash against the wall without looking to see where the basket was. He made it. Of course.

He continued toward the glass counter, toward her, with the same old deliberate gait. Slow, determined. Most people made the mistake of underestimating Jackson's easy, good-ol'-boy demeanor. But she knew better. He wasn't slow or uninvolved at all. He was always watching, always observing, always waiting. Patient. Like a hunter hiding in his blind, waiting for the perfect moment to strike down his target.

He stood directly in front of her, staring down with that teasing, quiet way he had. The way that made all her girl parts go tingly and her brain fuzzy. With only the glass counter and wooden swing door separating them, she felt too close, too exposed, and too damn raw. Dammit. It wasn't the reaction she wanted or expected from herself. She was bigger than the nonsensical hormones that had ruled her life so many years ago, the stupid emotions the darkly handsome man staring at her had threatened to unleash. Before he'd rocked her world with multiple orgasms and darkly sweet words, only to steal away into the morning without a word.

Jerk. That's what he was.

"Well, well, well." His deep voice rumbled over

her skin and burrowed into her chest, sending little tremors through her body. "If it isn't sweet little JamiLynn Dillon—queen of good manners and all things appropriate."

The air in the room felt stifling, thick, and steamy. Could he see her pulse pounding in her neck or the very unattractive bead of sweat forming on her forehead?

Awesome, counselor. Some cool-under-pressure lawyer I am.

"Jackson." It was all she could say. For once, Jami was at a loss for words. Not just figuratively either. So the "Jax" that Mason and Kevan talked about was none other than her college boyfriend. Her skin felt tight and her world was suddenly entirely too small and uncomfortable.

Jackson's lips twitched and a cloud of doubt—or something that looked a lot like it—passed behind his eyes. Or maybe not. It happened so quickly. And she'd never seen vulnerability in this always-confident man.

"How do you know my sister, Jax?" Mason's back muscles tensed, and his tone changed, became slightly more jagged, cautious. In an instant he transformed back into her overprotective older brother.

Jami cleared her suddenly dry throat. "School."

"We met during my misguided stint in law school," Jackson said, his eyes locked with hers.

It had been five years since she'd seen him last—two since she'd finished up law school and become a corporate law attorney—but his dismissive tone stabbed her heart a little. Screw him. And his beautifully decorated, sinewy forearms. And those damn cow eyes. A memory of him staring down at her, demanding she open her eyes and watch as he drove into her, flashed into her mind. Her neck and face warmed from the flush she knew stained her cheeks.

She shook her head. She wasn't that stupid girl anymore. The wild child she'd once been had been obliterated. Jackson Paige had almost brought her back, but thankfully he'd disappeared before she'd succumbed completely to his charm.

"Funny, she never mentioned you." Mason's voice was pinched, laced with suspicion.

"We barely knew each other. And he dropped out right after we met." She turned her attention back to Jackson, avoiding his hard gaze. "So this is where you ended up? A tattoo parlor."

"Ironically, working on your brother. Imagine that." His gaze flicked to Mason, who sat twisting his head to the side, trying to watch their discussion, confusion etching his usually stoic features.

"And about that. I'd like to have a word with Mason privately."

"Sorry. Too late. You're welcome to sit and talk with him while I start on the outline for his back piece."

"That tattoo is the reason I'm here."

"I have no doubt." He pushed open the swinging door and gestured for her to enter and sit on a chair next to his station. He looked so tall, so handsome, even in his loose, worn jeans and flannel shirt, sleeves rolled up to his elbows. "Come on. We're just getting started." His smile shifted her nerves from simply jangled to outright apoplectic. "You can watch, sunshine," he leaned over and whispered. The bright light from the open windows hid his devil horns under a false halo.

"What are you doing here, Jami?" Mason's deep voice interjected before she could respond to Jackson's nickname for her.

She tried to say something but nothing came out. She stepped past Jackson, trying to avoid touching him. One touch could send her spiraling back into the past, and she wasn't going back there. She could still feel a gravitational pull to him, insistent and undeniable. Even after what he'd done, her body still wanted his. Ridiculous.

"I asked you what you're doing here." Her brother looked to Jackson and back to her, lines of suspicion framing his eyes.

Jackson didn't need to know what he still did to her. And more important, Mason didn't either. Taking a deep breath, she smoothed her features. "What are *you* doing here is the question, big brother." She swept her hand across the room. "Isn't this all getting a little weird and desperate?" When she'd followed Mason here, she'd had every intention of approaching him from a position of pure reason, rather than emotion. He didn't respond well to direct demands or taunts.

Mason snorted, but said nothing as he stared at her. Could he see her reaction to Jackson?

"Well?" she prompted.

"Well, what?"

"What are *you* doing here?"

"Getting a tattoo, Jami," Mason said slowly, as if speaking to a child. Her annoyance increased tenfold. Why couldn't he see what he was so clearly doing?

She resisted the urge to roll her eyes and strangle her brother as she leaned forward to avoid yelling over the music and the buzz of the other tattoo machines at the back of the wide-open shop. "Yes, I see that. I meant, why are you doing all of this? The tattoos? The clubs? Quitting your job? You've changed, and I'm here to stop you from making any more mistakes and screwing up your life any worse than you already have."

The loud roar of Mason and Jackson's combined laughter rolled through the room. Her cheeks warmed and her palms began to sweat. Why was this happening now? Jami prided herself on her competence, her ability to focus on what was important. Only two hours ago she'd found the loophole in a client's intellectual property contract that might save the business over fifty thousand dollars. Totally competent. But when her brother and some bad-boy tattoo artist laughed at her, she turned into a timid little girl being bullied on the schoolyard.

So not gonna happen.

She put her hand on her hip. "You think your reckless journey into an early midlife crisis is humorous? Seems kind of pathetic to me."

"Just because I've decided to start playing by my own rules, and not yours or Mom and Dad's, doesn't mean my life is falling apart. When did you become so judgmental?"

"That's absurd. I'm very open-minded," she said.

Mason chuckled.

She *wasn't* judgmental. She was dependable. Intelligent. Thoughtful. Organized. Not judgmental. Like Mason used to be.

Or was she? She'd stomped all over her brother by barging into the shop. She hadn't even bothered to greet Mason or ask how Kevan was.

For the first time since walking in the door, Jami leaned over to see what foolish mistake Mason was making now. The stencil had left a purple sketch outline of music notes scrolling across her brother's wide back. Even with the barest hint of what the image would be, she could tell it was beautiful. And she knew from experience that Jackson was a gifted artist. The medium he'd preferred years ago had been colored pencils and watercolors, not needles and tattoo ink. Once, he'd even used her body as his canvas.

The buzz of the tattoo machine zapped Jami from her trance. As he dipped the vibrating needle into the small plastic cup, she watched the dark blue—almost black— ink draw up. When Jackson lifted his gaze, their eyes met for a brief moment, and an involuntarily shiver ran up her suit-covered arms and tightened her nipples.

They should add some damn heat to this stupid shop. Might make the customers more comfortable. Jackson's eyes flashed as though he could sense her discomfort, before they dipped down the front of her pale pink silk blouse. He dragged his eyes back up, then chuckled and said, "Ready, buddy? This outline is going to take a while."

Mason sneered. "Bring it." He didn't even flinch when the needle hit his back and began to etch the permanent lines into his skin.

Jami sat, mesmerized by the tattoo slowly appearing. The hum of the tattoo machine, the lines and curves being drawn on Mason's back, and the process of the inking, followed by Jackson's cleaning and wiping off of his canvas, then more buzzing.

This was not part of the plan. The plan had been to run in, grab her brother, and talk some sense into him. The plan had not included running head-on into her past. The past she'd left neatly behind in college. Jackson Paige was a complication Jami had no interest in exploring again, despite his dimple or the colorful ink decorating his rippling arms. Or his damn deep voice.

Jax was a professional. Sure, sometimes he acted like he didn't give two fucks about anything, and some of the time he didn't, but he did care about the quality of his work. In his mind, tattooing was serious shit. Not only was it art—and art was sacred—but it was permanent art embedded forever into someone's skin. When he created a tattoo, he was essentially changing the way a person looked. For-fucking-ever. And even though a lot of people got inked on impulse or when they were wasted, he tried to create something worthy of their trust and money.

Which was exactly why he was pissed as all hell that Jami—the hot monthlong hookup he'd had five years ago and desperately tried to drown out of his mind with every chick he'd drunkenly banged since—suddenly walked into Tatuaggio. Frankly, it was a shame to hide all that sultry hotness under that boxy beige suit she was wearing. A body like that couldn't be hidden, not even under a fucking clown tent. To make matters even worse, not only was she dressed as an uptight spinster, but she turned out to be Mason's sister.

He tried like hell to focus on the outline for Mason's epic back piece. It was a beauty. Might even be his best work so far. But Jami's soft sighs and the annoyed tapping of her short nails on her phone were as distracting as if she sat there naked. Well, maybe not quite, but close. For the most part she completely ignored him. Like he didn't even exist. Like he hadn't fucked her deep and hard and bitten those full tits until she cried his name so loud her neighbors had banged on the walls.

It didn't matter anyway. He'd made a deal with the devil, and his fate was set in concrete. Besides, he knew what she thought of him and his art. And now he knew she was his buddy's little sister. No matter how much he wanted to ruffle her prissy little feathers, he wasn't going there again. Not when he'd kill any one of his friends for touching his own little sister, Mandi. No fucking way.

An hour into the session, Mason got up and left for a bio break. Jax stood up, tossed his flannel on the counter, and stretched his tingling limbs. Out of the corner of his eye, he saw Jami wasn't completely unaffected; even from a couple of feet away, he could see her breath hitch and her eyes glaze. Good. He stretched with even more flair, letting his Norton Motorcycle T-shirt ride high enough to give her a glimpse of his abs and trail to paradise. She rubbed her hands up and down her arms like she was cold, but he suspected she might be getting a little warm.

"You're a lawyer now." He smirked when she jumped, flushing and obviously embarrassed she'd been caught ogling him. He remembered loving how expressive she was. How every emotion could be read on her pretty face. It had made it so much easier and so much more fun to pleasure and tease her. She immediately schooled her features into what she probably thought was an all-business mask. Looked more like a glare to him.

"Yes. I see you aren't." Her skill at shuttering her emotions so quickly was actually kind of impressive. When had that happened? The Jami he knew had worn her heart on her sleeve and her feelings on her face. Or maybe she really wasn't that affected by him anymore. Maybe he'd imagined her interest like a ghost of their shared past.

He looked her up and down, taking in her conservative but impeccable outfit. Jax would give almost anything to see if her hair—the same soft blond cascade he had wrapped around his fist—still hung like a river of white gold down to her shapely ass. The tight librarian bun at the back of her neck made it hard to tell. Where had that curvy goddess of five years ago gone? God, she was even wearing shiny beige pumps. Obviously expensive, but meant to disguise, not highlight, her firm, strong calves.

"Nope," he said. She didn't deserve an explanation, not after the reaction she'd given when he'd admitted his dream of pursuing life as an artist so many years ago. "Living the dream, baby."

"Apparently so."

"What are you doing here, Jami?"

"Trying to keep my brother from ruining his life." She smiled, but it didn't quite reach her eyes, those big, beautiful ocean-blue eyes that used to make him feel like he could float away in them.

Because getting a tattoo would definitely doom Mason to eternal hell. *Whatever*. "He's happy. Really happy. Why isn't that enough for you?"

She paled, and for a brief second he wanted to apologize, wipe the stricken look from her face, but a door shut down the hall, and her features went right back to neutral.

As she turned to watch Mason exit the bathroom, her tailored jacket slipped from her shoulder, giving him a peek at the thin strand of pearls she wore around her long, pale neck. Fuck. Jackson wanted to run his tongue along her collarbone and feel her satiny skin pebble in anticipation. When she looked back, their gazes locked, and her eyes widened. She knew exactly what he was thinking.

Mason cleared his throat loudly and clapped his hands together, breaking the awkward trance that had formed between Jax and Jami.

"Let's finish this outline, buddy," Mason said to Jax, turning dismissively from his sister.

Fuck, his *little* sister. *Yeah. Not going there. Again.*

"Mason, we need to talk."

"We can talk about this when you come for dinner tomorrow. You don't need to stay." Mason's sharp tone didn't seem to faze Jami, who stood, smoothing her completely unwrinkled skirt. Mason walked over to his sister, gripped her shoulders and leaned in, kissing her cheek. Jax remembered the feel of her peachy skin, creamy and soft under his mouth and his fingers.

He shook his head and turned to her, feeling himself fall back in time. "Yep. Another hour should do it for this sitting. Good running into you, Jami. Guess I'll be seeing you around."

Her brittle smile looked like it might snap into a million pieces as she nodded and waved, leaving without a word. Where was she going? Where did she live? Did he want to see her again? The way shit had gone down between them years earlier had not been good. He'd left her without an explanation. *But she'd deserved it. Hadn't she?*

The protective plastic squeaked as Mason sat back down in the tattoo chair, pulling him back to the moment. Jax pressed his foot down on the pedal of the tattoo machine, and it buzzed to life like a maniacal mechanical bee. His hands were steady, but if he were forced to admit it, seeing Jami after all these years had been a bit of a gut shot. And maybe a bit of a dick punch. He'd moved on, for sure. But her curvy body had starred in his fantasies for as many years.

And now she was an attorney…

His band, Manix Curse, needed a lawyer for their upcoming tours—one that spring opening up for Pagan Saints and then the Hellfire Heavy Metal Masters tour the following summer—and recording negotiations.

Shaking off that ridiculous thought, he glanced up as Conner walked into the room with his client. Conner tugged the hairband out of his long mane and ran his fingers through it. "Dude, who was that? She was hot in a prissy kind of way. I'd like to get—"

Jax started to warn his coworker and bandmate, but before he could say anything, Mason held up his hand, making Jax cringe. He lifted his foot off the pedal and the machine quieted.

"What are you, fifteen? That's my fucking sister, so shut the hell up."

"Whoa. Sorry, dude. She was kinda hot, though."

Yeah. You have no idea. No. Idea.

"Shut the fuck up, Conner," Jax snapped. When both Mason and Conner gaped at him, he shrugged and started priming the tattoo machine again.

"Just sayin'. Is she dating anyone?" Conner was like a dog with a bone. Or boner, more like it.

"What the hell?" Both Mason and Jax shouted at the same time, looking up to see Conner with a smart-ass smirk.

"Ha! Kidding. I get it. Little sisters are off limits." Conner yanked off the rubber gloves they all wore when working with clients and tossed them into the wastebas-ket. And that, in a nutshell, was the real problem, wasn't it? Even if he wanted a do-over or even just to ruffle Jami's feathers—*ruffle* meaning "fuck" and *feathers* meaning "pussy"—she was officially hands off.

Conner was still laughing as he cleaned up and left the shop with his helmet in his hand, no doubt off to meet with his latest girlfriend. Conner, the poor sucker, was a romantic who held out hope date after date, woman after woman, that his newest flavor of the week was the one. That he'd find true love like his parents had. Once you got him started, usually after a couple of shots, he never shut up about his parents and soul mates and all that shit. It was really annoying. Unfortunately, Conner looked for love in all the wrong places and with all the wrong women. Usually the chicks he dated were more interested in his rock-and-roll persona than him.

Jax continued working on Mason's back, but his thoughts drifted to Jami. She'd always held herself to a higher standard than anyone else, but she hadn't yet fully developed that hard shell she wore like armor now. Back then, her smile was sunshine. God, that fucking smile could do him in with barely a teasing upturned corner. That smile. Fuck, that mouth. Her pink lips. People used the cliché of bowed lips all the time, but Jami was the only person he'd ever met who actually had a bow-shaped mouth. The things she could do with that mouth.

Jax shook the memories of her from his head, but like a sticky spiderweb, the past wouldn't sweep clean. Their time together was best buried, along with any hope of one last taste from her sweet mouth. There was a reason he'd walked away from her. A good reason. They didn't fit. He knew it. She knew it. And her parents had made it abundantly clear that they knew it. Now he discovered she was Mason's sister. Even more reason not to cross that bridge to nowhere. Which is why it surprised the hell out of him when he opened his mouth to ask Mason about their upcoming tour and instead asked, "What kind of law does Jami practice? Maybe she could do Manix's contracts for the tour and record."

Chapter 2

THE NEXT EVENING, JAMI PATTED HERSELF ON THE back—well, figuratively anyway—for almost forgetting about her encounter with Jackson as she walked up the steps of Kevan and Mason's new house and knocked twice on the bright red oversized door.

Their house was in an older area of suburban Portland that featured some gorgeous, regal homes mixed with older beauties in need of a loving touch. The narrow cul-de-sac was always filled with kids and much more a reflection of their new life together than Mason's cold, modern monstrosity had ever been. This house, a run-down Craftsman, had had good bones when they'd bought it, but it had needed more than a loving touch. So Bowen, Kevan's brother, who'd recently completed his own personal rehab, stayed with them for a while, welcoming the opportunity to help them refurb their house.

Jami ran the toe of her ballet flat over the edge of the porch boards, broken and peeling only a couple weeks ago, now painted a glossy dark gray. Who the hell painted a classic craftsman home gray, black, and red? Kevan Landry, soon to be Kevan Dillon, that's who. The same woman who would be a better match for a certain tall, lithe tattoo artist than her brother. The same woman who had blue streaks in her hair and a diamond in her nose. The same woman who had completely upturned the life of her once normal and stable brother and turned him into a tattooed entrepreneur instead of the Armani-suited corporate CEO he had been. Well, maybe it wasn't all her fault. But Kevan was the catalyst for sure.

The door swung open, and Jami was pulled into the embrace of the taller bombshell herself. Jami instinctively stiffened. She wasn't really a hugger anymore, but relaxed into Kevan's arms. It was impossible to ignore the ray of freaking sunshine that was her brother's fiancée. Jami wished she could allow herself to open up to Kevan's playful warmth, but she was still struggling with all the changes in Mason's life. Trying to reconcile this new him with the old him was going to take some time, and she still held out hope that she could undo some of the damage without meddling in his relationship too much.

Kevan squeezed her tight before letting her go. "Oh, Jami, we're so glad you're here. It's been too long."

She dragged Jami out from the foyer and into the open great room of their new home, raising their linked hands. Mason stood at the dark granite counter chopping, but he looked up through the hair hanging over his forehead, and his face lit with a wide smile. A smile she couldn't help but feel in her heart like another hug. His eyes connected with hers and he winked. Like he always did. Like they had a secret connection no one else had. That wink meant something to them.

"Hey, sis." Mason rinsed his hands and dried them on a towel before he met her in the big open room and pulled her into a hug. Her brother glanced at the clock over what looked like a vintage double oven, but was probably some new overpriced reproduction. "Right on time as usual."

Kevan set a glass of chardonnay on the counter and pulled out a faux-leopard barstool. "Sit. Drink. Visit." She patted the seat for Jami and took a sip of her signature drink—ginger ale and cranberry juice. "Mason's finishing up the fish, quinoa is in the warming drawer, and the salad is made."

Once Jami had a few sips of wine, she tried to relax into the warmth of their home. A buttery garlic smell permeated the kitchen, and the large stone fireplace crackled and glowed, warming the cool winter evening air. Her brother sang under his breath as he finished preparing their meal. They chatted about Jolt Marketing, Kevan and Mason's boutique entertainment marketing company. The tension Jami always carried in her shoulders eased, and she found herself laughing and enjoying both Kevan and Mason's company. They obviously adored each other and yet teased one another mercilessly. It was kind of annoying. And kind of cute.

So why did she fight it so much? Why did she keep telling herself her brother wouldn't be happy in the long term? She knew it wasn't any of her business, but she couldn't help wanting to keep him from making the same horrific mistakes she'd made. But he was smarter and more grounded than her—always had been. His big rebellion had been dropping out of Harvard and going into the business world and not politics or science like their parents had wanted. Her rebellion, on the other hand, had started with a teenage party and cutting school here and there. It had culminated in a car accident and the death of her romantic teenage dreams.

But that was the past. She had rules now. Parameters for dealing with life's curveballs. When they deviated from their blueprint, people's lives got mangled, and bad stuff happened. She didn't want that pain for Mason. He deserved to be happy. With Kevan. But with rules.

"How are things at Quirk?" Kevan asked, referring to the nickname for Portland Community Women's Resource Center, the shelter and family services organization where Jami volunteered her legal and administrative skills.

Jami sipped her wine, mulling over the last few hours. "Today was hard. They brought in a young woman, really just a girl…" Her voice trailed off as the girl's bandaged face floated in her mind. "She'd been beaten up by her boyfriend, an older man." She swallowed, not wanting to reveal the rest of the story. The part where the girl had been kicked in the stomach so many times her body hadn't been able to hold on to the little life growing inside of her. The part where Jami had helped her get a room and clothing assigned and then set up a restraining order. The part where, hours later, she'd locked herself in Ella's office and sobbed silently for half an hour.

Mason's arm wrapped around her shoulders from behind and then grabbed her hand, squeezing three times—their secret code for "I love you." He kissed the top of her head. "You don't have to talk about it, Jami."

She hadn't planned on telling them everything, but his sweet words emboldened her to open up a little. She took a deep breath. "He beat her so badly she miscarried her baby. And he'd known she was pregnant and did it anyway. Maybe he did it *because* she was pregnant."

Kevan's eyes welled with tears and she jumped from her seat and gathered Jami up in her arms once again. "I'm sorry, Jami."

Mason reached over with his gigantic hand and squeezed hers. "I love you, Jami. You know that, right?"

Jami wanted to relax into their love. She really did, but she didn't have any more tears to cry. Not today anyway.

"I do. I'm okay. We did her intake and I filed a restraining order. He's in lockup. But you know how that goes. He'll be out in a day or two, begging her to come back, saying how sorry he is."

Kevan pulled back and smiled weakly. "No, I meant, because of what happened."

"I know. I really am okay." Mason squeezed her hand three times before pulling away. Jamie smiled, pushing away the past and the image of the poor broken young woman.

He took the hint and went to busy himself in the kitchen. Kevan apparently also understood Jami's need for space, as she sat back down and started talking about their current client list. The air in the room changed, lightened, as the conversation became less emotional and more upbeat.

When Mason reached up to grab a pitcher off a high shelf, his shirt collar pulled down and she saw the dark outline of his latest tattoo. The one Jackson had put on him the day before. Jackson Paige. His deep brown eyes drifted through her mind…and the way his gaze had floated over her when her jacket had lifted. Had she imagined his interest?

"Anyway, as I was saying, our latest client has a

couple offers right now and we need some legal expertise," Mason's deep voice rumbled.

Was he talking to her? Well, of course, or he wouldn't be staring at her like he was waiting for an answer. Nor would Kevan.

"I'm a corporate attorney. I don't know anything about entertainment law."

Mason's lips pulled down at the corners and his eyes widened with exasperation. He propped his fist on his hip. "For fuck's sake, Jami, aren't you listening? I just said your contracts experience is ideal."

"Don't swear at me. And it's hard to take you seriously when you're sporting an apron that says 'I like pork butts and I cannot lie.'"

Still scowling, he said, "Don't try and change the subject. You worked strictly on these kinds of deals when you interned in GEM's law department. You're perfect for what Manix Curse needs. They need a contracts expert, not an entertainment expert."

"I have a job." Besides, working six months for marketing giant Global Entertainment Marketing did not make her any kind of expert. Hardly. If anything, it proved how little she actually knew.

"Seriously, Jami?"

"What?" Geez, how long had she not been paying attention while she daydreamed about her law school hookup?

"We covered this. The band can pay you a small retainer and then a percentage of all signing costs and profits. It's great for them and it's awesome for you. Both the money and the experience."

When Jami didn't say anything, Kevan picked up

where Mason left off without missing a beat. Which was probably why they were so good in business together.

"They have offers for two tours, a couple merchandising deals, and a recording contract. They're going to be big, Jami, and we could really use someone we can trust." Kevan furrowed her perfectly lined brows and clutched her hands in her lap. She was nervous.

They were serious? They really wanted her. They did make some valid points. Jami was underutilized at the family-run firm she worked for. She hadn't admitted it to anyone, not even her brother and God forbid her parents, but they essentially treated her like a legal assistant and not an attorney.

Jami chewed on her bottom lip for a moment. What could it hurt? She could work for the band and still stick to her plan of proving she could be a successful attorney without her dad's contacts or firm. She looked back and forth between Mason and Kevan. Their shared enthusiasm hung in the air, making her believe she could reach out and grab it for herself.

"You're serious? You're asking me to represent your biggest act?" Something long forgotten rolled around in her chest and expanded.

Just slightly. Just a little. Just enough.

They both nodded.

They believed in her.

Tears wet and heavy pricked at the back of her eyes. She wouldn't cry. Nevertheless, it was hard to find the words to agree so she nodded back. "Have their manager call me. He can have the contracts sent to my house and I'll look them over. We'll see." Kevan startled her by squealing and wrapping her in a hug. Guess she was becoming a hugger, whether she liked it or not. Jami let the warmth from Kevan's joy wash over her. For a moment, she leaned into her. It was pretty awesome to be wanted. Appreciated.

"All right, Bettie, let my sister breathe," Mason said, calling Kevan by the nickname he'd given her in honor of the legendary pinup model, Bettie Page. "Let's go enjoy the rain and eat dinner on the patio. Grab a plate of food and a drink." He heaped portions on their plates and led them out to the huge glassed-in porch on the back of their house. The furnishings were an eclectic mix of shabby chic, antiques, and contemporary styles. But somehow it worked.

Kind of like Mason and Kevan.

Jami shook her head and laughed to herself as she plopped onto one of the mismatched but comfortable dining chairs, and wondered if maybe Kevan and the new Mason were beginning to grow on her.

After dinner, Jami helped Kevan wash the dishes while Mason handled the leftovers. Kevan nudged Jami's shoulder as they stood side by side at the sink. "So Mason told me how you chased him down yesterday at Tatuaggio and tried to talk him out of his new tattoo."

The warm blush of embarrassment crept up Jami's neck and heated her cheeks. Since Kevan was covered in tattoos, Jami didn't want her to feel judged. Just because she didn't think tattoos were appropriate for Mason didn't mean Kevan should feel bad about hers. Jami was starting to suspect that Kevan's vibrant personality might actually be a cover for a more sensitive, less secure woman.

"Well, uh, yes. It's just Mason...I know—"

"Hey, hey, relax. I was only teasing. We all know Mason's gonna do what Mason's gonna do." She smiled, and something cloudy, something dreamy lit her eyes as her gaze locked with Mason's over the counter. Jami felt that weird thing rolling around inside her, something like envy—not as ugly, but nearly as uncomfortable.

Thankfully, he hadn't mentioned her knowing Jackson or how she'd practically drooled all over him like a lovesick coed.

"So," Kevan started, pausing for a few seconds. By now, Jami knew Kevan said "so" as a prologue to something important or some kind of zinger, so she held her breath waiting for it. "How do you know Jax?"

The fork Jami was rinsing clattered to the counter, splattering them both with suds and water. Kevan laughed, but Jami knew she'd wait for the answer—or dig it out of her with the damn fork she'd dropped. Might as well confess.

"I met Jackson in law school."

"You were in school at the same time? He's older than you."

"He was a third-year student. I was a first-year. He TAed one of my classes. But he left, and I haven't seen him since."

Her stomach pitched. Seeing him again had brought her chaotic past rushing back to the forefront.

"Until yesterday." Was that a smirk on Kevan's pretty face?

"Yes. How do you know Jackson?" Jami thought she saw surprise flit across Kevan's eyes before she swung her gaze to Mason again. He raised an eyebrow and then quickly looked away. How did they do that?

Communicate without words and say so much? And what exactly was he hiding from Jami?

"My brother works at Tatuaggio. I used to do the books there. We've been friends for years." Jami's stomach was now flat-out free-falling. The chances of not seeing Jackson again were quickly diminishing.

"Like how good of friends?" she asked, keeping her head down and feigning great interest in the plate she was washing.

"Like, he's in the wedding party, friends."

Jami's blood sizzled through her veins, and her chest clenched with an odd mixture of trepidation and excitement. Well, damn. Looked like she was going to be seeing him sooner rather than later, since Mason and Kevan's engagement party was in two weeks.

"Oh." For the second time in as many days, Jami was out of words.

✵ ✶ ✵

Jax looked around at the assemblage of people sitting around the conference table. At the head sat his band's manager, Joe McKellar; next to him were marketing reps Kevan and Mason; and then his band Manix Curse, which included their singer Marco, bass player Conner, and his little sister, the guitar wunderkind Mandi. This was everything he'd worked toward the past several years: success as an artist, sitting on the tip of a rocket about to launch them into the rock-and-roll heavens, where he'd be a heavy-metal god.

He glanced at his phone. In about two minutes, the one chick he'd never really gotten out of his system was going to walk into the conference room, contractually obligated to share breathing space with him. Boo-fucking-ya. Maybe he'd get the chance to mess up her perfectly coiffed lady-bun. Maybe he'd turn on the charm and get her to go out again. One more night together. For old times' sake. Because one more night was all he'd ever get once she unburied the truth about their breakup.

Right on cue, Joe's new receptionist led Jami toward the conference room. What would she say when she realized he was in the band? Did she already know? Tingles of anticipation sparked up his spine, not unlike the adrenaline he felt spiking through his body before a show.

Had Kevan and Mason told her he'd be there? Probably.

They all stood as she walked through the open door wearing a pristine pantsuit and matching heels. She was giving off that school-principal vibe in waves, but he knew what hid beneath her overly practical clothes. White-hot fire burned under all that navy-blue ice.

She smiled, the type of smile most would accept as genuine. But he could tell the smile didn't quite make it to those blue eyes; it was a practiced, lawyerly smile. And as she began to shake hands with everyone and make her way around the table, Jax knew without a doubt this was the all-business Jami, the one she showed the rest of the world. He wondered again if the hair in her tight bun at the base of her neck still felt soft and satiny like silk. Would it snag on his calluses when he ran it through his fingers? And, more importantly, was it still long enough to wrap around his fist as he took her from behind?

Whoa. Time to cool your jets. Business first. Fun later. If he was lucky.

He cleared his throat, trying to shake the image of her heart-shaped ass under his palm as she walked toward the table, her gaze searching for her brother and then Kevan. Then…wait for it. Bam! Her gaze fell on him like a fucking hammer and she nearly dropped her briefcase.

So that would be a no. They hadn't told her. Interesting that she didn't make the connection to his stage name on the contract.

Jax couldn't hide the knowing smirk that spread across his face. He'd bet dollars to donuts the three of them were the only ones in the room to see her smile falter and the lines momentarily mar her otherwise smooth forehead. Oh yeah. He liked ruffling her feathers. He liked it a lot.

Regaining her composure, she held out her slim hand, her nails short, shiny with clear polish. A funny thing for him to notice because he was a guy and all, but she'd always done that to him, made him notice the little things.

"Jackson Paige, a.k.a. Jax Pain." Her lip curved up and the dimple in her cheek popped. The gleam in her eye said so much more than her words. "Mason and Kevan neglected to mention you were in the band."

His much larger hand swallowed hers. "JamiLynn Dillon, esquire." And then without thinking about it—because if he'd thought about it he wouldn't have done it—he pulled her all the way in for what looked like a chaste hug between old friends. But he could feel her slight tremble and hear the catch in her breath. God, he'd forgotten how tiny she was. How voluptuous and small, and how the curve of her body fit perfectly with his taller, leaner one. And her smell. Flowers. Sweet simple flowers. A soft edge to the sharpness she tried to portray to the world.

"Hello, sunshine. Miss me?" he whispered in her ear, brushing his mouth against her soft lobe. The sharp intake of breath and the way she melted into him before she pulled away meant he could still affect her. Good.

She laughed with a confident lilt. He bet only he could hear the slight tremor in her voice or see her throat move. "Well, I see Jackson hasn't changed. Much."

As everyone chuckled and shuffled back into their seats around the table, she sat between Mason and Joe. Jax sank in the chair directly next to his sister and across from Jami.

Mandi's glance flicked back and forth between Jax and Jami. Jax narrowed his eyes and shook his head, a warning to his pixie-sized sibling with the big mouth. But her eyes shone with glee. Dammit. Surprisingly, she didn't cackle evilly or rub her hands together in excitement.

"So, Jami...may I call you Jami?" Mandi asked as Jami's smile stayed pasted to her face like an emoji sticker. "I know you're Mason's sister, but how exactly do you know my brother?"

"We met in law school."

"Ohhhhh, you're *that*—" Jax grabbed Mandi's knee under the table and squeezed hard, but not before Jami's blond and perfectly arched brows furrowed, creating a single line, like a question mark, between her eyes. Although he hadn't told Mandi about Jami, per se, he had told her about "some chick" he'd been with in law school. That it hadn't ended well. Mandi probably assumed the mystery girlfriend was the reason he was a serial dater. She'd be correct in that assumption, of course.

"Yes. I suppose I am." Jami pulled the band's

contracts out of her bag and turned to Joe, the decision maker and official suit of Manix Curse. "I've gone over the contracts Joe had delivered earlier this week. While there is some predatory language and some terms we'll definitely want to negotiate, the three offers are fairly solid and have the potential to be quite lucrative. Of course, we're still waiting for the formal offer and contract from the record label. I don't expect those until next week. At that time we'll counter, if necessary."

Jax sat silently while she talked, but stretched his legs under the table, bumping her foot with his and making her fumble her words briefly. She never glanced at him, but he could tell his presence was getting to her.

He should quit messing with her. Let her go and do her job without interfering. But fuck, she was hot when she put on her bossy lawyer pants and took control of the meeting.

Joe smiled, but then again he was always smiling, so it was kind of hard to differentiate his moods. "Excellent. Then you're interested in joining the Manix team as counsel?" When she agreed, he slid a stapled stack of papers her way. "This is the signed contract of our agreement, along with the retainer we discussed on the phone. But, as specified in the contract, you get paid when we get paid."

"Great. Shall we go over some of these points while the entire band is here?" she asked.

★ ☆ ★

Hell's bells.

Jackson Paige was, in fact, Jax Pain, the drummer of Manix Curse.

That thing in her chest tightened around her ribs, making it hard to breathe.

This new little development was further complicated by the fact that she'd been hired by the band to negotiate their tours, sponsorship, and recording contracts.

As she slowly rinsed her hands in the sink and checked her updo for any out-of-place strands, she pretended it didn't make a difference. She had a way of doing things—rules, structure, plans—that worked for her now. And Jackson had no place in the calm order of her life. None. He was a blustering tornado that would rip apart anything good and calm she had, leaving behind only more mess. And his effect on her panties had nothing to do with real life. It was something to note and then forget. She took a deep breath, allowing the oxygen to fill her lungs and relax that pinch in her chest.

By the time she found herself striding back down the hall to grab her briefcase from the empty conference room, she'd slowed the pounding of her heart. She could do this. The soup of emotions boiling up from seeing him would go away. It would. She would be okay. She was not a frivolous, impulsive girl easily swayed by tall, muscly tattoo artists, let alone super-hot musicians. She was a damn lawyer. A respected member of the judicial system, a sworn officer of the freaking court.

Jami didn't like all these messy feelings. She'd gotten used to being in control. She smoothed her jacket down. Her outfit screamed conservative attorney. Or it asserted it politely, but resolutely.

Stepping into the conference room, she looked around for her briefcase. Not on the table. Not on the chairs. Dammit, she was usually more together than this.

She was turning around to go back through the door and see if someone had left it in the reception area when she heard the snick of the door closing. She snapped her head in the sound's direction, and a very tall, very sexy Jackson stood there, swinging her bag from his hand.

"Looking for this, sunshine?" His smile was wide, but slightly predatory, and his eyes narrowed in challenge. He needed a shave. Well, another man with that amount of scruff would need a shave. Jackson, on the other hand, looked knavish and naughty as heck, with his shadowy stubble and messy hair. Hair that was longer than it had been in school and shorter on the sides, brushing the collar of his gray-striped button-down shirt. The edges of a tattoo—what looked like swirls of blue water—peeked up over his shoulder and across his collarbone, tickling his neck. He had his long sleeves rolled. Color filled his forearms to his wrists, with the tongue of what appeared to be a dragon licking over the top of one hand. The muscles in his corded arms tensed and danced when he shifted her bag.

Why did she find him so damn hot, burning all rational thought from her head with just a glance, just a touch? Why him? She saw guys every day with this same look and never gave them space in her head. There was something in the relaxed but coiled way Jackson held himself that exuded pure sexual charisma. All rock-star charisma.

A rock star that had left her. Without explanation. Without a reason.

"Yes, thank you," she said tightly, reaching for her bag. He swung it out of her reach, pulling it to his chest.

Without warning, the room whirled as he grabbed her

shoulders and spun her. Her back hit the door with a soft *thunk* and she heard, rather than saw, her bag drop to the floor. She couldn't move, couldn't look away from his piercing gaze, which might as well have been a knife, the way it cut her open, exposing her. Heat from his body washed over her, blanketing her skin, overwhelming her. He didn't touch her anywhere but her shoulders, where his long fingers dug into her flesh, branding her through her jacket and blouse. They stood there staring at each other, her hands at her sides. Then he reached up and drew his index finger down from her ear along her jaw, flinting sparks off her body. Her nipples pulled into hard buds, painful as they ached for his touch. If she wasn't careful, those sparks were going to start a fire she wouldn't be able to put out. She couldn't afford to lose control. Not now and not ever again.

She wanted to close her eyes. Wanted to lean into his touch and let him take her over, like he always had when they were together. But she couldn't give in.

Not anymore. Not again.

When she moved to speak, he drew his finger over her lips, causing her to gasp. She sucked air into her lungs… air she so badly needed but couldn't quite get enough of. Big mistake, since his smell—that clean salty scent he always had, like minutes earlier he'd jumped off a surfboard after riding waves—kicked her sense memory in the gonads. And everything she'd been trying to forget about him came flooding back, making it hard to ignore the flutter in her belly.

Jackson shook his head, and an unruly lock of hair fell forward over his eye, lending him a sinister and mischievous look, like the forbidden devil he was. The air between them grew thicker, weighed down by ghosts of the past and a lust that had never gone away.

He leaned down, touching his forehead to hers. "I can't ignore the thing between us, Jami. Can you?"

Yes. She certainly could and would. But then she did something completely unexpected. Something she hadn't planned or even considered. Because if she'd thought for even one second, it would have never happened.

She wrapped her hands around the back of his neck and tugged his mouth down on hers. It was a light, sensual brush of her lips against his, but the little flutter she'd felt earlier—barely a blip on the Richter scale—became a full-scale earthquake, threatening to destroy everything. And yet she didn't care. It wasn't enough.

All rational thought, all control, all her rules flew out the window, replaced with a dark need she recognized on a visceral level, one she thought she'd obliterated a very long time ago. The mask she affixed firmly every day to keep order in her life fell off the second his mouth met hers. It completely disintegrated as soon as her tongue decided to lick the crease of his lips and turn a seductive taste into a feast. Instantly he took over, and his fire consumed her. Like it always had. It would sear her and then leave her like so much dusty ash on the floor.

A deep, low moan sounded in the room, and Jami's eyes opened. The groan came from her. *No. Not again.* This was not how this thing was going down. She was years over Jackson Paige. Years. Over. And now his band was her client, which definitely meant no kissing. Sweet or sexy didn't matter.

A cold, sharp clarity wrapped itself around her. She

pulled away and ducked under his arm, and the separation felt more like a slap than it should have. A look of confusion marred his handsome face for a moment before it was replaced quickly by his don't-give-a-shit-take-it-or-leave-it grin. Of all his looks, she hated that one the most. Though, at that moment, she was grateful for his cocky response, since it was a reminder of exactly why she shouldn't be kissing him.

Her hands balled into fists against her hips. "I'm sorry. I was clearly out of line. We shouldn't be doing this, Jackson. We shouldn't be doing any of this."

"I disagree. I think we should do it some more," he said, stepping forward.

She held up her hand, stopping him. "You gave up that right when you left me without an explanation or even a good-bye. Not even a 'screw you' so I knew where I stood. Nothing." She cocked her eyebrows, waiting for something. A response. Some shame. Anything.

But his expression never changed when he swept his hand through his hair. "Fair enough, but let's not forget you basically fucked me with your mouth, sunshine. This isn't over."

Guilt and desire and anger mingled hot in her throat. "Oh, yes it—" She stopped abruptly when he stalked toward her and leaned down, sending shivers up and down her arms.

Jesus, what was wrong with her?

"No," he said, close enough she could feel his breath feathering against her cheek. "You're right about one thing. We do have some unfinished business."

"Jackson." His name was an exasperated sigh on her lips. "You're a client now. So even if I did want to know why you ran off, and even if I did want to take it farther, I can't. We can't."

The half-lie half-truth rolled off her tongue more easily than she'd thought it would. He *was* a client, and they really shouldn't mess around. But the other side of that coin was that she really just wanted him to pick her up, hike up her skirt, and pull aside her soaked panties before he plunged his big dick into her over and over again until he gave her what she knew would be the best orgasm she'd had in a very long time.

But that wasn't going to happen. No matter how badly she wanted him in her bed again, he was no good for her. It had taken her far too long to get over him, and the recovery had almost been as bad as when she'd been a screwed-up teen. In a way, maybe it had been worse.

"That's where you're wrong. We aren't done." He pressed his face to her throat. Her breath hitched as he ran the bridge of his nose up her neck and bit her earlobe. The surprising nip sent sharp pricks of desire straight to her already aching nipples. He pulled back and chuckled before turning around and glancing over his shoulder.

"That's where *you're* wrong," she said. "We were done a long time ago. That was your good-bye kiss."

Something dark flashed in his eyes before he pasted that damn smirk back on his face. "See ya soon, counselor."

He strode casually out the door and into the empty reception area, leaving her raw and exposed, nerves sparking and jumping like live wires.

Like he always did.

Chapter 3

FRIDAY NIGHT, JAX WAS SITTING IN A LARGE BOOTH AT his favorite hangout, the Tiki Torch Bar and Lounge, with bandmate and coworker Conner Steele, Manix's bass player and all-around scary-looking badass, well on his way to a good buzz. His cell phone chimed in his pocket, making that six times in the last half hour. Usually, by this time on a weekend, especially after a long-ass week of slinging ink and three grueling multi-hour band practices, he'd have responded to one of his incoming texts. Would have picked his flavor of the month and made arrangements for dinner and a hookup. But one smoking-hot kiss from a short, curvy, stuck-up blond and all he could think about was getting her under him. Being inside her warm body again was beginning to become an unwelcome obsession.

Well, to be fair, he'd been losing interest in the game for a while. He couldn't even remember how long it'd been since he'd hooked up with anyone. Even after a show, when he was usually so fucking horny. Lately, he'd opted to take that energy and channel it into his artwork.

Fuck. He used to actually enjoy the pursuit, the date, the buildup before the big show. But ever since Manix Curse had started making news with their upcoming tours and recording deal, chicks had been coming out of the proverbial woodwork. At first he'd made the effort, courting them and shit. But they'd all made it clear they were in it to bang the drummer of Manix and didn't really give a shit who he was or what else he did. So now they all bled into one long one-night stand, with the occasional cheap date thrown in for shits and giggles. He had his pick of hot, available women every night. Hell, he could choose a type for each night. Curvy redhead for tonight, maybe? Petite brunette tomorrow?

He must have scoffed or grunted or something because Conner glanced up from his phone with an eyebrow raised. "What's your problem?"

"You mean other than that fucked-up haircut you're sporting, man-bun?"

"You wish you could rock this cut, dude. Chicks dig my luscious mane." His friend scowled, pulled the tie off his goofy bun, and flipped his long hair over his shoulder, exposing the shiny shaved sides of his head. "So fuck off, buzzkill."

"Buzzkill? Me? Dude, I'm a fucking chick magnet. Everyone knows the ladies love the drummer, not the bass player."

Marco Dane, Manix Curse's bearded but baby-faced singer, walked up with his arm around his girlfriend, Sabre. They'd been together, fighting and fucking, fucking and fighting, on and off, for years. When the gigantic Marco sank down into the booth and tugged Sabre in next to him, Jax guessed they must be getting along again. Maybe he'd be able to avoid getting in the middle of their next epic battle.

"Yeah, bro, and everyone knows the singer is the hottest ticket. Right, babe?" He took a sip of his beer and either pointedly ignored or, more likely, was idiotically oblivious to the hurt that shadowed his girlfriend's pretty face. She might be young, but she wasn't foolish enough to ignore her boyfriend's reputation as a manwhore on the road. Jax felt a little sorry for her. But he'd also seen her throw down in the middle of a bar during a show and fuck all kinds of shit up, and then stalk off with her own revenge fuck. So they kind of deserved each other, in a sick, twisted way, and he wanted nothing to do with it.

"Yeah, babe, I do. I'm a singer, too. Remember?" The look she gave him was dark, pointed, before she started peeling the soggy label off her beer bottle. Truth was, she was a damn fine singer. Could belt the shit out of blues and rockabilly like a cross between Elle King and Imelda May. She had real talent and would probably surpass them in popularity one day. Her gorgeous face didn't hurt her chances either.

Clueless Marco chuckled. "What do you call a beautiful woman on a bass player's arm?"

When no one offered an answer, Marco shrugged his overly muscled shoulders. "Duh. A tattoo."

"Dude, shut up." Conner punched Marco, but laughed anyway.

"Okay, totally serious. Did you hear about the bassist who was so out of tune his band actually noticed?"

Jax sighed. He loved his band and his friends, but he was getting so tired of all this shit. Shouts and a loud noise drew his attention across the room, where three guys were scuffling next to a pool table. Another damn bar fight.

Conner elbowed him, "Hey look, Shelby's actually making Carl and Tiny break that fight up."

"Yeah. Probably because they're not regulars."

Thirty years old and he was still hanging out in a bar. Kind of pathetic. But he was also sick of going home to a quiet and lonely apartment. Mandi was always either at school or studying. Although they didn't have a whole lot in common other than a father and Manix Curse, she was smart and driven and a much better student than he had ever been.

And, there he was back to thinking about school, which led to thoughts about Jami. JamiLynn Dillon and her furrowed brow and grim face hiding all that beauty, forcibly reining in a primal wildness she kept tethered down. God, how he wanted to watch her break free and fall apart in his hands.

He listened to the conversation and smart-ass retorts, and watched as others joined their growing group. Just another late-night party like every other Saturday. Except his buddy Bowen wasn't there. With Bowen still pretty fresh from rehab, a bar, especially the Tiki Torch, was not a safe place for him to hang out. He tended to opt for recovery meetings over barhopping nowadays.

"Hey, Jax, you're looking all emo over there. Something up?" Conner's tone was teasing, but his expression was serious.

"Nah. Tired. Getting too old for this shit." He tried to smile as he raised his voice over Halsey's remake of "Walk the Line" blaring and the raucous customers playing pool and unwinding from a long workweek. Tried to pretend he wasn't feeling as dark as he was. But Conner was his friend—part of his childhood wrecking crew, a ragtag group of boys who had been drawn together in middle school and had stayed friends ever since. Conner, Bowen, Nathan, and Jax had had each other's backs since way back in the day. Giving each other shit was their way of saying they cared.

"Yeah. Ditto, dude. I'm gonna finish my beer and walk home." Conner shared a small house with Nathan, who also worked at Tatuaggio and played in a band with Bowen called Toast. Their place was off the main drag in the Hawthorne district, around the corner from the apartment above the tattoo shop Jax shared with Mandi. Both places were walking distance from the Tiki.

"I'll go with," Jax said.

"Cool. I gotta get up early and visit Sunny tomorrow. Shouldn't be out late."

"How's she doing? Any better?" Jax drank the rest of his beer, hating to let it get stale and stagnant. Warm beer tasted like piss. Or he guessed it did.

Conner smiled. Not a happy smile, but one full of regret and pain. Those shadows had shown up after he'd come back from Iraq, and they'd never quite gone away. Sometimes they grew lighter, and sometimes they grew darker, flatter.

"Worse. She doesn't remember me at all anymore, man. Keeps calling me James." Conner's feelings were starkly obvious.

Jax nodded. Conner's older brother James was one of those slick fuckers who was so slimy nothing stuck to him. He had everyone fooled into thinking he was the golden boy, but he was simply a dick who didn't give a fuck about anyone, including his aunt Sunny, who had raised the brothers after their parents had died in a car crash. Conner was the one dedicated to caring for his aunt as she slowly lost her mind to dementia.

"That blows." Jax looked around the bar. The

bouncers had cleared the fight fairly quickly. The bar's owner, Shelby Henley, an ageless woman whose past no one really knew so there was much speculation, employed a couple of burly meatheads with sadistic streaks. They seemed to love nothing more than tossing drunk dudes out on their asses. Although they did seem to let regulars like the Tatuaggio crew work it out with their fists as long as they didn't break anything.

When had it gotten so crowded? Their group had doubled in the few minutes he'd been talking with Conner. The booth table and the second one that had been pushed up against the first were littered with half-empty glasses, drained pitchers, and the skeletal remains of buffalo wings.

As Jax and Conner pushed out of the booth and stood, two smoking-hot blonds from the scene—Kayla Something and a friend he sort of recognized—strutted up in their impossibly high platforms and tipped their chins coyly. "'Sup, Jax? Conner?"

"Hey, Kayla," Jax said and started to brush past them when Kayla and her friend both pushed out their chests and rubbed against him. Kayla laid her fluorescent pink dagger nails on his arm and squeezed. Instead of lust, annoyance shot through him. The only woman he wanted was the one he had run away from. The one who belonged in a mansion in Snob Hill, not a dive bar in Portland.

"You want company?" She smiled, her bright teeth almost glowing under the dim lights.

Had he found her attractive once? She *was* pretty, but not really his type. Strike that. She had been his type. For a while. He seemed to remember making out with her after a show, but not much else. He may have been a bit of a man-ho, but he definitely remembered the women he fell into bed with. Most of the time. It certainly hadn't been recently, since he hadn't taken anyone to bed for… for how long? Weeks? No, more like months.

"Nah, sweetie. Maybe another time." He tried to act playful. Sincere. But he wasn't feeling it.

Her smile dropped, and for a minute he was reminded of a different blond. One he *did* remember being buried in. One he couldn't seem to forget lately. One he needed to find soon so he could watch her prim and proper facade shatter as he slaked this crazy lust.

"You sure, sexy? We could make it worth your while." Kayla and her friend stepped back as he and Conner moved away from the table and said good-bye to their friends.

Conner grabbed his hoodie and yanked it on. Smiling, he said, "Seriously, another time, yeah?" he said, pulling Jax out the door.

The crisp late-night Portland air hit his lungs. He inhaled like a man taking his first breath after a very long dive. The stale bar smell of greasy food and old sweat drifted away, replaced by the sharp, damp smell of winter.

"Dude, what's going on with you?" Conner asked as they walked back toward Tatuaggio. "You seem off the last few days. Is it Bowen? Some chick?"

Jax considered how much to tell him. Fess up to the weird shit swirling in his head, or blow it off like he did everything else? What would it hurt to actually tell Conner the truth?

"Maybe a little of both. It's fucking lame that we can't find something else to do, something where Bowen can actually participate. Are we just about bars and metal and that's it?" Great, now he really did sound like an emo pussy. He should have kept his mouth shut and said everything was fine. Like he always did.

Conner pulled his hair thing from his pocket and gathered his mane back into a man-bun. "What's the deal with you and that pretty lawyer?"

Leave it to Conner to jump right into the meat and skip the side dishes. Jax chuckled. Not a sound of humor, but of gloom. Apparently he wasn't fooling anyone. "What about her?"

"What the fuck was that little show in Joe's office? Dude, you looked like you wanted to devour her right there in front of the band."

"That's what it looked like?"

"Yeah. That's what it looked like."

Jax sucked in the cool air and wished for the millionth time since he'd quit smoking that he had a cigarette. Something to distract him from the shitstorm in his head that had started the minute Jami had walked into Tatuaggio. He could really use the rush of nicotine right about now. Or maybe he should go for a run after he got home. Pounding the cement might knock loose the crap in his head and give him some relief from all his current angst.

"I was her tutor in school. She was uptight then, too, but not like now. Now she's a different person." He could feel the smile stretch his face despite his assertion. "But, oh man, she was hot. Big fucking brain, smart mouth. Hot."

Yeah. That was an understatement. He'd liked her. A lot. Until it had all gone sideways and he'd had to bail.

After he'd left, he'd wanted to talk to her, but then he'd force himself to remember how different they were. How they had different plans for their lives. Her parents were assholes, anyway, and he hated the way she jumped when they said "jump." Plus, leaving school had been his opportunity to finally cut loose from his dad's oppressive expectations and his mother's ridiculous manipulations. Unfortunately, Jami would have never considered standing up to her parents, let alone breaking free from their iron-fisted hold on her life.

So he hadn't called her. Figuring her parents were probably right, he'd taken the payoff and bailed. Over time, the ache had dulled, and he'd moved on to his new life. Who needed law school when he had his sister, his friends, his art, and his band? He discovered quickly that there were plenty of chicks from his side of the tracks who wanted the same thing he did: dirty sex with no attachments. He had everything he needed.

"So what happened?" Conner asked.

Everything. "Shit got complicated. I dropped out of school." They cut through the alley behind a row of small stores, the high-end boutiques the area was becoming known for.

"Dude, she seemed like she was pissed about something."

They continued walking, turning up his street. "Probably."

"Probably?"

Conner cleared his throat, and Jax realized they were standing in front of the back steps to his apartment. The curtains were drawn in their second-floor apartment, and no light shone through. Mandi must already be asleep.

"I left without telling her." It was dark so Jax couldn't see Conner's expression, which meant Conner couldn't see the guilt on Jax's face.

Conner chuckled, disbelief coloring his laugh. "That's pretty fucked up."

Jax scaled the steps up to his apartment door and shoved the key in the lock. "Yep. But hey, it was just a long hookup." Because that's all it had been, right? One monthlong hotter-than-fuck hookup. He ignored the niggling itch at the back of his thoughts calling him a liar.

"So what are you going to do about it now?" Conner yelled up at him.

He stopped and turned. Good question. What *was* he going to do about it now? "Not sure yet," he called down.

"You better figure it out soon. She may be prickly and abrasive, but Jami Dillon is hot. And hot don't stay on the market long in our world."

Jax could still hear Conner's laughter as he disappeared into the night.

He let himself into his darkened apartment and stumbled into his bedroom. He had women practically throwing themselves at him—women like Kayla, who were as lukewarm as old beer—but fifteen minutes in a conference room with Jami left him burning.

Without flipping on the light, he undressed, dropping his clothes in a pile on the floor. As he slid into bed, the soft flannel sheets caressed his heated skin, at once soothing and frustrating. He wondered where she was, if she was naked and in bed, thinking about him. He pictured her touching herself, her soft fingers pinching her rosy nipples, her other hand stroking her neatly trimmed pussy. Would she moan softly or cry out when she came?

He didn't want to lust after her, but if he was honest with himself, he couldn't wait to get beyond her boxy suits and boring-ass beige pumps to rediscover the sultry woman beneath. Apparently his dick didn't give a shit whether or not he wanted to want her. It had a mind of its own and wanted to teach her all the wicked things he'd learned since they were together in law school.

But how the fuck was he supposed to do that with so much history clogging up any kind of future?

The next afternoon, at Mason and Kevan's engagement party, Jami's gaze swung toward the front door every time the bell rang. Each time a new person or group walked into Mason's house, she held her breath. Jax would be there. Of course he would. He was in the damn wedding party. He had to make an appearance at the engagement party. She looked around the room and recognized only a handful people: Kevan's brother; members of Manix Curse; Joe, the band's manager; and a couple of Mason's college friends. Almost everyone else was a stranger to her. The growing party was a colorful one, a lot of piercings, tattoos, and a cacophony of hair colors and styles. Businesspeople, tattoo artists, music people.

She kept busy refilling food dishes and drinks, helping Kevan in the kitchen as well as out by the new pool. As she swung open the refrigerator door, she felt Jax's gaze like pinpricks on the back of her neck even from across the great room. His gregarious greeting for the soon-to-be newlyweds lifted above the voices and the music moments before she felt his hand touch her waist as she leaned into the fridge, pretending to look for more of…of…something someone had asked for.

"Told ya I'd see you soon." Jackson's long fingers wrapped around her waist as his other hand crept down between their bodies and squeezed her butt. She straightened up and spun, pushing the fridge closed. "Did you miss me?"

Yes. She had, dammit, but he didn't need to know that. In fact, she was going to do everything she could to purge any kind of desire for him from her body.

"Not even a little." Her voice came out a wobbly gasp, not a real protest. Great. She held up an unopened bottle of cranberry juice. "If you'll excuse me, Kevan's waiting for her juice."

"Liar," he laughed as she untangled herself from his long arms. "Looking good, sunshine."

She hadn't thought about him at all when she'd selected the pale pink dress from the very back of her closet. Not once. Okay, maybe just once.

Resisting the urge to preen in front of him, she snorted. He laughed again and leaned over and kissed her cheek before she could pull away. Her face heated as she glanced around and realized almost everyone had made their way out to the pool.

They were alone. Good.

They were alone. Not good. Whenever she was alone with Jackson Paige, bad things happened.

Well, things that *felt* good, but definitely *were* bad.

"I missed you. I can't get that kiss out of my head."

Me too. Shit. He was confusing her and invading her personal space.

"Not my problem, Jackson," she said, turning to grab a veggie platter to take out to the covered patio with the bottle tucked under her arm.

"See, I think it is your problem. You made it your problem when you kissed me." He stepped in front of her, barring her way and blocking her view of the party with his wide shoulders. "Have I mentioned how much I love it when you say my full name like that?"

"I can assure you I don't say your name in any special way."

"You say it all prissy and posh. Dragging it out, letting it roll off your tongue like a peppermint or butterscotch candy. Do you think of candy when you say my name, sunshine?"

She brushed her bangs out of her eyes. Maybe to buy herself a second. Maybe so she could see his eyes better. "I certainly do not," she said crisply, ignoring the visions of lollipops and her tongue and his cock…and… dammit, she was doing it again.

He softly ran his finger across her forehead and down her cheek, mimicking her movement. Only his finger drew a hot line, a river of lava, across her face. God, his heat was going to devastate her again if she wasn't careful.

"You do, sunshine. I have a proposal."

Screw his proposal. He'd thrown away any chance he had with her long ago. Didn't matter how melty he made her feel when he was near. Jackson was trouble. With a capital T. And she was not going there again.

"Apparently you're delusional. Get out of my way."

"No."

"No?" Her pulse pounded in her ears, and her cheeks warmed again, but for a totally different reason this time.

"Get. Out. Of. My. Way," she repeated.

"No." The smug look on his face finally threw her over the edge. She set the platter and the bottle of juice on the counter, then poked her finger into his chest.

"I can't even stand to be in the same room with you. Who the hell do you think you are? You left me. There is nothing for us to discuss." Heat rolled off his body, combining with her surge of anger, creating a dangerous cocktail of lust and rage that she hadn't allowed in her life for a very long time.

He wrapped his hand around the one finger she still held to his chest and lifted it to his mouth. She stared, frozen, as his lips surrounded her finger and sucked it in. Holy shit.

Her breath got stuck somewhere between her lungs and her heart. A low moan escaped her throat before she could tamp it down. His eyes never left hers, and the warm glove of his tongue slowly ground down every sharp edge she had. Her heart slowed and skipped three beats—one, two, three. Her eyes closed—she couldn't stare into the warm chocolate depths of Jackson's eyes for one more second or she'd be done. It would be game over before she even had a chance to forfeit.

He released her finger from his lips, but reached up to grasp it in his hand. "I keep telling you it isn't over between us," he muttered in her ear. Jami's eyes snapped open and she yanked her hand back from him. "But you're right. I owe you an explanation. Over dinner."

For a second, the cocksure drummer in front of her

looked vulnerable. She almost laughed aloud at that preposterous thought. Instead she shook her head and turned to grab the juice and veggie plate again. Her body fought every inch that she moved away from him, one heavy step at a time. She wanted to think they were opposites, like water and oil. Repelling, never mixing. But the more she saw him, the more she realized the attraction they'd had years before wasn't a fluke. They were more like magnets, unable to ignore the force dragging them together. She still despised him for sneaking out on her, but her body acted like they'd never been apart. Stupid vagina.

She stopped and turned. "No. I don't need an explanation. Frankly, I don't even care."

God, she couldn't breathe. She needed to get out of the room. Away from him and his crazy, sexy voodoo. He didn't need to know what he did to her insides. No. She had a good life now. Everything had a place. There was order. She was earning back her parents' respect. And there wasn't any room for an oversexed tattoo artist.

She stomped to the screen door, but before she could figure out how to get it open with her one free hand, Jackson's colorful forearm reached around to grab the door for her. Damn, even his forearms were corded with muscles. Why was she so damn obsessed with the man's arms? Clearly, she was completely out of her element with him. She always had been. When she got a chance, she was going to call her girls for a meet-up. They might have a better idea about what the heck was going on in her head…and her lady parts.

Before he pulled the door open, he said, "If you

go to dinner with me tomorrow night, I'll leave you alone tonight."

She scoffed. "Let me get this straight. You're offering to not stalk me at my brother's engagement party if I go to dinner with you?"

He nodded.

"That's basically extortion."

"Whatever gets you through the night, counselor."

Maybe she did want to know why he'd left her so many years ago. Maybe, once she heard the explanation, she'd be able to let go and move on. She felt her shoulders fall.

No. She couldn't risk it. The reason he'd left—if there was more to it than just the restless spirit of a wannabe rock-and-roll playboy—didn't really even matter. It wouldn't change what had happened, and it didn't affect her in the least now.

She looked out at the yard full of people laughing and enjoying the rare cool, but not cold day left over from the brief storm. The blue sky was full of billowy white clouds, and the sun shimmered high in the sky. Her brother stood taller than almost everyone, his arm wrapped tightly around Kevan, who laughed and talked with a red-haired man Jami didn't recognize. When Mason leaned forward and kissed the top of Kevan's head, Jami's chest tightened.

"Sunshine, go out with me. Just dinner," he repeated.

And she might have shivered. Like she always did when he whispered that particular nickname. The one he'd used in bed when he was commanding her body and winning over her battered heart. Remembering that phase in her life was smart. Holding on to the memory of the pain his betrayal caused would save her this time around.

She shook her head. "No," she said simply and squared her shoulders before walking out to the patio with a forced smile. But she did it without looking back at him, without giving in. That had to count for something.

Chapter 4

JAX WATCHED JAMI SWISH THROUGH THE OPEN DOOR and walk up to Mason, Kevan, some of the guys from Tatuaggio and the band, and Dan Cullen, the marketing guy from Hellfire, the sponsors of their big upcoming tour. Jami's pink dress exposed a lot more skin than she usually showed. Not to mention the mountainous cleavage and long legs the dress accentuated. When he'd walked into the house he'd seen her immediately, drawn to her creamy skin and perfect heart-shaped ass like a motherfucking tattoo machine to virgin skin. And hadn't it always been that way with her? Hadn't she always drawn him in with her prim and proper words and rules? Half the time he thought it was cute as hell how she tried to control the universe, and the other half he wanted to muss her up and leave her off-balance.

Jami was talking to her brother and Conner. Her pale blond hair was pulled back into a long ponytail that swung back and forth, the tip nearly brushing her waist when she tipped her head back to talk to Mason. Damn, how he'd love to wrap that long mass of golden hair around his fist and kiss that full mouth of hers again. She wore very little makeup, with a light shine of gloss on her lips and maybe something on her eyes. The high lines of her cheekbones were dusted with freckles. Fucking beautiful. And still totally out his league. Oh, and still his buddy's little sister.

She laughed at something Conner or Mason said, then spoke to Mandi. They both turned, and Jami pointed back at him, where he no doubt stood staring like an idiotic lovestruck teen. Was Jami calling him out on his threat to dog her the entire party before he had a chance to make his first play?

Mandi waved and started walking towards him, stepping to the side as partygoers strode past.

"Stick your tongue back in your mouth, loverboy, or Ms. Fancy Pants is going to notice you salivating over her." She punched her tiny fist into his shoulder. She was his physical opposite. Their politician father had gone from Jax's statuesque model mother to a younger, smaller version with Mandi's mom. Joseph Wade Paige was currently on wife number four and family number three with their seven-year-old brother and four-year-old sister.

His current stepmother, Brittany, had been a very friendly, very social cheerleader only two years ahead of Jax in high school. She had tried on more than one occasion to get him into bed at a party, and once after one of his shows, but she'd always made him a little wary. She'd been the kind of girl who manipulated situations and people with her cute little mouth and nice tits. And now she was his stepmother. Ew.

"Shut up, twerp."

"So she already knows you're still lusting over her body?" she teased.

"Yeah. She knows," he said before he could stop himself.

"Oh."

"Speechless for once?" He nudged Mandi with his

elbow and yanked the beer from her hand. "What the hell, Amanda? You still have to study tonight."

"You're no fun." She laughed. "But I was bringing it over to you anyway."

He took a long swig off the icy local brew, his eyes still locked on Jami. "She's hot, right?" Might as well get a woman's take on it.

"Yeah. Totally hot in a perfectly poised kind of way."

"Yep."

"So what's the problem? You're obviously into her, you have some history, and she's not seeing anyone that I know of."

"Our history is not exactly problem-free. And she's Mason's little sister."

"So?"

"Dudes don't fuck their buddies' little sisters."

"That's lame. Sounds like an excuse to me. You're going to have to explain what went down between you two."

"Another time."

Her eyebrows furrowed and her lips went flat. The Monroe piercing above her lip glinted in the sunlight. "Whatever. I'm going to mingle and then I have to get ready for my finals. Stay out of trouble, big bro." Sarcasm dripped from her tongue, honeyed with her sweet voice but stinging all the same.

He watched as Mandi walked away, annoyed at her. But also proud. She was working her ass off to get through school. Despite being in a heavy metal band and hanging out with a bunch of crazy tattoo artists, she had her head on straight. Even if she didn't know what the fuck she was talking about when it came to Jami.

Jax spent the next hour talking with his friends and meeting a few new ones. More than a couple of women at the party, while not overtly making passes at him, did a good job of flirting and making themselves available. He flirted back. No need to be rude, right? Plus, he was a guy. That's what guys did. But there was only one woman at the party—or anywhere, for that matter—who truly held his attention.

When he found himself part of a group that included Jami, he sidled up to her, but before he could say something or drag her away for some privacy, Kevan looked at him with those big blue eyes of hers. "So, guys," she started loudly enough for about a dozen people to turn and stare. "What's the deal with you and college? Friends? Friends with benefits? Same study group?"

The fuck?

He peered over at Jami as her cheeks turned pink and her eyes widened. He wanted to call her out and tell everyone about them. Or at least that's what he'd usually do. Because, really, he could give two fucks about what anyone else thought. Plus, he might have left, but it hadn't been totally his fault. But the anxiety shadowing her eyes made his chest hurt a little, reminding him of a younger, sweeter Jami. She stood so close he could smell her flowery body lotion, so close he wanted to reach out and brush his fingers against her soft skin. But he didn't. For once they were on the same side of the table and not battling each other on opposite ends.

He flung his arm across her shoulders in a manner designed to clearly say "old buddies" and not "old fuck buddies," and her body tensed for a moment before softening against him. Brushing his fingers along her bare shoulder—he was only human—he smiled. "Friends. I was her tutor."

When half the group gaped at him like fish pulled from their tanks, he laughed. "What? In law school. She needed help in a class I TAed."

Bowen—no longer the obnoxious life of the party he'd once been—was the first to break the awkward silence. "Dude, I think everyone's digesting the fact that you went to law school."

Bowen reached over and smacked his arm. Hard. Bowen knew about his law school background, knew he'd dropped out six months before graduation. Even knew a little—not the whole story, no one knew the whole story—about the girl he'd left behind. They'd spent many a late night hanging out and talking, drinking beers. Stuff came out.

Everyone laughed and the conversation flowed back to Kevan and Mason's upcoming wedding, as well as the band's tours and record deal. He tried to pay attention and not obsess about the woman standing next to him, the woman who kept shifting from foot to foot, the only sign that she wasn't completely in control of everything around her. She laughed at all the right times. Smiled appropriately. Even responded without prompting. But still she shuffled her feet and wrung her hands. Jami was nervous around him. Or the group. Maybe both.

She grinned, catching him staring again. "Thank you for not making a big deal in front of everyone," she whispered, placing her hand on his chest as she leaned up to his ear. Her fingers were like a brand, burning through his shirt, and her clean scent wafted over him. His blood pounded in his ears. And other places. Fuck.

One minute he was fine, having a good time at the party. The next, the touch of her fingers were giving him a semi.

Jax moved his hand to cover hers, pressing it into his chest, allowing her fingers to dig in slightly. "You're welcome. Come with me." Then, without stopping to think about it and before she could make up another reason to pull away, he turned and marched back into the house with her hand in his. Back in the day, Jami Dillon had liked it when he helped her relieve some of her decision-making…in the bedroom, anyway. Yeah, Mason was a good friend and all, but Jami was an adult.

And for once she didn't resist as he dragged her into the back part of the house where he knew there was a guest bedroom and en suite bathroom. She didn't pull away when he tugged her into the empty room and pushed her up against the closed door. Instead she dropped that annoying in-control mask she wore like a shield every day, and she smiled. It was small, but it was real. The kind of smile where cartoon animals started singing and butterflies circled around their heads. Zip-a-dee-fucking-do-dah-day.

"You still have a thing for pushing me up against doors, Jackson."

When his already-hard dick somehow grew harder, he realized he must really be a sick fucker. Because he got hard, like concrete, as the image of the last time he'd had her up against her bedroom door flitted through his brain. They had finished studying for an exam she had the next day and stopped for bagels and coffee. Halfway back across the Oregon State campus to her apartment, the sky had opened up and dumped buckets on them. He'd caught sight of the wet T-shirt molded to her curvy breasts, and their waterlogged breakfast had been forgotten on the entryway floor.

Flashes of legs wrapped around his waist, pulling him, fingers kneading his damp shoulders, teeth biting her neck. Her cry as she came all around his cock. Fuck. How had he let all that fall apart?

"So why me and not one of the dozen or so women following you around today?"

He snorted. She was jealous. "I haven't been able to stop thinking about that kiss. Now hands above your head, sunshine." She started to say something. Then her eyes grew wild and her mouth fell open, her body unable to resist the familiar command. She hesitated and a guarded look flitted across her face. "Try to trust me."

When she scrunched her brows and tilted her head, he smiled and cupped her cheek. "Trust me for now. Please."

He could sense the quiet battle going on in her busy head. She was listing the pros and cons as well as every possible outcome to every scenario. Her big brain was always burning bright, which was why he loved the challenge of getting her to stop thinking and just feel.

"Don't think, do."

She sighed deeply, maybe giving in to the battle in her head. Slowly her fingers crawled up his abs and over his chest, each tap of her fingertips burning through his T-shirt and straight to his cock. He loved it when she let go and gave in. When she lifted her hands from his chest and clasped them over her head against the door, he was simultaneously filled with regret at losing her touch and relief that she had allowed him back in. Then she dropped her eyes. Slightly, but enough to send him the consent he needed.

So many years passed, and yet they could still communicate without words.

His hands traced her hips and small waist before he dragged them up, outlining her ribs through the soft material of her dress. He caressed her curves as his thumbs grazed her nipples, sweeping back and forth against the hard buds he could feel tightening through her dress. With one hand he reached up and gripped her thin wrists. With the other, he kneaded one ample breast, marveling at how perfect her tits were for his hands.

Her hips jutted and pushed against him. God, he wanted to lift her up and take her against that damn door. But he wouldn't do that here, even if he sure as hell wanted to. He'd already messed with her head enough for one day.

"Jami, I'm not having sex with you."

Her face dropped. "Why not?"

He lifted her chin with his finger and dropped a quick kiss on her nose. "Because we're at an engagement party."

"Oh my God, I hate you so much right now." She pouted, her plump bottom lip poking out. That was new. "We could forget the past for right now and hump like bunnies. We can deal with the regret tomorrow." She pressed her hips into his.

"Yeah?" He smiled.

"Yeah."

"Nope." She huffed and pulled her chin from his fingers. Without warning, he picked her up.

She squealed, laughing. "What are you doing?"

"Taking the edge off," he said as he placed her on

the daybed against the wall and spread her legs wide with his hands. Reaching for the elastic band on her lace panties, he laughed, "Thank God you wore a dress."

"You are not taking my panties off here," she protested as he tugged them off. Cute but practical, of course. But still sexy as fuck.

"You're objecting? You were ready to let me screw you against the door two seconds ago and now you're a prude?"

She started to disagree, but her words dried up on a gasp as he tugged on her dress and bra. He wrapped his hand around her full breast and squeezed before dropping his mouth down and running his tongue over her hard nipple. She tasted so sweet, like sunshine and light, peaches and cream. God, he could do this all day, torture and taunt her gorgeous tits. Instead, he gave her a playful bite and her body bucked against his.

He moved back down her body and continued pulling her panties off slowly.

She smacked his hand, but lifted her hips, allowing him to pull them down to her ankles, where he yanked them free and stuffed them into his pocket. She panted and her voice caught. "See, not a prude."

"No," he teased as he pushed her legs apart and dropped to his knees, her heady natural scent overwhelming his senses. "You sure?" He began layering soft kisses up her inner thigh.

Falling back against the bed, she weaved one hand through his hair as he parted her folds with his fingers.

"God, you're so sexy, sunshine. Always so wet for me." He leaned forward to drag his tongue along her crease several times.

Her body arched into his mouth and her fingers tugged on his hair, the sharp pull causing his cock to pulse and harden even more as he latched on to her clit and sucked hard. She gasped and cried out his name, but he didn't let up. This wasn't meant to be a long, slow, casual buildup. This was meant to bring her to dizzying heights quickly and get her off. Chip away at the titanium shell she coated herself with.

When she began to rock her hips, he added a finger to her slick pussy. In and out. Over and over her body protested, trying to pull his fingers back in. Short pants burst from her lips, and she threw her arm over her mouth to squelch her own cries. Fucking hot. Then her entire body trembled and arched, frozen in pleasure. She hung there, absorbed in the roiling orgasm his fingers and tongue had just given her. And then her body crashed against the bed, while she struggled to catch her breath.

Jax stood, but kept himself solidly between Jami's athletic thighs. He bent and kissed her forehead. "Thank you," he said quietly and stroked her long ponytail.

"I should be thanking you." Her giggle hitching in her chest, eyes downcast as she adjusted her bra and dress. Her lips were puffy and her cheeks were ruddy because of him. Pride filled his chest. But why did she suddenly look so shy and embarrassed? He stood and pulled her with him, trying to gauge the blank look on her face.

Fuck. He should have known better than to drag her down to his level. What was he doing? Trying to pick up where they left off five years ago? If he insisted on bullying orgasms out of her, it was all going to crash and burn before he got a chance to really spend some time with her again.

Wait. Was that what he wanted? Another chance? Or to pick up where they left off, so he could get her out of his head and move the fuck on? Picking up where they left off might be a good start, but would it be worth the pain of letting her go again? Thinking too far ahead might screw it all up before it got started. He knew they'd have to deal with their past. And then, eventually, her asshole parents. That would probably end them for good.

"No, you're amazing. And I'm sorry. You deserve better than this," he said sweeping his hand across the room and then reaching for her, needing to feel her in his arms one more time before she shuttered her windows and pulled away. Like she always did.

"Jesus, Jackson, you don't get to decide what I deserve and what I don't." She pushed him back to look up into his face. "I'm a grown woman, and if I want a hot drummer to go down on me in my brother's guest room, then that's what's what's going to happen." She grinned.

"But..."

She reached around and wrapped her hands around his denim-covered rear and dragged him in closer. "But nothing. I know what I like and I know what I want. And right now, I want you."

Something happened when Jami spoke those simple words. Something changed, snapped into place. Maybe a couple of those broken pieces that had been rattling around in his chest clicked together.

I want you.

What if he was worth more than what he gave the

fans and his customers—more than his dad or her parents thought? Jami had thought so, once.

I want you.

Maybe he wasn't able to give her long-term. Maybe they weren't meant to be together. But one thing was certain, they had chemistry. And that would have to be enough for now.

What the hell just happened?

Jami knew guilt should be setting in. Maybe it would. Any minute now. Instead she felt euphoric. Floaty. If that was a thing. Maybe that was the mind-blowing, toe-curling, body-numbing orgasm she'd just had. Yeah. Probably. Holy sheep. How had she not known it could be like that? Or maybe she had. Maybe it had been like that with Jackson before, but she'd buried the memories of her physical reactions to him along with her emotional ones.

Jami's body was still tingling, but also felt very zen and relaxed. She was more comfortable in her own skin than she'd felt in years. Not willing to examine that particular thought, she watched as Jackson battled with something. His face changed: his brow rose and dropped; he opened, then closed, his mouth. With a resolute look, he began to speak, but instead her mother's muffled voice barreled down the hallway and into the guest room. Jami's warm, fuzzy feelings evaporated, and her entire body felt tight again, as though if she moved too quickly she might shatter into a million little pieces.

"JamiLynn. Your father and I would like a word with you." Carol Dillon never raised her volume above what was considered polite, and she certainly never yelled, but still her voice carried and had the same effect as if she had walked in on them screwing. Jackson's mouth snapped shut, and Jami began pacing and smoothing her hair and her dress. Her eyes darted back and forth from him to the door. Her heart raced with a heady mixture of the pleasure Jackson had dealt her and the anxiety that always tainted every interaction with her parents. His eyebrows furrowed, and lines she'd never seen before drew across his forehead. Whatever he'd been about to say to her was gone forever. She was torn between begging him to leave and begging him to finish what he'd started to say.

He'd already made it to the door when his hand froze on the handle. He looked over his shoulder, glancing first at Jami's hands and then dragging his smoldering gaze up to her face.

"Dinner, Jami."

"What are you talking about?" she whispered.

"I want a date, sunshine, and I want to talk about what happened. Promise me one dinner, and I'll get out of your hair and let you deal with your parents."

Jesus. He was blackmailing her after an insanely powerful orgasm. So not cool.

"JamiLynn, are you in there?" Her father's voice bellowed outside the closed door.

"Fine."

"Yeah?"

"Yes, Jackson. I will have dinner with you. Only dinner. But I can't until next week. Now leave."

"Why?" He almost whined. Was he jealous? Seriously?

"Oh, don't look so forlorn," she sneered. "I volunteer

over at the Portland Community Women's Resource Center. I have a shift I can't miss. Now go!"

Relief flooded his face as he pushed the door open and walked out. With her panties in his pocket.

Oh shit. Ice-cold fingers of guilt crawled inside her, filling her head with regret.

What was it with this man? Wasn't it usually women who wanted to talk and guys who didn't? Jackson had to make everything harder. Everything different. Everything…Jackson.

The bedroom door stood open, filling the room with loud music as her parents reached the doorway. The bed was a wreck, and the room smelled like sex. The look on her mother's face immediately filled Jami with shame and an overwhelming desire to run. Her hands shook, not a lot, but enough that she threw them behind her back so they wouldn't notice.

She swallowed, her tongue so thick and heavy in her mouth it reminded her of a wet towel. "Mother." She tried to smile, but as her father's tall body and grim face peered into the room, she couldn't force her lips to turn up.

"What are you doing here?" she asked before she could filter her words or compose her expression.

Her father's pinched expression deepened. "Don't be ridiculous, JamiLynn. Your brother is still planning on marrying that woman. Where else would we be?"

The last thing she wanted to do was antagonize her parents. She owed them so much. They didn't deserve her attitude. She took a deep breath and pulled herself together, aligning her thoughts and straightening her dress. "Of course. I apologize. It's great to see you. I

hadn't expected to see you until next Saturday's brunch."
She moved across the room away from the bed—the evil
and now rumpled bed—toward her parents, still standing in the doorway.

Completely ignoring her question, her father's eyes
swung from her face to the bed and back to her again.

Damn, damn, damn.

The look her parents gave her spoke volumes about
what they thought of their youngest child. Her father
stood with his legs wide, arms crossed, the tic in his jaw
jumping. Her mother stood stiffly, picking imaginary lint
off her spotless pastel pantsuit. Elegant. Untouchable.
Perfect. And Jami was the opposite, despite her constant
efforts to measure up, to fit into their country-club-
martini-sipping perfect world. It never mattered how it
looked on the outside; she would always be an impulsive, reckless screwup to them.

She was never going to change. She'd proved that
by letting the only man she'd ever really cared about,
the only one who'd ever really seen the real her, go
down on her in her brother's house during an engagement party. The same man who had abandoned her five
years ago. And somehow her damn parents had figured
it out.

Screw this, the little voice in her head whispered.
Screw them and their judgments. Jami almost covered
her mouth, sure her betrayal must show on her face, as
garish as clown makeup.

Her brave inner voice was back. The one that had
kept her company for so many lonely years as a child.
The one that had backed her up when her parents tore
her down as a teen. The one that had told her sleeping

with Dallas Gale at seventeen was not a good idea—
even though she'd ignored the voice and done it anyway.

Instead of cowering and explaining to her parents,
which she had started doing after "the incident,"
maybe she should do as they said and actually act like
a grown-up.

"What were you doing with that man, JamiLynn?"
her father asked with barely contained contempt etched
in the lines of his face.

"He's an old friend, Father."

Her dad snorted and glared at her. "He looks familiar.
Is he one of those volunteers at your clinic?"

"It's a family resource center. I'm an adult, and who
I speak to is really none of your concern." Her frozen
feet suddenly melted as she took two steps forward and
met her father's steely gaze, daring him to not step aside.

"Yes, you are an adult, and we expect you to act
like one."

"I know, Father. I'm doing my best." She smiled,
probably watery and weak, but she tried. Considering the
orgasm Jackson had given her and then this very uncomfortable confrontation, it was the best she could do.

Her father only grunted, but the unspoken words
hung in the air: the words she'd heard her entire life
about working harder, being the best, never settling.
Both parents stepped back into the hall and let her pass
with only a quiet, disgruntled sigh. It was never enough.
She was never enough.

Not only had she let her parents down again, but this
time she'd let herself down. She needed to get her shit
together and forget all about Jackson Paige.

"Mother, Father, there's a bar and food out in the

backyard. I'm going to use the restroom and I'll meet you out there," she called over her shoulder.

And now her inner voice was telling her to throw her shoulders back, hold her head high, and go get her god-damn panties.

"I'm telling you guys, it's sweet."

Jax listened as Joe described the new bus the band was getting for their tour with Pagan Saints. The tour was a big fucking deal, and everyone was stoked about it. Everyone but him. He wasn't feeling it. He wanted to. Knew he should. But this last tour had been only nine days, and he'd still come off the road feeling old and lonely.

Mason and Kevan were another story. They'd started that trip as enemies competing for the band's business and ended as lovers and business partners.

He cringed and blew out a long breath, shoving his hands in his pocket. When his fingers wrapped around something soft, something lacy, he almost yanked it out in front of the group he was standing with in Kevan's fancy kitchen before he realized what little jewel he held in his hand.

Panties. One hot little blond's panties, to be specific. He reined in the smile threatening to give him away.

It was highly unlikely that Mason would get a big kick out of Jax pulling Jami's cute panties out of his pocket and fondling them. Nope. His reaction would probably resemble something more along the lines of a punch in the face. Or, at least a swift escort out of their new house. Better keep his hand where it was.

Dammit, where was she, anyway? Once he'd seen her parents on the other side of the door, his heart dropped from sixty to zero in two seconds. As he brushed past them in the hall, he wondered if they recognized him. They'd only met the one time outside Jami's apartment, but it hadn't been that long ago. One minute he had felt the spicy hint of adrenaline pumping through his veins from having his hands on Jami again, and the next he literally had to force himself to put one foot in front of the other and make it down the hall. He needed to get away from the two people he'd never wanted, nor expected, to see again.

Maybe he should have turned around and stood by her. A unified show of strength against two dicks he knew hadn't changed since the day he first met them five years before.

So why hadn't he gone back in? Maybe it was that dark shadow of doubt he'd kicked in the ass so long ago. Or thought he had. Could he have handled another rejection from Jami, even if it was once again orchestrated by her parents?

Of course he could. Who the fuck was he trying to kid?

Sure, Jax had never forgotten Jami's haunted eyes or petite curves. And long after he'd left her, he'd marveled at how well they'd fit together despite a foot's difference in height. Her tiny package fit so perfectly with his it was burned into the memory folds of his brain. Unfortunately, so was his last meeting with Jami's parents.

The first few months after he'd left school, and her, he'd gone back to work at Tatuaggio. He felt shame for leaving, shame for falling for her, and shame for falling into old patterns of behavior. He'd quickly become Bowen's partner in crime again—like back in high school—and he'd fucked and drunk his way through the Portland music scene. He'd needed to drown out the guilt and embarrassment for how he'd left. His desperation to prove that Jami hadn't gotten under his skin—that she'd been just a silly fling, nothing more, nothing less—drove him to screw every groupie and hot willing fangirl. His goal to burn Jami's scent from his nose and the feel of her skin from his fingertips hadn't really worked.

Then he'd come to his senses, with a little ass-kicking from his bandmates and Tony, the shop's owner. He'd slowed down on the chicks and the booze. Started working seriously as a tattoo artist. When Bowen really began to fall apart—missing appointments, going drunk to practice with his band Toast, or skipping out altogether—Jax had had to reevaluate his life, and he realized he might be following his buddy right down the same path.

But he still couldn't nail what the hell was missing or wrong with his life. For fuck's sake, he had an awesome band that was a goddamn rocket ship on the way up. He had awesome bandmates. His sister was almost done with school, and his schedule at the shop had a significant waiting list. He'd even started dabbling in art other than tattooing. But he'd still felt hollow, like a puppet merely going through the motions with someone else yanking the strings.

Then JamiLynn Dillon had walked into Tatuaggio and thrown his world back into chaos. But maybe it was a chance at fixing the past, at least his part of it. But then her parents showed up and fucked with his head as well as hers. No matter how many times he told himself another story. Another lie. Another fairy tale. They would always be there, the morality devils sitting on her shoulder telling her what was appropriate, how to act, how to live.

A sharp stab to his side startled him from his pathetic little jaunt down memory lane. "Don't you think, dude?" Marco looked at him expectantly, his long hair loose and falling forward over one eye.

"Huh?"

"Dude, what is your problem?"

Good question.

What the fuck *was* his problem? Her parents were her deal, not his. And they were the main reason he'd left her without a word years ago—and why he needed to stay away from her now. They'd made it clear she had a plan, and he wasn't part of it. Yeah, it had hurt, but it turned out for the best, hadn't it? Her parents were everything he detested: judgmental, superficial, achievement focused. A good reminder of the family he'd run from. The family he had no interest in being part of. "Sometimes your words start blending together and all I hear is 'whaaaa whaa whaaa whaa wha,'" he said, affecting the drone of a Charlie Brown grown-up.

Marco looked stricken for a minute and then tapped Jax's gut with his fist. Jax welcomed the physical play and protected his belly from another shot. Usually he could shoot the shit all day and socialize for hours. Not today. Not when he could still taste the sweet tangy flavor of Jami on his tongue. Could still smell her honey in his nostrils and hear her muffled cries in his head. He gently jabbed Marco in the gut, then stuck his leg behind his knee and pulled him down to the wooden floor, flipping him onto his back, laughing and cajoling him to tap out.

Voices rang out around him, mixed in with "Collapse" by Zeds Dead pumping through the house from the sound system.

Kevan's house. Mason's house. A nice, upscale house and not some hangout dive.

Fuck. If he was resorting to wrestling at his friends' engagement party, maybe it was time to get the hell out of this party. But instead of shrieks of anger or threats from the hostess, Kevan yelled from the patio for Marco to kick Jax's ass.

Apparently the woman had no loyalty.

As he continued to roll on the kitchen floor with the taller, bulkier singer, catcalls from their friends and family rang out. Mason's big boots appeared as a blur in Jax's line of sight next to the full black and white polka-dotted swing skirt of his future bride.

"So, losers, you guys really going to do this here?" he asked as Marco rolled over Jax.

Kevan had her fist planted on her hip, but a big grin betrayed her amusement. "At my engagement party?"

"Is this normal for you people?" That uptight voice brought an entire room full of metalheads and tattoo artists to a hush. Kevan's cheeks burned red, and she snapped her focus to her soon-to-be father-in-law. Unfazed, he continued, "Rolling around on the floor and playing this horrific noise?"

Jax attempted to untangle himself from Marco's

stranglehold, but not before giving him a firm elbow to the nose. For fun and shit.

Marco sucked in a jagged breath, but didn't say anything as Mason stepped in front of Kevan with a measured but feral look in his eye, a controlled burn on the cusp of jumping its fire line. "Dad, Mom. I didn't see you come in. Welcome to our home." He spread his arms wide and discreetly grabbed Kevan's hand, tugging her into his side. Jax smiled to himself. He really liked this guy. No apology. His words said "welcome to my world," but his tone said "take it or leave it, because I don't give a shit what you think."

"And to our engagement party," Mason said.

Without acknowledging the people standing awkwardly staring, Mason's dad's expression was equally controlled. Just a shadow of a sneer twisted his narrow face. Mr. Dillon still stood tall, nearly as tall as his son, but much thinner, with the slight build of someone who rarely saw the inside of a gym or soccer field, like Mason.

"This is how you greet your parents? Who are these people, son? They're dressed more like thugs than guests at an executive's engagement party. We found your sister in the bedroom with one of them, and your future wife is egging on the same miscreant to beat up another *friend*." His father stood with his arms crossed over his chest. His wife clutched her purse with both hands and stood closely behind her husband.

As Mason's face flushed red and he started to move toward them, Jami stepped out from behind her parents. "Our mother and father are forgetting their manners."

She moved to place her body in front of Mason

and spread her hands out. "These *people* are Mason and Kevan's friends and family. The people they love and respect."

Before her dad could reply with his usual vitriolic response, she continued, "This is Mason's fiancée, Kevan." Jami's smile never wavered in the face of her parents silent judgment in that room of strangers. Jax's chest filled with something warm and a little sweet. She'd probably been ripped to shreds by them moments before, and yet here she was, rescuing them all from the Wonder Twins, Ice Queen and Asshole Man.

"It's great to finally meet you both." Kevan stuck out her hand, and they stared for a moment before Mrs. Dillon finally shook the tips of Kevan's fingers. Jax nearly expected her to dig the hand sanitizer out her purse. Kevan smirked. Yeah, she was thinking the same thing.

"Thank you for the invitation, Kevan. It's nice to finally see where our son lives."

Not "It was nice to finally meet you. You have a lovely home. It's great to see where you both live." Nope. Mason and Jami's parents were calculating and cutting with every word that came out of their mouths. How could he have forgotten?

"Yes, well, we've done a lot work over the last few months since we bought the house. I'd love to show you around." Kevan and Mason led them back toward the kitchen and then out onto the deck and backyard.

As the people standing around began to dissipate in search of food, beer, or boobs—or a combination of the three—Jax turned to Jami.

"You didn't have to do that."

"I did."

"You didn't," he insisted. His chest squeezed with something like pride for the way she stuck up for her family and smoothed over such an awkward situation.

"I did."

"Why are you so damn stubborn, woman?"

"I'm not."

"You are. Stop fighting me, sunshine. Or I'll use these panties in my hand as a gag while I spank that sweet round ass of yours." He smiled to himself as he watched her eyes darken and widen.

"Jackson," she scolded as she reached for him and the wadded material in his much bigger hand. "Give those to me."

"When you have dinner with me."

"That's not for a week," she whined.

"Friday night we're playing a surprise show at the Tiki. Be there by ten and maybe I'll let you have them back." He pulled his hand from hers, then walked out the door with her panties in his pocket.

Chapter 5

JAMI HAD NO INTENTION OF GOING TO SEE MANIX Curse play. Instead she found herself at Grape, the local wine bar, on that Friday night. And it was hopping. Maybe not hopping, but pleasantly boisterous, like a wine bar should be. The music filled the tall, open room with an upbeat, calming pulse, giving it a more intimate feel than a traditional bar. The deep burgundy color of the booths popped against gray walls and huge sparkling chandeliers. Jami could imagine couples meeting there in the early stage of a relationship, with the possibility of love charging the air. The perfect place to share a seductive look, a firm caress, a lover's secret fantasy.

For someone else, of course.

After a craptastic week of feeling useless at her office, where the only challenge was the courier delivery of the recording offer and contracts from Joe, Jami was ready for the weekend. She had been looking forward to curling up into a fetal ball on her couch with her cat Aubrey when Ella had texted about meeting up with Gabby at Grape. She'd nearly said no and gone home to evaluate the band's contracts over an exciting microwaved meal of leftover pasta paired with an even more exciting glass of sparkling water or wine from a box.

But Jami was always alone. And she was starting to like having girlfriends. She knew very little about them, but hoped to have the opportunity to learn more.

Gabby had survived some kind of trauma when she was younger, which was why the savant programmer volunteered so many hours every week at the women's resource center. Ella was divorced. Her bad marriage was what had led her to working with the program as a full-time social worker and family counselor. She was the single mother of twin four-year-old daughters, Maya and Amelia, whom Jami had met a few months before at a barbecue Ella had hosted. Since then she'd spent quite a bit of time with the girls and Ella. At first she'd felt awkward around the kids, and a weird mixture of yearning and fear wove through her first couple of visits. But the girls didn't know about her stiffness. The girls didn't care about her past. The girls liked her. Truly liked her. And she was beginning to fall for them, too.

Crossing her ankles and tucking her legs under her chair, Jami leaned forward to hear the rest of Ella's story about her latest case at the Portland Community Women's Resource Center, or Quirk, as they called it. Supposedly, there was an interesting story behind how the acronym CWRC transformed into the nickname Quirk, but no one could remember it.

After her "incident," as her parents still referred to the most horrifying events in Jami's life, she'd dived into her studies and then her career, leaving no room for making friends. In law school, she'd started to shake loose the rust that had formed in place of her nonexistent social skills. Had even taken a chance and gone on a date with the tall, tattooed, lanky third-year law student who had pursued her until she not-so-reluctantly gave in.

And then he'd left without a word. Poof.

She took a small, measured sip of the red zin, savoring the oaky flavor and the hint of tartness. She rarely allowed herself the luxury of a glass of wine, let alone the wacky-hedonistic-party-girl second glass.

No, she thought wryly, no wine for you. Not too often, anyway.

"What are you laughing at?" Gabby poked her shoulder with a skinny finger.

"I wasn't laughing. I'm being pensive."

Gabby raised her auburn eyebrow, throwing doubt left and right. "Smirking and giggling is not being pensive."

"*Au contraire, mon ami*, for me it is."

"Don't try and distract me with your lawyerly tactics, Frenchy. I know that look. I would bank a billion that you're thinking about—"

Ella gasped, and said, "A guy! You're getting all weird about that guy you mentioned"—she tapped her perfectly trimmed nail on her bottom lip—"the one you met in college. What was his name?"

Ella and Gabby stared with their mouths slightly open. Gabby, with her fresh face and long, wavy red hair pulled back into a messy bun, completely clueless about every man who stared at her in the popular wine bar. And, Ella with her severe but chic black bob and Cleopatra makeup. Her friends. She couldn't help but smile. Her heart softened a tiny bit with their simple act of showing interest in her—in her thoughts, her life. Jeez, had it really been so long since anyone gave two shakes about her? The real her?

Maybe it had.

And maybe they deserved a little honesty. Because friends shared stuff, right? Frick, she needed a guidebook.

"Jackson Paige. He's a tattoo artist and the drummer in that band Manix Curse," she said, and they melted into squeals. The two women, usually serious and professional, basically morphed into teenage girls right there in front of her.

"You just turned five shades of red and rolled your eyes," Gabby said.

"Did not."

"Did too."

"No, I'm sure I haven't rolled my eyes in at least five years."

Ella shook her head. "No. You totally did."

"Whatever."

The knowing smirk on Ella's face struck a little too close to home, reminding her of her parents. "It's not a big deal. Can we drop it?"

Ella rested her hand on Jami's. "If you want. But we're your friends, Jami. You can tell us stuff. That's kind of the way it works."

Although they'd been friends for less than a year, Jami felt a special connection to Ella, and was starting to trust Gabby too. She took a deep breath that sounded more like a hiss than anything else.

"He was my tutor for a criminal law course in school. Despite his, uh, different look, we got on right away."

God, he'd made her laugh with his goofy impressions and the laid-back way he approached everything. She'd been trying so hard to impress everyone and keep her parents off her back that she'd forgotten how to laugh. He reminded her how to have fun again. And taught her things about her body and sex that she'd forgotten.

Gabby chuckled. "By *different look* do you mean super hot?"

"I guess so. At first I was pretty intimidated by how good-looking he is and all that ink. But he was very persistent about asking me out. Even started making a game of it. Finally I gave up resisting."

"Right. That must've been hard…resisting, I mean," Ella said. "What? Every guy in that band is gorgeous," she continued with a shrug.

Jami nodded. Yes, she'd acted like it was no big deal, but not giving in to Jackson's overtures had been harder than finding a loophole in a celebrity prenup. "I kept my guard up. I had a really bad breakup in high school and barely scraped through college. Jackson and I had a fling. We flung."

She took a sip of her wine, stealing a moment to remember the first time he kissed her—so commanding, but kind and sensual. Like nothing she'd ever felt. Before or since.

"What happened to the flinging?" Gabby asked, her voice quiet in the loud bar.

"I'm not sure. One morning we were in bed talking about art and the future and school. Then he went off to class and I never saw him again. He disappeared from school."

Gabby's eyes went wide, while Ella's narrowed. "You mean he never said anything?"

Jami shook her head. Nope.

"Even now, you don't know why he left school? Why he left you?"

She shook her head again.

"And he suddenly showed up? Out of the blue?"

"No, no. Two weeks ago, I decided to confront

Mason and talk him out of more tattoos at the tattoo parlor. Guess who his artist was?"

"No," Gabby and Ella said at the same time.

"And somehow I let Mason and his fiancée Kevan talk me into representing and overseeing the band's contracts. His metal band. I don't even like heavy metal anymore. That's what I get for trying to talk my stubborn brother out of anything."

"So are you going to see him again?" Ella asked. "Have you seen him again?"

Heat crept up her neck and burned her cheeks at the memory of his hands, his mouth on her. She lifted her fingers to her collar, knowing they probably couldn't see her blush in the darkened booth, but wanted to stop the warmth from taking over. Stop the delicious recollection of Jackson between her legs that had been haunting her since the weekend.

"We saw each other at Mason's engagement party. And then he left."

"That was it? Five years and…" Ella prodded.

"Other stuff happened."

Gabby smiled. Or she gave a look that passed as a Gabby smile. "Sexy stuff?"

"Yes. Okay? We messed around. My parents showed up. Jackson wrestled with his friend on my brother's kitchen floor and left."

"Without saying anything? Seems like a pattern, if you ask me." Gabby crossed her arms. The simple gesture loosened something in Jami's chest. These two women actually cared for her.

Jami chose to chew on her lip and stare at her nails. And not respond to Gabby.

"Oh, what exactly does 'sexy stuff' mean? Was it good?"

"No."

"Liar."

"Not really."

"Total liar."

"Fine. It was always good with him. That wasn't the problem," Jami admitted.

Ella squinted her eyes and tilted her head, evaluating Jami. "You're holding something back. I can tell."

Jami took a sip of her wine and released a long sigh. "He told me the band was playing tonight at the Tiki Torch and that I should go see them play."

"*Whhhhatt?*" Ella nearly shrieked, drawing attention from a group of suited men to their right, but then she lowered her voice and dug into her purse. She whipped some money out of her wallet and threw it on the table before grabbing Jami's hand and yanking her to her feet. "What the hell are we doing here?"

"Where are we going?"

"We're going to the Tiki Torch," Ella said, sharing a smile with Gabby. "But first we're going to get changed. The girls are with my parents, and I have all night to play."

☆ ☆ ☆

Word must have gotten out that Manix Curse was playing the Tiki again, because the club was nearly at capacity, wall-to-wall flannel and denim as far as the eye could see. Everyone from Jax's middle-school girlfriend to his high-school art teacher had come up to congratulate him on the band's success.

It was cool. But, frankly, it was fucking exhausting

always being on. Always smiling and acting the good ol' rock star. It was bullshit. Half the time he felt like a poser, and the other half he just felt tired. Until he got up on stage behind his drum kit. Then everything else faded away—the crowd, the lights, the women. All the chaos narrowed into a fine laser point where the only thing that mattered was the music, his band. They became a fluid, unified entity.

Jax rolled his drumsticks in his hand and playfully tapped out a beat on his much shorter sister's pink head. Mandi, apparently, didn't appreciate his brotherly affection and attempted to punch him in the stomach, despite the fact that she was a dinky little squirt with fists the size of his big toes.

"What is it about you guys and punching each other?" A familiar, husky voice broke through Zakk Wylde's remake of "Ain't No Sunshine" booming through the club.

Jami. She actually came.

His head snapped up, and his blood felt like lava, burning him from the inside out as it flowed faster through his veins. Unfortunately, his shock gave the dinky devil next to him an opening to punch him hard in the gut, doubling him over with a cough.

"What the hell, Mandi?" He choked, trying to stand up straight and hold his belly. But his sister waved at Jami, smirked at him, and ran off toward the green room.

He turned back to Jami and realized she was wearing a short jean skirt—short enough he could see her creamy thighs—and a long-sleeved plaid cotton shirt. And even more surprising, if that were possible, she had it unbuttoned far enough that he could see the top curve of her full breasts, held tightly in a lacy tank top. She was hotter than any woman he'd ever laid eyes on.

She threw up her hands. "Well?" She huffed, blowing out a breath that lifted her loose, long blond hair. Long, gorgeous hair that he hadn't seen down in five years. He smiled, trying really hard not to look predatory. He couldn't help it. Despite her douchebag parents and her odd attachment to everything boring and beige, his body instantly reacted to hers. She looked awesome. But instead of telling her so, he motioned with his finger for her to spin. He had to know how long her hair fell down her back and what those black heels she was wearing did to her pert, round little ass.

She tried to hide her blush, which he always found so cute, but slowly turned, her arms still spread wide. How she could be so wild in bed and still get embarrassed at a little lascivious attention was pretty damn funny. When she started turning, he realized he wasn't the only one watching her swivel her hips as she circled. He turned his glare at the table of assholes eyeballing Jami and the two standing against the bar. The blond goddess in front of him remained completely clueless about her audience.

It was only a moment before her back came into view. Her hair wasn't as long as it had been back in school. Oh no, it was longer, curling over the round lift of her ass. Enough hair to grab and wrap around both fists as he imagined bending her over and driving into her. His chest tightened, and he took a step forward. Placing his hands on her shoulders, he felt her tremble under his touch. He loved that feeling. The way he affected her. No matter how much she fought their connection and their past with her words, her body betrayed her lust. Every. Damn. Time.

Jax bent over her, letting his hand trace her shoulder, linger on her collarbone, and brush the side of her breast before spreading across her soft belly. He loved Jami's body. Always had. Her insane hourglass figure made him drool. Even when she hid it in boxy suits and wore her no-nonsense bun and lawyerly demeanor. She oozed sex innately. She knew it. Hated it. Fought it. But not tonight. Tonight she wore it on her sleeve. Owned it.

And Jax was arrogant enough to believe it was all for him. "Did you wear this for me, sunshine?" he whispered into her ear and ran his tongue over the soft curve of her lobe.

She stiffened for a fraction of a second before melting back into him and shaking her head. Such a little liar. He smiled against her neck, her soft, flowery scent filling his lungs like it was oxygen itself. "Did you come to get your panties or did you come to see me play?"

"Both." Her words were low, a smoky whisper. "I thought it would be a good idea to hear my client's music. And you do have something that belongs to me."

"You'll have to stay for one to get the other." He ran his nose along her neck and bit her softly. He didn't need to feel her up in the middle of the dingy club to know her nipples would be hard as two little bullets. Experience and her sharp intake of breath told him that.

"Please stop."

He turned her in his arms and looked down into her blue eyes. "I will if that's what you really want. Or we can pretend the past doesn't exist, like you said at the party. For one night." Wrapping her long hair around his fist, he angled her head where he wanted it. Where he needed it.

"I'm going to kiss you now."

"In the middle of all these people?"

"Yeah."

Her eyes widened, and while she seemed to consider it he ran his hand along her neck and cupped her face. She nodded, hissing slightly when he gave a sharp pull of her hair. He heard the band announced as Conner ran past him and bumped him with his shoulder. "Time to rock and roll, playboy!"

Jax took Jami's mouth. There was no other way to describe it. He took her full, bow-shaped lips under his and tried to convince her with his tongue to stop screwing around. There was no subtle buildup, no gentle touch of lips brushing together. He needed to fucking kiss her again. And hard. So he did, leaving no question as to what he wanted from her, fucking her with his tongue and rubbing his hard cock against the soft give of her body. He was going to combust into flames if he didn't get back inside her sweet curves soon. He moaned into her mouth and held her tighter when she mirrored his desire with a low groan of her own.

The lights flashed and dimmed as he contemplated how quickly he could get her into Shelby's office without breaking the connection. Reluctantly, he pulled back, noting the dazed, glassy look in her eyes and how hard she pulled her hands around his neck. *Good.* He slowly tugged her panties from his pocket and tied them around his wrist. Before she realized what he'd done, he pulled his drumsticks from his back pocket, twirled them in the air, and winked.

Then he turned and ran up toward the steps of the stage, wondering why he was always running away from her and not toward her.

Chapter 6

"Did he just wrap a pair of women's underwear around his wrist before going up onstage?"

Jami turned slowly, still in a Jax-induced haze. Ella and Gabby stood behind her. Oh shit, had they witnessed the whole scene play out between her and Jackson? That was exactly why she shouldn't be here. Why she had to stay away from him. He was dangerous. He made her think wearing a short denim skirt, heels, and a tiny top were good ideas. That coming to a heavy metal show in downtown Portland was a good idea. Or that letting a tattooed, pierced, six-foot-four wall of narrow, twisting muscle wrap her hair around his fist in a packed bar and kiss her breathless was a good idea.

It wasn't. Not a good idea. Definitely a very bad idea.

She stared at her friends. What had Ella asked her?

Behind her, a guitar began to play a slow, pulsing melody. Soft, sweet, building to something bigger. More solid.

The steady beat of a bass drum. Then more drums.

Ella and Gabby pointed to something on the low stage behind Jami. The band. Of course, the band was starting. More specifically, Jackson's band, her client, Manix Curse, were beginning their set. Her heart dropped into her belly. She swiveled around, her eyes tracking the hundreds of hands with their fingers held up in heavy-metal salutes.

The lone spotlight shone down on the tall and shirt-less Marco Dane as he tossed back his mane and bel-lowed to the sky about the cruelty of love. His perfect torso was already glossy with the sheen of sweat. But it was the tall, rangy man beating the drums with feral efficiency that made her blood boil with prurient lust. His head hung low, but his short, messy hair was already dark with sweat despite the fans circulating air around the stage. Conner leaned into a mic in front of Mandi and they joined the chorus.

Jami watched in awe, mesmerized by the pure raw power of the four band members and how seamlessly yet viciously they tore apart and reconstructed the song. She'd never seen anything like it. Never heard any band with such vitality and brutality, and yet a dash of melody. Even in her wilder youth, when she'd snuck into every concert and club possible, she'd never seen anything quite like Manix Curse.

Not one for crowds or other people actually touching her, Jami barely registered the audience members push-ing into her, clamoring for a closer look at Manix Curse. Or even the couple of losers who attempted gropes before Ella—or she assumed it was Ella—slapped away a restless, errant hand.

The band abruptly ended their song and the crowd went wild, screaming their names and favorite songs into the chaos.

Marco growled into the mic, and the women in the crowed squealed. "You guys here to see Manix Curse?"

The crowd screamed louder.

"You here to rock the fuck out?"

They yelled louder still.

Then Jackson raised his head and searched the crowd. The smirk that transformed his face when his eyes locked on Jami's could only be described as wolfish. The voice in her head began to whisper again, filling her with all kinds of dark and dirty thoughts. Because gone was the laid-back, easygoing Jackson everyone knew. In his place was the man she'd met years before.

Sexy.

Dangerous.

Pure sin.

And her blood turned from liquid into steam and evaporated from her body, leaving her a hollow shell of need.

He flipped his sticks around his fingers in a manner that, for some unexplained reason, made her wet. Then he pointed one stick at her, and sure enough her freaking panties were wrapped around his wrist like some ridiculous rock-and-roll talisman. People turned to stare at her, obviously wondering what, or who, had caught the playboy drummer's eye, but she just stared at him.

He yelled into his mic, "One, two, and three, and four!" before breaking into a fast-paced beat. His long arms moved so quickly she could barely keep up with his movements, except for the flexing and undulating of the well-defined muscles in his shoulders.

Lord above, the man was sheer muscle and raw sex. She'd never understood the appeal that rock stars and other celebrities had for some women. They'd always seemed so uncivilized and, frankly, so self-centered that she couldn't see herself ever having interest in one.

Until now. In this moment, if Jackson jumped up from his drums and walked up to her, demanding she drop to her knees in the middle of that dirty club and suck him off, she totally would have. He was that hot. And she was that hot for him.

When an elbow flew past her head and nearly hit her temple, she realized her friends were trying to drag her out of the way of the mosh pit that had opened up like a tempestuous storm in the middle of the club. She let them lead her to the edge of the crowd.

Gabby turned to her, her cheeks pink and her green eyes wide. "Dude, what the fuck was that?"

"That, my dear friends, was Jax Pain. Drummer extraordinaire and bad-boy tattoo artist. He's the whole thing."

"Yeah." Gabby laughed, her eyes never leaving the stage. "He certainly is."

"Anyone ready for some more booze?" Ella yelled over the blaring guitar and deep bass.

"I'll have one more since I'm taking a taxi home," Jami said.

Gabby held up her water bottle and shook her head. "I'm good."

When light bursts circled the room, Jami spotted a familiar tall figure leaning against the far wall. He was turned away from the band, looking toward the far end of the room. Jami followed his gaze to where she knew her future sister-in-law would be.

Yep. Her big brother had his eye on Kevan, eyeing her with pure adoration and bold-faced love. Jami's heart stuttered, and a twinge of something old, something long forgotten, began to unfurl in her chest. Damn, was that jealousy? In the beginning of their courtship she'd been more afraid for her brother than anything else. Afraid he was losing his mind, or that the crazy woman he'd fallen for right in this same club would somehow hurt him.

But after spending time with them, together and apart, she'd learned pretty quickly that there was definitely more to Kevan Landry than her pinup look and love of tattoos. A lot more. The bond Kevan and Mason shared was evident after one dinner. They were the real deal.

Opposites really did attract in some cases.

Spying an empty booth along the wall, Jami directed her friends to the table. After several songs, she stood and let them know she was going to say hello to her brother and his fiancée.

As she walked up to Mason, he glanced her way. She almost laughed when he did a cartoonish double-take and his mouth fell open.

"Holy shit, Jami, put some fucking clothes on."

"Nice to see you too, big brother," she laughed. "You don't like my outfit?"

"I'd like it if there was more to it. I don't think I've seen you wear something like that since high school."

Jami's stomach pitched. She was not that girl anymore, and yet here she was in a club dressed like that girl. She took a deep breath and willed her pulse to slow. "I'm a grown woman, Mason. I can dress how I want."

His brow furrowed, giving her his version of a hurt look. "Meant you look nice. What's the occasion?"

"I came to see what the big deal is." She leaned against the wall next to him and looked up at the stage. Marco was swiveling his hair in a large circle and yelling his anger into the retro-styled microphone, while Mandi was on her knees at the front of the stage, her fingers nearly invisible as she basically owned her guitar and the song. Calm, cool Conner stood to the side with his long hair pulled back to expose the shaved sides. In the center of it all was the drummer.

Jackson Paige was all that and a box of spiked leather wristbands as he beat the holy hell out of his drum kit, pounding out a sound filled with angst and intensity, yet tinged with a sorrowful melody. He made her core heat and her panties wet.

"Yeah, they're awesome, aren't they?" Mason yelled, scanning the crowd and smiling when his eyes connected with Kevan's.

"Yes. They are." She tried not to look at Jackson. Really tried to talk-yell with her brother in the noisy club, but Jackson's drums, the steady unrelenting beat that somehow reminded her of crazy wild mad sex, kept drawing her attention. Up on that stage, he was a beast, a man completely in his element and at ease with himself. A shiver ran up her spine and into her hairline. A man whose calm control of his world manifested itself into something all-consuming and dark in the bedroom. Something Jami had fought against in the years since he'd left.

"Gonna grab my woman and head for home in a few. You still coming to brunch tomorrow?"

She nodded, eyes locked to the ferocious band on the stage. "I wish they'd move back to Texas." Jami had moved from Texas with her parents when Mason had left for college and she'd been in middle school. Her mother had retired from the Space Science Institute to support her husband in his role as partner in his new Portland firm. That's when Jami's life had started to spiral. Without Mason around, she had been left on her own and spent a good deal of that time hanging out with the wrong people doing inappropriate things.

"You and me both. You better be there tomorrow. After that shit they pulled at our party I'm definitely not going if you're not."

"I'll be there. Go get Kevan. I'll see you in the morning," she said as Jackson flipped his head back, his hair wet with sweat, but still so hot. So freaking hot.

When Jackson's eyes connected with hers everything in that room disappeared. Like in a damn movie. Only this movie's soundtrack was set to a heavy metal grind and not some Top 40 ballad or hokey country song.

"I will find your darkness," Marco growled into the mic. "And add my own."

Mandi's fingers slowed and her guitar cried, drawing out the melody.

"I will drag you into the light." Jackson's arms moved at a more languid pace, his muscles flexing and twitching, the movement hypnotizing.

"Because now I know for sure." Conner's bassline pummeled the audience—building, digging deeper, climbing higher.

Marco looked up through his mane, a huge lion of a man, and screamed, "You were meant to be my home!" At the same moment Jackson jumped up, kicked his stool back, and pounded his drums in a blurred fury.

The air in Jami's lungs left with a whoosh. She couldn't breathe. And despite the loud wall of sound circling her like a hurricane, she could hear the swooshing sound of the blood pulsing through her ears.

Jackson was glorious. A magnificent metal god.

As the song ended and he ran up with his bandmates to take a bow, he brought his wrist—his panty-covered wrist—to his nose and smiled that untamed one-sided grin again, before running offstage.

By the time the band wrapped up their three encores and the bright overhead lights illuminated the club again, Jami was making her way toward the door with Ella and Gabby when the band's newly hired roadies started loading out the equipment. Suddenly, a damp tattooed arm wrapped around her waist, and she felt herself pulled into a solid, slick body.

Before she could yank herself free and reprimand the asshole messing with her, Jackson's dark voice whispered into her ear. "Say good night to your friends."

Her nipples hardened as if on command, and the heat she'd been feeling all night in her chest dropped down between her legs. He pulled her tighter, snug against the hard cock pressed against her back.

She didn't even consider the remote possibility of saying no. Instead, she waved to her friends and assured them she'd be fine as Jackson was already pulling her back through the crowd toward what she assumed was the office and backstage area. Maybe tonight she'd give into her lust for him. A shiver crawled up her neck and her heart raced. Maybe one night was what she needed for closure.

✷ ✷ ✷

Jax was on a performance high and wanted nothing more than to pounce on Jami. They were stopped by three different women before he finally pulled her into the owner's office and kicked out a couple making out on the couch. He'd barely slammed the door behind them before he twirled her and pinned her up against the door, his hand on the fleshy globes of her sweet ass. He growled when she wrapped her hands over his shoulders and pulled herself up his body, her legs winding naturally around his waist.

She had once told him his sheer strength and size had always made her feel safe, protected. That she always found it erotic as hell. He felt just the opposite right then, like he might be too close to losing control. Like he might be the furthest thing from safe right then.

His rock-hard cock throbbed against the zipper of his ridiculously tight jeans. Somewhere in the back of his adrenaline-infused brain he knew it was wrong to rub his show-sweaty body all over her sexy but tidy outfit. All he cared about was touching her, feeling her, feeling the hot glove of her pussy around him again. He was tired of waiting, of playing games.

"You were taunting me from the stage weren't you, sunshine?" He rubbed his scratchy beard along the edge of her jaw. The sharp intake of her breath followed by the increased pulse in her neck told him two things. One, she was as turned on as he was. And, two, he could have her right then and there if he wanted. A part of him wanted that very much. "Eye-fucking me the whole time."

She didn't answer for a moment. Their panting crowded the air between them.

"I was in awe," she said finally, her voice sounding low and hoarse, like velvet wrapped around his cock. He pulled back to look into her eyes. "I didn't expect...I didn't know...I..." She stared up at him, the blue of her eyes so vibrant it almost looked lavender, but she looked so confused and lost.

"You were so beautiful, Jackson. So powerful. I had no idea your music—that you—were like that. I mean. I don't know. I just didn't know."

He smiled and licked her neck, stopping to nibble her ear. His normally articulate lawyer seemed flummoxed, at a loss for words. "Men aren't beautiful."

"You are. And, oh my God, so freaking sexy."

He chuckled. "I love how ready to be fucked you are right now, and you still can't swear properly."

She pinched his shoulder. He squeezed her ass with his hands. Hard. She gasped and leaned forward, pressing her mouth to his, "Then stop talking and fuck me, bad boy."

He sucked her full bottom lip into his mouth and bit. "So now who's getting bossy?"

"Jackson!" She pleaded. And he liked the edge in her voice—jagged with lust and need. "I want you."

I want you.

There it was again.

"Want you, too, babe, but not here."

And then Jami did something for the second time that blew him away. She pouted, sticking out her luscious bottom lip again. "Why not?"

A fist pounded on the door next to Jami's head, and he let her slide slowly down his body, savoring the press of her curves into his harder edges. He moved her to the side, keeping his arm firmly around her waist. She was done running for now. He knew that, but he wasn't giving her a chance to hide anymore. Just in case.

He swung the door open where Mandi and Conner stood, obviously still riding the high from the show. "We're going to Conner's for a while, you ready to go…" His sister stopped her grab for his arm when he shoved the door all the way open with his boot.

"Oh. Hi, Jami."

"Hi, Mandi. Conner. Incredible show." Jax didn't have to look at her to know her normally gloriously pale skin glowed bright pink.

"Jami. Wow. You look hot tonight. Not like a lawyer at all."

His sister turned to their bass player and punched him in the shoulder. "Really, Conner? You're so fucking classy." She turned back to Jax and Jamie. "We're having a little after-party at Conner and Nathan's house. You're welcome to come, Jami. Kevan and Mason might show up."

Knowing Jami was going to start panicking and bolt any minute if this conversation went on much longer, he thanked his sister and friend, but made an excuse about an early breakfast with Bowen the next day. Then he turned to Jami, expecting a deer-in-the-headlights look. Instead, he saw a sultry, needy leer.

"We can go to the party." She blushed deeper. "I mean, you can go. But I'd go with you. Damn. I mean…"

"Next time. We're not going tonight, though."

"No?" Her cute brows pressed inward.

"No." He took one short step toward her, closing the gap that might have been inches wide or miles long, and grabbed her hip probably a little too hard, judging by the sharp gasp she gave. He yanked her hips toward his body and leaned down, whispering against her lips, "I'm going to take you home and rip your clothes off. Then I'm going to take my time relearning every curve, every sweet crevice. Slow. So fucking slow. Then I'm going to devour you."

"Yeah?" she asked, her voice breathy and nearly a croak.

"Yeah."

"We need to get the hell out of here."

Jami practically ran from the room, her perfect ass swishing back and forth as she tugged him through the loitering crowd and nearly ripped his arm out of the socket when he was stopped and congratulated for the fifth time. Who knew such a tiny woman could be so strong?

He loved her impatience. It was hot as hell. He'd let her drag him around the club for now, but as soon as they were in the door she would be all his.

And he wasn't walking away this time. Not for anything.

Chapter 7

JUDGMENTAL JAMI, THE DIVORCE ATTORNEY, DAUGHTER of the frigid Robo-Dillons and reformed wild child, had left the building. She couldn't keep her hands off Jackson in the cab, touching his face, running her hands through his beard and his now messy rockabilly-style pompadour, feeling his corded arms under his leather jacket.

They pulled up in front of her house on the quiet family street in her safe, well-lit neighborhood. When he had to untangle himself to pay the taxi driver, he laughed a deep, dark chuckle full of promise that filled her with wicked thoughts and warm honey-like desire. She had her keys in her hand and was halfway up the porch when he tugged her back and took her keys, fumbling with the locks. He spun her the second they were in the door, his long hard body pressed to her short curvy one. An unlikely pairing, yet they fit perfectly. Like sweet caramel and sea salt.

A loud long beep filled the room, reminding her to reach over and disarm her alarm system before it alerted her security company and the local police. That would definitely derail her plans for sexy times with Jackson.

When she leaned over and quickly pressed in the code, his hand pinned her arm against the wall. The look he gave her raised the hair on the back of her neck and sent shivers down her spine. Her already-hard nipples tightened further, bordering on painful, and her once dormant pussy clenched in desire.

It was the look, the one he used to give her years ago that quieted the committee in her head and made her want to do whatever he asked, whatever he demanded, without question.

Then he pulled back and ran his hand up her hand, tracing each finger with his own, drawing circles on her wrist. His lips followed, awakening every nerve, every cell, along her arm, making her feel light-headed, drunk, even though she'd only had two glasses of wine the entire night. At the same time, he dragged her other hand up so she stood with her arms straight out against the door and wall as he ran his hands across her body and followed with his tongue. It was too much and not quite enough all at the same time.

"More," she whispered. "Please, I need more."

"I know what you need, don't I, sunshine?" he asked before opening two buttons on her blouse. She watched as he leaned over her, loving the way his much taller body curved over her, mesmerized by the sheer beauty of him. "I should probably go take a shower before we fall into bed."

She shook her head fiercely from side to side, making him smile again. When he mouthed her breast through the satiny material of her tank top, she shot off the wall and gasped, finally able to pull a full breath into her starving lungs.

"Like that, do ya?" Oh, that smirk. If she were in her right mind, and not drunk with desire for the cocky man with his mouth on her breast, she would definitely have something smart to say.

She screeched when he mouthed the other one and swung her into his arms. Jami, like a lot of vertically challenged women, did not appreciate being called "adorable" or being picked up like a doll or child. However, when Jackson picked her up with that evil sex twinkle in his eye, she couldn't find the resolve to fight him. And, actually, she liked the way he made her feel—safe, sexy, special. She swallowed down the niggling doubt threatening to bubble up and ruin her mood. Later. She'd deal with her feelings later.

"Bedroom," he said, looking around the great room, trying to figure out what direction to go in.

"Door at the end of the hall."

"Thank fuck."

He carried her down the hall, which seemed quite a bit longer now than it had the night before. He toed open her bedroom door and set her on the platform bed. As he started to tug off his boots, she began unbuttoning the remaining button of her blouse.

"Stop."

She looked up, confused. Were they done already? He smiled. "I'll take the rest off for you."

Relief flooded her chest as she leaned back on her elbows to enjoy the scenery of Jackson Paige's body. The last time she'd seen him naked, he'd had some artwork, some smaller pieces, but he was full of colorful ink now. The dark room, lit only by the moonlight shining through the backyard-facing window, was too shadowed to really see what the images were. Not that he'd give her the chance.

Hell, not that she wanted the chance now anyway. No, looking at his body as he undressed, she marveled at the changes in the few years since she'd seen him last. He was a runner like Mason. He'd always been fit—running every day burned off his excess restless energy—but now he seemed so much stronger, wider, and more powerful. He had a man's body.

When he pulled down his boxer briefs and his long, hard cock sprang free, Jami almost jumped. She didn't remember him being quite so thick. And long. And it had been a while for her.

"This is your last chance for me to go clean up first."

Oh no. She wanted him fresh from the stage with his rock star sheen still on him, so when he was gone his masculine energy would linger for a bit. "I want you to get me dirty."

His look went dark as he crawled onto her bed on all fours, his taut muscles rolling and bending. She nearly squealed when he wrapped his hands around her knees and growled. And JamiLynn Dillon, esquire, did not squeal.

But when he tugged her under him she did actually squeal. The smile he gave her lit his mouth and eyes from within. God, he was stunning. Maybe he might just be out of her league.

Too hot. Too tattooed. Too everything.

"Oh, sunshine, you are so gorgeous." His voice caressed her as his hands unzipped her skirt and pulled it down past her toes. "So much sexy packed into one little package."

He stuck his fingers under either side of the narrow bands of her pink lace thong. "Did you wear this for me?" She looked up into his gorgeous brown eyes glazed with hunger, his dark lashes making it look like he had on eyeliner. Such a beautiful, dangerous man. What had he asked her?

"Did you wear matching panties and bra knowing I wouldn't let you go home alone tonight, counselor?"

She shook her head, not wanting to show her hand too early in the game.

"Really?" He cocked a brow.

Screw it. Who was she kidding? Game over. She nodded, her tongue too thick to speak.

"Tell me."

She blew out a long, stilted breath. "Yes, I wore them for you."

The second the words were out, he dragged her panties off, then kissed each of her hipbones and began to run his tongue up her belly.

"Raise your arms," he ordered, sending desire spiraling through her body like a damn hurricane of lust.

He pulled her blouse and tank top off in one tug, then unsnapped her bra with another growl. Jami decided she really liked that sound. A lot.

"Your tits are fucking perfect. Perfect," he panted as he tested her by nipping sharply at one nipple. Her cry of pleasure told him everything he needed to know as he bit the other harder. She arched her back and pushed her heaving chest into him. She'd never been able to keep her reserve up when she was with Jackson—why had she thought that would change now?

Leaning back on his heels, his eyes caressed her body from head to toe and then back up to her face. He reached out and cradled her cheek with his hand. For some reason, tears welled, and she had to close her eyes for a moment to push them back. Tonight was about sex, not sentimentality.

"Look down at your body, Jami. Do you see the way your skin glows bright in the moonlight? You fill the world with light when there isn't any. My sunshine in the darkness."

Oh, Jackson, if only that were true.

The truth would reveal itself to the contrary soon enough. For now she chose to let him believe it. And to allow herself to let go for just a little while. Because eventually he'd walk away, and she had a life she was happy with. But, for now, she would have this moment with him.

Jax hadn't meant to be so honest about how he felt about her. He hadn't meant to say it out loud, but it was like his brain was on autopilot around Jami. And now that he finally had her naked and under him again he couldn't help telling her how gorgeous she was.

Jami propped herself up on her elbows, jutting her breasts out even more, and looked down her own body. She gazed back up at him and giggled, her laugh filling his chest with that warm, liquid feeling again.

The smile on her lips was contagious. Sweet. Sexy. He didn't deserve her, but he was going to selfishly take tonight and as long as she'd continue to give.

His sunshine. Nope. Erase that. This wasn't going anywhere. They'd tried the relationship thing before. This was just fucking.

"Are you wet for me, gorgeous?"

Her body stiffened, then almost melted back into the

bed. Looking down into her crystal blue eyes he saw so much, but desire most of all, causing a low rumble to form in his belly.

"Did you just growl at me?" She giggled again. He loved that sound. Loved that the stiff, conservative divorce attorney looked like a wanton seductress laid out for his very own personal feast.

"Maybe."

"God, you really do have an amazing body, Jackson. It's a work of art. A beautiful body to match your artistic soul," she said, her voice thick and rough.

The muscles in his shoulders bunched, pulled tight. And he shook his head. She wouldn't think he was beautiful once she knew the truth about why he'd left her all those years ago. In the harsh light of day, everything would look different. Reality was ugly.

He leaned back over her and ran his tongue between her breasts. The sweet and slightly tangy flavor of her skin flooded his senses when he reached her nipple, imprinting her in his brain. When she extended a soft hand and circled his hard cock, he let her stroke him once, twice, three times, before the tingling sensation at the base of his spine became too much. He wanted her hands on him, all over him, but two weeks of foreplay had taken their toll. "No, sunshine, if you keep touching me like that, it's gonna be all over."

Jax's much larger hand encircled her wrist and pulled it over her head, dragging it slowly, purposely against the soft flannel blanket. Her full lips curved down, but the hitch in her breathing told a whole different story. Leaning back on his knees, he ran his other hand over the curve of her hip and up her rib cage, his callused fingers teasing her fair skin, until he grasped her other wrist and placed it above her head. "Keep your hands there," he ordered, looking directly into her hooded eyes.

She hesitated for a moment before nodding slightly. He watched the lines in her neck and shoulders tighten momentarily. Then she relaxed, as if a lever had been pulled from off to on. The pulse at the base of her jaw fluttered, a silent tempo beat out by their racing heat.

He sucked hard on one nipple. As she squirmed under his hand and moaned her pleasure, he smiled. "What do you want me to do?"

She growled in frustration. "Anything. Touch me."

He lifted his head from her tits and their eyes met. "I am. Be more specific. Tell me what you want."

"Fuck me, Jackson. Please!"

He removed one hand from her breast and trailed it down her soft belly, tracing all her curves until his fingers parted her pink lips. Her shuddering breath and glassy eyes made his cock harder, making his skin feel almost too tight for his body. When he plunged two fingers into her sweet pussy, she cried out, arching into his hand as he rubbed his thumb over her hard clit. Dragging his fingers through her slick heat once and leaving the tips at her entrance, he said, "No, baby, fuck yourself on my fingers."

Jami's body began to undulate on the bed as she pushed herself, at first slowly then faster, onto his hand, over and over. Faster and faster, until she was moving her head back and forth on the pillow and her fingers turned white where they were clasped in a death grip above her head. When he felt the narrow, warm walls around his hand begin to pulse, he pinched her clit and she cried out, his name rolling from her tongue on a sob as he felt her orgasm tremble around his fingers. Slowly he pumped in and out of her. Slowly he stayed with her through her release. Slowly he felt himself fall a little bit off the cliff for her. Again.

With her chest still heaving, he grabbed the condom and suited up before he moved over her and cupped her face with his hand, caressing her check, he looked into her eyes and smiled. "Okay?"

"Okay." She grinned lazily, the dimple in her cheek indenting her beautiful face, and wrapped her pale legs around his thighs. Without warning, she tugged him into her, his cock finding its way without direction. If he'd had any control left, her simple, eager motion had obliterated it. He was no longer a thinking being, but a man of pure sensation only. And all he felt was Jami wrapped around him as he plunged into her soft, tight, warm canal for the first time in years. This was perfect. She was perfect. No one else was ever like this.

He shifted back, letting his knees bear his weight, and reached under her to grab her ass, one round globe for each hand. Pulling her hips up and down on his throbbing cock over and over, until they were both moving as one. Until they no longer worried about the past or even the future. They were no longer separate entities, but one unified thing with one path and one goal.

"Look at me, Jami. I need to watch you come apart. Watch what you do to me."

She opened her eyes and gazed directly into his soul. When her body began to shake and her breath shortened, he fucked her harder, deeper, angling to get so far in her that she'd never forget him, never forget what they'd shared.

"Oh my God, Jackson!" She howled as she came, tipping him into ecstasy that started at the soles of his feet and shot up his legs and his spine, finally settling in his balls as he shot his seed into the condom, wishing for a moment that he was bathing her with his come. With a growl, he kissed the dampness from her cheeks. He pushed his forehead against hers, and the world slowly came back into focus—still the same, but somehow completely different—when he realized the dampness on Jami's face was not only sweat, but tears.

Chapter 8

THAT DARK, NASTY GUILT CLOUD WOULD BE SETTLING over Jami's parade any minute now. It always did. She just had to wait for it to cover her in a blanket of shame, sucking the joy out every triumph or happy moment she had.

Any minute now.

It wasn't a question of if, but when. She was programmed from years of impulsive behavior, followed by inevitable regret, followed by her parents' reprimands. After their move to Oregon, when she'd had so much anger at being left to her own devices, she'd rebelled much in the way a lot of teenagers did. Sneaking out, parties, boys, a little weed, a little drinking. Most of it had been harmless. Most of it—until she met Dallas at a college party she was too young to be at. Then it had all gone to hell. She shook off the past and waited for the darkness.

Waited.

Nope. Nothing. Actually, she felt euphoric. Floaty. If that was a thing. Maybe that was the mind-blowing, toe-curling, body-numbing sex she'd just had. Holy heck.

Still gasping for air, she realized Jackson had come back from ditching the condom and was sitting on the side of the bed staring at her. Expectant. Worried.

"Huh?" she said, not recognizing the husky, slurred voice coming from her body.

"I'm sorry. I think I hurt you…"

"What?"

"I'm sorry I hurt you. You drove me crazy, but I lost control."

"What are you talking about?" She reached her hand over to caress his muscled thigh, twirling the hair on his leg and tracing her finger along the outline of the large colorful dragon tattooed there.

"Jami, you're crying."

"I am?" She brushed her hand across her check. "I am."

"Because I'm a fucking monster and you're so small. And I didn't treat you like you deserve."

"What?"

"Jesus. You deserve so much better than me."

"Oh, for Pete's sake, Jackson. That was intense. I was overwhelmed. The last thing you did was hurt me." No, in fact, she'd felt a new, sexual Jami unfolding from within, coming out of hiding, demanding to be recognized. This new Jami had been only a thought in the club, and had taken form tonight when she'd made the last-second decision to wear lingerie under her clothes before going to meet her friends. New Jami required Jackson's full attention and whatever he had to offer. New Jami was not old-screwup Jami. "It's been so long, and you've been teasing me for days now."

Sweet concern crept back into his eyes, chasing off the shadows of doubt. The way he scrunched up his nose and peered at her with his big chocolaty eyes was so sexy and adorable, softening the harder planes of his angular face. She laid her hand on his cheek and leaned up to kiss his mouth. "I mean it. That was incredible."

His lips curved into a dazzling smile. "Yeah?"

"Yes."

He flopped onto his back and pulled her into his side, her body fitting perfectly to his, like missing puzzle pieces snapping together. Setting her hand on his broad chest and wrapping her leg over his, she kissed his pierced nipple and curled around him. Jackson's hard muscled arm cradled her head, and his big hand lazily stroked the small of her back.

When she sat up and scooted back against the headboard, he settled his head in her lap. She found herself rubbing his scalp and rolling his hair through her fingers, loving the soft, scratchy texture of his dark hair on her sensitive skin.

God, if only it was all this simple. No outside world to interfere with their little bubble. No past. No future. Just now.

The little voice in her head remained quiet. No admonishments or judgments. No gut-punching fear that she'd somehow derailed her life and was once again riding the Jackson Paige train to hell. Just the soft breath of the incredibly hot and sweet man with his head on her belly.

For the first time in what seemed like forever, she felt calm and peaceful. And for the first time in a long time, she chose not to question her feelings or tear them apart and analyze them to death. For once, she chose to lean into the moment instead of run from it.

"You know what I'd really love right now?" Jax, with his head in her lap, stared up at the ceiling as she dragged her fingers through his hair over and over. His bones were gelatinous goo, melted from rigorous sex, and his mind was finally quiet. The constant restlessness that dogged him was gone.

She looked down at him, her eyes wide and her smile wider. He loved how the corners of her full mouth tilted up, giving her a sweet smile even when she tried to look like a bossy lawyer.

After the gymnastics they'd done, he couldn't possibly want more already. "You can't be serio—"

His stomach chose that moment to share its opinion. She threw her hand over her mouth, smothering a giggle.

"Holy smokes, you must be starving," she said, realizing they'd never eaten. She scrambled from the bed, pulling on a long T-shirt with "Portland Community Women's Resource Center" printed across the front and tugging on some boy shorts that didn't quite cover her butt.

"I was." He smacked her ass. "Now I'm just hungry."

She pulled open the door, and a huge blur ran into the room and launched itself toward him on the bed. He barely had time to protect himself from the monstrosity by pulling a pillow in front of his body before the world's biggest cat—was that even a cat?—pummeled his knee with what looked like its head.

"What the fuck is this thing, Jami?" he yelled as the animal continued to aggressively request petting by slamming its enormous head into his knee.

Jami wrapped her arms around her middle and laughed so hard tears—actual fucking tears—streamed down her face. She collected herself enough to walk back over to the bed and pick up the giant furball, holding it like a baby. Obviously she wasn't worried that the thing, which was more like a dangerous cougar than a cat, would maim her.

"This is Mr. Aubrey Beardsley. He's a rescue, so I'm not sure what breed he is, but I think he's part Maine Coon and maybe part Ragamuffin."

"Beardsley, after the art nouveau artist?" he asked, venturing to pet the killer cat purring louder than Conner's Harley. "You're a fan of art nouveau?" He glanced around her room, noticing the décor for the first time. A pale lavender bedspread with embroidered flowers was piled on the floor along with some pretty pillows. The wall sconces in the room were obviously art deco, as well as the inlaid wooden vanity. Jami's room was striking and soft, just like the woman.

"Sort of. I'm a fan of art deco…didn't you see my living room?" She blushed when he raised a brow. "No, I guess not. Anyway, I love deco, and his cute little beard seemed to fit, and Beardsley was sort of the catalyst for the art deco movement, so there it is. Are you a fan?"

"Art, yeah. Mountain lions masquerading as cats, not so much." He was an artist, after all. Maybe she thought it was only about tattoo art. Other than that last conversation they'd had, he'd never told her how much he loved traditional art. He'd wanted to, but never got the chance.

He shoved the old memories—old mistakes—back down. They had no place in her bedroom that night. Soon enough she'd want to talk about it. He hoped. But not now. Eventually, he'd have to tell her everything.

She smiled—sweet like honey and warm like tea— and looked down at Aubrey. "I remember, you know."

She looked up slowly and met his gaze. "I remember that day."

He did, too. Like it was fucking yesterday. Her lounging on the floor, supported by a myriad of colorful thrift-store pillows, covered in his art from head to toe. Her gorgeous body marked, highlighted by his designs. What fun they'd had turning her into his own vibrant creation. Then he'd sketched her and made love to her on those funky pillows. Maybe that was when he'd fallen in love with her. But before either of them could stop the momentum of that love or whatever it was, the train had derailed completely.

Thanks to him.

"I remember it, too." Unfortunately, he hadn't kept the picture he'd drawn of her. He'd left it at her apartment. She'd probably destroyed it the minute she realized he'd dropped out of school and her life.

Speaking of trains, Aubrey began to purr loudly.

He dipped his chin toward the cat. "Where'd you get him? Shelter?"

She nodded, grabbing a pair of thick black-rimmed glasses from the side table. Those fucking glasses threw gasoline on the smoldering coals still burning in his gut and basically lit his dick on fire. Zero to eighty in two seconds. Every single hot-secretary fantasy he never knew he had came to life in living color right at that moment.

"What? Oh heck, is there something on my face?" she asked, swiping at her nose.

"Um, no." He reached under her shirt and palmed one warm breast in his hand, wrapping his other hand around her neck and pulling her close. Her hooded eyes blinked. Once. Twice. And then closed as he caressed her mouth with his, tongues slowly dancing to their own song as she hummed that little sex sound she made whenever their lips met. That little sound went straight to his already straight-up-hard-as-fucking-steel cock, making it spasm.

A low growling noise that seemed to go on forever echoed in the room. They jumped apart, then fell into laughter when they both realized it was his stomach again.

She set Aubrey on the bed and stood, primly adjusting her glasses and her shirt. "I need to feed you."

"Only so I have more energy for you."

She snorted and started to walk out of the room, stopping and glancing back over her shoulder, completely unaware of how sexy she was. "You can take a shower in my bathroom, if you'd like."

"Only if you join me."

"Maybe next time."

"I'm going to hold you to that." He laughed, then walked toward the master bath.

He thought he heard her say "I hope so" as she made her way down the hall.

☆ ☆ ☆

Still damp from his shower and wearing only a fluffy yellow towel around his waist, Jax walked into Jami's living room—or great room, as she called it. In the kitchen that was technically part of the great room, he watched Jami bang around, clanking pans and rummaging through the cupboards and her tall built-in stainless fridge.

"Hope you still like scrambled eggs," she called out as he investigated her home. The three walls of the big open room were a silvery blue shade of gray, giving it an elegant, fresh feel. She still obviously loved her books. Her entire living area had wall-to-wall built-in whitewashed bookshelves. He picked up a book from the arm of her couch. The cover featured the torso of a muscled dude with a very scantily clad woman blindfolded and kneeling before him. The words *The Professor* were scrawled across the cover in dark styled text. Apparently, his studious and ever-so-serious attorney liked to read naughty books.

Jax smiled to himself and set the book back down. "Sounds great. Do you have any bacon?"

"Actually, I'm sort of a vegetarian." She smiled up at him. She probably didn't even realize she was humming and dancing slightly as she stirred the eggs. Why the hell did he find it so damn hot? Why did everything she do turn him on?

"No way, since when?" he said. He missed this. Her. Why had it all fallen apart?

Oh yeah. Her parents. His decision to let them chase him off with a threat and a big check.

"Always."

What?

"But I remember getting burgers with you in Eugene." Didn't he? It *was* Jami, right? Not some other nameless chick in a line of shallow trysts?

"I thought I'd try it out the first year of school, but got sick later that year and went back to being a pseudo-veggie."

"I don't remember you getting sick." Wow. He really was a dick. He thought he'd remembered everything about their time together. "Sorry."

She stirred the eggs and looked up over the counter, her face slightly shadowed by her hair. "Oh, it was after you left. And technically I'm a pescatarian, since I still eat fish sometimes." She fluttered around, wiping up splattered eggs and cleaning off the counter as she cooked. "Anyway, it was nothing," she said without meeting his eyes.

Within two seconds, he hopped up and was at her side. Laying his hand on her shoulders, he slowly turned her and tilted her chin up to meet his eyes. "What's going on, sunshine?"

Every time he used her old nickname, his chest tightened, either from guilt or from lust or from the way her body softened. In any case, it did something to him. Took away the malaise that had been eating at him lately, and brought him back to her. To them. To life.

"Hey," he said. She raised her pale lashes and he could almost allow himself to get lost in those icy blue pools. "What's going on?"

She brought her hands to his chest and pushed. "I'm fine. Nothing. Don't want to burn the eggs."

He reached around her and turned the burner off without breaking eye contact. She swallowed hard and took a deep breath. "After you left, I got sick. Dehydrated. I was in the hospital for a couple days. No big deal."

Jax's stomach dropped into his feet, a free-falling elevator with no bottom, and he suddenly felt nauseated. He'd known he was a dick to leave and accept her parents' ultimatum, but they'd told him it was for the best. That he was fucking up her life. Instead he'd sent her to the hospital.

Wait. Shit. "Were you…oh, fuck, did you…"

The look of horror on her face was like a kick to the groin, so real he almost reeled back. "No, but I thought maybe I was."

"What happened?"

"I caught some superbug that was going around. That's all." She stared intently at the eggs and then turned to butter their toast.

Why didn't he believe her? Maybe because she'd spent the last few years learning to mask her feelings. It was what she did for a living.

"We're going to have to talk about what happened."

"We just did."

"No, I mean why I left." They could never both move on if they didn't look at the past. She needed to know the truth.

"I know."

"Not now though, huh?"

"Not yet," she said.

Then she did something spectacular. Mind-blowing. With one hand on his bare shoulder, she cupped his face, leaned in, and pressed her nose against his neck, drawing in a long breath. He smelled of sex and soap and her flowery shampoo. Then she kissed his pulse. Soft and long, but sweet and chaste.

God, his skin tightened again, and his heart might have dropped down to his feet to keep his stomach company. This tiny woman was too much. Had always been too much, but as a young fool he'd burned all memory of her away. He'd tried to cauterize the hole in his heart that she'd left, that had burned through his soul like a motherfucking bullet. He'd tried music, art, drinking, and women, and every combination in between, but they had only dulled the ache.

And he knew why. Stodgy, conservative, closed-off JamiLynn Dillon was not what she appeared on the outside. For some reason she'd never disclosed to him, she wrapped up the sensuous, kind, sparkling star of her personality into some kind of homogenized version of Lawyer Jami.

"What are we doing?" he whispered when she lifted her lips from his neck. The spot still burned from her fiercely tender attention. "What are we going to do?"

She shook her head and offered a watery smile. "Have breakfast in the middle of the night and then go back to bed?"

Yeah. That's what they were going to do, and fuck all if he wasn't starting to think he was screwed. Again.

Chapter 9

STILL BUZZING FROM HIS NIGHT WITH JAMI, JAX swung into Tatuaggio to pick up the printout of his appointments for that week. Then he planned a couple of hours of sketching before a quick run. Quick being the operative word, since his all-night escapade with Jami had left him less than perky.

Lost in thought, as he pulled the door open, he was surprised to find the shop lit up and music playing over the sound system so early in the day. Tony Martelli, the shop's owner and de facto sage-leader-slash-father-figure to most of the artists, stood next to Bowen's station, where Bowen was doing a touch-up on one of his regular customers. They shouted greetings and Jax bumped fists with Tony.

"Tony, whatcha doing here?" Jax asked, worried he might be there to keep an eye on Bowen.

The older man laughed, but the circles under his eyes looked a little darker than normal. "I know what you're thinking, and it's not that. I'm doing all the paperwork until the woman I hired to replace Kevan starts next week. Came out to say hello and invite Bowen over to dinner tonight." The older man pointed his thumb back toward the office and piercing room. "I'm going to finish up, Bo. Meet you at the house tonight around five…maybe watch the game?"

Bowen snorted. "Dude, if it ain't hockey, it's not a

game. But, yeah, I'll see ya later." He pressed the foot pedal and dipped the needle into the small plastic inkpot filled with dark purple tattoo ink.

Tony shuffled down the hall, looking a little slower and a little older than he had before. Jax wondered if the old man was taking care of himself. He hoped Isabel, Tony's only child, was keeping an eye on him. Guilt clawed at his chest. They all should be taking care of Tony, since he'd spent the last ten years taking care of them.

The buzz of Bowen's tattoo machine stopped as he peered up through the dark fringe he'd let grow since his last stint in rehab. He raised his eyebrow and looked from Jax's boots to his face. "Didn't you wear that shirt to the show last night? Walk of shame, dude?" Bowen's client, Carmen, took the opportunity to adjust herself on the table and jut her boobs out into Bowen's face.

Jax laughed. "Nah. Just the opposite."

Bowen smirked and shifted away from Carmen's blatant offering, turning his attention back to her ankle. "Sweet."

His client's sigh was audible over the noise of the tattoo machine. Less than six months ago, Bowen would have been all over that. Probably would have waited for everyone to leave, cleaned up her new tattoo, and then fucked her on the counter. That was the old Bowen. Jax was still getting to know this new version of his best friend. He thought maybe Bowen was still trying to figure himself out, too. At some point they were going to need to talk about his epic downward spiral. But Bowen didn't seem ready to talk about it yet. He seemed to be content to take shit slowly…one day at a time, so to speak.

"You have any clients today?" Bowen asked. "Wanna grab some java?"

"Nobody scheduled today. Practice later, though. How long before you're done?"

"I'll be done with Carmen in about twenty minutes. I'm free for about an hour, then I have some color work on a new client's sleeve."

"I need a quick shower. Text me when you're ready."

Jax jogged down the hall and climbed the back stairs to the apartment above the shop, which Tony let him and Mandi rent for dirt cheap. Loud music blared through the thin wooden door as he let himself in. His sister sat on their oversized leather couch in a pair of worn jeans and a newly designed Manix Curse shirt, picking at her ancient, beat-up Gretsch.

"How the fuck can you hear yourself play?" he yelled, fully aware he sounded like an old man and not a tattoo-artist heavy-metal drummer. So what. He turned the music down a notch and waited for her to react.

When his sister ignored him, Jax made his way to his bedroom, grabbed some fresh clothes, and jumped into the shower. His second of the day, if he counted the middle-of-the-night shower. Two more bouts with Jamie—in bed and against the wall—had left him smelling like sex and flowers. As soon as the warm water hit his skin, his brain was flooded with memories of their night together.

He'd left before Jami had woken up. He needed some time to think, and he was sure she'd need some space to process what had happened between them. She'd been so unguarded, so beautiful sprawled out on her bed. He'd run his hand from the crown of her head down her supple body to her calves, wanting his hands to memorize every dip and curve. Wanting to sit next to her on the bed and run his fingers through her golden hair. Funny how his body still knew hers so well, like they hadn't spent years apart, time with other lovers. Her body gripped his like it always had, like they were fucking meant for each other.

The time would come when he'd have to dig deeper into that. Despite their history, Jami wasn't a love-'em-and-leave-'em kind of girl. At some point, he would need to let her go for good, so she could have the two-point-five kids with a more appropriate partner than he could ever be. But the thought of walking away from her again made his chest tight and his stomach drop.

Now that he had her back in his life, he couldn't imagine any kind of future that didn't involve her. If only he could get her to loosen up and stay that way. Although, truth be told, he did love watching her arrange her little rules and rituals, like folding down the bed even though he had every intention of messing it—and her—up again and again. He even found it a little hot to watch her methodically clean her dishes and place them in the dishwasher after they ate. Or insist on running sanitation wipes over the counter before and after he fucked her on it.

Fucking adorable.

He toweled off and ran some pomade through his hair before throwing on a pair of old jeans and a JD McPherson T-shirt, then walked barefoot into the kitchen and tore open the fridge door.

"What's up with you? You're smiling like a little girl with a new Hello Kitty coloring book."

His sister stared at him as he stood in front of the open fridge holding the carton of orange juice he'd apparently pulled out.

"What does that even mean?" he asked.

"Hello Kitty. Duh." His sister rolled her eyes and moved toward her room with her guitar slung across her slim back. "It's like you don't know me at all."

"Where you going?"

"To grab my backpack, then to the coffee shop to study. Where've you been?"

"None of your business."

She turned to look him up and down. "Yeah. Right. You screwed the lawyer, didn't you?"

"None of your business." He chugged the rest of the juice and tossed the empty container in the trash.

"Whatever. Where you going?"

"Grounds."

She turned and stuck her pierced tongue out at him. "You can't go there. I called dibs."

"What are you, five? We can go to the same coffee shop. And grown-ups don't call dibs, squirt."

She planted her hands on her hips and raised both brows.

"They don't," he insisted.

"Really? Bowen called dibs on the last piece of pizza last week. You called dibs on the front seat of Mason's car just a couple days ago."

"I called shotgun. Totally different."

"*Right*. So you're all Mr. Maturity now that you're banging a lawyer."

"No." He scrubbed his hand down his face, feeling the rasp of his growing scruff. He should probably shave. But then an image of Jami shivering, her nipples hardening when he ran his chin down the inside of her thighs, popped up in his head.

Nope. Not shaving. Maybe he was a dick, but he liked the idea of leaving a red tinge from his beard on Jami's fair skin.

"No, what? You're not fucking the lawyer or you're not a mature grown-up?"

"I'm—" Jax's phone buzzed on the counter, and he grabbed it. Mandi shrugged and disappeared into her room. He swiped across the phone's screen and a text from Bowen popped up.

Done with my client. Ready for caffeine.

Down in a minute. Shoes.

Mandi burst from her room and stomped past him with a backpack at least twice as wide as she was thrown over her shoulder. "Going to the library. See you at practice later."

"Hey." He put his hand on her shoulder to stop her forward momentum. "You can study at Grounds. We won't bug you. Promise."

She smiled, transforming her face and making her look like a pink-haired angel. "I know. I really do need to study. Gonna go to the library and sit in a back carrel." Then she rose up on her toes and kissed him on his cheek. It had been a couple of years since she'd done that. He was so surprised his hand flew to his face as if he'd be able to hold the kiss there.

"Don't go getting all mushy, big bro."

Then she was gone.

Mandi had moved in as a teenager, but he'd only started

seeing her as an adult for the last two years. She made no secret of her attraction to guys and sometimes other women. Mandi was interesting, intelligent, and definitely not introverted. She loved being the center of attention and really came alive onstage. But she wasn't egotistical or lazy about her natural beauty. Just the opposite.

But this might have been the first time he acknowledged how much his little sister had changed over the last five years. That scared him a little. When he'd come home to visit the shop after the fuckup with Jami, Mandi had been there, looking for him. Since they shared a father, but had different mothers, they hadn't grown up together. But Jax had tried to stay connected to her through FaceTime and social media. He'd driven down to visit her against his mother's vehement objections every summer since the year he'd turned eighteen.

When she showed up at Tatuaggio looking too thin, too young, and far too stubborn to go back to her man-happy mother, he'd known for sure that law school wasn't in his future. That Jami wasn't in his future. And that he wouldn't be going back to Eugene. Mandi and he had moved into the vacant apartment above the shop, and he'd gone right to work. It had taken him several months to break through her hardened shell to get to the scared and lonely girl on the inside.

Mandi hadn't wanted their dad to pay for school, so she'd waitressed for a couple of years, and they'd saved so she could go to college full-time. Since they hadn't grown up in the same home, they'd taken a while to really get to know each other. In the end, it had been the forming of Manix Curse that had finally brought them closer together.

Now his past had imploded all over his present, which meant it was time to face his demons if he wanted to move forward. Now that Mandi was an adult and nearly done with school—and Jami was back—it was time to figure out just what the hell he was doing with his life. The first place to start would be to figure out where this thing with Jami was going.

Jax stared down at the foam bear drawn on his cappuccino. "What the fuck is up with this shit?" He pointed at the image and stuck his finger into the hot liquid, stirring it. "When did Grounds go hipster?" He looked up from his coffee and glanced around the busy café. Still the same mixed clientele, one part starving student, one part businessfolk, and one part wild card. He considered the Tatuaggio crowd as part of the wild card contingent.

"Chill, bro. It's only coffee…fancy, froufrou coffee, but still just coffee." Bowen laughed and sat at a corner table near the front window.

"As opposed to your manly triple shot with coconut milk and a fuckton of sugar?" Jax sneered and plopped down across from him.

His best friend snorted. "It's all I got left. Gave up drugs and booze. Avoiding women. What's left? Bacon, coffee, and sugar."

The casual tone in Bowen's voice lifted a boulder of guilt and stress off Jax's chest. He suddenly felt like he'd been holding his breath until his buddy started acting like himself again. But, no, the old Bowen was gone. Now there was this new guy Jax didn't really know. He wondered if Bowen even knew himself that well.

"So, speaking of women…"

"We weren't. Dude, what's up with you? How're things in your new apartment? I feel like I haven't seen you much since you got out…of…"

"Rehab? You can say the word, Jax. Reeeehaaab." Bowen's big fist punched him lightly in the arm, shaking the table.

"I know. I don't want to make you feel weird. I think you're fucking awesome, but I'm not sure yet what's cool with you and what's not. You're gonna have to help me out."

"Yeah. I appreciate that. It's all new for me, too. All that shit they say about one day at a time and living in the moment is fucking true. Sometimes it's an hour-by-hour thing. Breathe in. Breathe out. Hippie shit. But it works for me. I don't want to fuck up everyone else's good time because I'm the one with the problem. Not you. Not Nathan. Not your band. Not my band. It's just me."

"I get it. But we're adults, Bo, and we're your friends. So you gotta let us…me…in. Okay? You don't have to do this shit alone."

Bowen's eyes looked watery, but clear. Clear as the sunny, butt-ass cold, Portland sky outside. He nodded, and his face looked so damn serious.

"Enough of my fucked-up ass, let's talk about yours. Don't tell me you broke your dry streak and finally stuck your dick in some hottie last night."

Bowen didn't know any better. This was usual banter for him and the guys, but thinking of Jami as "some hottie" made his gut clench. "Nah."

He took a sip of coffee, wondering what, if anything,

he should tell his best friend. Jax wasn't the kind of guy who talked about his fuckbuddies in detail, but he and Bowen had had their share of discussions regarding the women they banged. Then there was that one time they'd shared the singer from Hellion years ago, after a long drunken night of debauchery.

"Nah you didn't get lucky, or nah she wasn't hot?"

Jax chuckled. "I got lucky and she was smoking hot. But I didn't just stick my dick in her."

Bowen's eyebrows shot up. "No? Special then?"

Yeah. You could say that. He shrugged.

"Someone I know?" Bowen asked.

He nodded.

"The lawyer."

"Also known as Jami Dillon, Mason's little sister." Jax dragged the words out slowly, letting them hang in the air before they clanged on the table one by one.

"So."

"Sooo, I'm having sex with Mason's little sister. Not sure he's going to appreciate that."

"Uh, dude, he's fucking marrying *my* little sister."

Holy shit. Jax hadn't even thought of that. Would Mason see it the same way when he found out? Because he would find out. He still didn't know where this thing with Jami was going, but he did know one fucking thing for sure. He wasn't ready to let her go. Not yet. And he sure as hell wasn't going to hide that he was sleeping with her from his friends, including her brother.

"Fuck. You're right. But, to be fair, you and Mason weren't buddies. He may be our promoter now, but he's also a friend. A real one. And I'm not eager to go and fuck that up."

Bowen shook his head. "No. I wouldn't either, but I don't think it's gonna be an issue."

"Why?" Jax was confused. Wouldn't Mason be pissed his princess of a little sister was screwing around with a metalhead tattoo artist? Frankly, Jax hoped even his little sister would find someone better, more stable. Of course, Mandi had a crazy mind and did things the Mandi way…and not the Jax way.

"Are you planning on seeing her again?"

He nodded, unable to consider not holding her again.

"Planning on fucking other chicks when you're with her?"

Jax didn't even bother shaking his head. The thought of being with another woman left him cold, empty.

"You're a good guy, Jax. Mason knows that. We all do."

"I don't know. Am I? He's seen me on the road. Seen the chicks I've taken back to the bus or the hotel. I haven't exactly been a saint."

Bowen laughed, probably remembering specifically when Jax had not been a saint.

"Does any of that appeal to you anymore?" He smiled when Jax cringed. "I didn't think so."

They sat quietly sipping their coffees. Jax watched a dark-haired woman at a corner table sitting with two young boys. The boys were coloring in books, but would occasionally punch each other without looking up or even bothering to stop their tasks. Then they'd laugh and quiet down for a minute. Their young mom—he assumed she was their mother, anyway—sipped what looked like tea and watched them with a quiet, amused expression on her face. Until her gaze fixed on something in the parking lot and she froze. Her cup dropped noiselessly to the floor and the lid popped off, sploshing liquid all over her tennis shoes. As a tall soldier still dressed in his fatigues walked through the door, the woman squealed, startling her boys. When their mother ran into the smiling soldier's arms and he lifted her, swinging her in a circle before kissing her senseless, the young boys started yelling, "Daddy!"

By that time the entire shop had turned to watch the family reunion. A weird longing crept into Jax's chest as the woman started laughing and sobbing at the same time. Everyone in the shop clapped and hooted for the family. The soldier waved with a huge I-own-the-world grin and led them out of the shop.

The longing in Jax's chest crept into his heart and burrowed in, firmly planting itself deep. It didn't exactly feel good. Instead it was irritating. Scratchy. A little uncomfortable.

Jax turned back to his oldest and best friend, feeling like he was looking at everything with a new pair of eyes. What had seemed so murky and muddled a few minutes ago suddenly seemed clear.

"Fuck me," Jax whispered.

"What?"

"That right there," he said to Bowen, jabbing his finger toward the door where the family had walked out. "I think that's what appeals to me now."

"So make that shit happen."

"I wish it were that easy."

"You like her. She likes you. Can't get much easier."

Jax laughed. *If only*. "Remember when I dropped out of law school?"

"Sort of. You came home to take care of Mandi, right? That whole period of our lives is kind of fuzzy." He laughed a little nervously, unable to meet Jax's eyes.

Jax bumped his fist onto Bowen's hand to get his attention. "Dude, when you gonna stop beating yourself up over the past? The past is the motherfucking past, right?"

"Yeah. Maybe. Some days that works for me. Some days it's all I can do to just get up and move forward." The sharp stab of Bowen's darkly honest admission cut him open.

"Do you miss the partying?"

"No. Not at all. That's the weird thing. I don't want to drink or get high. But now that I'm not high, I have all these fucking feelings and shit. At first, I was numb. I felt nothing, but then the dam broke. And bam…emotions. I mean, like all of them. It blows." He took a deep breath and shook his head. "That's enough of my shit for now. Tell me about the lawyer."

"She's the band's new attorney. Gonna handle our contracts. We were together in law school before I dropped out."

"You have history. That's a good thing, right?"

Jax shook his head. "Not the good kind of history. We were pretty serious. I was, anyway. And then we had this awkward conversation where she sort of dismissed me wanting to pursue my art more than law. Said it was a waste of my degree and three years of law school. It was the first time I felt like she didn't really hear me. That she was stuck on the idea of us both being this upwardly mobile couple. And it freaked me the fuck out. I never wanted to be an attorney. I thought I did, but I was too much of a pussy to admit I was doing it for the old man. Until then."

Bowen nodded. He'd been around long enough to know that Jax had spent most of his childhood trying to get his dad's attention. "What'd she say when you told her?"

"Nothing. I never told her. At first I was pissed, but I thought maybe we'd talk about it later. I mean, she seems all ice cold and shit, but she's the only woman that's ever really understood me. At least, I thought she did until that morning."

Shadows danced behind Bowen's eyes as he nodded. "Yeah. I get it. Still don't understand what the hell happened. And why you never mentioned her before."

Jax took a deep breath as memories flitted through his head. God, that day had gone downhill fast. Now that he was actually letting himself think about it after so many years, he was beginning to realize how fucked up it had been to walk away.

"I ran into her parents as I was leaving her apartment. Had already decided to go grab some scones and coffee and skip my class and finish our conversation. But her parents made it clear they were there because of me. Specifically, to get me out of their precious daughter's life."

"Hell no. What'd they say?"

Deciding he needed to come clean with Jami before he told anyone else the full story, he gave an edited version of the truth. "Basically that I was a piece of shit. That she, apparently, was some kind of impressionable former wild child. That she had a plan and someone like me was just gonna fuck it up."

Bowen's pinched mouth and raised brow were calling bullshit. "Yeah, not buying it. That wouldn't have stopped you, especially if you were falling for her. You were, weren't you?"

Not bothering to lie, he nodded. "Yeah. But then they said the best thing for her would be for me to get out of her life because she had a boyfriend back home."

"Whhhhat? She was cheating on you?"

"Nah. I knew it was a lie. But all I heard was everything I hated about *my* parents. All they cared about was how shit looked, not how it really was. Nothing important mattered. I mean, dude, her mom was wearing a peach-colored pantsuit with matching heels and shit. Her dad was wearing a monkey suit, too. It was a fucking Friday on a college campus. You saw them at Kevan and Mason's party. Tight Sphincter City."

He still felt that gut punch and stabbing ache thinking back to that day. He'd known they were lying, and yet he'd taken the chickenshit way out and run like a coward. But he hadn't been able to face her and confess his run-in with the Dillons. Because maybe they were right about him. Maybe he hadn't been good enough. Shit, maybe he still wasn't. Now that she was back in his life, he couldn't find the courage to let her go again. But how would she feel about why he left? Even when he told her the truth, how would she forgive him? Fuck, he couldn't even forgive himself.

"They called dear old dad and made a donation to his campaign. Apparently, in exchange for him threatening to pull my tuition."

"Assholes."

"No kidding. And then Mandi showed up. Seemed

like the choice was made for me. So I said 'fuck it.' My poli-sci degree was useless on its own. Felt like I'd been coasting. But now I'm thinking maybe it was just an excuse."

"Dude, I'm the king of regret, remember? The past is the past. Let it go." Bowen suddenly sounded so wise.

"I'm trying, but I'm not sure it'll be enough," Jax said, his voice low.

"Does she know about her parents?"

"Nah. I'm gonna tell her, but I don't think it'll matter. I left her." Just like his dickhead father each time he got tired of his current family or needed an upgrade to his image. He left and never looked back.

"Jax, do you love this girl?"

Did he? Could he really love anyone? Or was he going to let his shitty history and rock-and-roll lifestyle dictate his life forever?

Yeah. He might love her.

"I don't know, Yoda, I think maybe I could. Not sure it matters, though. She has this plan for her life. And she's still attached to the puppet strings her parents yank around."

Bowen startled him with the first real Bowen belly laugh Jax had heard since the man had gotten clean and sober. "Well, fuck me. Another motherfucker bites the dust. First my sister and now you. Who the hell is gonna fall next?"

"Didn't you hear me? There's too much in the way."

"Bullshit. Look at Mason and Kevan. It doesn't get much more fucked up than them. And they still ended up together."

Jax couldn't refute that. Mason and Kevan had started

out enemies and competitors and ended up working together, and were now planning their wedding. "Maybe you're next, bro."

"Not gonna happen. I've made a career out of screwing up and just plain screwing. I plan on staying away from anything with a vagina for a while. Need to get right with myself before I bring anyone else into my own private shitshow."

Jax laughed. "I'll believe it when I see it."

"Believe it. Anyhow, what're you gonna do about Jami?"

"Don't know. Guess I'll just see what happens next. I do know that I'm not running away this time."

They bumped fists, and Jax smiled, glad to have his buddy back. But he knew if he decided to jump into the deep end, winning Jami back was going to take a fuckton of work. Even back then, before he screwed everything up, there was still something keeping her from really giving herself to him.

Now it was going to take double the work to chip away the concrete shell she'd built around her heart.

Chapter 10

I HATE THIS STUPID DOOR, JAMI THOUGHT, STARING AT the gaudy oversized door to her parents' home. Before knocking, she ran her tongue over her teeth and straightened her blouse and slacks. She knew her clothes were impeccable, but old habits died a hard, noisy, painful death. She took a deep breath and knocked twice. Through the intricately colored stained glass, she saw movement and then the shifting patterns of someone walking to the door. Obviously not her mother or father, since they would never have enough spare time to spend on such a mundane task as greeting their children for a family meal. Like Jami, Carol and Robert Dillon respected order, formality, and civility. Unlike their daughter, it was natural for them, like breathing or sleeping. Or making money and being judgmental.

The door swung open, and she was pulled into the arms of the woman who had been the one touchstone of compassion during her tumultuous teen years. The soft cushion of Erma's firm hug filled Jami with longing. She loved Erma, and had always been drawn to the older woman's warmth, like a plant starving for light. Even as a rebellious teen, she'd loved to help Erma in the kitchen or even do the laundry together. She'd craved her attention and wished her mother could be more like her.

Erma laughed and held Jami at arm's length. "Feels like I haven't seen you in years, instead of months,

JamiLynn. Let me get a good look at you." She motioned her hand in a circle. "Turn."

After holding out her arms and circling once, Jami smiled. "Nothing's changed. Still me."

Erma's eyes wrinkled more at the corners, and she placed her fists on her ample hips. "Hm. Something's different. Care to—"

The sharp click clack of her mother's heels sounded down the tiled entry, filling Jami's gut—and the room for that matter—with a weighted dread. She'd always mused that her mother's impatient heels should be accompanied by Darth Vader's theme music. "Erma, stop fussing with JamiLynn and bring her into the house, since she's already late." Her mother's crisp Texan accent greeted them as she whisked through the hall in a flowered sheath dress and pale pink stilettos, then turned and walked back toward the main section of the house, where Jami knew her father waited with a mimosa in his study. King of his castle.

The older woman quickly hid her smile before tucking Jami's hand around her arm. "Yes. Mrs. Dillon, we're on our way now." Erma smiled at Jami and whispered, "Heaven forbid you actually be on time."

That's why she loved this woman. Erma always had her back, making life so much more bearable. It had been Erma, not Jami's own mother, who had nursed Jami's broken body and sewn back her broken heart after her accident. It had been Erma who'd given her the courage to go back to school after she'd gotten sick. After Jackson had left her.

Jami smiled. Jackson. He'd been gone that morning when she woke up from the deepest sleep she'd had in years. Her cracked heart ached a little when she spied the empty indention he'd left. She'd reminded herself they were having a fling…catching up on old times. But when she'd seen the daisy picked from her flower box and the note he'd left next to a muffin, her pulse beat faster. He'd left his number and asked her to text when she was done with her parents.

He hadn't pushed her for more or for less. He kept saying they weren't done and they needed to talk about the past. Part of her wanted to know—no, needed to know what she'd done to drive him away. Part of her wanted to leave it alone. What did it matter anyway? She was fine. She'd been a stupid girl with big romantic dreams. More than once, those dreams had epically gone up in flames. Bonfire flames. Volcano flames. Regardless, the only thing love ever got anyone was ashes. No matter how bright something burned, that's all that was ever left.

"If it isn't our daughter, the disappearing attorney."

Jami's stomach rolled as her father's deep voice greeted her from his study. Although her mother's touch infected everything in their sterile home, this room was by far the most masculine, with its traditional plaid wallpaper and dark wood accents. Except for the far wall, classic hunting art decorated the room.

Her father's wall of achievement was different, holding his various certificates, awards, accolades, trophies, pictures with politicians. His altar of success. While Jami, the great disappointment in her parents' lives, had chosen the tawdrier avenue of boutique corporate law that focused on smaller companies and individual entrepreneurs, her father had spent most of his life in one political appointment or another, with the last several years dedicated to his own private firm, which focused on any number of lucrative corporate paths. It was what had brought them from Texas to Portland when Jami was barely a teen.

She walked into the room and moved to peck him on the cheek, but he pointed to the club chair across from him.

Cheese on a freaking cracker. Now what?

"Sit. Your mother and I have something we want to discuss with you before your brother gets here."

Jami's roiling stomach lurched as her mother perched on the brown leather couch at the opposite end from her husband, legs crossed neatly at the ankle and back straight. Jami sat in the chair across from them, thinking maybe the low narrow seat was designed to make the sitter feel smaller. Inferior.

"We're concerned about that man we saw you with at Mason's engagement party. He appeared quite unsavory and we're worried you might be walking down a less appropriate path. Like before."

Jami's stomach pitched again, and her mouth felt clogged with sand. When her father took a sip of water and cleared his throat, Jami realized she should settle in. His throat-clearing and her mother's silence usually meant one thing: lecture time.

"I went to law school with Jackson, actually."

Her mother made a sound resembling a snort. But Dr. Carol Dillon, retired rocket scientist and trophy wife, didn't snort. Regardless, the subtle sound carried all kinds of meaning and bore a lifetime of history. Disbelief, to begin with. "That's the truth. He was my tutor. We were friends."

Her parents stared expectantly at her. The Dillons weren't ones to waste air on too many words or too many social niceties. Yes, they were exceedingly formal, but always pointed. And patient as vultures. They'd stare—blinking robotically at regular intervals—until their victim felt too awkward not to reply or expand. But Jami was so tired of being manipulated by her parents. She was exhausted by her constant need to prove to them she wasn't *that girl* anymore. Why was it so hard for them to see who she was now? Responsible. Hard working. Mature. She'd always admired how Jackson had been able to live his life the way he wanted despite his parents' constant concerns about public perception.

Instead her parents refused to let go of damaged Jami. They seemed to cling to her past even more than she did. Did she still see herself that way? Forever a screwup? Forever unreliable? Forever broken?

For the first time in a very, very long time, Jami looked around the room. Really looked at it. Then at her parents, who gazed at her, apparently willing to wait her out until she cracked and her words flowed like spilled water from a busted pipe.

It was like a blanket was suddenly pulled off her, and the harsh light made everything so much more real. So detailed. And it dawned on her...

They were the ones who never changed.

Her dad's study had looked exactly the same—same certificates on the wall, same damn crystal paperweight in the shape of an oversized golf ball—no matter where they lived. Her mom's expertly trimmed hair and the creases in her dad's trousers. *All. The. Same.*

She locked eyes with her mother, no longer uncomfortable enough to look down or away. "You realize I'm an adult, right? That I'm a practicing attorney? I own my own home and do all kinds of regular grown-up shit every day."

Her mother's eyes widened for a second before a lifetime of practice kicked in and she neutralized her features. "You sound like a petulant child. And we fully realize how far you've come since…"

"Since the accident, Mother. You can say it. The accident I had after my boyfriend beat me because I told him I was pregnant. It happened, Mom. A long time ago."

A flush of anger crept over her father's face. "Yes, the *incident*," he sneered, sending a jolt of regret zinging through her body. Perhaps she was pushing too far. As usual. "Where our teenage daughter got herself pregnant, beat up, and then crashed her car into a ditch. Do you have any idea what that did to us? How people in this community looked at us?"

Were those actual tears forming in the corner of her mother's eyes? Of course, it must have been horrifying for them. Such an embarrassment.

"Are you fucking kidding me here?" Her brother's deep voice boomed through the room. Jami dipped her head, the ice of shame filling her veins, replacing the prideful courage that had just flowed there. "Did I just hear you tell your daughter her horrific accident and the loss of her unborn baby was embarrassing for you? *For you*?"

Kevan strode across the room, like Wonder Woman, impenetrable to the bullets of disdain shooting from her parents' eyes. She knelt by Jami's chair and grabbed her hand. "Look at me," she said while Mason and his dad began to discuss loudly the conversation he'd overheard.

"I'm so sorry you've been pulled into this," Jami whispered, looking up into Kevan's face and expecting to see disgust. Instead she saw compassion. At that moment, Jami knew she would never doubt Kevan's love for her brother. Never doubt her role in their messed-up family. And never doubt her future sister-in-law's sincerity.

"No, sweetie. You have nothing to be sorry about." She leaned over and brushed tears from Jami's cheeks. "We're done here for now. Mason won't put up with this shit, and I think it's time to go."

She wrapped her arm around Jami's shoulders and pulled her up. Mason tugged them both toward the study door when her dad stood up.

"You both are huge disappointments to your mother and me. You had such potential and you choose to throw it all away on gangbangers and tramps. We got rid of that tattooed idiot five years ago and everything was great for you, Jami. Wasn't it? Everything right back on track despite your indiscretions. Look what you've accomplished."

Jami sucked in a gasp as her brother pivoted. He took three long strides and stopped toe to toe with their father. "I'm going to pretend you didn't say that. But if you say it again, we're going to have more than words."

Before she could ask her father what he meant by *five years ago*, Mason had his arms around both women and was passing Erma in the hall. She blew them a kiss and shooed them out the door.

Kevan held out her hand. "Keys."

"What?" Jami asked, numbness taking over where she'd felt such hurt moments before. "No. I'm fine. I'll just—"

Mason was already pushing Jami into his M5 when he squeezed her hand three times.

Three squeezes were all it took before she burst into tears.

Jax's phone beeped as he rounded the last corner of his run. His heart raced, and the blood in his veins pumped hard, making him feel strong. Alive. He slowed to a jog and walked back and forth in front of Tatuaggio until his heart rate slowed.

Yanking his phone off his arm, where he strapped it when he ran, he slid his finger across the screen. The text was from a local number he didn't recognize. Jami's maybe.

> *Done with my parents.*

Nothing about their night together. Or how was his day. He shook his head and rolled his eyes. *Dude, you're turning into a freaking teenage girl. Cool it.*

He jabbed at the screen, punching out a text.

> How'd it go?

> *Fine. We can talk about it later.*

Well, normally that would be a terse answer, but this was Jami.

You sure it's all good?

Yes.

He climbed the stairs to his empty apartment. Weird that his sister was almost never home lately. He glanced at his watch.

Fuck, he was going to be late for practice. That's probably where Mandi was.

He fired off another text.

Want to talk about it?

No.

Seriously? A guy offers to talk about feelings and usually chicks go cray. ;-)

I'm not like most chicks.

True dat. I have practice in a minute. I'll call you when done. How do you feel about sexting?

I don't know what that is.

Liar. Minx. Dinner with me tomorrow night?

Yes.

Yes?

Yes, I'll go to dinner.

Awesome. Call you later, sunshine.

Feeling a bit like a giddy schoolkid, he showered and ran out to his truck in under fifteen minutes. He tapped out a quick text to his band members and then drove the twelve miles to the Tigard warehouse where they practiced.

Even from outside the building, he could hear Mandi and Conner trying to outdo each other in some heavy metal real-life version of Guitar Hero.

He swung the door open and was hit with a wave of noise and the unique smell of their practice space: beer, sweat, carburetor fluid, and those damn crème brûlée candles Mandi insisted on burning. He fucking loved it. For the first time in what felt like forever, he was stoked to be there in that tin shack and really stoked to be playing with his band.

"Hey, fucker, where you been?" Marco yelled. He leaned into the old fridge they kept there and tossed a beer at him.

"Sorry, guys. Hung out with Bowen, then went for a run."

His sister flipped him off and pulled her guitar off her shoulder, setting it on the stand. She hopped off the platform and punched Jax in the arm. "Sure it wasn't your girlfriend?"

She smirked and grabbed an open beer bottle from the table, or more accurately, the pressboard plank on two cinder blocks that pretended to be a table. Very heavy metal.

Jax flicked his bottle cap at his sister as she walked back to her guitars, bouncing it off her shoulder.

"Asshole."

"Brat."

"Ewwww, so mature."

"What girlfriend?" a very deep, very familiar voice asked from the door he hadn't heard open.

Before Jax could answer Mason's question, Mandi laughed and answered for him. "Oh please, I was kidding. My brother hasn't gotten laid in months. That's why he's been such a prick." The pink-haired monster spun to grab her guitar. "So, losers, we gonna play some rock and roll or what?"

Ignoring her, Jax turned to see Mason and Jami walk into the center of the large open warehouse. Before he could censor himself, he smiled and took a step toward Jami. He thought he saw her shake her head. Apparently now was not a good time to out them as a couple. They *were* a couple, right?

"What are you guys doing here?" The red around Jami's eyes worried him. "Come to watch us practice at being awesome?"

He grabbed a set of drumsticks from the holder he kept next to the stage. His stomach flopped when Jami remained quiet, unreadable, next to her brother.

"Only here to bring you the promo schedule for the tour and some copies of the changes Jami made to the agreements," Mason said.

Settling onto the stool behind his set, he called down, "Hey, Jami, bring 'em up here, sweetheart."

Sweetheart? *Oops*.

She glared lasers at him as she climbed awkwardly up onto the raised platform and stomped over to his practice drum set. When she stubbornly stood in front of his kit, contracts in one hand and her other fisted on her hip, he smiled. He hadn't realized how little sleep they'd gotten until he saw her eyes. Even red-eyed and peeved, she was gorgeous. Still hotter than fuck.

She mouthed something to him and cocked her head to the side. Looking around to make sure no one was paying attention, he confirmed the rest of the band members had gathered around Mason and had their backs to him.

"Come here. Can't hear you."

"Jackson," she scolded in a whisper.

"Sunshine. Come here."

Her eyes widened slightly and he heard the soft little intake of air. But he noticed. He always noticed, even the infinitesimally small changes to her demeanor. She kept herself so tightly wound sometimes that it was only the small details that gave away her mood.

When she reached him, he stood and took the contracts from her small hand and let his fingers linger across her palm and wrist. He smiled to himself when the pulse in her neck beat faster and she closed her eyes for a moment. Setting the papers on the table at the edge of the stage, he patted his drum stool.

When she looked confused, he stood behind her and grabbed her shoulders, pushing her toward the stool.

"Sit." He could see the goose bumps on her arms as the soft bursts of his breath hit her skin. When he pushed her down, firmly, he saw her lips curve up demurely.

Man, oh man, what he wanted to do with those lips.

Focus, dickhead.

"What are you doing?"

"Teaching you to drum."

"Why?" she asked.

As he wrapped her fingers around his sticks and then his hands over hers, he realized he was already hard. Damn woman. "To prove you have an ear for music."

She giggled, sending tingling jolts of lust straight to his cock. "Doesn't mean I'm going to karaoke with you, Jackson."

"We'll see." He settled on the back of the extra-wide stool behind her with his legs framing hers. Her body stiffened, her arms turned into steel rods. He snorted. "Honey, you have to relax."

The tension melted out of her muscles and she leaned back into him. She wiggled her little ass and said, "I can feel you."

"Ms. Dillon, are you flirting with me?"

She snorted.

"Such a charming woman. Now I'm gonna play the bass drum, set the beat, okay? Then we're going to start with a slow tap on the snare drum…that one there, got it?"

She bit her lip, and he hit the bass drum at a slow, even tempo. She wiggled in his lap and he groaned. His girl was hot. When she nodded, he took that as a sign that she was ready, so he flicked her wrist slowly on the downbeat. With the other hand he started tapping his high-hat.

They played for a few minutes, a simple but solid beat, and when he lifted his hands from hers and settled them on top of her thighs where no one could see them, she slammed the crash cymbal. His band members and Mason broke into applause. Jami's cheeks turned pink and she stood. She took a bow and motioned for Jax to do the same, so he grabbed her hand and threw their arms up like boxing champs and bowed with her.

He jumped off the stage and helped Jami down, letting his hand dust her perfect ass before shaking hands with Mason.

"Ladies and gentleman, the new backup drummer for Manix Curse."

"Hey, who knew my tone-deaf sister could play the drums." Mason laughed.

"She only thinks she's tone deaf. I'll turn her into a headbanger soon enough."

Mason's eyes drifted to Jami, who was staring up at Jax, his face blank. Jax didn't want to look back on this moment and have regrets. He wanted to look back and remember how important this was. And not as "that time Mason punched Jax out for fucking his little sister."

"Yeah?" Mason raised a brow.

"Yep, that's the plan." Making his move—his statement—right there in front of her brother and his band, Jax placed his hand at the small of Jami's back. She looked up at him, but didn't move away. Instead she blew his mind by smiling wide.

Jami laid her palm on his abs. "We'll see about that."

"Okay," Mason said, dragging out his words and raising one brow at Jax. "Hope you know what you're getting into."

"I do." Jax replied. Because he did. He'd been thinking about it since he saw her at the shop. He wanted Jami Dillon for his own. For a while, anyway. Forever? Maybe.

Jami pulled away, grabbing his hand and giving it

three quick squeezes before she reminded everyone she needed their contracts back by the end of the week and telling them to call if they had any questions.

"I'll see you out," Jax said as they walked toward the door, where a stack of old pallets partially hid them from the rest of the band and Mason.

"No. Practice. That's why you're here. But thanks for the lesson, and thanks for turning my crappy day back into a good day." She cupped his face briefly, but her eyes still looked shadowed, hiding that sad, broken thing she refused to share with him.

"Was it bad?"

Her eyes glittered. The last he thing he wanted was to make her cry. "The morning was great. The brunch was not."

"Come to my house tonight. Spend the night."

She glanced up to the stage, where his sister conferred with Conner on something. "Your sister."

"What about her? She can have dinner with us."

"I have work in the morning."

"Bring a bag."

She rolled her eyes and paused for a moment before replying. "Okay. I concede."

"Really?" he asked, hating how he sounded more like a squeaky pubescent boy than a heavy-metal rock god.

She smiled and nodded. "What time?"

"I have to run by the store, so sevenish?"

"I'll be there."

Right then another missing piece clicked into place, or maybe an extra piece shook loose. Either way, he felt a shift in his world. One minute everything made sense and was perfectly aligned. Or seemed like it should be. Then the next it was all mixed up and confused. And now it had realigned itself in a new, more perfect way. A way he had never expected and had not seen coming.

Because right now, right here, Jax Paige knew only one thing for sure: he wanted JamiLynn Dillon more than he wanted his next drum solo, more than he wanted a multimillion-dollar contract.

Even if he didn't believe he deserved her.

Jami wasn't surprised when her parents showed up at her house later that afternoon and bullied their way in under the pretext of resolving their altercation at brunch.

"JamiLynn, are we boring you?" The sharp edge of her mother's voice snapped Jami's head up. "That's the fifth time you've looked at your phone in the last thirty minutes."

"I doubt that, Mother. More like the second."

Her mother raised her brows briefly, the subtle recrimination that said so much in one small expression. But she was right, Jami had looked at her phone almost half a dozen times in a half hour.

Jami picked at a loose thread on her casual cotton pants, the ones she had changed into for an evening with Jackson and maybe his sister. She was now at a turning point. She either had to tell her parents the truth, that she did indeed have plans, and they needed to leave. Or she had to text Jackson and let him know she wouldn't be making it to his house for dinner—or anything else for that matter. Her stomach rolled and her palms felt clammy.

"Darling, quit fussing. We're here to discuss your behavior this morning and see what we can do about the issue with your brother."

Jami laid her hands in her lap and took a deep breath. She was tempted to focus on Mason and his "issue," which she assumed was his impending nuptials. What a relief it would be to have the burning focus of Mr. and Mrs. Robert Dillon off her for once. And Mason was so strong, so self-assured, surely he could take their meddling shenanigans. But her feelings about Kevan and Mason had changed.

"Of course, we want to give you a chance to explain yourself. We're nothing if not fair," her father said, apparently taking her lack of response as agreement.

Maybe that's what they'd always assumed: that, because she didn't fight back, didn't stand up for herself, she agreed with them. They never really asked, and she never really offered. After the accident, she'd worked so hard to earn any little bone they'd throw her. Even a subtle nod or "good job" would hold her over, and they led her to believe it was enough and that she didn't deserve much more.

But maybe she did. She was just having a little fun with an old friend. And, dammit, she was so tired of being treated like a wayward teen. She was a successful attorney—she had gotten her life together and gotten into college, then law school. She had a decent job she'd acquired without her family's assistance. A home she'd purchased with her own money. She volunteered, and she had friends.

She deserved some respect.

"Right. Fair. Father, you told Mason and me that

we were huge disappointments. Disappointments. I made some mistakes a very long time ago. But I'm an upstanding member of the community. And Mason is hugely successful. First as the CEO of a corporation, and now as an entrepreneur. When is it going to be enough?"

"You're hardly successful at your little firm, and your brother threw away the opportunity of a lifetime, even if it was in the music industry. We raised you to be more," her father answered.

"More than what? You raised us to be robots!" Being attacked by her parents twice in one day was twice too many. She was exhausted. Done. It was too much for her to keep it all together at the moment. Too damn hard to live up to their exacting, unattainable standards.

"We raised you better than some tattooed losers who hang around filthy, rock-and-roll musicians." The hitch in her mother's voice was the only outward indication she was anything other than pleased with the situation. "That environment is not acceptable for any Dillon."

"My God, Mother, do you even hear yourself? I do everything you ask of me. I tow every line and dot every damn *i*, and even *I* know you sound insane."

When her father jumped from her couch and took two strides to her, she stood up, shivering with a dangerous mix of fear and pride and rage. In a flash, without warning, he struck the side of her face.

All the air in her lungs rushed out. Tears pooled involuntarily in her eyes. Her fingers felt icy where they pressed against her heated skin. Already she could feel a bruise forming on her cheekbone where her father's palm had hit the hardest. A tremble began in her hands and quickly moved through her entire body until she began to shake uncontrollably. She wanted to run, to hide from her father, her parents.

"You do not talk to your mother in that tone. It is appalling and will not happen again." Her father's voice was only slightly louder than normal, but otherwise he sounded completely calm. Like it was perfectly acceptable for him to smack his adult daughter, which he'd only ever done when he'd disciplined her as a young girl.

Jami pulled a deep breath into her lungs, letting the air fill her with courage. Glancing over at her mother, she noted a new look her eyes. Was it fear?

Breathe out.

Jami sucked in another long breath, praying to the universe for more courage.

Breathe out.

"Do you understand?"

Willing her voice not to shake, she forced a watery smile. "I understand you just assaulted me." The words hurt to say, hurt like jagged pieces of glass in her throat. How could they have come to this?

"This is ridiculous. You and your brother are ungrateful idiots. Come, Carol. We'll speak to you later, JamiLynn. When you're less emotional."

Her mother stood and looked as if she wanted to say something, making a motion like she was going to step toward her. Jami's heart grew with hope, until her mother's expression hardened and she allowed herself to be pulled away by her husband.

"Mom?" Jami's voice cracked. But her mother never turned back toward her.

Jami closed her eyes and heard the door slam as she

slid down to the floor and tucked her knees up against her chest. Hoping the tighter she held, the easier it would be to keep her tears in and the pain in her heart from leaking out all over the floor.

Jami didn't know how long she sat there holding herself—maybe minutes, maybe hours—before she became aware of a subtle beeping sound and then a pounding. Someone yelling.

"Jami! Open the fucking door now!"

"Jackson?"

She unwrapped herself and stood, making her way to the door.

"Open the door, sweetheart. Please open the door." Panic laced his voice.

"What are you doing here?" she asked. She barely had the chance to swing the door wide before Jackson leapt into the room and wrapped her in his arms. He quickly led her to the couch and pulled her into his lap. She rested her head on his solid shoulder, taking comfort in his body and the steady beat of his heart under her ear.

Thump.

Thump.

Thump.

"Are you okay?"

She nodded against him, not wanting to break their connection.

"How did you know something was wrong?" She looked up into his dark-fringed eyes. His handsome face transformed—eyes narrowed and mouth pinched. His knuckles brushed her cheek gently, a total contradiction to the tension in his body.

"You didn't show up at my house. You didn't call.

You wouldn't answer your phone. What was I supposed to do?"

The big bad metalhead her parents seemed to think was such a horrible person had come looking for her.

"What the fuck happened?" His voice was low. Feral. A scary calm swirled around him like a silent hurricane. She pulled her shoulders forward as an ugly heat burned her cheeks. "Hey, what happened?" he asked again, cupping her face and forcing her eyes back up to his. What she saw surprised her. Something gooey and warm, honey and tea. Not anger, not disgust.

She took a deep breath meant to ground and cleanse, like she'd been taught years before at the center.

"It's nothing. Really." She instantly realized how flat and silly that sounded, especially since Jackson was a protector at his core. He was fun and good-natured, but his true essence was one of responsibility. The hurt in his eyes burned more than the bruise from her father.

"Do I really need to explain this to you, sunshine? I'm pretty sure you're not ready for what I have to lay down. So tell me what happened. Now."

She sighed. No, she wasn't ready for Hurricane Jax yet, but he was here with his big heart and warm body, and she wanted to lean on someone. For once. "My parents came over. They wanted to discuss brunch this morning and Mason's issues. Whatever that means."

Jackson continued to stroke her cheek and hold her. The slow, steady pull of his strength was grounding, but did she really need to burden him with her family crap and her baggage?

"I know that look. Don't even brother. Whether you want to admit it, we're already in too deep. I want to know. I need to know." He kissed her nose and pulled back to stare directly into her eyes. Damn man pushed all her buttons, shoving her out of her comfort zone every time.

"They demanded an apology for this morning at brunch. And—"

"What happened this morning?"

"They said some very cruel things. Mason and Kevan showed up and dragged me out of there. My parents wanted me to say I was sorry for being a huge disappointment. And, for once, I called them on their bullshit. I said something to my mother...I don't even remember what I said, and my dad smacked me. Then he called me an ungrateful idiot and marched out."

"What the fuck? *He did what?*" She could feel his arms tighten around her. What did it say about her that, the stronger his hold on her, the safer she felt, more cared for instead of pinned down? "I want to fucking smash something right now, preferably your dad's face. But I can't let you go."

She knew he meant he couldn't let her go right now, but for a moment she let the words sink in as if he'd meant something else altogether.

"Jackson, this isn't your fight. It's mine. I wasn't always like I am now. When I was younger..."

He grabbed her face again, gently, and stared right into her eyes so intensely she wanted to look away, but didn't. Couldn't.

"Don't you dare start making excuses for them." His

barely controlled anger filled the room. "They don't deserve it. And you deserve so much more."

"They're my parents," she said, sounding unconvincing even to her own ears.

"So what, Jami! They don't get to hit you and continually tell you lies about yourself." He kissed her cheek and then rubbed his thumb over where she knew a bruise was already forming. "No parent should hit their children, and no man should ever hit a woman."

She lay her head back onto his strong chest, and sighed. Jackson was here, feeling all the rage her shock was filtering.

"Motherfucker," Jackson whispered and tucked her closer to his chest. "He's a cocksucking motherfucker."

She laughed. No one called the great and powerful Robert Dillon a "cocksucking motherfucker." Well, except maybe the badass Jackson Paige.

"Yeah."

Jackson's long fingers tangled in her hair. "Say it."

She shook her head. No. Saying it aloud was too much. Too hard.

"Say it, sunshine," he growled.

Instantly her hormones came to and flooded her body with all kinds of naughty thoughts.

He gathered her hair and wrapped it around his fist. It was like he knew intuitively that his dominant gesture was exactly what she needed. It erased the real violence her father had thrown at her with his hate and anger. Jackson knew her darkness, the shadows she kept deep inside with her shame and self-doubt, and he brought them out into the light. Showed her their value and then added them to his own.

"My dad is a cocksucking motherfucker." She giggled. She seemed to be doing that a lot.

"What else?"

She mumbled her answer.

"I can't hear you when you mumble, little one."

"I don't deserve how they treat me. Happy?"

"Not yet, but getting there." He let her hair down
and cupped both sides of her face, his thumbs gliding
back and forth over her jawbone. "Gonna tell you something…don't get that panicked look in your eyes, it's not
what you think. Well, maybe it is. Ready?"

She nodded, but couldn't breathe past the boulder of
emotions choking her.

"This is on me. This is not your fault. Not gonna let
this shit happen on my watch again. Feel me?"

"Jackson, you can't protect me from life. I'm an
adult—"

"Sweetheart, I'm not saying you can't take care of
yourself. I know you can. I'm sayin' you don't have to
anymore. I got your back. I was too busy pussyfooting
around to realize it."

God, all the emotions. Every damn one. Fear. Hope.
Gratitude. It was all too overwhelming. So she simply
nodded and laid her head back against the wall of
warmth under her.

"Don't have anything to say to that?" he asked.

What could she say? That she was afraid—terrified
of her growing feelings for him, panicked at the very
idea of him leaving her again? No, he didn't need that
kind of power over her again. No one would ever have
that kind of control of her emotions ever again. Not him.
Not her parents.

"You can't blame yourself for how my parents behave." She patted his chest and let him fold his arms around her.

"True. But I won't let them hurt you again. I've already let them get away with too much."

Any thoughts of asking him to clarify that statement dissolved as his hand snuck under her blouse and caressed her breast.

Chapter 11

THE FOLLOWING NIGHT, JAMI FOUND HERSELF staring at the reflection in her bedroom's full-length mirror. "Are you sure this looks okay?" She nervously tugged at her short dress. The much-shorter-than-usual dress, which she'd put on after Ella and Gabby had muscled their way into her house and stared aghast at her outfit. She turned her backside to the full-length mirror and looked at her behind over her shoulder. "I mean, if I bend over you'll probably be able to see my panties."

Ella tapped her finger on her bottom lip. "That's the point." She stepped into Jami's small walk-in closet. "But there's still something missing."

"I think she looks hot as hell," Gabby added from where she lounged on the lilac and gray duvet on Jami's bed. "Fucking smoking hot."

"Gabby!"

"What, Jami? You never swear? Please. Wait until you get to know me better. I've been on my best behavior." Gabby smirked as Ella exited the closet with a folded black mess of leather and tulle.

Jami's stomach pitched.

"No, no, no, no. I am not wearing that thing! It's…" Oh jeez. It was bad enough she was standing around in this ridiculously short dress, getting ready for a date that really wasn't a date with a man who had already broken her heart once. But then Ella had found her secret. Well, one of them anyway.

Gabby stood and snatched the outfit from Ella, shaking it out with a long whistle. "Whoa. I would never have guessed."

"It was a costume. In college. I was in a steampunk play." Jami lied, spitting her words out like bullets. "I could never wear that in public. On a date."

Ella shoved it into Jami's hands. The soft leather melted in her hands and the subtle smell tugged hints of the past from her brain. No. She wasn't going back to that heartache again. Opening herself up to another human, letting him do things to her that no one else ever had or would, was too out of control. It wasn't who she was anymore.

She tossed the dress on the bed. "Nope. Not wearing that ever. I didn't even realize I still had it." Gabby picked it up and placed the dress in Jami's hand, closing her fingers around it.

Gabby gave her a rare smile. "I see that look in your eyes. I recognize the fear, Jami, because I see the same thing in the mirror every day. I see it in the eyes of the women we help at the center. Don't live in that place anymore. Beneath all that baggage and lawyerly bullshit, I know you're all glitter and unicorns. Come on, lead us out into the light."

"It won't fit." Tears swam in Jami's eyes, but she couldn't look away from the raw truth Gabby was trying to share with her. Both her friends ignored her comment, so she took a deep breath. "I'm scared."

Gabby brushed her hand against Jami's cheek in the most tender gesture Jami had ever experienced from any woman. "I know."

Ella stepped forward, dwarfing both of her friends with her willowy height, and threw her hands wide and smiled. "Group hug?" She wrapped her long, toned arms around them both. "Now go put the fucking dress on."

This date thing was a bad idea. When Jackson had suggested dinner at the party and then again when she'd stayed the night, she'd agreed. Without hesitation. But now that the weekend had rolled back around, she wasn't so sure.

Some careful pulling, tugging, and wiggling later, Jami found herself in front of the mirror with her friends standing behind her. Jami barely recognized the exotically elegant woman staring back at her. Who was this sexy, confident woman? The soft black leather dress accented and celebrated every curve, every hill and valley, on her body. The sweetheart collar not only highlighted her full breasts, it put them on display, yelling "boobs" to the world. The tight corset was boned, cinching her waist before dropping down to a short, full skirt. The tall, simple T-strap heels Ella had found buried in the back of her closet—still in the box and stuffed with the shaping paper—didn't exactly give Jami stature, but they made her legs look great and her butt pert.

"This wasn't a costume, was it?" Gabby asked.

Nope. When she'd found it in a women's clothing consignment store her first year in law school, she'd instantly fallen in love with the dress. Her heart raced as she remembered how she hoped Jackson would take her out and show her off in it. But he'd never seen her in it, since he left her the next week. "No. Never wore it, though. Not my style."

"Well, it is now. And it still fits," Ella said in a quiet voice.

"And it's fucking amazeballs, bitches," Gabby whispered as theirs eyes met in the mirror.

"Really?"

"Yeah, really," Ella and Gabby said simultaneously. Then they both bent over in laughter. Jami would have joined them; however, she was afraid she might not be able to bend at the waist at all.

After Jamie took a couple of practice walks up and down the hall, Ella was finishing Jami's makeup and the doorbell sounded.

"Oh, hell's bells," Jami whispered. "He's here. Dammit. Dammit. Dammit." Her hands began to tremble as a tornado of emotion welled in her chest. And for a moment she was back in that apartment, studying for some class she'd long forgotten. Waiting. Waiting for a man who had broken through walls. She remembered finally reheating the fettuccine one last time and eating a plate for herself before trying his cell phone one final time that night. Tonight she would find out why. Why he'd left. Why he made her believe in love again and broke her heart anyway.

And she would listen and try to understand, forgive him, and finally move forward.

Ella squeezed Jami's shoulder and slowly pivoted her body toward the bathroom mirror. Ella and Gabby exchanged a look—maybe of admiration, maybe of understanding. Her reflection displayed a new Jami. While she looked different—glamorous and carefree—this was not the old wild child Jami. But it wasn't divorce-attorney-love-sucks Jami either.

This was someone new. Maybe this new Jami could finally move beyond her past, keep her parents happy and off her brother's back, move up in her firm and be taken seriously, and have a fling with a sexy-as-hell drummer and tattoo artist without getting her heart shattered again.

Maybe New Jami could be all the things Old Jami couldn't.

Jax followed Jami into the Pearl District restaurant with his hand resting on her lower back—fitting perfectly into the indention below her waist. The soft leather felt fluid, alive under his palm—so much so that he caressed it with his thumb, gently rubbing it back and forth over that sweet dimpled spot that teased him beneath the material. He couldn't see her face as they walked behind the hostess into the lush, dark cavern of a room, but he knew her well enough to know her cheeks would be flushed with desire. He let his hand drop for a second to brush the rounded curve of her perfect ass, and smiled to himself when he heard a soft gasp.

He'd picked The Duke's Gallery for its unique alcove booths and private tables. The rich tapestries and plush velvet seating were a bonus. The local favorite had a long, torrid history that included years as a brothel and later as a speakeasy. The dark wood and eclectic mix of antiques lent an outlaw yet elegant flavor to its colorful history, but the art deco sconces and wall pieces were what really drew him here. Because the beautiful woman in front of him with her flowing blond hair and seductive yet innocent leather dress fit the room like she was born to it.

He scooted into the private booth after Jami so they sat angled toward each other, side by side, still close enough for their knees to brush. The chaste touch of her bare knee burned his leg through his Ben Davis twill pants, and the fire continued straight to his cock, which he'd been trying to keep below full mast since she'd flung open the door to her apartment and he'd seen her standing there. In that dress. And those fuck-me heels.

Though they texted or talked on the phone every day, they'd both been busy all week with work. Plus, he'd had practice and she'd had several volunteer shifts, so he hadn't seen her since the morning after her dad had hit her. He'd been excited about their date—and anxious about telling her the truth. He was pretty sure he'd stopped breathing for nearly five minutes when she'd opened that door. He'd certainly stood there like a dolt until Jami's tall friend, Ella, and their quiet friend, Gabby, had started making excuses and run out the door like they were being chased by Cthulhu. That was right about when he realized he was probably going to pass out if he didn't suck in some oxygen.

Guess she had literally taken his breath away.

"What?" Jami asked, breaking into his thoughts, and bringing him back into the moment.

"What *what*?"

"You laughed."

"I did?" he coughed, covering his surprise. Or trying to.

"Well, actually, you kind of giggled."

Oh, hell no. "Yeah? No. I don't giggle."

"Whatever you say."

"Whatever *I* say?" He could definitely get on board with that.

"Jackson." She smacked his bare forearm and sparks shot through his veins and straight to his dick. Again. *Fuck*. He was in for a long night if every time she touched him she started his blood boiling and got his cock hard. But he loved when she called him Jackson. Loved the possessiveness, the propriety of it. Loved how she looked so wantonly hot in that leather dress, but still clung to her manners.

Jami's chest and neck turned pink. Adorable. He was about to lean forward and whisper something inappropriate enough to turn it bright red when the waitress showed up and shared the specials. The younger red-haired woman was professional and discreet, but kept peering over her order pad at Jami, while Jami kept her menu high and allowed her hair to fall forward, covering much of her face.

He wondered if Jami was embarrassed to be seen with him. Was she worried she might run into a colleague while she was out with her bad-boy hookup? More likely it was her discomfort in her outfit. For some broken reason he didn't quite understand yet, his girl felt more comfortable in her boring suits than in the dress that fit her like a glove.

Fuck that. Maybe he wasn't good enough for her. Maybe there wasn't anything he could do to make amends for their past. But he could try. He threw his arm across the booth and let his hand rest on her shoulder. As usual, her body went rigid as rebar before he squeezed gently and she relaxed. With his other hand he leaned across her body, accidently-on-purpose brushing his fingertips across the bodice of her dress, and tucked her hair behind one ear. At the same time, he nipped the soft flesh at her neck and whispered, "You look so fucking beautiful tonight, it almost hurts to keep my hands off you."

The waitress made it a few feet before she slowed and then swung back to their table. She looked right at Jami's face. "I don't mean to be rude, but I feel like I know you." As panic began to darken Jami's eyes, Jax stroked her collarbone lightly with his index finger. The waitress's face lit with recognition. She pointed to herself. "It's me. Diana O'Conner, Ms. Dillon. You helped me and my son get away from my shi—uh, jerk ex-husband. Remember? You got us into the center, then helped us find housing."

Jami's lip trembled as her lawyer face clicked into place. "Of course I remember you, Diana. It's just so dark in here. And how is Jacob?"

Diana's smile stretched across her face. "Fantastic. He's getting ready to start seventh grade. Very excited." She leaned forward and lowered her voice. "You probably know my divorce was final a couple months ago, right? And Johnny is going to be in jail for a long time."

Jami nodded. "I do. I filed the paperwork myself."

"I'm sorry. I know you're having dinner." The other woman scanned the dining area, probably to make sure her boss wasn't around. She smiled at Jax.

"Oh, this is my friend Jackson."

"Nice to meet you, Diana." He smiled at the waitress, not sure what else to say. He seemed to remember her working at a higher-end law firm, not one that would help out a struggling waitress.

Diana blushed. "I wanted to say thank you for every-thing you've done for us. I'll be back in a minute for your order."

Instead of explaining, Jami began to line up the silverware and rearrange the table setting. Jax could practically see the gears and springs moving around in her head.

That's okay, baby. I'll give you a minute.

He waited for Diana to come back and take their order before he covered Jami's twitchy hand with his to still her fingers. Slowly, she pulled back the silken curtain of her hair and he caught her gaze. One second he was in control and calling the shots, the next he was a helpless fish gasping for air, caught on her line. Did she have any idea that she reeled him in completely with a simple, honest glance from her arctic blue eyes? Did she feel any of what he did? The chaos inside him, swirling around them…was it in her, too?

He took a slug of beer. "So how do you know her?"

Her chest rose and fell several times before she took a sip of wine and sighed. "I've mentioned it before. I volunteer at Quirk a few nights a week and a couple weekends a month." She shrugged.

"Quirk?"

"Quirk is the nickname for the Portland Community Women's Resource Center. No big deal."

"Of course it's a big deal," he said, with a swell of pride at the idea of her selflessly helping others. He knew she volunteered at a women's center quite a bit, but she didn't usually offer any details. She fussed with her glass, centering it above her fork. He placed his finger on her chin and tilted her face toward him.

"That's pretty fucking cool, sweetheart. You work all day sorting through the wreckage of people's relationships and then you go give more of yourself to people who—"

"Women."

"Give yourself to women who really need your help." Shame filled him. What the hell did he do for anybody that didn't have some ulterior motive or address his own agenda? Not a thing. Not one fucking thing.

"You make it sound so altruistic."

"It is."

She shook her head. "Nope. I could never give enough time or enough money. The need is just too great."

"Uh, yeah. How'd you get into it?"

"I started tutoring and helping in the kitchen my senior year of high school. I needed something to be involved in." She smiled, lost in the past. "I went back during the summers after you left me…left school."

"I'm sorry, Jami."

She shrugged dismissively, and looked up, apparently overjoyed when Diana brought their food. She immediately busied herself arranging her napkin neatly on her lap and taking a big bite of risotto.

Her groan thrummed in his chest and her eyes went wide. "You just growled."

"No, I didn't."

"Yes, Jackson, you did." Her lips tipped up on one side, and she threw him a knowing smirk. "How's your steak, carnivore?"

"Haven't tasted it yet."

Too busy staring at you.

He took a bite of the nearly raw filet on his plate, but

it could have been diamonds or dust, it wouldn't have mattered. All that mattered was sitting right next to him.

"Why did you pick the women's center to volunteer at? Why there?"

Jami put her fork down and rested her hands in her lap. Patrons' voices drifted above the soft blues music playing over the sound system. A clink of glass meeting glass. The click of forks touching plates. A laugh. The murmurs of intimacy floated all around them. As he was about to take her hand and tell her to forget it, she lifted her eyes to his.

"I first went there for counseling when I was a teenager."

"Baby…"

"No, it's okay. It was a long time ago." She smiled but it didn't reach her eyes. Instead, she had a faraway look, like she'd left the room completely.

"Basically, I got into some trouble senior year of high school with my boyfriend. When I needed his help, he turned on me. Then he ran off with one of the girls I thought was my friend. I think they're still married and have like three kids in Tigard or something."

Suddenly Jax wasn't hungry. Suddenly he wanted nothing more than to beat the fuck out of the asshole that had hurt Jami. Then he wanted to pull her into his arms and hold her tight.

Forever.

And then he realized he'd been just another asshole who'd hurt her. His eyes met hers. Hers were so full of sadness it was a wonder she had any room left in there for the pride he also saw. He wanted to run from the room and pummel something. For her. Well, probably more for him. But the realization that she'd let down her guard and actually told him something about herself—something real—overpowered his anger and calmed the storm rising in his chest.

Was this the beginning of trust? He reached over and pulled her hands into his, angling his body so he could look into her face. "Did he hit you?"

She nodded. One simple curt nod of her head. But instead of acting on the rage bubbling in his gut and giving in to the darkness clogging his ability to reason, he chose to see her as she needed to be seen. As a survivor. A beautiful fighter. He'd come along a few years later, she'd started to open up again, and he'd left her high and dry. No good-bye. No explanation. No nothing. He brushed a kiss on her bruised cheek, hoping some of her strength would rub off on him, hoping to quell the rising tide in his chest.

Was he any better than her asshole ex just because he hadn't raised his hand to her? He knew now that he'd fucked with her head and maybe even her heart when he'd left.

"I'm sorry."

"It wasn't your fault. He was bad news and I should have known better than to get involved with him. But my parents kept pushing Dallas and me together. Said we were perfect together."

"Dallas? Do you mean Dallas Gale?"

She nodded.

What the fuck? His family owned half of Lake Oswego. The sleazeball had been two years ahead of him at school, which would have put him at twenty-two to Jami's teenage seventeen.

A warning look crossed Jami's face. "Jackson, don't

go getting any ideas. He has a family, and I moved on the second his fist connected with my body."

A rush of heat hit Jax's face, nearing an explosive temperature. That scumbag had hit this tiny woman when she'd been still a child. Who the hell did that shit? His vision began to narrow, and his temple throbbed. Jami yanked her hands out of his.

"You're hurting me. And it was a long time ago."

"I'm sorry," he said, and he meant it. He had no intention of ruining their first real date in five years by focusing on some dick from the past and not the leather-clad woman next to him. It seemed like all he did was hurt her. And he wanted desperately to change that.

She grabbed her wine and took a neat sip. "Stop saying that. Like I said, not your fault. Can we get back to dinner?"

"Sorry about the past. About leaving. About getting angry now. So fucking sorry about everything." Shit, he needed to tell her the damn truth. But then they'd be done for good. Once it was out there, she'd never forgive him.

She shrugged in that dismissive way again. He'd had about enough of that for now. "I tried to force you to be something you weren't. I'm so sorry for that."

"Stop doing that. I hurt you. Much more than you hurt me."

"Fine. What do you want from me?" she hissed.

"I want you to stop acting like what we had didn't matter. I want you to stop pretending it wasn't totally fucked up for me to leave without telling you why. I want you to let me explain."

"What if I'm not ready?"

"You are. You have been," he said, surprised at how the strongest woman in the world had no idea of her own power.

"Why is it so damn important for me to know why you left school?"

"Because we can't move forward until we talk about it."

She smiled that sad smile again. "What if I don't want to move forward? What if I want to stay right here?"

"But I don't. And I don't think you do either. Who knows, maybe you won't forgive me and this will be our last dinner, but I respect you too much to not tell you the truth."

✶ ✶ ✶

Why did it seem like Jackson was always right? It was starting to get annoying. But she did want to know what had happened to make him run from her five years ago. So long ago she'd buried those feelings of want and abandonment under something she could control. Discipline. Control. And school.

Jami felt completely unnerved under Jackson's frank gaze. Afraid to know the truth, if he thought it was so bad that she might not ever forgive him. But he stared at her like he knew her, like he could see deep down into her dark places, and he maybe still liked her anyway. The weird, soft, twisty thing she'd felt unfurling before began to unwind more, stretching its warm tendrils.

"You gave me something. A piece of you. I want to give you something back."

Her throat clogged, like there were jagged pieces of glass she couldn't swallow down. "I'm afraid," she managed.

His long thumb, the one with the black heart fashioned at the base of it, gently stroked the top her hand. The motion was both reassuring and unsettling. Every touch, accidental or calculated, sent sharp reminders of her body's need for Jackson Paige. Was this addiction? Was this why it had hurt so badly and had taken so long to recover from his blow to her heart?

Now here he was playing the part of avenging angel and attentive lover, practically begging for a chance at redemption. What if she didn't get the closure she'd needed so desperately for so long? What if his answers didn't quite meet her expectations?

As if he could read her mind, he gave her a lopsided smile. "I'm not looking to make amends, Jami. I'm looking to give you an explanation. One that's probably pathetic at best."

She simply nodded.

"It wasn't you. It was never you."

Her heart, beating double-time since they'd sat down, suddenly stopped and dropped to her feet. The grim look on his face quickly transformed to horror when he glanced up. "No, no, no. I said that wrong." He brushed his hand over her hair, tucking in a long tendril. "I meant I didn't leave because of anything you said or did."

After taking a sip of water, she found her voice. "Then why? Because everything seemed pretty great."

He smiled weakly. "Do you remember what we talked about that morning?"

She shook her head. No, not really. They'd made love so sweetly and slowly, chatted in the afterglow about school and art. Then he'd left for class. "We had sex and talked about school."

"We made love. And it was fucking epic. We talked about art." He watched her closely, his eyes narrowing, waiting for her memory to come clear. Her cheeks burned like they'd caught fire. Jackson remembered their lovemaking the same as she did.

Yes, his art. And how he'd wanted to balance a law career with being an artist.

"And you wanted to do a showing at the campus gallery."

He nodded, waiting.

Her heart started beating again, hard against her ribs. "I laughed." Ice flooded her veins. She had laughed, speculating he'd be too busy with his career as an entertainment attorney to be able to pursue his hobby. "But I didn't laugh at you. I thought you'd be in so much demand as a lawyer. Oh my God, Jackson, I dismissed your passion like it was a silly little whim. I'm so very sorry." Exactly as her parents had done to her when she'd wanted to go into nonprofit or environmental law.

"I know, sunshine." He squeezed her hand. "I was going to skip class, went to get us coffee and scones. I was all set to come back and finish the conversation instead of leaving it hanging there."

"But you didn't come back."

"No. I didn't."

"Why?" She hated how shaky her voice sounded, how the short word came out as a whine.

"I ran into your parents walking back to your apartment."

If the center of that elegant restaurant had opened up right then with a huge sinkhole, Jami would have happily stood up, said good night, and jumped in feet first. As an attorney she dealt with often contentious contracts and dissolving partnerships. She was more than used to her share of uncomfortable conversations. Those inter-actions had nothing on this one. Not a damn thing.

She ran her hands up the side of her face and through her hair. "I don't think I want to hear the rest of the story."

"I know you don't, baby, I know."

She placed one elbow on the table and covered her eyes with her hand, but he wouldn't let her hide and yanked it down. "See, this is what you really need to hear. What they said to me, what we discussed, was not your fault."

"They're my freaking parents, Jackson," she said still not able to look at him. "I brought them into your life."

"Look at me, sunshine." His tone was firm, and she could never refuse that voice.

Slowly she raised her eyes to meet his, flinchingly prepared to see the hurt of the past, the anger and humil-iation, anything except what she saw.

But what she saw instead in that dark, cozy eatery took her breath away. Tenderness. Kindness. Compassion. Maybe something even stronger. Something more.

"They told me what I already knew. They told me I wasn't good enough for you. That you were getting your life together and that a fuckup like me would ruin your progress. Get in the way of your opportunities. They said you had a boyfriend back home. I didn't believe them about the other guy, but the other stuff kind of hit home. They were very convincing."

Her stomach ached as her well-ordered life spiraled even more out of control. How could they do that? How could he? She couldn't breathe. "They had no fucking right." She gasped for air, struggling to fill her lungs.

"Whoa. I don't think I've ever heard you say the f-word outside of bed. I'm impressed."

"Don't try to distract me." Was she hyperventilating? She blinked several times and began to count through the panic.

One, two, three.

He lifted and dragged her into his lap. His long, powerful arms wrapped around her body and stroked down the low open back of the dress. They were in public. She should push him away. She should insist she was fine and continue to drink her wine. She should not soften in his arms like heated butter.

But she couldn't do any of those things, any more than she could stop the heavy tears from sliding silently down her face.

She was exhausted. So tired of holding up her walls and protecting herself. Tired of all the rules. Tired of fighting her feelings for the big man holding her heart in his hands.

He whispered words that soothed her jagged edges like an ocean forming sand from craggy rocks. "Breathe deeply. Slowly. Not like a gulping fish, baby. Take a nice long cleansing breath. There you go. Now slowly let it out. Good." He continued to hold the back of her head with one hand and rubbed her back with his other, tugging her in closer against his body.

Time passed. Maybe five minutes, maybe fifty. Jami didn't know. She didn't care. Someone was carrying her burden for once. Jackson was on her side—holding her, helping work through the past with his actions. God, she was so sick of words. Vicious words thrown back and forth between divorcing couples. Fearful words from frightened women. Cruel, controlling words from her parents. Even her own judgmental words to her brother, who for once in his life was actually happy.

"I'm getting your shirt wet."

"I don't care."

"I'm a mess."

"Yeah, you are. My fucking beautiful mess with the face of an angel, body of a goddess, and heart of a warrior." He brushed his lips across hers. "God, I missed you so fucking much."

She snorted, which made him laugh. "I'm so tired."

"I know you are. Thank you for letting me take care of you."

She tilted her head up, searching his eyes. Did he really mean that? He was thanking her for being a hot, sobby wreck in his lap in the middle of an upscale Portland restaurant?

"I'm sorry."

"No, I am. I'm sorry that asshole Gale hurt you. I'm sorry your parents are so cold and constantly trying to make their choices yours. But mostly I'm sorry I didn't trust us enough to talk to you about what happened."

"I wish you had trusted me, talked to me before you left."

He nodded. "I'd planned on it. I was pretty pissed, though, and thought I should calm down. As an insurance policy, they offered my dad a contribution to his campaign—I think he was running for state senate or some shit then. He threatened to stop paying my tuition if I didn't break up with you. That really pissed me off. I was so done with being manipulated. I never wanted to be a fucking lawyer anyway. I only went to law school as a sad ploy for daddy's appreciation."

"Jackson," she whispered, unable to say anything else. Haunted by the dark look in his eyes.

"I know I should have called you. But when I drove to the shop to talk to Tony—get his advice—Mandi was there, and she needed a place to live. I didn't want to be dependent on my asshole father anymore. And a little part of me believed what your parents said about me being in your way. So Mandi was my excuse to run away. I went back to slinging ink, and we started the band. That's the story."

This was all too much. He was too much. Too many feelings. He looked away for a moment and pinched his dark brows together. She could tell there was more to the story, but she couldn't take another word. Not one more.

Jackson kissed her. When he pulled away, her hands went reflexively to her still-warm lips.

"Tell me something, Jami. Tell me you hate me. Tell me you forgive me. Tell me anything."

"I don't hate you. I never have. I was…I didn't…" She wasn't quite sure what she'd been. Broken. Crushed. Lonely. But those were all things he didn't need to know—didn't get to know—at least not yet. "I was so hurt and sad. I'm glad you told me. And I understand."

She smiled, and he kissed her lightly on the nose again. "I'm so sorry," he whispered.

"I know you are. And I am, too. For not letting you know you could talk to me, trust me to work through it." But he knew that she would have never turned her back on her parents. She would have done everything they asked of her, because she'd been so afraid to revert back to her old self. So terrified to be left really and truly on her own.

But she'd had enough of this discussion. It was emotionally draining—and not exactly ideal date conversation.

"I'm like a groupie sitting here on your rock-star lap." Her laugh sounded shrill to her ears. All she wanted was to ease the intense tension from his so-serious face.

He gripped her hips hard and pulled her tight. "You are nothing like a groupie. There is no one like you, JamiLynn Dillon. You are unique and fucking glorious. Do you understand?"

What? Her heart pounded double-time against her ribs again. *Thump thump. Thump thump. Thump thump.*

When she didn't answer, he asked again.

Her words were lost. God, how did he keep scrambling her brain like that? Once again, nodding was the only way she could communicate with him.

"Say it."

When Diana arrived with their cheesecake, Jami was thrilled with the reprieve from his…everything. After they were alone again, he repeated his demand.

She shook her head. No. She couldn't say it. Not aloud, where it would become real, like a contract or love signs written in sand. "Say. It."

No. The words felt too heavy. "Why?"

"Because I know you don't believe it yet. But if I get you to say it enough times, maybe you'll start believing it. Say it."

"No." No, no, no!

"Now."

"Fine. I'm not a groupie. There's no one like me. I'm unique and effing glorious."

"Next time without rolling your eyes, counselor." He pressed a quick kiss to her nose and lifted her back to her seat next to him. "Enough mindfucking for tonight. Eat your cheesecake and then I have a surprise for you."

Jami smiled and let him feed her a bite of the strawberry cheesecake while her mind reeled. She was pretty damn sure neither her head nor her heart could take another surprise from Jackson Paige.

Chapter 12

JAX TRIED NOT TO HOLD HIS BREATH WHEN THEY walked into the Drake Martelli Art Foundry. He held his back straight and ignored his clammy palms. He was nervous as a teenage art nerd on his first date with a girl way out of his league. But when he saw Jami's lips curve up into a stunning grin, he released a rush of air, because it wasn't just a polite grin. Nope. It was a big fucking-happy-rainbow-farting-glitter-unicorn smile.

Thank fucking God.

All day he'd played the date over in his mind, each time with a different outcome. Sometimes it would end like the last morning he'd seen her in school, right before running into her parents in the lobby of her apartment. He'd laid his heart out and she'd eaten it for breakfast. Before he'd had a chance to recover and talk to her about his plans, her parents had shown up and poured rock salt into the gaping wound. At the time, he had rationalized it all by acting like he didn't have any interest in ending up in a relationship with a woman who was programmed by her parents to be superficially perfect. That, coupled with his need to get out from under the stifling control of his dad, made his options pretty clear.

His dad was the gold standard for the type of parent kids shouldn't try to emulate. All he cared about was his latest campaign or superficial cause. As an Oregon congressman, his father had always catered more to public perception than reality. But despite his dad being a major dick, Jax had spent many years trying to make him proud. After apprenticing and then working at Tatuaggio for the first couple of years out of high school, he'd finally caved to his father's relentless bullying and enrolled in college.

Oh yeah, Joseph Wade Paige had been thrilled when Jax graduated from the University of Oregon. And when he decided to forgo his MFA for law school, ol' Joseph threw him a fucking party and everything. Of course, he hadn't bothered to invite any of his actual friends or even Jax's mother or other siblings from other wives, only people he thought would be good for his political career.

But maybe Jax wasn't like his dad, and maybe he'd sold Jami short, not given her the opportunity to make a choice on her own. So here he was, bringing her into his semi-secret life. He glanced around the gallery. Isabel and Jewell had done a spectacular job cleaning up the former butcher's shop. Three walls were painted wood, white to highlight the art pieces, and a fourth brick wall was left untouched. The exposed ductwork and industrial lighting created an artsy feel without being too contrived.

As he looked around the gallery filled with people, he realized he didn't know most of them. He'd struggled with the idea of putting his art out there for the world to see, to judge. But he'd never know how it would be received if he didn't try. He didn't really care if others didn't love his art. He hoped they would, but his self-worth didn't hinge on others' approval anymore.

When Jax had resolved to let Jami in again, on the off

chance that they might be able to actually move forward instead of backward, he'd tried to convince himself it really didn't matter anymore what she thought, but that was bullshit. It mattered. That was the real problem. Jami had always mattered. But when he couldn't quite pull the trigger and give her the full story, he realized he might be doomed.

He really was falling for her all over again. Something about her bossy little ways and prim attitude fucking *did* it for him. And those flashes of time when her shield was down were moments to be celebrated. Despite what anyone thought, Jami carried some dark shit around with her, and he'd always known it. He suspected he still wasn't the only one keeping a secret, that there might be more Jami hadn't told him. Whatever it was colored everything she did and said, turned her bright yellow sunshine to a manageable gray. But, slowly, he was peeling back that armor, one tiny bit at a time. Once he had her open and exposed, he was going to prove that he could take care of her, that he'd do anything to keep her this time and to make up for the past.

But first he had to break open his chest and bare his heart and soul. After that, it was in her hands. He wasn't quite sure either of them was ready for that, but taking her to the gallery was the beginning. A spike of uncertainty shot like a bullet through his chest. Was the risk of losing her again worth the benefit of keeping her? After all, her parents were always going to be in the picture.

Jax shook the thoughts away and kept his eyes on Jami. He moved her into the gallery with its eggshell-white walls lined with backlit art pieces. He was so focused on reading all her expressions, he didn't realize the young woman standing next to him had wrapped her hand around his other bicep and had said something.

"I said, 'Hello, Jax, welcome to your showing.'"

"Hey, Isabel, and thanks."

Jami tried to pull free when he leaned over to hug Isabel, but instead Jax tugged her in front of his body. "Jami, this is Isabel. This is her gallery. Isabel, this is Jami, Manix Curse's new legal counsel."

He thought he saw Jami wince slightly, and his heart sank a little. Should he have introduced her as his friend? Surely, not his girlfriend. Yet. He didn't want to spook his brittle lover.

Jami took the taller woman's hand in hers. Jax noted how Jami looked pointedly at the gallery owner's face. "Pleased to meet you, Jami. The gallery is only half mine. My business partner, Jewell, is away visiting her family. Please take a look around. Eat some treats. Drink some wine. I'll do your intro"—she glanced at her watch—"in about ten minutes."

His girl nodded curtly. Professionally. Was she jealous of Isabel?

Jax sighed and turned back to her. "Well, what do you think?" He touched his fingertips to her lower back. He could really get used to the feel of leather molded over her curves.

It was hard enough keeping his hands off her in her lawyerly getups. Add in all that other girly shit like mani-pedis, makeup, and matching accessories, and it would probably only overshadow all the beauty and curvy sex appeal.

"I think she's lovely. This gallery is beautiful. I love

the artistic use of light. A couple of the attorneys at my firm have been talking about this place for months."

His heartbeat thrummed loudly through his veins. "But what about the artwork? What do you think?"

"I love it, why?" Her confused expression was replaced with interest as she moved toward the wall. She squinted and she pulled her sexy thick-rimmed glasses from her bag. His pulse increased as his blood boiled with a heady concoction of nerves and lust. She stood in front of the first piece for nearly five minutes, never saying anything, just examining it closely. Then she stepped back and moved on to the next, where she did the same damn thing. Love them? Hate them? Something. The air felt so charged with tension he could almost reach out and bunch it in his fist. The low electronica music playing throughout the room added to the energy, and the occasional laugh or clinking glass sharpened his sense of the woman studying his art. But he stood quietly, greeting the occasional well-wisher, waiting for her.

When she turned to him, her demeanor was stolid, her face unreadable. He watched as her full rosy lips parted and her pink tongue curled over her bottom lip before she reached for him, grasping his hand in both of hers, and started to say something.

But someone punched him in the arm hard enough that he took a step away from Jami. He turned to see Bowen and Tony standing behind him. His stomach pitched as he glanced nervously around for his other bandmates and coworkers.

"What the hell? How did you guys…" Jax trailed off when Bowen flicked his gaze toward Isabel. Of course she had told her dad, and then Tony had to drag Bowen along with him down to the circus.

"So what the fuck, bro? A gallery opening and not one word to your BFF?" Bowen's eyes followed the female server walking by with a tray full of champagne flutes sparkling in the light. He ran his fingers through his hair and chuckled hollowly. "Not the booze. That chick is hot. Anyway, my problem is my problem, Jax. You can't fix it for me."

He whacked Jax on the back with a thump. His friend was getting physically stronger, and maybe some of that strength was reaching his head, too. Maybe things would be okay for Bowen.

"Nah, dude, I know you're good. I didn't want everyone making a big deal. I'm not really ready for everyone to know about my art and shit." Jax shook his head and took a deep breath.

Bowen raised a dark brow and offered his hand to Jami. "When you gonna to introduce me to your friend, Jax? Trying to keep all the hot girls to yourself?"

"Slow your roll, ladies' man, this is Mason's sister, Jami. You both met her at Kevan and Mason's party."

The comical look on Bowen's face received a laugh from Tony and Jax. Jami cut in and shook his hand. "I'm dressed a little differently. I wasn't expecting to see any of Jackson's friends or coworkers tonight."

Tony smiled. "Ignore these bozos, honey. It's obvious they don't know how to treat a beautiful woman. It's good to see you again."

A loud gong sounded throughout the gallery, echoing off the walls and partitions set up around the old butcher's store. The room grew quiet. Jax grabbed Jami's hand and pulled her to his side. Where she belonged. This time she didn't stiffen first, but immediately let herself melt into him, filling his sharp edges with her soft curves. Like maybe she was meant to.

In the center of the room, Isabel cleared her throat and held a full flute of sparkling champagne. Her dark hair was pulled back into one of those weird messy girl buns, and she wore a fitted, brightly colored dress. "Thank you for coming out to the Art Foundry tonight for our debut showing of multitalented multimedia artist Jax Paige." To Jax's utter disbelief, the room broke out into applause and hoots when she pointed in his direction. The applause was loud, but polite and structured—so different than a Manix show, yet it filled him with the same warm pride and confidence of a gig.

"As you can see from his work, Jax excels in several media, including mixing photography, watercolor, oils, and charcoal. His unique perspective and artistry produce an often amusing and always provocative result. Jax is also an award-winning tattoo artist at the local studio, Tatuaggio." Her short announcement was followed by some *ooh*s and *aah*s and a smattering of applause.

"Please take your time to peruse this varied collection and have some drinks and food. Keep in mind that all the pieces on display are for sale. And Jax will be available for at least the next hour to answer any questions or discuss his artwork."

The next hour was a slow slog of overenthusiastic women and some general interest in his artwork. After the first ten minutes and the constant assurance from Jami that she was fine, he let Bowen and Tony drag her off to mingle and check out his art.

His art. On the walls for everyone to see. And judge.

Jax pasted on his best business smile and rubbed his clammy hands on his pants one last time before glancing over at the only woman in the room who drew his interest. His anxiety evaporated when he realized she really was fine. She was in a small group of well-dressed guests and seemed to be engaged in an enthusiastic conversation. A tall blond man in a dark suit laughed, flashing huge straight white teeth, and flung his arm around Jami.

What the ever-loving fuck?

An angry heat burned in Jax's lungs as he moved toward the fuckwit with his arm around Jami. But before he could take another step, a familiar tattooed hand wrapped around his forearm.

"Give her a minute to work it out, son," Tony rumbled in his ear.

"That douche…he's touching my woman." Jax replied without taking his eyes off of the hand that now stroked Jami's dress where it met her shoulder.

"She's a big girl. And she doesn't strike me as the type to need rescuing."

Jax took a breath, forcing air deep into his lungs and making himself look at the scene unfolding with clear eyes. While Jami's body had stiffened, she kept smiling as she deftly twisted her body out from under Douchebag McGee's arm and looked up to catch his gaze from across the room. In his mind, the lights in the studio dimmed, losing power from the intense crackle of electricity their connection demanded. Hell, people were going to get hurt if sparks started flying.

If he thought Jami had a grin on her beautiful face

before, he'd been wrong. The smile she flashed at him now was the kind a man remembers his whole life as the moment he first saw light. Or the exact second he discovered love. Because that's what Jax felt right then.

It was a punch to the heart. But that's what it was, nevertheless. Love.

Fuck.

She motioned him over to where she stood, but he stayed still for another second, wanting to absorb everything about that moment. Love. In an instant, he saw their future. A real forever, with a wedding and babies and a life. And it suddenly scared the shit out of him.

When her smile faltered and he felt a shove from behind, he realized he must've been staring. All the eyes gazing at him openly pretty much confirmed it.

"Dude, go get your girl," Bowen's low raspy voice chuckled from behind.

✕ ✕ ✕

"So who's the loser rocker guy?" Jami's boss and resident jerk-off, Carl Horndecker, asked. He'd come in late and immediately wrapped his arm around her. As she tried to brush the slime from his touch off her shoulder, she flashed a rigid smile.

"That would be Jackson Paige." Jami pointed around the room. "This fabulous art exhibit is all his work." She couldn't hold in the smug smile that tugged at the corners of her mouth. Not only was Jackson the star of the gallery, but his artwork was truly breathtaking. She kept her eyes locked on his as he rushed across the room with only a hint of the aggressive intensity that had ruled his features seconds before.

"That's Jax Paige?" Carl's jaw dropped, which was a completely new look for the always-on divorce attorney.

"Yeah." She sighed. "That's Jax Paige. Artist, tattoo expert, and rock-and-roll drummer."

"In the flesh, baby," Jackson hissed right before he pulled her forward, his hand spread wide on her neck. Possessively. She could feel her breasts pushing, practically pulsing, against his muscled chest before he angled her head up to look at him. Everyone and everything faded away when he looked down into her eyes and leaned over and brushed her lips with his. "Miss me?"

She inhaled his clean, beachy scent, and her heartbeat doubled, reminding her of one of his frantic drumbeats. "Yeah."

Wow. He had officially reduced her to monosyllabic nonwords. Lovely.

His thumb massaged the back of her neck, causing little spikes of pleasure memory to stab at her core. "Are you going to introduce me to your friends?"

She shook her head, trying to chase away the tunnel vision he seemed to induce every time he touched her with his masterful hands. His artistic hands. His huge, commanding hands. The thought of them on her triggered her Pavlovian response. Instantly, wetness pooled at the V between her legs.

"Well?" He chuckled and thrust his palm toward Carl. "I'm the boyfriend."

Her gaze snapped to Jackson's face and then back to a still-stunned Carl, who at least remembered his manners and shook Jackson's hand. Curiosity coiled in her chest. What was going on with him tonight? The confession. The looks. Calling himself her boyfriend when earlier he'd been surrounded by a swarm of heaving boobs.

"Interesting development." Carl cringed slightly when Jackson let his hand go. "We didn't know Jami had a boyfriend. Did we?"

"Well, I didn't know she had a....what exactly are you, buddy?" Jackson still smiled, but his eyes took on a competitive gleam Jami had never seen.

"Boss, actually. I'm sure since you're her boyfriend she's mentioned me more than once or twice." Carl smirked at Jami, making her stomach roll.

"Sorry…" Jackson shook his head and snaked his arm over her shoulders before tucking his big hand around her rib cage, his fingers splayed across the stiff bodice above her waist. His possessive hold had the unexpected result of making her feel cherished, cared for. Jackson's touch was becoming so familiar that even a light graze was grounding. "We don't do a lot of talking about the office when we're alone. Do we, sunshine?"

His warm chocolate eyes bubbled with mischief, and just a little mirth. She smiled, lost for a second in his gaze, before laughing and turning back to her coworkers.

"Jackson, I'd like you to meet the Horndeckers— Carl, his brother Victor, and their sister Suzanne. They're the partners of the firm I work for."

Jackson politely shook each of their hands.

"It was lovely seeing you here tonight. See you at the office Monday." She turned to lead Jackson back toward his images. She was dying to walk through again and discuss them with him.

"Actually, Jami," Carl said, and she turned back. "I was going to call you and see if you could finish up the Harriman notes tomorrow. I know it's Sunday, but I have an early hearing Tuesday morning." At least he had the decency to look apologetic. And working weekends wasn't all that unusual at the firm.

Jackson gripped her waist harder for a moment, and she chewed her lip. They hadn't discussed plans for Sunday, but she had hoped that since they hadn't been able to see each other since the previous week, they'd be able to spend the day together. Disappointment coursed through her, but she was a professional. She'd been raised to believe the job came first, above all else.

"Yes, of course, Carl," she said with a stiff nod. "Now if you don't mind, we're off to celebrate Jackson's art show. I hope you enjoy his work as much as I do."

As the Horndeckers made their way out of the gallery, Jackson quickly dragged her across the room and into a small alcove. Before she had a chance to say anything about his boyfriend comment or Sunday, Jackson crashed his mouth over hers. Arousal quickly replaced irritation as need pooled in her belly. When his tongue pried her lips open and merged with hers, everything fell away except the feel of him and the touch of his hands over her body. No stress about their past. No worries about their future. Too quickly he pulled his lips away, leaving her fuzzy and needy.

"God, you amaze me, Jackson. Amaze. Me." She began to stroke the scratchy hairs of his beard. "Your work. It's so beautiful and dark and complicated."

"Kind of like my woman," he said as he kissed gently down the soft shell of her ear and neck.

His words filled her with a sense of feminine power

she had only ever felt with him. Ironically, trusting him gave her the strength to let go of her constant and exhausting iron-fisted control and let him take the reins.

But she could get lost in his easygoing chaos and languid heat. She wanted Jackson. She wanted him to desire her. But she didn't want to lose herself to him again. How could she indulge in him and still walk away with some dignity—and more importantly, keep him from melting the ice walls around her heart? If she let her guard down and Jackson wasn't interested in ditching his playboy ways, she couldn't keep going with this thing between them. Even if he did, she still had her parents to deal with. Yes, they were controlling jerks, but they only wanted to prevent her from replaying old behavior. Although the game had definitely changed when her dad had hit her and then gone radio silent all week.

Jackson stopped peppering her with kisses and looked down into her eyes. "Need you to know that you are my girlfriend. Before you say anything, let me say this. I'll be honest, sunshine, I haven't been a saint. But that reputation thing is urban legend. Wipe that look off your face. I'm serious."

She smiled to reassure him that it didn't matter. That she didn't care since this thing between them couldn't go anywhere. "You don't owe me an explanation. We're just…"

"We're just what? Having fun? Fucking? Maybe. Maybe not. All I'm saying is that my reputation is mostly hype. Sure, I screwed around. But I haven't for a long time, and now all I see is you."

Jami snorted. His provocative art was making her feel

vulnerable, emotional…and then his words. He was getting to her.

"Just you," Jackson lowered his voice, running his hands down her back and cupping her bottom.

Jami's eyes watered. She needed to stop thinking, which his hands on her body facilitated quite quickly. Then she needed to let this play out. Have sex, have fun, and move on, just like Ella said. But Jackson was making it difficult to remember that was the goal.

"Not sure what you're talking about," she mumbled.

She gasped as he nipped her neck. "Liar. Mmmm. You smell so good. Like roses. Did you wear that for me?"

"No."

His hand snaked up her back and brushed aside her hair.

"What happens to bad girls who lie, Jami?" He hissed and bit her earlobe, firing bullets of desire straight to her nipples. "Tell me."

She shook her head, but he wrapped his fist around her loose curls and looked down into her face. The overt show of dominance anchored her in the moment to the open gallery past the dimly lit recessed corner, where people continued to admire his art and drink the free wine.

But that wasn't what happened. Panic didn't flood her system, nor did her internal voice shout a warning to run and hide. *Warning, warning, this man is dangerous*.

Nope. Instead she sank into his possession, and her body felt both hyperaware and fully relaxed. Not unlike being slightly tipsy. Not fuzzy, but focused.

"Tell me. Won't ask again." His low growl triggered her nipples to contract so tightly they almost hurt as they rubbed against the leather bodice of her dress.

She took a deep breath, sucking air she desperately needed. "Bad girls get spanked."

"Yes, they do." He chuckled against her neck, sending tremors down to that spot between her legs that he seemed to have a direct connection to. "But it's not really a punishment, is it?"

A flash of memory. Lying across Jackson's lap the first time he'd suggested smacking her ass. Her horror at being so aroused. Her fear he wouldn't stop. Her terror that he would.

She shook her head, a curl pulling loose from his grip, and then looked up directly into his beautiful dark brown eyes. "No, not when you do it."

He threw back his head and groaned. "Holy fuck, woman, what am I going to do with you?"

"Show me your art and then take me home and fuck me?"

"I love it when your proper little mouth goes all street on me."

"Ha! There are more ways for my mouth to go street on you, Jackson." She untangled from his grasp and grabbed his hand. "Let's go check out the rest of your art."

She'd stuff down her worries about his past and her family and her plan to become a partner in a law firm. She'd ignore the warning signs that she was, once again, falling for Jackson Paige.

For now.

Chapter 13

JAMI'S OPINION MATTERED TO JAX, WHICH WAS THE sole reason he let her tug him around the gallery for an in-depth discussion on each piece. He answered every question she asked. Her curiosity about his creative process and her probing questions into his inspirations were thoughtful and sometimes too nosy. But he'd made a decision to quit hiding from her. And if that meant telling her about the loneliness he'd felt lately, then he was going to barf up all the ugly truth. He didn't even need to explain it—she recognized it in his work, calling his pieces "darkly stunning" and "poignantly lonely." He smiled and kissed the light freckles on her nose. The sugary taste and soft texture of her skin under his lips was intoxicating, so sweet to his savory.

His resolution lasted all of an hour before he couldn't keep his hands off her round ass, cupped so lovingly by the leather pleats of her dress, any longer. Frankly, he had mixed feelings about the damn dress. He was a little jealous of it, and yet loved it for making his woman look so amazing.

Regardless, it was time to go. His signal was a sharp nip to her neck before finally dragging her out of the gallery. He only stopped to kiss her desperately against his truck before lifting her in and buckling the passenger seat belt.

He climbed into the driver's seat and slammed the

door, making the window rattle. Maybe he was a bit too eager to get Jami home and into his bed. It had been nearly a week since he'd been inside her, seen her writhing beneath him, making those sexy little sounds he loved, and he vowed to never again let so many days go without her. But Jami didn't know that yet. And he didn't want to scare her away with his newfound light. She still had her demons and, with a little trust, maybe she'd let him be her backup when she chose to face them. He still had a tour—make that two—to manage this year. And the truth that he still hadn't shared. How was he going to explain the check her parents had given him? When she found out, it wouldn't matter that he'd never spent it and that it had been sitting in a savings account for five years.

They'd cross those bridges when they came to them. In the meantime, he'd ignore the acid pooling in his gut.

"I can do that myself, you know."

"What?"

"My seat belt. I have two degrees. I'm pretty sure I can handle my own seat belt, Jackson." She stared at him as the truck roared to life. God, he loved his truck. He'd really love to fuck his girl in this truck. Not now, but sometime. Sometime soon.

He moved the gearshift into drive and glanced at Jami before pulling out of the parking lot and onto the main road. "I'm fully aware of your intelligence level. Sometimes my inner manly man likes to take care of you. Because I want to. And it makes it all the sweeter that a strong woman like you lets me do so."

She mumbled something.

"What was that, sunshine?"

"Your inner alpha, you mean."

He snorted. "You read too many romance novels." He silently thanked the universe that her rigidity did not bleed over into their sexual exploits.

She reached across the seat and ran her fingers from his knee up and around his thigh. "Are you complaining?" He could see her sly smirk in the lights reflecting through the cab.

"Nope."

She unfastened her seat belt. When he started to protest she slid over to the middle of the bench seat and wrapped the lap belt across her waist. Instead of putting her hand back on his thigh, she placed it on the center of his chest and twisted her body toward him. He could feel each fingertip through his shirt, pressing in and setting fire to nerve endings in his body. It was so insane how two people could be at odds most of the time, and yet their bodies could have such a fierce connection, like metal shavings to a magnet.

He stared straight ahead, keeping his eye on the road, but could feel her hot breath against his neck and smell her sweet scent. The semi he'd been sporting most of the night became fully engaged the second her slick little tongue connected with the hoop in his ear. Like a light switch flipped, flooding a dark room with light. Her teeth snagged the metal of his earring and tugged.

Flick, or lick, and then instaboner.

Jax's laugh at his little inside joke caught his throat when she began to nibble his ear while one hand caressed the back of his neck. The hand on his chest slowly snuck down to his abs. Waves of want filled his belly, twisting and tangling, short-circuiting his brain.

Then he pretty much forgot his own name.

"Did I tell you how hot you looked tonight, Mr. Paige?" She pulled his shirt out of his pants and tucked her fingers under the material to stroke the ridges of his abdomen. Her soft ministrations caused his muscles to bunch and jump. "Did I mention how incredibly attracted I am to your body?"

He shook his head. He wasn't feeling so cocky anymore. It wasn't her sizzling touches or words, although those were hotter than hell. Her playfulness felt deeper, heavier than her husky questions. Yes, she was talking about his looks and his body. But he was beginning to see through her, beginning to understand that when she said one thing she often meant another. Jami was so practiced in pushing down her feelings and conforming to her parents' demands that she'd created a means of communication that only a careful listener, someone attuned to her moods and reactions, could decipher and translate.

He listened. He watched. He understood.

What Jax heard was Jami telling him something that had roots. Something deeper than the superficial words she was saying. For one, she was the aggressor, running her hands over his body and her lips up his neck and jaw. Telling him she found him sexy. What she was really saying, without letting herself be too honest, was that she was proud. Proud of his artwork and his gallery showing. She didn't know how to say the words because no one ever said them to her, so she tried to show him with her body.

The thought made his chest tighten and his heart skip a beat. He wanted to be the one to tell her he was proud of her, that she was fucking spectacular and no one could darken the sunshine inside her, even though she tried to tamp it down.

"Jackson?" The vulnerability in her voice was subtle, but he heard it there, hidden underneath the sexual bravado.

He drew her hand from under his shirt and kissed her wrist before laying it across his thigh. He chuckled to diffuse the thick heaviness of the moment. "You better stop fondling me, sweetheart, or we'll never make it back to my house."

Her smile, while soft, seemed tinged with relief. "Well, thank goodness we're almost there."

They sat in silence the next couple of miles. He held her hand on his thigh and stroked his thumb over her open palm until they pulled into the lot behind his building.

It took them approximately five minutes to get from his truck up the stairs and into his apartment. After assuring her several times that Mandi was staying with a friend on campus and would not walk in on them, he finally picked Jami up and tossed her over his shoulder.

She smacked his back and squealed in protest as he laughed and threw her onto his bed. "Roll over." His pulse slowed and became languid as he watched how easily she followed his direction in the bedroom. He popped his phone into the speakers and selected a playlist, while keeping one eye on Jami spread out on his bed, waiting for him to do something.

She squirmed, her gaze soaking up his every move as he undressed. "What's this song?"

"'Powerful.' Major Lazer and Ellie Goulding." He

tossed his shirt on the dresser and kicked off his dress shoes, never taking his eyes off her face. Her lashes fluttered down and she began to move her hips on the bed. It was mesmerizing. Hypnotic. When she let her walls down a little it was confusing how that made *him* feel powerful, full of masculine pride.

"I like it. Very sexy. Not very heavy metal," she teased. Her full pink lips curved up and her eyes opened, pinning him with a gaze he didn't recognize. It wasn't really penetrating, more intensely curious. Maybe he wasn't as great at reading her as he thought.

"Hmmm. I'm a lot more than just that, sunshine." He pulled his socks off and undid his belt and the top button of his pants before kneeling at the side of the bed. Her expression changed to hunger and lust. Good. That was where they met in the middle; in bed, there was order and no secrets for either of them. In bed, his unworthiness vanished, and her inability to share herself evaporated. *Poof.*

"Yes," she sighed. "I'm beginning to see that."

The throb of the low bass pulsed throughout the room. A determined, languorous feeling began to build in his chest. He gathered her hair in one hand, the silky strands sliding through his fingers, and pulled it to the side. The pale luminescence of her flawless skin drew him in, and he had to touch her. So he dragged two fingers along the collar of her dress, reveling in the contrast of her softness against his callused, tattooed hand, until he reached her zipper.

He leaned forward and kissed the base of her neck, inhaling her heady mix of leather, roses, and arousal. As he began to unzip her dress, her sigh turned into a strangled breath that he swore expanded his chest with something heavy and warm, something he didn't recognize, something a little scary.

That thick, syrupy feeling was a sign. A sign he should heed. Because Jax knew he should pull away if he wanted to save himself the pain of the path they were barreling down. This was his point of no return. If he took her dress off and made love to her tonight, there would be no going back.

"Jackson..." Jami implored, startling him back to the moment, where he realized his hand had frozen at the end of the zipper pull. "Are you okay?" she asked, lying belly down on his bed, seductively looking over her shoulder.

The quake in her voice gave him what he needed: the answer to his own question and a clue to her real feelings. She felt vulnerable. His tough-as-nails woman was nervous. Good. Because so was he.

Yep. He was all in.

"Everything's perfect, sweetheart," he whispered, which sounded more like a growl, as he tugged her dress off and stared at her round ass and delicious curves. "Absolutely perfect."

Jackson placed a chaste but somehow lascivious kiss on the back of her neck. "Sunshine." His lips move against her neck, and his words thundered through her body, setting fire to her nerve endings and making her wet. Instead of pulling away and trying to take the situation back in hand, she did what she always did when his mouth was on her.

She caved. She needed. She begged. "Please..."

Gently he rolled her over to her back and kissed her neck before wrapping his hands around her wrists and pulling them above her head. He wrapped her fingers one by one around the wooden slats of his headboard. "Keep your hands there. Don't move them," he said in his bossy sex voice, sending more shivers across her skin. But his eyes, those deep dark beautiful brown eyes, said something completely different. She knew him well enough to recognize how they pleaded forgiveness, how they begged for another chance.

She sighed, letting her eyes drift closed as she sank into the oblivion of feeling his hands and lips all over her body, leaving a trail of fire wherever he touched or kissed. Light splashed across her closed lids as his whispered endearments washed over her. He massaged her shoulders and bit her tender breasts until she cried out, begging him to stop, to not stop.

When she opened her eyes again she was surprised to see him staring at her face, that same look of openness tinged with something like…like fear. He looked almost broken, and a little lost. More like how she'd felt when he left her, and not how he should feel after the cathartic conversation they'd had earlier.

When Jami lifted her hand from his headboard and caressed his cheek, his eyes narrowed. But before he could rebuke her for disobeying, she placed her hand over his lips. He didn't say anything when she cupped his face with both hands. He leaned over her with that same odd expression and let her pull him down to meet her lips with his. Only this time, the kiss was soft, sweet, painfully tender in a way that was more revealing than their passionate ones.

He didn't try to take back control when she pushed on his chest so he'd roll over on his back. He didn't move her body how he wanted it when she swept soft kisses across his face and down his neck. He shivered when she reached his nipples and slowly wrapped her tongue around them, tugging on the sexy barbells piercing them.

It was only when she went to take his swollen cock into her mouth that she heard the crinkle of the condom wrapper and he tugged her with one strong arm up to kiss him again.

"I want you," he whispered against her mouth with such need it made her quiver with desire. He handed her the condom and she pulled it down over him, loving the way he twitched under her fingers, filling her with a sexual power she had only ever felt with Jackson.

He curved his hands down over her back and over her ass, squeezing hard before dipping his fingers into her wet pussy. Jami arched into his hands and rocked her hips into his before he lifted her over his cock and gently pulled her down on him. The sweet, slow ecstasy of his power and control surrounded her, overwhelmed her, and she cried out, surprised by the ferocity of their connection.

The cords in Jackson's neck strained, and his muscles were rigid bands of steel, but he never increased the speed of her descent, nor did he break the intensity of his gaze on her.

"Sunshine," he panted and then rolled her over, with his large body framing hers. "I will never get tired of your body," he growled. "You're so damn sweet and so incredibly beautiful."

His thrusts became less controlled as his angular jaw tightened and beads of sweat formed on his forehead. Jami clamored to meet his every push with her own, their bodies colliding in the rushed, liquid sound of passion. She became lost in his eyes, in his body, a receptacle for all his focus, his desire, anything he wanted to give her.

His cock throbbed inside her, filling her. She froze, keening as she came all around him. Her orgasm was brutal in its suddenness, overwhelming in its complexity. It was like an earthquake centered on her clit, then spread out over her entire body in seismic waves until not one single nerve ending was left unaffected.

He slammed into her again, and an aftershock made her walls quiver and her breath catch. When Jackson came, he shouted her name, pumping his climax into her three more times before he collapsed on her, panting. She could feel his breath on the side of her neck, his pounding heart through her skin, and his sweat-slicked chest on hers.

Yes, she'd given up a little piece of herself to him. For him. She wasn't going to get it back when he left. But it was worth it. So worth it.

✯ ✯ ✯

Jami woke up gradually. Swimming up from the cloud of sleep, she heard Jackson's voice raised in argument through the closed door of his bedroom. *Is he on the phone?* she wondered. Did his sister come home early?

Heavy footfalls tumbled down the hallway, stopped, and started again. When the steps stopped outside his room, Jami's heart began to race as she realized she was still naked. She looked around for some bit of clothing to throw on, but she couldn't see her dress anywhere. Letting him tear it off her had seemed like a good idea at the time. Not so much now. She reached down and tugged the soft flannel comforter up over her body to cover herself from the intruder who seemed determined to burst the little bubble of intimacy they'd created.

Someone jiggled the door handle. Jami pressed her elbows into her sides as her legs begin to shake. Who the hell was fighting with Jackson? Surely his sister couldn't be that angry. The rattling stopped and she heard Jackson say something with a sharp tone before the door swung open.

Jackson stood there in a pair of black boxer briefs with his phone pressed to one ear, twirling a small paintbrush in his hand. His long torso was covered in stunning tattoos layered over sinewy muscle. Jami noted something new added to his body art, a streak of blue paint across his forehead and a red smear on his shoulder.

"No, Dad. I don't give two fucks what you think." His face reddened as he walked into the room. He set down the paintbrush on a book and grabbed a T-shirt, tossing it at Jami. Tugging on the shirt and then her panties, she hopped up and ran to clean up in the bathroom. Through the door she heard muffled snatches of the conversation. Words like "fuck off," "none of your fucking business," and "no thanks, fuckhead," leading Jami to believe he still didn't have the best relationship with his father. Did it have anything to do with the donation from her parents to his father's campaign?

After washing up, she walked into the kitchen and immediately noticed the smell of cinnamon mixed with something more chemical, like paint. Then she saw Jackson's back, which was covered in an ornate Asian dragon, so realistic and rich in colors it seemed to move along with his muscles as he worked on something his body blocked from view. On the counter of the surprisingly spacious kitchen-and-living-room combo sat two ridiculously huge cinnamon rolls dripping with frosting, next to two steaming mugs.

Opting for the hot painter, not the hot coffee, she stepped quietly across the carpet and wrapped her cold arms around his warm body. Jackson cleared his throat and paused briefly, but continued painting even when she laid her cheek against his back. He smelled like paint. And man.

"Why are you always so damn warm?"

He chuckled. "Why are you always so damn cold, woman?"

"Were you talking to your dad, Jackson?" she asked quietly. He didn't respond, but stopped painting and set his brushes down before turning and wrapping her in his arms.

He sighed. "Yeah."

She led him over to the kitchen counter and grabbed the coffee and cinnamon buns before settling into the quaint cottage-style kitchen table. "Thank you for breakfast."

He moved a stack of small canvases to a chair and sat next to her.

"If you don't want to talk about it, we don't have to," she said. Truthfully, she wasn't sure if she could take any more honesty and conversations about parents or the past—or even the present—but he'd been so open with her. He deserved to be heard, even if each little admission took her farther and farther away from the point of no return.

He took a bite of his roll and chewed it thoughtfully. Annoyingly. Fine, if he didn't want to share then he didn't have to, but it was his move. She crossed her arms and looked at Jackson.

"After I left school, both my parents—who could never agree on anything—dogged me relentlessly. I mean, they kept showing up here and the studio. I finally had my dad's attention now that I didn't want it anymore." Jackson made a hollow sound.

"I'm sorry," she said, picking at her roll, suddenly not hungry.

He tipped her chin up with his finger. "Hey, this didn't have anything to do with you."

Heat crept up Jami's neck and cheeks. It *was* all her fault. "Yes, it did. I brought my parents to your front door. And they did what they always do."

"Bullshit. That whole thing was just another excuse, another way to control me, sunshine. What they didn't realize is that it set me free. I didn't have to pretend to be someone I wasn't or play by their rules anymore."

Without warning, tears sprang to her eyes. She'd been prepared to take responsibility for her parents and their actions, but hadn't expected that the very thing that had crushed her battered heart had granted Jackson his freedom from his oppressive family.

"No, baby. You don't get to own that. I meant I was free from my parents' expectations. Not you. I missed you. I hated myself for being such a coward. I keep trying to figure out how not to fuck this up again."

She gasped at the needy look in his eyes. So much want and lust, and maybe something more…something she wasn't ready to put a name to yet, because it was too scary and dangerous.

"Thank you," she said quietly. And because she didn't know what else to say she shoved a chunk of cinnamon heaven into her mouth.

He snorted. "Do you have any idea how beautiful you are?"

"You know flattery doesn't work on me," she lied, melting a little under the fire of his intense gaze. "Can I ask you something completely off topic?" She tried to keep her tone even, pretending she didn't feel the tightening in her chest. She noticed, for the first time, another smear of blue paint on his forehead that she desperately wanted to trace with her finger. But she didn't. Wouldn't.

"Sure," he said with his head cocked slightly and his eyes narrowed in that cute way.

"All those women, the ones at the show and then at the gallery…did you go out with all of them?" Her cheeks burned. She so didn't want to be the jealous type, but her heart hurt thinking about him dating other women while he was seeing her.

He shook his head vigorously and ran his hand up and down her arm and over her hip. "I may have hooked up with a couple of them, but I've only been in one real relationship."

The grip around her lungs constricted. Maybe she didn't want to hear what he had to say. Maybe she didn't need the truth. She swallowed and smiled, but didn't say anything. Instead, she began to list in her head all the contract stipulations she needed to discuss with the band. Push those damn feelings down. Control. Calm. Composed.

"Hey, I know what you're doing." He squeezed her knee, forcing her back into the moment. "You wanted to have this discussion, so we are. You don't get to drift off into Jami Land, where you make all the rules."

"I'm not…"

"You are. Don't bother lying."

"Fine. You've only been in one real relationship. But you have a reputation, you know. I know all about Jax 'Manwhore' Pain."

"Whoa. That's a little extreme. I haven't been a saint, I'll admit it, but I wasn't that bad."

"You just admitted that you screwed some of those women, Jackson. And we have all this messy history…"

When she tried to pull away from him, he held her firm. "Look, what happened with us fucked me up. I really liked you. And then the thing with your parents sort of exploded my world. I was lost for a while. I went a little crazy with partying. I don't know what I was doing. Maybe I was trying to screw you out of my head. It got old fast."

"Until you met the woman special enough to have a relationship with?"

He blinked. Once. Twice. A third time. The look of confusion on his face was comical. "What? No! That was you, Jami. You were the only one."

"Me?" That couldn't be true. The tightness in her chest expanded, lightened.

"Only you. You were the one that got away."

"Well, technically, you're the one that went away, not me."

"Yeah. I know." He took a sip of his coffee and leaned back in his chair. "You know what's strange to me?" She shook her head. "That Mason is your brother and I had no idea."

"Does it freak you out that I'm his little sister?"

"A little. At first, anyway. We talked a little about you when we were on tour."

"About me?" She asked, her voice too high.

He chuckled and kissed her forehead. "Yeah. Only I had no idea it was about you. Life is fucking weird." His deep sigh filled her with joy. And desire.

It was all beginning to feel too real, too complicated, too big for her to handle.

"No more talking," she whispered and pulled him up from the table.

"Oh yeah. Why's that?"

As she ran into his room and jumped on his bed, she said, "Because my mouth is going to be full."

Lucky for her, or maybe for him, he was already half hard when she dragged his boxer briefs down and drew her tongue up his warm, pulsing cock. He stopped talking completely.

She had the perfect plan for killing the two hours before she had to be in the office.

Chapter 14

JamiLynn Dillon was all Jax's, and he couldn't be happier about it. Instead of agonizing over why he cared so much or when he was going to tell her the rest of his story or what he was going to do when he left on tour or even whether or not he deserved her, he chose to move forward. Maybe if they moved fast enough, they'd outrun their past. Since he'd made a split-second decision to trust his gut, he knew everything would work out. He was going to do everything in his power to ensure that it did. He was done fighting his demons. For now, he would help Jami battle hers.

After she'd left for her office that morning, he'd laid in a bed that smelled of her. Flowers and fucking. Did it make him some kind of pussy when he leaned over and put his head on her pillow? How about when he dragged in a long inhalation of the sweet floral scent the pillow still held from her soft body?

When he strolled into her office later that morning, he smiled at the stern look she threw at him. Cute how she couldn't hide her smile when he held up the bag of tacos he'd brought. The smile turned to a wide grin when she discovered they were veggie tacos.

Yeah. He remembered.

"What are you doing here, Jackson? I thought you were painting," she said as he pulled the chair in front of her desk closer.

"Seriously?"

"Yes, seriously."

"I'm bringing you lunch. Duh." He leaned over and kissed her cheek before settling into the chair across from her. "Of course, I'd really like to throw you over your desk and bury my cock in your hot pussy."

Her glossy lips fell open and she stared at him as her face turned an adorable shade of pink. "Um. Okay. Thank you," she said and took a bite of her soft taco. A low moan bubbling from her lips was all it took before he had a semi. She chewed and swallowed her food before flashing him a bold half smile. "You know I'm the only one working today, right?"

Instaboner.

Fuck this, he *was* going to screw her on her desk.

"Put the taco down, sweetheart," he said. She froze midbite, and her eyes widened as he stood and stalked around the desk to where she sat. She didn't budge as he removed the half-eaten taco from her fingers. Didn't say anything as he picked her up and set her on the half of the desk not covered with paper and file folders. She didn't make a sound as he leaned her back and flipped her so her chest pressed against the cool wood surface and her legs dangled over the edge. But she gasped when he smacked her ass, then pushed her flowy flowered skirt up and covered her mound with his hand, squeezing. She did, however, arch into his grasp, making him smile, and that warm, heavy thing expanded in his chest.

She felt hot, scorching his hand through the panties separating her from direct contact with his fingers. God, she was beautiful, with her blond hair fanned out on the desk and her knuckles turning white where she gripped the sides. Beautiful. And all his.

If only she agreed. If only she truly forgave him.

The trust she placed in his hands was awe-inspiring. A gift he had no intention of taking advantage of ever again. He marveled at the honest and natural sensuality that rolled off her. For him.

With her lying across the desk, fully clothed, he was tempted to take her like he'd told her he wanted to. But they'd said too much and not enough, and he wanted to see her bright eyes roll back as she came apart in his arms. Really, he shouldn't even be messing around with her at work. If he weren't such a selfish bastard, he'd wait until she was done and he could take her home.

But he needed her. Needed to feel himself inside her.

"Don't move," he ordered before moving to lock her office door. He might be a perv, but he wasn't a total jerk.

Settling himself behind her again, he pulled on her hips and fell back into her chair. "Sunshine, turn around, I want to see your face."

She stood and her skirt dropped down as she slowly turned, her hair looking a little wild and messy. A sexy smile shaped her mouth. She tugged off her cardigan sweater before she hiked her skirt up around her waist. In under a minute she stood before him in a lacy thong and a colorful striped bra that pushed her full breasts together. A wave of heat rolled from his chest down to his already hard cock pushing uncomfortably against the zipper of his jeans. He unzipped his jeans and then lifted his hips to drag his pants down to his knees. Her eyes followed his movements as he donned a rubber he'd pulled from his pocket.

He curved his finger into the waistband of her panties and pushed between her legs. The glazed look of desire in her eyes filled him with pride as he reached up to pull the cups of her bra down and release her full breasts. She leaned forward and brushed her lips against his. The kiss quickly escalated and her tongue invaded his mouth as she yanked her panties to the side.

Her lips never left his as she crawled up on the chair and wrapped her hands around his neck. He put his hands under her ass, and she threw her legs over the arms of the chair as he slowly lowered her onto his hard dick, savoring the unhurried burn of her velvet embrace. Finally breaking their marathon kiss, she pushed forward against him, her panting breaths bursting against his mouth. His arms quivered and burned, but still he controlled the descent of her body onto his, until finally they were fully joined.

He couldn't move for a second. The feeling—the smell of their sex, her floral scent, the soft, wet feel of her pussy around him—was all suddenly too overwhelming to process.

"Jackson, please," she begged.

He attempted an evil smile. Best to have her think he was completely in control, that not moving was all part of his evil sex genius master plan.

Once he felt like he had it back together, he whispered in her ear, "Fuck me, sunshine."

As if she'd been waiting for the words, she threw her head back and began to move up and down on him, not soft and sweet like the night before, but needy and fast like she couldn't get enough of his cock, of him. He leaned in and bared his teeth to her long, exposed neck, and the bite seemed to ignite her fire even more as he moved his hand and mouth to her dusky pink nipple. First licking and sucking, and then nipping ever so slightly. Her loud moan filled the small office as he gripped her waist and he began to thrust his hips up into her. Hard, harder, his cocked throbbed in her pussy.

She cried out, "Yes, harder, Jackson…oh my God!"

Her bottom lip began to tremble as her climax became inevitable. Her eyes rolled up toward the ceiling, and her whole body shook and then went stiff. He immediately began to feel his balls pull tight and that feeling of electricity surged from his spine to his cock as he shot his seed deep into the condom, into her. One, two, and three thrusts. He wrapped his arms around her and pulled her hard against his body, their greedy breaths filling the room with sound. He kissed her crown, knowing he was too rough and not able to stop himself.

Something about this woman brought out all of these sex-barbarian tendencies. He knew she didn't warrant his roughness, his darker self, and yet it roared to life the second he felt her soft curves under his hands. She deserved so much more, someone so much better than him. Someone who didn't spend months out of the year on the road, someone who could afford the lifestyle she'd grown up with.

He had this feeling of drowning and losing control, like he was falling under her spell. He was terrified he was going to drag both of them down into his darkness before it was over. And yet he couldn't stop.

After they'd unlocked the door and each made trips to the restroom, Jackson settled across from Jami in a stiff chair, another piece of furniture designed to make people uncomfortable. She did her best to smile when he handed her the red-and-white-checkered paper plate from one of the most popular food trucks in the area. She'd mentioned to him just the other night how she wanted to try their tacos.

"So, sunshine, why no decorations? No family pictures. Just your degrees, and those aren't even hung up?"

She nearly snorted. "You know, I really love law," she said sincerely. She had always found a grounding comfort in knowing what the rules were for any given situation. "I even enjoyed corporate and patent law in the beginning. I loved working with the law counsel after my internship with GEM. Loved the challenge of helping community members start businesses or figure out leases and contracts."

"So what happened? You don't seem to *love* it anymore."

Jami shrugged her shoulders. "I guess focusing on strategic alliances and partnership dissolutions is starting to chip away at my love of law. One little chunk at a time." He nodded, of course. Jackson always seemed to have some weird insight into her head.

Initially, she'd been so thrilled to have landed a position on her own, without the long-armed of influence of her father. That excitement had quickly dissolved into boredom as she realized she was no more valued as an attorney than the receptionist. Now, she dreaded coming to the office and only found true solace in her work at Quirk.

"Besides, the partners are siblings. I have almost no chance of moving up beyond my current position," she said, surprised she'd finally admitted it out loud. While she was a firm attorney, they had yet to trust her with anything challenging or more complicated than straight-up legal assistant work. Every week it got worse. But instead of confronting the issue and asking them point-blank what her role in the firm was, she hadn't. Maybe she didn't really want to hear their answer. Maybe she was afraid she might have to make a change, move on. Maybe she was terrified of rocking the boat and disappointing her parents. Again. Because despite everything, a small part of her still hoped they would someday look at her with pride.

"Why not do something else?"

"Like what? I never thought I'd be anything other than a lawyer. Like my dad." She suddenly felt a little lost and a little alone, even with Jackson sitting across from her asking deep questions and reading her damn mind.

"Where is your boss, cupcake?" Jackson smirked and stretched his long denim-clad legs up on her desk.

"Not sure. Not here."

"You sure he's not here? Because you did just let me fuck you in your office. Wouldn't want him to walk in and get a show."

"Let you? Pretty sure I helped in the actual humping, Jackson."

He quirked a brow…another of his annoyingly sexy and clever habits. "Is that a little humor there, counselor? And, yes, I'll concur. You did have an awful lot to do with laying yourself on your desk like a tasty afternoon treat."

As if on cue, her stomach growled and she laughed, but Jackson jumped up, grabbing the forgotten bag of tacos. "Shit. Sorry. I got carried away the second I saw your cleavage, and the next minute I had to have you bouncing on my cock."

His crass words should have her bristling and reminding him to mind his manners, but Jami was beginning to know this man. Or this version of the man she had thought she knew five years ago. What was he doing to her? What were *they* doing? This was supposed to be fun and games. They were supposed to let their attraction run its course so they could move on and go back to their lives.

That was what she wanted, right? Her life back?

"Hey, what just happened?" he asked, concern etching lines around his dark eyes, making him even handsomer, if that was even possible. He reached across the desk and brushed his callused fingers along her cheek and tapped the end of her nose. "It's just lunch, okay? Just sharing a meal with my girlfriend."

Jami's heart squeezed in her chest. His girlfriend.

Just sharing a meal with my girlfriend.

That's all it was. But it wasn't, was it? That entailed a commitment…a commitment between two very messed-up people with a screwed-up history together. A boyfriend was someone you leaned on and asked for help.

But Jami didn't ask for help. Not from anyone. She didn't like owing anyone. Is that what was happening here?

"Eat, sunshine. Don't think," Jackson said quietly. "Then you can get back to work."

She nodded. "Of course." She bit into the now cold half-eaten taco, letting the flavor invade her mouth. "Oh my God, this is so freaking good."

He reached over and wiped juice from her chin, then demolished his own burrito before leaning back in his chair and patting his belly. "Pretty fucking great, if I do say so myself." He looked down and tapped his foot nervously before glancing back at her. "Uh, so, I wanted to continue our conver—"

"Well, well, well. I certainly hope you're not billing our client for time you're sitting around socializing, Jami." Carl's voice rang off the walls, making her jump and drop the rest of her taco into her lap.

Great.

Jami brushed the mess into a napkin and looked up at the last person she wanted to see at that moment. "Carl. I didn't expect to see you here on a weekend."

"I thought I'd pop in and see how you were coming along on the Harriman case. I'd like to get the list of assets to opposing counsel by the middle of next week."

If she were a second-year student intern that might be difficult, but she'd been practicing law for a couple of years now, and he still treated her like an admin. What did she have to do to get a little respect around here? Blow someone? Geez.

"Of course, Carl. I emailed it to you about an hour ago. I was going over the Harriman partnership agreement and trying to figure out why the client is insisting on ten years of tax returns. If he's sincere about the partnership, shouldn't five be—"

"That's not really our concern," Carl interrupted, his tone placating, like a parent speaking to a child. She didn't miss his annoyed look as he waved his hand dismissively. "We don't determine the client's motivations or feelings regarding their legal needs. Our job is making sure their demands and needs are met."

Okaaaay. Basically he was telling her not to care about the client and bill, bill, bill.

Again, why was she doing this?

"Of course. I thought…"

"Don't. Think, I mean. Your job is to do what we ask of you." His smile was forced and didn't meet his eyes as he turned to Jackson. "Nice to see you again, Mr. Paige. Your art showing was quite a success. My sister bought at least three of your pieces. Apparently she's your biggest fan."

"Cool," Jackson said, without breaking eye contact with Jami. Standing, he stretched his long, hard body, turned to her boss and smiled that smile…the one that made grown men and law partners willing to walk on water for him. "It was great to see you again, Carl. Gonna say good-bye to my girl. Then she's all yours. Well, not quite," he said and waited for the other man to move from the room, mumbling that he'd be back in to check her work later.

Moving around her desk like a panther, all lean long muscles and focused concentration, Jax leaned over her and pressed his lips to her cheek, sending silken tendrils of warmth down her spine. He smelled of sex and paint and the ocean. "I'll see you later, sweetheart? I have practice, then we're all going out to plan the bachelor and bachelorette parties."

"That's right. Kevan texted me." She nodded, until she remembered she had plans that night. "Oh, sorry, I can't go. I'm watching Ella's twins tonight."

"What time are you done? Come by later." He rubbed his short scruff against her neck, the tendrils sharp against her sensitive skin, making her feel needy for his touch. "It's your brother's last stand."

"I won't be done until late. And I have to work tomorrow."

"It's Mason's wedding, Jami."

"Fine. I'll text you when I'm done."

"Perfect," he said in a low voice, making her insides go liquid. What was happening to her? She was already getting in too deep with this man.

"Perfect," she said despite the dark shadows lurking in the back of her head telling her to jump ship before it was too late and all her plans went to hell.

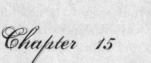

Chapter 15

"WE KICKED ASS TONIGHT, BRO." CONNER SMIRKED AS he tapped the edge of his glass to Jax's bottle.

"Fucking A, we did."

Seemed like the more they played together the better they got. For some, that seemed to be a given, but it hadn't always been the case with Manix Curse. They'd started playing together as their version of a pissing contest. Who could nail this Megadeth lick or that Volbeat blast beat on the first shot? Until recently, Bowen had always beat them, hands down and tied behind his back. He had a musician's ear and could reproduce any melody, any riff, after hearing it only once. But Bowen had drifted in and out, and Mandi had eagerly replaced him, jumping in and filling his shoes seamlessly.

Her age and gender had never worked against them onstage; rather, they were part of her appeal. She looked sweet and colorful and young, and then she started playing her guitar. It gave him chills every time she got into that zone. He was proud, yeah. But more than that. He was awed by her skill. Her ferocity.

Maybe he should tell her more often. Jax glanced over at her leaning against the bar, talking to some guy she'd recognized from school. The dude obviously dug his little sister, but she seemed completely oblivious. More interested in ending the conversation and getting back to her band.

His phone buzzed in his hand and he flipped it over.

Too late? Little tired, but I could come say hi.

Just getting started. Crystal Rose Grill on
Burnside. Text me when you're here. I'll meet
you in front.

Conner got up, presumably on the prowl for chicks or
beer, and Mandi slid into the booth next to Mason. "You
were pretty awesome tonight, you know," Jax said.

Her cheeks pinkened, and she smiled wide. "Thanks.
Your mojo seems to have returned. Have anything to do
with a certain anal-retentive blond legal eagle?"

"Nah." He shook his head. "Okay, maybe. I don't
know what it is about her, but she's always had this
anchoring effect on me. Or some shit."

"Whoa. I don't think I've ever heard you talk like that
about some chick before."

Nope. Never. "She's not some chick."

"No. I guess not. She's kinda the one that got away."

"Yeah. Well, that was all on me." He suddenly felt a
surge of shame for how he'd left Jami years before. He
didn't really think of himself as a dick, but he had been
one when he'd bailed on her. He'd convinced himself
Jami hadn't really understood him and her parents were
exactly the kind of family he despised. Controlling.
Robotic. Superficial.

Just like his dad and his do-over families.

But that wasn't Jami's fault. And they were working
through that shit. It was out there between the two of
them, and it was getting better.

Mandi reached across Mason and patted Jax's hand. "I know you stayed for me, Jax. If I hadn't needed you so much, you would have gone back to school. Back to her."

Immediately, he jumped to deny it, but her pursed lips and I-dare-you-to-tell-me-I'm-wrong look stopped him. Made him reconsider. "Maybe, sis. Maybe not. I don't think I was really ready for her. For what was happening. I was still so angry about everything."

Mandi shrugged and sipped her beer before turning back to the planning of what was turning out to be one party for the bride and groom instead of two.

He kept his eye on the door for what seemed like hours. The planning continued with the occasional tease thrown his way, until Jami finally walked in and slipped into the booth next to him. She looked beautiful, and the bruise from her father's slap was almost gone, but she had dark circles under her eyes he hadn't noticed earlier. Was she working too much? Did he keep her up too late? Was it the side stuff the band had her working on? He made a note to remember to talk with her about that when they were alone.

As casually as possible, he threw his arm over the back of the booth and ran his thumb and forefinger through her silky hair. She seemed happy to chat with Marco, Kevan, and Bowen with her hand on his thigh and his arm around her, while Mandi, Mason, Conner, and Nathan argued about something on the other side of him. Funny how Jami could be all business, all about manners and rules, but deep down she was a funny, vivacious woman. Now, instead of keeping that part of herself hidden, she seemed to be blossoming back into herself.

Fucking cool. He laughed at some stupid joke Conner told them as he scanned the room for their waitress. He could really use another beer.

A familiar couple stood at the entrance of the bar, looking as out of place as a couple of goats in church. Bile boiled in his gut and adrenaline flooded his system, making his skin itch with the need to confront, agitate, fight.

Jami's parents. What the hell were they doing there? They'd pretty much made it clear they'd washed their hands of Mason's wedding. At least, that's what they'd told Mason when he called to yell at them about their treatment of Jami.

Jax elbowed Mason and jutted his chin toward the door.

"Why the hell are they here?" Mason snapped.

"Dunno." Jax was already pushing up and out of the booth. "I got this."

A hand wrapped around his arm. "Jackson, please don't. Let's see what they want, okay?" The wide-eyed panic in Jami's eyes made him check himself. The last thing she needed was a damn bar fight between her boyfriend and her parents. That would send her skittering off for good.

He patted her hand. "No worries, sweetheart. Just going to find out what they want. You with me, dude?"

Mason was already walking toward his parents. "Yep."

Mr. Dillon flashed his corporate smile when his eyes connected with his son, and then quickly changed when Mason stood with a scowl before his parents.

"What are you doing here?" Mason asked, his voice deep and tight.

"There's no need to be hostile, son. We're here to

talk about the wedding, since you mentioned your little planning meeting at your party."

"No need to be hostile? You left a hand-sized purple bruise on your daughter's face. That's a fucking problem in my book."

Without looking at him, Jami's dad pulled his wife to his side. Like she needed to be afraid of *them,* as opposed to the asshole who had assaulted her daughter. "We want to be involved in the wedding. It's not every day our oldest child gets married."

Mason laughed. Not an ironic chuckle, but a real belly laugh. "Not gonna happen, but thanks. You've made it clear how you feel about Kevan and our wedding. You hit Jami. We're done. You don't have any place in our lives. Got it?"

Robert Dillon took a step toward his son and bent in close. "Obviously, we need to spend more time together as a family. This situation is spiraling, and your sister is out of control again." His eyes darted to Jax before he started to say something else. But Jax had had about enough of this bullshit. Jami's parents didn't give a shit about the wedding or even their daughter. They were there strictly for damage control—whether to control the spin on their son's nuptials or to get Jami back under their thumb.

He stepped from behind Mason and reached forward, grabbing the lapels of the older man's suit jacket. "You fucking attacked her in her own home. You've sabotaged Mason and Kevan every chance you've had. He said you're done. I say you're done. Now get the fuck out of here."

"You have no say in what we do. You're nothing.

Just another fool we bought off once. You're trash."
Mason's father sneered, his voice low, and pushed him
back. Jax stumbled, but kept his balance long enough to
land a punch on the other man's chin.

That's when all hell broke loose, of course.

Jax crashed to the floor with a thud. Jami's father
leaned over and pointed in his face. "Stay away from
my daughter or I'll send you to jail for assault. Got
it, loser?"

Mason started yelling. "Get the fuck out of here."

Jax looked up to see Mason push his father toward
the door. "Mom, I'm sorry, but I don't want to see either
of you before my wedding. You're not invited. I don't
want you to be a part of our new lives."

Other than a slight nod, his mom never even flinched.
She'd stood there almost politely during the entire
exchange. Maybe a flicker of sadness or something
behind those pretty unreadable eyes, but nothing else.
It was like she was dead inside. Jesus, no wonder poor
Jami was so fucked up with her emotions. Look at her
goddamn role models—it was a wonder she wasn't
totally crippled by her feelings.

Jax watched as the bar door swung closed behind the
Dillons. Mason turned and offered his hand, tugging Jax
off the dirty bar floor. Not like he hadn't been in that
same spot many times before. "Sorry you got mixed up
in our family drama, buddy. Didn't realize you knew
my parents. What the hell was my dad talking about?"

"He wasn't just my tutor." They both whipped around
at Jami's monotone. "We were dating. They chased him
down. Told him I was too good for him. That I had a
boyfriend. So he left. Left me. Left school."

Her tone was cold, and it sent chills down Jax's neck. It reminded him of the blank look on her mother's face. Shit.

Mason stared at Jax, his brows high. "For fuck's sake. She's kidding, right?"

Jax shook his head. No reason to deny it or hide anymore. He took a step toward Jami, but she held up her trembling hand as Kevan and Mandi walked up behind her. She looked so small, so young.

"I can't do this, Jackson. I don't belong here. And you heard what my dad said." Her voice cracked on the last two words.

Fine, he'd give her some space to process everything, but he wasn't afraid of her father. Fuck, he had a whole bar full of witnesses to prove he hadn't made the first move. Jami's dad had clearly shoved him to the ground. Besides, her parents were done calling the shots.

She tucked her purse under her arm. "I need to go."

"No," he said. She couldn't drive all jacked up like she was. Even though she stood there with that calm demeanor, he knew better. Inside she was a jittery mess.

"No?"

"No."

"Fuck you, Jackson Paige," Jami nearly spat. The venom in her voice was a slap to his face. "Fuck you and fuck your violence. You don't get to tell me what to do any more than they do."

Her words were sharp little stabs to his heart, each one pushing in deeper than the next. But the pain didn't overshadow the very glaring fact that Jami had finally let her walls come crashing down. All it had taken was him popping her dad in the chin. His girl was pissed, no longer holding her shit together, letting it ooze out all over the place. Poor Jami was finally cracking wide open. It was beautiful. Because if she let it all out, they could finally move on. She could heal and stop being afraid, stop pushing down her fear and all the rest of her feelings.

Either that or she'd be good with him gone forever. But he couldn't believe that. Couldn't let them fall apart again. Never again.

"Hey, I'll take you home, okay?" Kevan grabbed Jami's hand, and for some reason an ugly stab of jealousy stuck him in the gut. Someday, would he be the first one she always chose to comfort her? Or would he be the one she needed protection from?

Kevan kissed her fiancé on the cheek and patted Jax's arm. As she walked out hand in hand with his girl, he realized something. Something really fucking important.

Jami *did* belong here. With them. They could be her family.

Because she was already his.

✯ ✯ ✯

Jami sat staring at the wall, petting Aubrey's soft fur. His loud purring rumbled through her lap, making her smile. She covered her mouth. Why on earth would she smile right now? Of all the things she should be doing, smiling wasn't one of them.

Jackson had punched her father. Right in the face. Of course, her dad had started it by shoving him and trying to throw him to the ground. Then he threatened him. Again. A needle of despair pierced her lungs, taking her smile and her breath.

God, why couldn't they just let her be who she was? Why was everything so hard?

She leaned over and took a sip of tea, burning her tongue and the roof of her mouth.

"See, Aubrey, I deserve that. This whole mess with my parents and Jackson is my fault."

Aubrey didn't respond, but kept purring.

Her phone chimed again. Surely another text from her brother or Kevan. Kevan had made her tea, gotten her settled in her pajamas, and then left after kissing her on the forehead and hugging her tight.

Yeah. The jury was in on that woman. Who the hell wouldn't love her? Jesus, she was a mother-freaking ray of sunshine. Thank God Mason had found her and realized how awesome she was.

Her phone chimed again with an incoming text. And again.

She glanced at it.

Jackson.

Picking up the phone, she swiped her finger across the screen.

> I understand if you don't want to talk, but pls
> text me. Are you okay?

She took a deep, long breath, trying to unravel all the different emotions rolling through her head. Guilt… always guilt. Sadness. Fear. And oddly, hope.

Quickly she tapped out her response.

> *I'm fine. Please don't worry.*

Can I call you?

No. We can talk tomorrow. I'm fine.

Call me if you need me and I'll be right there.

I will.

Good. I don't want to scare you or anything.
I'm not a creeper, I swear, but I'm sitting on
your deck.

What?

In case you need me.

You're crazy.

About you.

"You can come in, creeper," she said as she swung
the door open. The sweet, eager face on the tall tattooed
man sitting on her step almost made her laugh. But
laughter would be too much. Too much to process. Too
much effort.

"Are you sure?" He grinned that sexy-as-hell lopsided smile, and she knew right then that she would
forgive him. Yes, the darkness she saw in him—the
ability to throw a punch at her father, for Pete's sake—
scared her. She had spent the last several years learning
to separate herself from Dallas and their violent past.

But she wasn't ready to move on from Jackson. Not again. Not yet.

Who knew? Maybe not ever. She pushed that ridiculous annoying gnat of a thought away. When his hip brushed her belly, she leaned into his body before pulling back. She shut the door and pressed herself against it. What would happen next? Yes, she would forgive him, but would she be able to trust him again? And then it hit her.

She already did trust Jackson. Trusted him with her body wholeheartedly, and was beginning to trust him with her feelings, maybe even her heart a little. Well, she had until he'd hauled off and slugged her dad.

Jackson was all fierce fire and hotness, but that was in bed. She knew he would never hurt her because in his mind, he had been defending her. Years ago, and even now, he'd had plenty of opportunities to lose his temper, push their sex games too far.

He stood by her couch, wearing fitted jeans that hung perfectly off his slim runner's hips and a faded black Red Fang hoodie. Today he wore motorcycle boots instead of his usual Vans or running shoes. His hair was longer on top and starting to grow out on the sides. It was messy, like he'd been weaving nervous fingers through it. And it was sexy as hell. *He* was sexy as hell.

More than anything she wanted to wrap her arms and legs around him, and wipe the sadness from his eyes. But something held her back. It wasn't her past any longer she was so afraid of. Now it was more the future. Or the present.

"I'm sorry," he whispered as she brushed past him and walked into her kitchen.

"Do you want some tea or something to drink?"

He shook his head and tipped his chin toward the couch. "Can we talk?"

She nodded and filled a glass with water, setting it down on the coffee table and motioning for him to sit. Sinking into the opposite corner, she pulled her legs under her body and turned toward him.

"I'm sorry."

"Yes. You said that. But somehow I'm not sure you mean it."

"I do."

She shook her head. "Nope."

"Come on, Jami. I am sorry."

"For what?"

"For punching your father."

She shook her head. "Nope. Don't think so."

"I am."

"Nope."

"Jami! Stop saying that. I said I was sorry. And I am. What else can I do?"

"You can be honest with yourself and with me about what you're really sorry about."

Jackson's face colored slightly, and his eyes darkened. "Fine," he said with an exaggerated sigh. "I wasn't going to hit your dad. I had planned on asking him to leave…if that's what you and Mason wanted. But when he shoved me, I reacted. In my head I kept seeing the bruise on your face. And he fucking pissed me off. God, he's such a dick…I *am* sorry. I'm sorry I upset you."

"I know. I realized that after I left. I didn't know how to process it all. I mean, I was still trying to deal with him hitting me." She closed her eyes, suddenly overwhelmed with confusion. She still felt the phantom throb on her cheek from her father's hand. And she still felt the throb in her heart from watching Jackson defend her. But then she saw his eyes again just before he threw his fist into her father's face. Neck and cheeks red, mouth drawn and eyes narrowed with calculating aggression and anger.

Not impulsive, out-of-control rage, but planned. He'd done it on purpose.

"What? I can tell by the look on your face you just figured something out."

Geez Louise. It's like she couldn't keep anything from the man. "You knew you were going to punch him, didn't you?"

He smiled morosely and nodded. "Yeah."

"Why?"

He looked up and their eyes connected. "Wanted him to pay for your pain. Wanted him to feel the hurt and humiliation you felt. Wanted him to know someone had your back. Can you understand that…even a little?"

Jami scooted closer to him and pulled his hand into her lap. "I get it, Jackson. I do. But the violence is what I have a problem with. I hate it. Just as much as I hate the screwed-up relationship I have with my parents. Do you understand that?"

He nodded and smiled. "I do, sweetheart. And that's what I'm really sorry about."

"But you couldn't help it."

"But I couldn't help it."

"He recognized you. Remembered you from before," she said. Her father had even seemed a little more than unhinged that she was there specifically with Jackson.

He paused, almost like he felt the need to answer carefully. "Yes."

"He said they'd paid you off. I assume he meant the money he gave your dad's campaign. In Robert Dillon's little black book, that meant he owns both you and your father."

Jackson leaned over and brushed his thumb across her cheek in that sweet, sexy way he had. "No one owns me, sunshine. Although you might be getting awfully close."

She smiled. Still tired, still confused, and still sad about finally having to come to terms with her parents' hypocrisy and the ridiculous standard they held her to. But she wasn't alone for once. She had Jackson there by her side, holding her hand and kissing her tears away.

"Are you interested in making it up to me?"

He waggled his eyebrows and flashed her a stunning grin. "Hell yeah."

She laughed. "Not like that. Come to the center with me. Help me at Quirk. Maybe you'll understand how I feel about fighting. You can see what real violence does to families. And more importantly, how we help them move on from it."

She knew he'd seen plenty of violence in his life and had a pretty clear picture of what abuse and suffering looked like. But at that moment, she wanted him to understand the underlying fear she felt when fists flew. The sudden pain in his eyes made her chest ache. He pulled her hand into his and then her body into his lap.

"Name the time and place, and I'll be there."

Jami held his face in her hands, trying to convey the gentleness that he always rained down on her—sweet, reverent. When she leaned forward like she was going to kiss him, he closed his eyes. Instead she pressed her forehead to his, and he opened his eyes in surprise.

"Can you make it Wednesday morning around seven? We can meet at my house and go from there."

He nodded. "Or we can spend the night before together."

Instead of eliminating obstacles between them, she needed to start setting boundaries. This sweet, charming, sexy, protective, complex man was burrowing back under her skin. Who was she kidding? He was already living there and making dinner.

But tonight wasn't the time to make her big stand of independence. The night had been fraught with far too much emotion. She hated all those damn feelings. Her parents. Jax's anger. The apology.

Too much to process right now.

"We'll see about the sleepover. I have to look at my work schedule."

"More excuses, sunshine," he whispered and cupped her cheek, stroking her jaw with his thumb. Her nipples drew up into tight buds, and arousal flooded her limbs. Her body was heavy with an emotional hangover, and still his gentle caress brought her to attention.

He pulled her to him, and she pressed her head tighter to his chest, the beat of his heart loud in her ear, merging with hers and settling into a singular rhythm.

"And, Jackson?"

"Mmmm-hmm." His deep voice thrummed through her body, straight to her dumb vagina.

"Promise me, no more punching people in my honor."

He shifted his legs and cracked his neck. Obviously he didn't want to make that promise—it was his nature to protect. He wanted to always have her back and take out anyone who made her feel threatened or less than. He'd said it more than once.

"Jackson, promise."

"I won't let anyone hurt you again, sunshine," he said sullenly.

"Promise. Me."

Instead of answering, he swallowed the words like a bitter pill and nodded. Then he wrapped his arms around her tighter.

Chapter 16

WELL, THAT'S NOTHING TO LOOK AT, JAX THOUGHT, AS they pulled into the parking lot of a nondescript building in an old, abandoned strip mall and drove around to a hidden lot in the back filled with cars.

The long structure was separated by what looked like four stores—four very sad, neglected stores—a facade of chipped paint and a matching droopy awning decorated each section of faded gray-blue, brick red, lemon yellow aged to dirty ocher, and a surprisingly bright green. All the windows were either covered with plywood or darkened from the inside, and "NO TRESPASSING" signs were posted every few feet across the entire structure. When Jami punched in the code to the door nearest the end of the building and the heavy steel door swung open, he realized the condition of the shops was a carefully constructed ruse to hide the chaos and life teeming inside.

Beyond the glassed-in front desk of the lobby, Jax could see women and children milling about in different stages of everyday life. Everywhere he looked, someone was finishing dressing for school, running out the back door, or running in.

Jami grabbed his hand and tugged him into the lobby and in front of the receptionist desk.

"Hey, Gabby." She smiled at a familiar petite redhead through the glass as she threw the window open. "You remember Jackson, right? I'm going to show him around. Jackson, you met Gabby. She's also a volunteer here."

"Nice to see you again. Are you a lawyer, too?" he asked, thinking she looked more like a gamer than an attorney.

"No. I'm a certified geek." She smiled shyly, grasped his hand, and dropped it quickly. "Software developer."

"Cool. Nice to see you again." He smiled and took the nametag she'd filled out for him.

"You too." She turned to Jami. "Ella's in her office. She mentioned you might be bringing someone by. Oh, and she has a surprise."

After they signed the log and Gabby took a photocopy of Jax's license, she buzzed them through the door. "You probably figured out the building is low-key on purpose," Jami said as she led him into the main area of the building. "The lobby is another layer of security. A lot of these women are leaving bad relationships or are by themselves, having either disconnected from or been abandoned by any family. But some of them are coming from really bad situations. Dangerous homes, controlling husbands, gangs, the streets."

Jax felt a surge of pride for the courageous woman by his side, which was immediately followed by a cold shot of fear. Was she at risk working at the center? Her small hand wrapped around his arm, squeezing his bicep. He could feel the heat from her fingers through his flannel shirt, and it instantly centered him.

"It's perfectly safe. Did you notice the office next door to the entrance…the one with the big window?"

He shook his head. "I noticed the window, not the office."

"We have an armed guard there twenty-four seven. Staff and client safety is a priority. It's funded by a special grant." She removed her hand from his arm and knocked on a closed office door. A muffled voice shouted, "Come in."

"Hey, Ella. Remember Jackson?" Ella jumped up from her desk and shook his hand. She was tall. Really tall for a woman. He hadn't noticed that before.

"Jax Pain. Nice to officially meet you," Ella said with a dark twinkle in her green eyes and a mischievous lilt to her dark red lips.

"Instead of what?"

"Instead of you dragging Jami off after your show for whatever debauchery you had in store for her. Or the other night when you picked her up for her date." She glanced at Jami. "Oh, Miss Bossy Boots, is that an actual blush on your cheeks? I think I like it."

Jami's laugh was like a gentle caress to his groin. Man, he was gone if a chick's giggle was enough to get him hard.

"Don't pay attention to her. She's a ridiculous hopeless romantic," Jami said.

"Oh, pshaw, I'm as jaded and cynical as they come."

Jami tugged on his sleeve and pulled him toward the door. "Keep telling yourself that, Ella Bella. Gabby said you had a surprise."

Her friend's smile beamed wide. "Yep. We received an anonymous donation of $15,000 earlier this week."

"What?" Jami squealed. Her joy filled the room. "That will cover the food budget gap from losing the Cortello Foundation grant and pay for furnishing the three new family suites."

"Exactly. Anyhow, you kids run off and have fun," Ella teased.

"Right, boss, we're off to *play*."

Ella's response was muffled by the door Jami kicked shut behind her.

Over the next few hours, Jami took Jax from room to room and person to person. He helped make lunch for the center's fifty-plus residents and a hundred other guests. The center provided transitional housing to over a dozen at-risk women, most with children and some pregnant, and functioned as a community center for up to one hundred women plus their children every day. Jax was surprised to learn that such an extensive operation depended on only five full-time employees and a legion of rotating volunteers. All client families were eligible for counseling, medical help, transportation, relocation support, clothing and basic household goods, as well as help with recovery and study groups, vocational and life skills training, and recreational classes.

From the front of the building, a person could never guess the sheer extent of the operation behind those faded multicolored storefronts. No one would suspect the number of lives being saved and transformed beyond. And that was the point. They were hidden in plain sight from exes or anyone who might want to find them when they didn't want to be found.

"You've been so quiet the last half hour. Do you want to take a break?" Jami asked as he finished the remaining sandwiches for the next day's school lunches. She tucked the last two into plastic bags and folded the tops down before placing them in a cardboard box on the counter.

Was he tired? No, he was overwhelmed with emotions, but he was definitely not tired. He shook his head and pulled the disposable food prep gloves off his hands as she did the same, tossing them in the trash. Voices both young and old filled the room, combined with announcements over the PA system and ringing phones, and he was only vaguely aware of it all as he locked onto Jami. He leaned his hip against the stainless prep table and took in—really took in—the woman fussing with the paper bag lunches. She was beautiful, and her prim, preppy style only accentuated it instead of hiding it. He'd always known that. Always loved the way she tried to hide that luscious body under boxy suits and boring cardigans. Loved how she tried to tame her blond, silky curls by forcing them into a tight ponytail or twist. Loved how she could never be bothered to enhance her own innate beauty with more than a swipe of mascara to lighten her pale lashes and some pink gloss over her full mouth.

All those things were givens—details he'd never forgotten from their time together years ago. But now he saw past her beauty. Beneath all those layers she wore like fucking armor was something unique, something so stunning it almost hurt his eyes to look at it. It was like sunlight.

What did that mean?

It meant he was in love with JamiLynn Dillon, but more importantly, he always had been.

✷ ✷ ✷

Jami looked up to see Jackson staring at her, his eyebrows scrunched together and his mouth pinched. "What?"

He blinked twice and his gaze connected with hers. "You."

"Me?" What the heck was wrong with him? "Do you need to sit down? Do you feel okay?" She moved closer and slid her fingertips along his wrist, making electricity dance up her arms and down her spine.

He looked down at her fingers and grabbed her hand in his palm, turning it over. Keeping his eyes on her, he brought her hand to his lips and kissed the fluttering pulse, sending points of desire straight to the V between her legs. "You're fucking." Kiss. "Amazing." Kiss. "And beautiful." Kiss. "And every day you show me something new, about yourself, about the world." Kiss.

Then he tugged her into his arms, and if she hadn't been breathless she'd have thought of some clever response, something sexy and cute to say to all his heat. But she couldn't. As usual, his Jaxness overpowered her normally rational thought. And his scent—now slightly tinged with peanut butter and jelly—filled her nose. Her circuits overloaded. All she could see, hear, or smell was Jackson. All Jackson. How had she ever lived without him? And how could she go back to before? Before Jackson.

"Hey, Jami, do you have the last box of lunches for the kids?" Calvin, a teenage volunteer who had once lived at the shelter, popped his head into the kitchen prep area. Instead of jumping from Jackson's arms, she smiled apologetically and slowly pulled from his embrace. "Yes, we have them here."

The young man smiled and ducked his head, looking at his feet. "Uh, so, uh." He glanced at Jackson and then flicked his gaze to Jami.

"Was there something else you needed?" Jami asked, grabbing the final box off the counter.

The boy shook his head and stepped forward to alleviate her burden, but Jackson intercepted him. "Hey, cool shirt, used to love Black Dahlia Murder. I'm Jax, by the way."

Jami was shocked when the normally stoic teen blushed and grasped Jackson's hand firmly. "Yeah. They used to be my favorite band. I'm Calvin."

"A bit dark for me, but Trevor's a pretty cool guy. Who's your favorite band now?"

Calvin's grin lit his face. His words were nearly inaudible. "Manix Curse."

If Calvin's smile had been big, Jackson's was gigantic—a big, goofy, I'm-a-rock-star grin. "No kidding? Well, I happen to be in Manix, dude."

"I know. I saw you guys play last summer at the Monster Royale festival and I basically lost my shit." The kid looked down at his feet before glancing at her. "Sorry, Ms. Dillon. They are pretty awesome."

She smiled and nodded. "Yes. They are."

Jami set the box of bagged lunches on the table before stepping back and watching her ultra-sexy rocker-slash-tattoo-artist-slash-painter boyfriend—if that what was what he was—hold the longest conversation she'd ever seen Calvin have in the over three years that she'd known him.

"Well, thanks," Jackson said. "Do you play any instruments?"

"Nah. We can't really afford a drum set or guitar, and the lessons are pretty pricey around here."

Jackson's head swung to Jami. "Why don't you offer music lessons here?"

She shrugged. "Outside of some key staff members,

almost all the services are offered by volunteers. We try to keep all real resources available for emergency and rescue situations." Sadly, they had too few of those reserves and needed to use them way too often.

"You mean if you had volunteers for things like music—"

"Or art, or math and English tutoring, or culinary skills, or whatever."

"—that you would offer those things?"

She nodded slowly. Was he offering to help? The thought filled her chest with an unusual ache—want bordering on pain. But then she shook it off. Volunteering at the center was a huge commitment. Not only was an extensive background check required—Jackson had been allowed in for the day because of Jami's relationship with Ella and Gabby, and because she'd worked there for so long—but a real commitment was required. The families here needed stability, and they needed to be able to count on the people to be here for them…maybe for the first time in their lives.

"But it also requires the supplies and equipment. It's a big deal to start a new class or support service here. It takes money, time, resources, and people power."

Jackson's smile faded a bit, but the spark still showed in his dark eyes. He suddenly took out his wallet and dug around, pulling out two folded passes. "Here are two tickets to our show next weekend. It's all ages."

The look on the kid's face was priceless. "Cool, but I'm not sure I can get there. I don't have a car. I take the bus here a couple times a week to help out."

"How about Jami and I pick you and a friend up

early? We'll take you to dinner and then to the show. My treat."

"Really?" The slack-jawed, wide-eyed look of disbelief on Calvin's face broke Jami's heart. He, his sister, and his mom had been through so much and had come so far. They'd dealt with so much disappointment. She stepped forward to reassure him, but Jackson beat her to it, wrapping his big hand around the boy's slender shoulder.

"Yeah. Really. Does Jami know where you live?"

Calvin nodded. She'd helped them move into their tiny Gresham apartment. Karen hadn't stopped smiling the entire day. Her confidence and pride showed through in the strong set of her shoulders. Their road to independence had been long and brutal. Her husband— now ex-husband, since the judge had finally approved the petition filed last year—was currently serving twelve years under Oregon's Measure 11 law for attempted murder and sexual assault of his wife. When Jami looked at them, she saw not just survivors, but winners. The day she helped them move and saw them laughing in their new tiny living room, Jami remembered wanting to keep that snapshot of a memory in her head forever as a reminder of why she needed to do more, give more to the center. Quirk changed lives. The more time she gave, the more she could help them do that. Too bad her job was always getting in the way of that.

"Dinner at six?" Jax asked.

Jami smiled to herself, knowing Jackson was helping the boy save face by providing a ride and meeting his mom. Her heart couldn't take any more of this man's sweetness. If it grew any more, she might think she was falling in love with Jackson Paige.

After exchanging numbers and making arrangements to pick up Calvin for dinner and the show, Jami found Ella and Gabby in the small conference room off the main living area.

"So how'd it go?" Ella asked, smiling at them.

"Great. Jackson was awesome. We should sign him up to volunteer all the time," Jami teased.

"I'd love that," he said quickly, surprising her. "Was thinking about what it would take to start an art and music program here."

Ella's playful grin transformed into all business. "You offering?"

Jackson nodded. "Jami mentioned that funds and approval might be an issue. I've only been thinking about it for less than an hour, but maybe my band can do a fundraiser or something."

Jami's heart began to beat double-time. Damn this guy and his crooked smiles and sweeter-than-sugar ways. Now he was going to help start a new program? Before she could raise her objections, he placed his warm hand around her wrist. "Not pretending I know the ins and outs of that kind of thing, but I can play music and I dabble in art. Maybe we can put something together."

And now self-deprecating. This was too much. He was too much.

Breathe, her inner voice coached. *Just breathe*.

He's just trying to help. Would that be so horrible?

"Jami's brother and fiancé own a marketing firm, I'm sure they could help with posters and PR. I know the band would be on board. How much does it cost to get something like that started and running for a year?"

"Instruments, art supplies…they can be pretty pricey."

Gabby stepped forward. "My company does art and graphics software. I bet I could get them to sponsor or provide some of the art supplies…maybe even on an ongoing basis." She looked at her feet and then up at them.

"That's awesome, Gabby."

"Thanks." She smiled.

"If we had the equipment and art supplies I could help with teaching. What? I totally could."

"Hey," Jami laughed. "I didn't say anything."

"Saw the look on your face, sweetheart." He smiled, and she could feel the heat from it warming her cheeks. Or maybe she was just blushing. Again. "When I'm not touring, my schedule is pretty flexible at the tattoo shop. I'd love to figure out something regular. Like once or twice a week."

Her stomach lurched. *Tour*. Of course. He would be leaving on tour in a few months. And he would keep leaving, because he was a rock star on the rise. She should have remembered, since she'd been working on the contracts for the tours and merchandising.

"Well," Jami started. "Let's not get ahead of ourselves. Let's see if we can put together a fundraiser and get some supplies before we go launching a whole new program. Maybe we should run it by Kelly."

Ella's forehead scrunched up, making her look much older and reminding Jami of Erma when she was unhappy with her or Mason. "Actually, I think it's a great idea. Oh, Jami, I forgot to tell you, Kelly's husband just had a bad PET scan. She's going to be taking a little time off from running things to take care of him. I was hoping I could talk to you about it later. Privately."

What could she possibly do to help Quirk's managing director and Ella? "Poor Paul. Kelly must be so worried. Sure. I'll be in tomorrow night for my tutoring shift, we can talk then."

Ella nodded and they said good-bye, promising to go to Manix's show that weekend. She didn't fight him when Jackson grabbed her hand as they pushed through the door into the early afternoon sunlight. But the silver lining that had been shining over her all day had gone slightly gray, and she found herself wondering how long he'd stick around this time before he had to leave again. She couldn't go back to being that girl.

Chapter 17

JAX GLANCED AT THE SHOP'S WALL CLOCK FOR THE tenth time in the last half hour. What was taking her so long to call? Ella had been scheduled to stop by Jami's office with some "big news" when they hadn't had time to meet after Jami's volunteer shift the night before. Jax was dying to know what the news was. Jami had promised to call before they met for dinner later.

"You're starting to give me a complex," Nathan said as he stretched his back. "You don't think I'm as pretty as she is?"

"Who?" Jax asked, not fooling anyone.

"Who?" Nathan's voice was pitched high and he fluttered his eyelids.

"Whatever, dude. Fine. No, you're not as pretty as Jami. Not even close."

"You know you're acting like a chick, right? Are you done with the outline or what?" His friend nodded toward his arm, stretching to see Jax's work on his shoulder.

"Yeah. Let me clean you up and wrap it, then you're good to go until the next round."

"You done for the night?" Nathan asked as he walked to the back and opened the fridge. "Wanna a beer?"

"Not sure if I should. Gotta get home."

"Ha. Ha. You're a fucking funny asshole." He cleared his throat. "So what's the deal with you and this woman? Getting serious?"

Jax nodded and took the Rogue Ale Brutal IPA from his friend. He took a long sip. "I think it is. At least for me."

"What's her problem?"

The question made Jax's nerves bristle in her defense. "What the fuck does that mean?"

Nathan held up his hands as he sat back down. "Whoa. No offense, bro. Only wondering why she's so special? You got women throwing themselves at you, and this one seems to be playing coy and shit. What gives?"

Jax cleaned Nathan's fresh ink, patted it dry, and smeared some petroleum jelly on his shoulder with a tongue depressor before covering it with plastic wrap and taping the edges down. "Not her fault. I bailed on her in college without a word, and before that she dated some douchecanoe that fucked her over bad. She has every right to be cautious. But I'm working on it." He pulled off his gloves and tossed them on the plastic wrap covering the table before gathering it all up with the used ink cups and tape and throwing it in the trash bin. Jax sprayed his station with alcohol and opticide to disinfect and clean the area.

"Bowen mentioned you were trying to put together a fundraiser for the women's shelter she works at."

Jax smiled, grateful for the change in subject. "Yeah. It's this fucking amazing place, mostly women and their kids trying to get their lives back together. Going to school, getting jobs, and stuff. Jami does almost all their legal work pro bono—divorces, restraining orders, visitation rights, rental agreements—the whole nine yards. Thought it would be cool to give the kids art lessons and teach them about music."

The more he let the idea take root in his brain, the more he really wanted to make it happen. Music and art had been his salvation more than once in his life, as it had been for the whole lot of his motley crew, so he knew Nathan would get it.

"I talked to Declan and Bowen and they both want in. If you want Toast to open for you at the fundraiser, we'd love to help," Nathan said.

"Wow, man. That would be awesome." He really did have a great group of buddies.

Nathan cleared his throat and leaned his hip against the counter in a deceptively casual manner. "I know you're usually the guy everyone comes to for advice, but I've known you forever, so I kind of know some shit, right?"

Jax nodded. His gut churned, dreading what came next, but he'd known Nathan almost his whole life, and he was right: the dude knew some shit.

"I heard about the thing with Jami and Mason's dad." He held up his hand. "Wait. Hear me out." He waited for Jax to nod. "She doesn't really sound like the kind of woman you can swoop in on and rescue. I know that's what you want. You're that guy. I get it. But if she's as damaged as you say, you need to be patient with her. You need to put it all out there and then let her make the decision. Sounds like she's done letting other people run her life and make her choices."

It hit Jax hard, like when he'd realized he loved Jami. Nathan had nailed it. Something Jax couldn't even see right in front of him. Jami had to choose him this time. He needed to give her every reason to make that choice, including being honest about his feelings for her. But, in the end, it would have to come from her, otherwise it would never work long term. And he sure as fuck wanted her long term. Like forever. Now that he had her back, he couldn't imagine any kind of life without her in it.

"Yeah. I just hope she'll choose me. I fucked up pretty bad."

Nathan smacked him on the shoulder. "Then you have your work cut out for you. In the meantime, what can I do to help?"

"With Jami?"

"The girl and the fundraiser."

Jami stared at the closed door of her office. The same door Ella had just walked out of after dropping a bomb in her lap, laughing, and leaving. As usual, Ella pulled no punches, got straight to the point, and then moved on. *Bam. Bam. Bam.*

When she'd called and said she was on her way to Jami's office with "big news," Jami thought it might be related to the fundraiser for the arts program at the center.

Without preamble or any of the social niceties that Jami depended on to feel normal, Ella had jumped right to it. "Kelly's not coming back, Jami. She wants to spend more time with Paul before he's gone," Ella had said. "We'd like you to come help run the center with me. Co-directors."

At first, Jami wasn't sure if she'd heard correctly. The words made no sense, it was as though Ella was speaking another language. "I have a job," she had responded numbly. How could Ella even ask that of her? How could she leave her dream of being a top attorney? Once she spent a couple years with Horndeckers, her plan was to move on, maybe partner in a bigger firm or work as part of a corporate legal team. Not move into the thankless bottomless pit of the nonprofit world. What the heck was Ella thinking?

"You hate your job." Ella laughed hollowly. "Don't deny it. It's on your face when you walk into the center. Then the mask drops and the real Jami comes to life." Ella spread her arms and cocked her head in challenge.

Okay, so she didn't like working at this firm. They didn't really value her work, nor did they provide any opportunities to move up. But she had plans. Goals that didn't include working full-time for a nonprofit.

"Quirk is not part of my plan. I do it…I do it for me. It's not a career. It's to help out. It's not…" Even she knew that sounded lame.

She lined up the pens on her desk and shuffled a stack of already well-shuffled papers.

"Look, promise you'll think about it. Take the weekend. Then we need an answer. Kelly wants to go to the board next week. I'll email you the details of the offer. Okay?"

Jami nodded, and Ella left as she sat and stared at the door, counting to ten as she breathed slowly, urging her pulse to stop racing.

She lined up her notepad and paper clips. Nice and neat. Like she wanted it. Like she needed it. The organization she craved, her bosses admired, and her friends teased her about, kept her demons at bay. Kept her ducks in a row. And, frankly, her ducks were getting a little messy—definitely not in a row. Jackson. Work. The center. The band.

Ducks run amuck.

She pressed her palm to her forehead and tried to silence the beating drum of her heart. Glancing at her computer screen, she realized it was past six thirty, and she was due to meet Jackson for dinner in less than thirty minutes. Worse, she hadn't called as she'd promised.

She really needed everything to stop. Or at least to slow down enough for her to catch her breath. Jackson would understand. It's not like they were serious about each other anyway. They'd tried that and it had failed miserably.

By the time she'd reached her car she felt good about her decision to apply the brakes. She'd sent a quick text to Jackson about needing to reschedule and was driving up her street feeling pretty grown up, with an A plus in Adult Relationships 101. No out-of-control wild child here. No sirree. Just über-responsible grown-up JamiLynn Dillon making very adult decisions.

She was so busy patting herself on the back she didn't notice Jax leaning against her front door until she was almost unlocking it.

"Meeting over early?"

"Uh, no." She fumbled with her keys.

"No, you're still in your meeting, counselor?" His words were playful, but his face was anything but. He leaned down to take her keys and peer into her face, so close she could see the light flecks of black and gold in his eyes and the long dark fringe framing them.

"No. I didn't have a meeting. I'm just tired."

He turned and quickly opened the door and pulled

them both inside before kicking it closed. He took her briefcase and set it on the floor by the small catchall table and led her to the couch. After she settled down, he moved to the kitchen and began making her tea. Something tight in her chest loosened. She'd basically lied and bailed on him, and his reaction was to make her tea.

Jackson was a good man. Probably too good for her. Of course, that's not what her parents said about him. Just the opposite. But, at that moment, the last thing Jami wanted was to think about her parents.

Aubrey jumped in her lap and began meowing loudly. "Time to feed him?" he asked. She nodded and pointed to the cupboard. The cat jumped off the couch and began to circle his legs, begging for food. Jackson scooped some kibble into the cat's bowl, and the begging stopped as Aubrey dug in.

"How about you? Are you hungry?"

She shook her head.

"Sure?" He banged around her cupboards until he found the one filled with canned goods. "How about some soup?" He waggled his brows, and somehow talking about canned soup made him seem even sexier. How was that even possible?

She laughed. She couldn't help it. He was making it difficult to keep her perpetual walls up.

Get a grip, Jami. What happened to putting distance between you two?

But watching him cook in her kitchen—even the mundane tasks of opening the can and pouring it into the pot, heating the water for her tea—was doing all kinds of crazy things to her insides, filling the hollow feeling she carried around all day long with something she wasn't quite ready to put a name to. Was it possible to get wet from watching a man make dinner? Apparently the answer was yes. A big, fat, sloppy yes.

He was so much more courageous than she could ever be. He'd been able to walk away from school and break away from his controlling parents. Despite everything, she was sure she'd never be brave enough to stand up to her parents. Add that to his kindness in the face of everything, and the man was nearly perfect.

Jackson set the bowl and spoon on her coffee table next to the cup of tea.

"Why do you keep doing this, Jackson? Why do you keep coming after me?" she blurted before she could stop herself. Because if she was honest, she really did want to know why.

"You need me to. For now. You know that at some point I'll stop chasing you, right? At some point you'll need to make the decision to come to me. Until then, I'll keep fighting for you."

She knew in her heart she'd probably never be able to go after him. Because the part of her that would let her be a couple, that could feel real love—that part had been broken a long time ago. By Dallas, by her parents, and maybe a little by Jackson himself. And good riddance to it. She'd had enough of that gut-wrenching pain of heartbreak to last a lifetime and wanted to never experience it ever again. But what did she have left?

Her nice tidy life, that's what. Order. Rules. Simplicity. She'd learn to live again like she'd done before.

"Maybe I won't know how to do that, Jackson," she said quietly.

"You won't know if you don't try."

Maybe she deserved a little light in her life. For once, it was time to actually be the adult she kept claiming to be. She pushed aside thoughts of her lofty plans and her judgmental parents as he settled his long body onto her couch. His jeans pulled snug against his hard thighs, and his shirt sleeve rose up as he threw his arm along the couch to reveal his drool-worthy bicep ripped with cords of muscle. "What happened tonight, my sweet sunshine?"

She sighed and smiled at the sexy man lounging next to her. When he pulled her legs into his lap and yanked her shoes off, the heat from his hands infused her feet, warming her cold, brittle bones, as it traveled up her legs to slowly melt the panic she'd let control her.

"If you keep doing that I'm either going to fall asleep or attack you. Either way, it's a totally different conversation." She tried flashing him a sassy smile.

"Not dodging this conversation."

"No. I suppose not." He continued rubbing her feet, feathering his strong fingers up her calves. "I got a job offer tonight."

"Annnd…"

"And I can't take it."

"Okay. Do you want to?" Somehow he'd moved from sitting at the end of the couch with her feet in his lap to having her entire body in his lap and his fingers kneading the back of her neck and shoulders. She always seemed to end up in the man's lap.

She moaned. She couldn't help it. He was like human muscle relaxant. She suddenly became aware of his erection under her butt. She smiled to herself, loving that she could get a hotter-than-sin man like Jackson Paige hard. Just. Like. That.

"Focus. I know what you're trying to do. And we're not going there, despite my instaboner. Not yet," he said, grabbing her hips and holding her still.

"That's not making it better."

"No," he growled low, but went back to rubbing her neck and shoulders. "It's not. Tell me about the job."

"Ella said Kelly, the center director, is retiring, and the board of directors wants us to run Quirk. They figure her social work and counseling experience coupled with my legal and business background will make us a great team."

"You don't agree?"

She agreed wholeheartedly. Jackson would never understand the cutting disappointment of her parents or her need to stick to the plan. To stay the course and not fall back into old, irresponsible habits. "I do agree. We'd be awesome."

"Then what's the problem?"

She sighed. Not a la-di-da happy-day sigh, but a deep, you're-not-going-to-want-to-hear-this sigh. "I have a job."

"Do you love your job?"

She shook her head, rested it against his lean shoulder, and hugged him tightly.

"Do you love working at the center?"

She nodded, liking the way his flannel shirt felt against her cheek. Soft. Warm. Like home.

"Is it the money?"

She shook her head again. "No, it's not the money,"

she said. Her voice sounded hollow, distant to her ears. "I'm a lawyer, Jackson, not a social worker."

"Do you even like the firm you work at, sweetheart? Don't bother answering. I know you don't. So why not do something you love?"

"It's not part of my plan." It sounded ridiculous after saying it aloud. But instead of ridiculing her he just petted her hair, letting his fingers tangle with her heavy locks.

"Can you picture yourself working there? Imagine the good you could do on a full-time basis."

Of course he didn't understand. She knew he wouldn't…couldn't. He did what he wanted. Made art. Played music. Drew pictures. He knew when something wasn't meant for him, so he did something else. But she wasn't like that.

"I do what I can now. I'm not a social worker."

"So you keep telling me. They're not looking for a social worker, Jami. They're looking for a sharp-minded attorney. They want you."

When she didn't answer, he cupped her face and tilted it toward his. "You think I don't know, that I don't understand what this is all about. But, believe me, sunshine, I get you." He tapped her nose with his index finger. "The real you. Not the bossy attorney in the boring clothes with a shitload of rules. I see you. And I'm falling for you all over again. Hard."

No! No, no, no.

They were just having fun.

Right?

Yes, fun in the form of lots of mind-blowing sex. With some meaningful conversations thrown in for good measure.

Deep down, she knew the truth. And she realized suddenly that he might actually see the real her—a scared, muddled mess. Recognized it in his eyes and in the caress of her cheek.

For a moment, she considered what her parents would say. And then she realized something astonishing—she didn't really care. She was beginning to realize that her parents didn't have a say in her life anymore. They'd ended that with a slap and then chased it with the fight with Mason and Jackson. She should've realized a long time ago that she'd never live up to their standards. But it didn't change anything. She still had a plan that didn't include Jackson, and he had a lifestyle that didn't include her; one that meant months on the road away from her.

"Jackson, you are a good man. A man with integrity that knows what you want and go after it. You're also a really amazing and talented musician on the rise. I can't compete with that. More importantly, I don't want that." He deserved his shot at fame and fortune, and someone like her, someone with a train car full of baggage and fear, would only hold him back. He wouldn't see it like that. Jackson might even stay for her. He'd stay, thinking it was for love, but it would really be an obligation he felt to not let her down again.

He deserved his dreams, and she couldn't live like that.

She *wouldn't* let him live like that.

She couldn't bear to end it now. Not yet. But she'd have to let him go soon. Before the tour. He needed to be free of the tether she represented, so he could go and entertain the world.

She could give him that gift.

"I just said I was falling for you, and you give me some bullshit about integrity and music?"

"Yes, you think you're falling for me. But I'm not ready for this yet. Not tonight." She squeezed his shoulder. "But, how about if I don't say no yet. I'll think about it. I have the weekend to decide before they go to the board with a plan. And we can talk about…about other stuff later."

"Yeah. Good idea." He sounded doubtful, but he let it go. She knew he'd bring it back up soon enough, and she'd need to dodge his questions again.

Chapter 18

JAMI LOOKED UP FROM THE CONTRACT AND STARED AT the wall. The papers spread out on her desk told the whole story in detail. Jax was leaving, and not only that, but one of the two tours would keep him away for months. Months on the road in the U.S. and Europe, beautiful women throwing themselves at her equally beautiful man.

Her man. She groaned and pulled her glasses off to rub the bridge of her nose. When had he gone from just casual to "her man"? The night before, when he said he was falling for her and that he saw the real her, she might have panicked a little. Okay, maybe a lot. But, strangely, it hadn't been the actual idea of being with him for the long term that had freaked her out. It wasn't her parents. It was what his leaving her again could do. If she allowed herself to picture a life with Jackson, the image settled a kind of soft peace into her otherwise cold bones.

One thing Jackson had gotten wrong were the reasons for her rules and the way she dressed. The rules were to keep the chaos at bay. The clothes were her way of blending in. He was cute for thinking it was her way of toning down her "beauty," as he put it.

But then he'd gone and dropped the L bomb. Okay, maybe he hadn't said love. It was more like a "like you a lot" bomb. But still. Suddenly everything was swirling around her again like that scene in *The Wizard of Oz*. Any minute now, the Horndeckers would fly by on their brooms, screeching "and your fat cat, too."

Her computer dinged, notifying her of an incoming email, which reminded her that she should finish up the contracts and send them off to the attorney for the primary tour sponsor, a big energy drink company.

Her attempts to focus on the paperwork in front of her were interrupted by moments from the night before. He'd seemed so sincere when he held her face and rubbed his thumb across her bottom lip before telling her that he saw her, really saw her. Wasn't that the goal? To make a real connection with someone who saw beyond all the mousetraps and false fronts a person put up?

It had been her dream a very long time ago. When she still believed real love conquered everything. But it didn't, did it? Real love got you pregnant as a teen before getting you punched in the stomach and thrown against a wall by an abusive boyfriend. Real love sucked.

It was almost time to meet Jackson at the shop. They were going to dinner with Calvin and his sister Carey, and then taking them to the Manix Curse show. She was staying the night so she could go over the contracts with Jackson before she briefed everyone the following week.

She packed up her briefcase and was walking toward the elevator when her boss stepped into her way, stopping her abruptly.

"Leaving early?"

"It's almost seven o'clock, Carl, on a Saturday," she said, realizing she'd been working on her side project with her boss in the other room. Geez, what was happening to her? Her professionalism was flying out the window, along with her good sense. "Except for Wednesdays, I'm here by seven thirty every morning and I rarely leave before eight."

"You're never going to make partner if you don't put in the hours. Didn't they teach you that in law school?" He smiled, a pathetic attempt to pretend his barb was in jest.

It wasn't. She wasn't a fool. It wasn't quite a threat. No, more like a test. Usually she'd have a quick, appropriate response at the ready. Tonight, she was tired…so heavy with fatigue. Of the firm, of fighting her feelings for Jackson, of pretending she still gave a shit what her parents thought. Exhausted.

"I'm not an idiot, so please don't treat me like one. We both know I'll never make partner here." His face turned a reddish color, reminding her of a turnip, but he didn't respond. She walked around him before he stomped back down the hall. She was rather proud of herself when she pressed the elevator button gently, because she really wanted to pound that taunting little red arrow. Smash it through the wall with her finger.

She raced home to take a quick shower and change into something more appropriate, something good for dinner, but also for a Manix Curse metal show. By the time she reached the tattoo shop and had parked in the lot next to the building, she'd moved past Carl's pathetic taunt and calmed down.

As she pushed into the shop, she reminded herself to take deep cleansing breaths, count to ten, and smile. All the stupid things she did a dozen times a day to keep disorder at bay and her emotions in check. The effect, on this day, was not positive. Her pulse increased and her breath sounded ragged. The anticipation of seeing Jackson again preempted all other preventive measures.

Jackson Paige preempted everything.

Jami walked into the now familiar tattoo shop and looked around at the activity. The strong scent of green soap and rubbing alcohol hit her nose, and she smiled. The first time she'd barged into the shop, she'd known instantly that she didn't belong. But now she strolled in and Quinley, the new office manager and full-time piercer, greeted her with a wide smile, and Tony wrapped his arms around her. The first time he'd done it, she'd gone stiff as board. He'd laughed and squeezed her shoulder, telling her he was a hugger and she'd get used to it.

Strangely, she had. And rather quickly. She leaned into his embrace instead of away from it. The man had a natural warmth she was drawn to, much like Kevan, only paternal. At first she'd judged him based on his dress and scraggly beard. She'd done that with all of them—the band, the artists, Kevan. She'd been wrong from the very beginning. Like she'd been wrong about the shop.

Today the music blaring from a dozen hidden speakers seemed to have a techno vibe; a high, beautiful voice rang through the shop. Aww, Purity Ring—she recognized it from the other night. Jackson had played her a whole playlist of electronic music featuring female vocalists. He did that. Picked a musical theme and tried to broaden her horizons.

"Jax ran up to take a shower. He'll be down in a few," Tony informed her. Just then, the bell attached to the door beeped, and Kevan walked in with Bowen.

"Hey, sistah." Kevan grabbed her for a quick hug. "You going tonight?"

"Yes. We're taking a couple kids from the center to dinner and the show."

Bowen's eyebrows rose. "The women's shelter. Hey, I was going to ask you about that. Jax and Nathan mentioned some ideas for a fundraiser. I was thinking the week before, maybe we can offer a percentage of all profits from the shop to go to the fundraiser for supplies and stuff. Also, some of us would like to help with the classes." He shoved his hands into the pockets of his worn motorcycle jacket and smiled, flashing his dimples before they quickly disappeared and he looked around nervously. That was officially the most words she'd ever heard Bowen say at one time.

"Really? You'd do that?" Yeah. She'd misjudged these guys. Big time.

He nodded. "Fuc...uh, yeah. I already talked to everyone and Tony. They think it's a great idea. We can hand out flyers here for the fundraiser, too. Win-win."

"I don't know what to say. This all happened so fast. I mean, a couple days ago it was something Jackson threw out there. Now it's becoming a real thing."

"We want to help. He was pretty affected by his visit there. Was on fire about teaching music and art." Kevan jabbed her elbow into Bowen's ribs. "And this guy is pretty excited to help with art and guitar, right?"

"Yep." The stoic artist and musician nodded. Jami looked at him closely. He was one of the best looking men she'd ever seen, but he had a haunted darkness in his eyes. She knew he'd recently gotten out of rehab and was trying to get his life together, but he definitely still had ghosts swimming around in there. She knew the look well.

"Where the hell did you people come from?" she muttered aloud.

"We've been here the whole time." Kevan smiled and sat on one of the couches in the front waiting area. She slapped the empty spot next to her. "Come sit while you're waiting for your man."

"He's not my man."

"Sure, cupcake, whatever you say," Kevan said, patting Jami's knee when she sat.

Bowen flopped on the chair across from the couch.

"If he's not your man, then what is he?" Bowen asked pointedly.

"So we're doing this now? The what-are-your-intentions-with-our-friend talk?" Jami asked, amusement in her voice.

"Nah. It's none of our business. You know Jax and Mandi have different mothers, right?"

She nodded. Jackson had made a flippant comment about his dad and how he liked to start new families when the old ones got…well…old. Apparently he was on his third family now. Married to an ex-classmate of Jackson's. She remembered thinking how awkward that must be for them. Despite the dysfunction of her family, at least she didn't have to contend with a ton of extended-family issues. Nope. Just one big screwed-up family.

"His dad is a douchebag congressman, but I guess his constituents don't mind when you leave your family for a younger version every few years," Bowen sneered.

She couldn't help feeling like she was betraying Jackson. She knew his dad was some kind of politician, but if he wanted her to know this information, then he should be telling her. "Why are you telling me this?"

Kevan turned and looked Jami in the eye. "Because he won't. You need to know Jax has a fucked-up view about families and doing things to keep up appearances."

"Like my parents."

"Like your parents." Kevan smiled. "I know it's different, but it's this weird hair trigger for him. It makes him do stupid shit and act like an idiot."

While it was annoying, it was also kind of sweet that his friends were meddling in his relationship. They loved him. He had this crazy group of friends who cared about him no matter what. Now through her brother, and maybe through Jackson, she was being welcomed into the same group with open arms. They wanted what was best for their buddy, but they seemed to want her too. When had that happened?

"His mom was a model and B-movie actress. She cares about herself pretty much exclusively. She remarried some land developer and moved out to Florida a few years ago. Now she considers herself high society."

"How does her tattoo-artist metal-band-drummer son fit into that equation?" Jami asked, already knowing the answer.

"Yeah. He doesn't," Bowen responded. "Davida doesn't like her only child's relationship with his sister. She refuses to acknowledge his other siblings. It's kinda ugly."

Right then, the man they'd been talking about strolled into the shop from the back hall. Her eyes locked onto his the moment she saw him, his lanky body reminding her not for the first time of a predatory cat, with his muscles tensing and undulating as he moved. Goddamn, yes, Bowen was attractive, but Jackson was the most gorgeous man she had ever seen, and he was looking at her like he wanted to eat her for dessert. And she was ready to change her name to Cake.

She'd never been a fan of leather-clad men. Leather pants on a man had always seemed a little too '80s hair band to her. She immediately changed that view when she caught sight of Jackson in tight black leather pants thin enough that she could see his lithe leg muscles flex and roll under the soft fabric.

She stood and sucked in a ragged breath. His classic David Bowie tour shirt pulled snug across his wide chest and muscled shoulders, but hung loose over his torso. His messy long pompadour was brushed back, sharp.

Jax Pain was in the house, and he was so fucking hot her eyes nearly burned to ash.

✷ ✭ ✷

Jax saw her before she saw him. His gaze was drawn to her no matter where she was in a room. Like a fricking magnet. Or a laser beam. A goddamn laser beam magnet.

God, she was stunning. So beautiful his chest hurt from the throbbing pulse of his heart. He moved toward her again and she looked up. The unusual sapphire blue of her eyes glowed from across the room, drawing him toward her. He didn't have a choice any longer—he'd follow her anywhere. Because he had to.

When he'd hopped down his steps and turned the corner, whistling along with the song playing over the speakers, he had wondered if she was going to think his clothes were silly. Too rock and roll.

Her eyes said, "No, not too much." But despite the lust he saw there, he saw fear too.

Well fuck. Fuck, fuck, fuckity fuck. Jax was screwed. Royally. And not only because this felt an awful lot like love.

So what had he done? Had he come up with a plan to not scare his skittish woman away? Nope. He'd pushed her and revealed his hand too early in the game. Now she was probably spooked and on the run. Just like he had predicted, but still hadn't been able to stop himself. No, she hadn't physically jumped up and run from the room, but he'd recognized the moment flight had won out over fight as her brow furrowed and the pulse in her neck flitted like an angry bee. It signaled "Code blue! Run for the hills!" But there she was, sitting with Kevan and Bowen.

She stood when he reached her so he grabbed both her hands and spread them wide with a wolf whistle. "Damn, sunshine, you are fucking hot." He laughed and took in her outfit, from the pale pink leather wedges that made her a whole four inches taller, to the perfectly fitted jeans and pink, nearly see-through blouse tight enough to suggest her rocking curves, but loose enough to force a man to use his imagination a little. Her hair, which was usually pulled back in a tight bun, hung in long natural curls, with one lock falling over her shoulder and curling delicately under her breast. She'd brushed on a little dark eyeliner and some red lipstick, and she looked like a freaking model.

He wrapped his arms around her small shoulders and crushed her to his chest, not caring who was watching. Then he brushed his mouth against her ear, peppering small kisses to the corners of her lips until he swallowed her small gasp with his own mouth.

"Thank you," she said when he pulled back. The blush on her pale skin wasn't makeup, and he marveled that he could still have that effect on her.

The bell rang over the door and Mason walked in with Joe. "Dude, what the fuck are you doing to my little sister?" he growled and stepped forward.

Kevan grabbed his arm and yanked him back. "Easy, cowboy, remember we talked about this?"

Mason's Texan drawl got more pronounced when he was agitated or inebriated. Funny how Jax rarely heard Jami's accent at all unless in the throes of passion.

Mason's scowl softened—like it always did when he looked at the woman he loved—and made a half-assed attempt to smile.

"Is that a smile, big guy? Keep working on it." Jax laughed and turned his body to face Mason, but kept one arm firmly around Jami. He reached over and socked Mason in the shoulder. "I was telling your sister how gorgeous she looks tonight. Don't you agree?" He raised his brow.

Jami's brother looked down and shook his head. He'd get used to them being together soon enough. Better to get it out in the open now. One, it would give Jami fewer reasons to run away. Two, and most importantly, Jax didn't like having to keep his hands off her. His big hands fit around her sweet curves so perfectly. He didn't give a shit how fucking cliché he sounded—she was the big missing puzzle piece. She filled the gaping hole of disillusionment and loneliness that he'd just started to realize he had. But he wasn't naive. He knew she was scared shitless, and it wasn't going to be easy to convince her he was in it to win it this time.

Claiming her out in the open was a good start. He'd tried to keep her close and still be respectful of Mason the other night at the bar, but it was time for big brother to deal with it. To kick that point home, he dropped a kiss on the top of her head.

"Oh, I almost forgot." Jami pulled a thick folder from her huge shoulder bag. "I have copies of the two tour contracts. I'm still working with the sponsors on the merchandising agreements, but we need to get these finalized before they can put you on the bills, and you"— she looked pointedly at Mason, then Kevan—"can start working on promotions."

Jami smiled, like she always did, but her mouth seemed tight and she appeared almost nervous as she passed out the copies, leaving the extras for Marco and Conner, who were still finishing up work on clients, and giving Mandi's copy to Jax. "Look them over this weekend and we can discuss any questions you have at the meeting next week."

"We're heading out to dinner. What are you guys up to?" Jax asked as they were getting ready to leave.

"So we decided to couple the center fundraiser with the band's announcement of their Pagan Saints tour. We're going to hash out the details now and work on some marketing materials. Maybe come up with a little promo piece before we meet you at the club." Kevan said.

"I can't thank you all enough for what you're doing," Jami said, her voice wavering. "You really don't—"

Kevan reached out and covered Jami's hand with her own. "Yeah. We do."

Jami nodded with unshed tears making her eyes sparkle under the shop lights. "Thank you."

Jax said good-bye to his coworkers and friends, the whole time mindful of the quiet woman under his arm. Was she so unused to help that it brought her to tears? Or was it something about the contracts? Maybe she didn't want to handle their legal work any longer. He made a mental note to ask her about it later when they were alone. When she couldn't look away or try to get out of telling him the truth.

Whatever it was that had her worrying, he would find out.

He considered making Jami happy his new mission in life.

✬ ✬ ✬

White fairy lights covered nearly every vertical surface—and some of the horizontal ones, too—giving the restaurant an ethereal, dreamlike glow. The place was a lot like one of those upscale beer pubs where Jami had met with clients and other attorneys more than a few times in the past for lunch or a late-night meeting. Except this place had a quirky, rugged edge and wait-staff on roller skates. It was fun and funky, like Kevan, who'd recommended it. And Jami hadn't gone anywhere for fun in a long time. Come to think of it, other than her date with Jackson, she hadn't actually gone anywhere for a meal for something non-work-related in years.

Years since she'd had a meal out just for the company and good times.

Years since she'd been with a man that made her heart sing and her core quiver.

Years since she'd let herself enjoy a cold beer and laughs with people she actually chose to spend time with.

Her eyes caught Jackson's gaze as he belly-laughed at something Calvin's sister, Carey, said. His eyes crinkled at the edges, and a wide smile stretched across his face—across the damn room—before he threw his head back.

She smiled, not at the joke she missed, but at his open, honest lust for life. He didn't get caught up in appearances or what was considered good social behavior. No, he got caught up in the moment. He was the real sunshine in this relationship. She was just another moth.

The ache in her lips brought her attention to the too-wide, too-happy smile on her face. It was getting close to the end of all this. She knew it, and she suspected he did too. A couple more nights and few more days, and they'd have to deal with reality. And reality was that Jackson was an up-and-coming rock star. He was on a rocket ship to a galaxy that didn't include her and that she would never fit into.

She smiled when Calvin's voice broke as he sang one of Manix Curse's popular songs in a loud voice. The power ballad was even starting to get airplay on the local indie and rock stations in Portland. One of the paralegals at the firm had mentioned he heard it in a Seattle club the week before. Jackson's dreams would all be coming true soon.

"So Calvin here is definitely not singer material." Jax winked at the blushing teen. "But I'm thinking he'll kick ass—butt, I mean butt—on the drums."

"Sweet, dude, then we can start our own band," Carey said. "Maybe I can learn to play guitar like Mandi." She tipped her head down and gazed up through her purple fringe of bangs.

"Sure. Mandi's thinking about giving some lessons too. Maybe she can teach you herself."

Jami swallowed, her throat gravelly and dry. She took a sip of water. Gah, his sweetness was killing her. A stabby feeling in her heart made her eyes start to water. Damn allergies. "Don't get too ahead of yourselves. We still have to throw the fundraiser and get some actual instruments, let alone recruit qualified teachers."

"No worries, sweetheart," Jackson said in the low, languid way she loved. He sat across from her at the table, but the caress of his words washed over like she was sitting in his lap. "I've seen the proposed budget. No problem."

Calvin stared at Jackson, hanging on every word. She had to admit, if only to herself, his confidence drew people in. Made them believe his words and want to follow him anywhere like the heavy-metal Pied Piper.

"Hey. Jami. It will be okay. You believe that, right?" He reached over and covered her hand, his callused thumb brushing her knuckles. His eyes were wide with anticipation, willing her to believe in him. Like it wasn't only about the benefit. Like it was about so much more. Like it meant something.

Nodding, she took a bite of her polenta to buy herself a moment. "Of course. I only want to manage expectations," she answered. And in the flap of a bee's wing, the vulnerability was gone, replaced with the cocky smirk of Jax Pain.

"Keep trying, sweetheart, but you know there's no managing me." Well, wasn't that the darn truth?

Calvin and Carey snickered and looked at each other and then quickly away. For a moment, she'd forgotten they were even at the table. As usual, Jackson's intense focus on her narrowed her vision to him. Pressing her hand to her chest, she tried to push down the weird achy feeling. Even in a group of people, the effect he had on her was disconcerting. Overwhelming.

"You guys excited about the show?" Jami asked. That took them off into another, safer direction, one not fraught with peril.

Because peril was exactly where this thing with Jackson was headed.

Thankfully, the kids took the bait, and the rest of the meal was filled with music talk that Jami thoroughly enjoyed, but didn't understand one word of. Other than a couple of fans at dinner and the throngs of obnoxious women at the show, the rest of the night passed like a heavy-metal dream.

✲ ✲ ✲

After the show, Jackson drove Calvin and Carey home in his giant man truck. When they were finally alone, Jami once again unbuckled herself so she could slide next to him and stick her hands around the massive erection he always seemed to have after a show. Partly because she couldn't keep her hands off him and partly because he'd promised her punishment on their first date and never delivered.

Finally, back at his place, she sat on his bed while he showered, excitement zinging through her body. When he walked into his bedroom completely naked, she froze. The way he stood there, his hip cocked against the doorframe, the evil smirk on his lips, made her want to fall to her knees in front of him if only to worship his body. Then her eyes moved to his hand where he draped a blue silk scarf and her body heated.

"Take your clothes off, sunshine," he said quietly, firmly. "And lay down on the bed."

Jami tugged her jeans off, her heart pounding so hard she thought it would jump from her chest, and threw them on the floor, followed by her blouse, bra, and panties. She quickly crawled onto the bed, and he came down on all fours behind her.

"I want to blindfold you now. Are you comfortable with that?" His warm breath feathered against her throat.

Was she? It had been so many years since he'd done that to her, and since he'd walked away she'd kept her assignations strictly vanilla. The things she'd done with Jackson years ago, the things she fantasized about when she was alone and touched herself in the dark, required trust. And this time, when it was over, he would take with him more than just her trust; he'd take a piece of her. A piece she wasn't quite sure she'd be able to grow back.

His hand stroked her hair while his mouth continued down her neck and across her shoulders, sending little spikes of pleasure to every part of her body. His breath heated her, like fire against her already inflamed skin. "We don't have to do anything you're not ready for. We can stop any time you want."

She should not want this. She should not want to make herself more vulnerable to him. But she did. She always had.

"I'm ready," she whispered against the sheet.

His body left hers for a moment before he wrapped the soft scarf around her eyes and knotted it at the back of her head. The silkiness of the material contrasted with the rougher texture of his fingers against her cheeks, down her neck. The forced darkness made his touch so much more pronounced. Every caress of his lips or hands left behind a tingle—every breath was a blast of fiery heat, every word a deep rumble of meaning.

When he finally made his way down to her butt, his hands grabbed her hips and tugged her up onto her knees, and pressing her chest back down onto the bed with his hand on her back, he nudged her thighs wide and spread her open. His sheer strength and command of her body made her head spin. When he moaned behind her, her chest swelled. *She* did that to him. She made the hottest guy she'd ever met—ever seen, for that matter— moan with desire.

He ran his hands over her bottom and dragged two fingers down her folds, testing her wetness, discovering how eager she was for him. Hot, needy, and wet for him.

She arched into his hand to help direct him to where he should be, but instead of granting her release, he pulled back. "Greedy girl." His hand came down on her ass with a burning smack.

"Ow!" She cried into the darkness. His hand rubbed the sting out with small circles, replacing it with a liquid warmth.

"That's for lying at the gallery on our first date." He continued rubbing the sharp tingle and morphed it into deep pleasure. The kind of dark desire she'd denied for so long. She moaned before she could stop herself. Then his other hand came down on her other cheek. Hard.

This time she didn't cry out. This time she leaned into it, felt the burn of his hand, anticipated the rush of endorphins and the reassuring caress to follow.

"That's for placing yourself in danger by taking your seat belt off in the truck. Again."

Smack. Moan. Burn. Rub.

Her nipples were so hard they almost hurt as she pressed her chest into his bed and raised herself to meet his hand.

"And that's because I love to see your ass turn pink under my hand." This time he kept one hand on her backside and leaned over to grab something, probably a condom. She didn't care. She was floating. Waiting for Jackson to take her. To claim what was offered. Her trust. That little part of her soul she knew she was never getting back.

She was vaguely aware of the warm wetness between her legs. She should probably be embarrassed or cover herself. But that was against the rules. He kissed the base of her spine, then pulled back for a moment and rubbed the head of his cock up and down her swollen folds, stopping only to prop himself at her opening. She moved her hips from side to side, wanting desperately to push back. But she knew the rules. In this game, Jackson was in charge. In exchange for her trust and her submission, he gave her what she wanted. And he always knew what she needed. Always.

The same moment his hand came down on her ass, he pushed his steel-hard cock all the way into her. "That's to remind you that you belong with me. You're mine."

Her body sparked and crackled with electricity as Jackson bent over her and licked from the back of her neck to behind her ear and bit the lobe. The sharp snag of his teeth coupled with the thrust of his cock threw her under a tidal wave of lust, where she became a passenger to sensation and nothing more.

He lifted her and angled her hips. Pulsing deep into her on a roar, he called her name and pumped one more time before he stilled, panting against her neck. Jackson kissed her neck before whispering "Mine" in her ear and gently untying her blindfold. He rolled off the bed, giving her bottom a swat. "I'll be right back. Don't go anywhere, sunshine."

After he'd cleaned up, he lay down on his back and pulled her onto his body, gently stroking her hair and back.

As they fell asleep that night, Jami realized she was really going to miss all of this. Jackson. The sex. The shop. The music. Everything.

Chapter 19

AFTER THE SHOW, THEY FELL INTO THE CLOSEST THING a tattoo-artist metal musician and divorce attorney could call a normal routine, despite the clockhand of time hanging over their relationship like the executioner's axe. Jami spent some nights at Jackson and Mandi's apartment, and others Jax spent at her house. Either way, they almost always stayed together. Despite Jackson's late nights, he was an early riser. She loved to bring him coffee before the sun rose after his predawn run and then watch him paint in her windowed porch, where he'd set up a temporary studio.

But how temporary was it? Jami tried to live in the moment and take what she could from what Jackson gave her, but she felt this dark cloud of impending doom getting closer and closer. Soon it would open up and rain down on her, washing away the past and the future and leaving her alone. Soon there would be no way back from the edge where she perched now.

Jami looked around her great room now. Every chair was filled, as well as several pillows on the floor around the coffee table and next to her. The hulking figure of the man-child Marco sat between Mandi and Kevan on the couch, his long mane piled up in a funky bun. Both women had chosen to dress down for the last-minute planning session and wore jeans and hoodies. Jami had also attempted to dress down, but her definition of "casual" was apparently slightly different, as she stood in dark gray linen pants and a blue silky top. The rest of the seats were taken up by Mason, Sindra—the graphic design intern for Jolt Marketing—the rest of the band, Bowen, Ella, and Gabby.

The group had spent the past three hours brainstorming and planning the benefit concert for the center's art program. They had started out as one big group and soon broken off into smaller workgroups to hash out the details for the show. In a million years, Jami would have never imagined they'd get as much work done as they had. In her day job, work took time and often proceeded at the proverbial snail's pace. Contracts were drafted, submitted, responded to, redrafted, negotiated. These people were all about action and just got shit done.

Not only had a date and location been finalized early on, but a schedule assembled, talent acquired, and a full on marketing and promotional plan implemented.

Bam. Done. Just like that.

"Who are you people?" she asked loudly before realizing she was thinking aloud. The group stopped talking and snapped their attention to her. She could feel the heat flooding her cheeks. "Um, I meant…uh…"

Mason laughed and stood, unfolding his tall, broad body, and pulled her into his side. A warm, happy feeling settled into her muscles as Mason hugged her. These people were somehow becoming her tribe. One she'd never known she'd wanted, let alone needed.

She looked up into his hazel eyes and saw her thoughts mirrored there. He knew what she was thinking, knew the moment she had realized it. This was what he'd found with Kevan and this group of amazing and crazy people. He had been trying to pull her into the vortex of it all for the past several months, and she had fought and resisted like a whiny baby.

In an instant, the connection she'd been trying to rebuild with her brother for years was suddenly solid again, stronger and more powerful than silk strands, optic cables, and steel rods merged together.

Mason's smile reached into her chest and squeezed her thawing heart. "We want to help, Jami. And this is the perfect project for this group."

"You're my brother. You're supposed to help me." She glanced up in time to see Mandi pinch Jackson's arm and give him a "see, asshole" grimace. "But I can't believe how generous you all are with your talents and your time. And your money. I don't know how to thank you. How to repay you."

"Hey, lady, you're the one who gives all your free time to a women's shelter. We're a bunch of metalheads and ink slingers." Marco laughed.

Yeah right. "Thank you," she said, her whisper barely audible over the music playing in the background. Her glance snagged on a familiar pair of dark brown swoony eyes, and her body flooded with another kind of warmth altogether. And the smirk on the rogue's lips said it all. He knew exactly what she was thinking, which made her pussy a little more wet and her nipples a little harder.

What the heck was with all this mind reading going on around her lately? What had happened to her no-nonsense persona? Jackson and his friends were melting her frozen heart as well as softening her hard edges.

And then, being the show-off he was, Jackson blew her a kiss. Shaking her head, she walked back over to

the dining table where Kevan was seated with Sindra.
Ella stood with Gabby, bent over a laptop, where Sindra
was working on the final layout for the online graphics
and social media messages. Sindra's long, curly auburn
mass of hair was pulled up on her head in a ponytail
and she wore a T-shirt and jeans with well-used running shoes. Ella clapped her hands like a small child and
grabbed Sindra in a hug. "You're freaking awesome,"
she said and motioned Jami over. "Look at this. This
shit right here is top-quality work. Oh my gosh, I swear,
we should hire you guys to redesign our logo and all our
marketing crap."

"We could totally do it for cheap, too," Kevan
laughed. She shrugged when Mason glanced at her.
"What? It's for a good cause, cowboy." Then she
wrapped her arms around her future husband like he was
already wrapped around her little finger.

Ella poked Jami in the side. "Did you just sigh?" The
look of horror on Ella's face was surprising.

"No."

"You did. You sighed like a lovesick teenager,"
Gabby said from her other side.

"Shut up. I did not."

"You totally did," the usually laconic Sindra said
quietly, without looking up from her screen.

"How long you going to keep lying to yourself
and keep that hot piece of manmeat on the hook?"
Ella asked.

"I'm not..."

"You are. And he basically looks up to find where
you are in the room every ten seconds. Or when he hears
your voice."

Jami rolled her eyes. "Okay, fine. I sighed. Big deal. I'm happy for my brother."

"Sure." Ella smiled before looking back over Sindra's shoulder at the screen. "Keep telling yourself that."

Before she could respond, Marco's deep laugh rolled through the room, and she walked back to the couches. Jackson stood up behind her and wrapped his arms casually around her waist. She wanted to push him away, to show him he couldn't act that way in front of everyone, but she didn't. Instead, she practically dissolved into his embrace. When he leaned down and nipped her ear, she sucked in a sharp breath. How easily he took her from zero to sixty. Screw that. More like zero to one hundred sixty.

"We're about done here, counselor. How about we send everyone on their way and spend some time alone." The last word was a growl, and she felt it rumble through her chest and shoot right down between her legs.

As if Jackson was sending subliminal messages or Morse code through his body language, the group began to fold up lists and shove them into folders and put away laptops while standing and stretching. The excitement in the room was palpable. This group of talented people was putting together an amazing benefit for some really heroic women and their families. The art and music classes were going to bring a much-needed layer to their daily routines, in the ability to express themselves creatively, but also to harness the beauty in their lives with paintbrushes and instruments.

And it had been all Jackson's brainchild. This amazingly compassionate, gorgeous, enigmatic man. Her man. For now, anyway.

Until she ended it all, so he could go live the life he was meant to, the life he'd worked so hard to build. And she could get back to her plan. Although, the more she thought about it, the less appealing her plan sounded.

For the middle of the week, the local brewpub was brimming with activity. People were energized by the recent break in rain and reveling in the glorious spring-like weather. Beer was flowing and burgers were being devoured. Jax had decided to meet up with the group for a quick beer and late-night meal while waiting for Jami to come by with Kevan and Mandi. Mason had told him earlier that Kevan had invited them to meet her at a wedding shop so she could ask them to be in the wedding.

The plan was to meet at the Hole in the Wall and then stay the night at Jax's apartment. She was due to arrive any minute, and he'd just checked his phone for her text when a commotion near the front door snagged his attention. A group of guys walked into the bar, making a noise and basically being douchey, acting like overaged frat boys. One guy, in particular, looked familiar. Dark blond hair a little shorter, a little heavier in the gut and chest, but it was him.

Dallas motherfucking Gale.

Gale was prancing around, looking like he owned the crappy bar and grill, slapping backs and cracking jokes while his buddies followed him around. By the time he was sliding in to the last empty table, Jax had stood without even a second thought about what he was going to say. Gale probably wouldn't remember

Jax from school, as Gale had been two years ahead of him, in the same class as his current stepmother. But Jax remembered Dallas. Everybody's buddy. The dick had used girls by cashing in on his parents' money and his football-player status for years.

Dallas was about to learn a much-needed lesson about how to treat women.

A hand on Jax's arm snapped him out of his single-minded focus, and he looked up and realized he was already halfway across the room.

"What are you doing?" Mason's fingers dug into his bicep. "This isn't your fight."

"The fuck it's not. He hurt the woman I love," he said, before he realized it might not be the best time to tell Jami's brother how he really felt about her, especially since he hadn't actually told her yet. *Too late*.

Mason's eyes went wide, and he shook his head. He stood tall in front of Jax and squinted, then cocked his head slightly to the side. "Yeah? I've been waiting a long time to get that fucker alone. A. Long. Time."

"He's not alone."

"Neither am I." They stared at each other for a moment and then glanced back at their group. A moment weighed down with the past. Mason appeared to come to some conclusion and nodded before turning back toward the table of assholes, now twice in number with several women joining them.

"Hey, asshole," Jax yelled when they reached the crowded booth. Why bother with niceties when all he wanted to do was fuck some shit up? Gale was the cherry on top of his ass-kicking sundae.

Two of the four guys at the table snapped their heads

up, their jaws tight and eyes glowing—ironically, both men wore wedding rings. Jax would've bet big money the young women sitting with them weren't the wives attached to those rings.

"What the fuc—" Dallas started, but then his ruddy face suddenly paled. His head whipped from Jax's face to Mason's. He might not have recognized Jax, but he sure as hell recognized his ex's brother. Big. Time. "Are you kidding me, here? What the fuck do you want, Dillon? I told you then and I'll tell you now, it's none of your fucking business. It was between Jami and me. So get outta my face and let me enjoy my night." Gale's hand shook slightly around his beer—enough to let both Jax and Mason know he couldn't quite back up the cocky swagger as he turned to the redhead next to him and threw his arm across the back of the booth.

Fuck this noise. Jax leaned across the table and caught the eye of Gale's young friend. "Honey, did you happen to miss the ring on this jackass? Or maybe you don't mind taking another woman's sloppy seconds? Regardless, shit's going down, and it's gonna get ugly, so I suggest you and your girlfriends take this time to go to the ladies' room."

The women made quick excuses, nearly running from the bar before Gale and his buddies jumped up and pushed the table toward Jax and Mason. They stood with their feet wide and fists clenched at their sides, looking ready to back up their idiot friend who stood slowly, still behind the table.

Jax smirked and crossed his arms over his chest. Good. These fuckers wanted a fight. Perfect.

"Seriously, dude, it's ancient history. I've moved on.

She's moved on. Why the hell do you want to rehash this shit? It was nothing. It's over," Gale said, a man used to getting his way.

Lightning quick, Mason's arm reached over the table and grabbed Dallas by the front of his golf shirt. "It wasn't nothing," the big man growled. "You punched her in the stomach and threw her into a fucking wall. Nearly ruined her fucking life. What kind of man does that?"

Jax could feel the heat rolling off Mason in waves. He could almost touch his anger, not just hanging in the air, but swirling and bubbling, drawing Jax in. How the hell could a man hit a woman? It was horrifically unfathomable to Jax. But this asshole? Jax could definitely hit him. Hard and repeatedly.

Dallas Gale was a punk-ass little shit. He hated that Jami still carried around some of him in her heart, keeping her from Jax. Close enough to want more, but far enough away to not get it.

Gale's buddies had stepped back, while Conner, Marco, Nathan, Bowen, and Tony had quickly spaced themselves out behind Mason and Jax. Jax noticed the two bouncers and the bartender watching them closely, but didn't make any moves toward the group.

Mason pulled Dallas up closer and glared down into his face. "What kind of *man. Hits. A. Woman*?"

"I was young. It was an accident. I didn't know she was pregnant," Dallas wheezed.

What the hell? Jami had been pregnant? Jax's heart raced, and the bar got very quiet around him, thick with anticipation.

"Fucking liar," Mason spat. "When she found you

at the party with that other girl, she told you. And what did you do, Dallas? What the fuck did you do to my little sister?"

The heat that had surged through Jax moments ago suddenly chilled. He felt cold. Like ice. It felt like hours he stood there waiting for Dallas to answer. But Dallas wouldn't say anything, just jutted that cocky chin out, almost begging for Jax or Mason to punch it.

When Mason finally answered for Dallas, Jax had to lean in to hear what he said. "You punched her in the stomach and shoved her into a fucking wall right before she drove her car into a tree, motherfucker."

A red haze fuzzed Jax's brain and clouded his vision. Before he could really process the words, he was on Dallas. One punch to the jaw jarred Dallas out of Mason's grip. A second to the gut felled him to the floor, where Jax kicked him in the ribs before he jumped on him and started pummeling.

Motherfucker. *Punch*.

Going to kill him. *Punch*.

Could have lost her forever. *Punch*.

Could have never had her. *Punch*.

Will never lose her again. *Punch*.

Jax's pulse pounded in his ears, in rhythm with his crazed fists. He thought maybe someone was screaming, others yelling. Then he was being pulled away from the asshole who had hurt the one woman he'd ever loved.

His head was dizzy, but the cloud that had fogged his brain was beginning to lift as Gale's loser crew pulled him up and dragged him toward the door. His focus shifted when something moved in his peripheral vision. He glanced into the mirror behind the now empty booth and caught the red, watery eyes of Jami. Turning slowly, swallowing and gulping for air, he wiped Dallas's blood from his hands onto his jeans. Jami's full lips were partially open as if to yell, but she only stared at him.

Jax shrugged off the hands still holding his shoulders and stepped forward, but she took a telling step back and held up her hand. He'd brought those tears to her gorgeous face. He was an animal. Not worthy of her. And he'd proved it.

How could she be standing there, so close but so fucking far, when only hours ago her gloriously round breasts had been in his hands? But instead of sadness or even anger, her face showed fear mixed with horror.

Shit. Anger he could diffuse with a smile. Sadness he could charm away. But this fear…he had no fucking clue what to do with that.

"Jami…" He held his hand out toward her but dropped it when her gaze ran over his bloody knuckles.

"How could you?" Her voice was a dark whisper, catching like sandpaper over his jagged nerves. "Anything but this, Jackson. Anything."

"I had to." He took another tentative step toward her, only vaguely aware of the activity around them. "I couldn't…I didn't…he hurt you…"

"*You* hurt me. You promised."

No. No, he'd done it for her. For him. Dammit, he couldn't be the source of more of her pain. Mandi and Kevan stood on either side of Jami, but didn't say anything. Their expressions were unreadable, but their support of Jami obvious by their wide stances and jutting chins.

The skin around Jami's blue eyes bunched and she

crossed her arms over her chest, rubbing her biceps as if cold.

Kevan put her hand on Jami's shoulder and whispered something in her ear. She nodded and shot Jax a look loaded as surely as any gun—and more damaging.

A heavy hand thunked his shoulder, and he turned to see Mason. "We'll take care of her. She needs some space. Violence freaks her out."

Jax shook his head. "I fucked up. I shouldn't have done that. I promised I wouldn't."

Mason laughed. Actually fucking laughed. "No. She shouldn't have seen that, but you definitely should have done it. Been wanting to kick that fucker's ass for years. You're my goddamn hero. She'll get over it."

Jax wasn't so sure. He watched Jami walk out the door with Kevan and Mason without so much as a glance back in his direction.

☆ ☆ ☆

Jami's first reaction when she'd seen Jackson punch the man who'd broken her body and her heart was overwhelming sadness. She'd thought that part of her life was finally over, fading from her present and staying firmly rooted in the past where it belonged. But when she'd seen the man she might love beating the man she'd once thought she loved, she'd wanted to run home, curl up in a fetal ball, turn on *The Princess Bride*, and eat a box of chocolate macaroons. Alone. Forget Dallas Gale and all his stupid friends. Forget the hot dumb asshole who was punching him silly.

Jami's second reaction was anger. A gloomy anger that quickly turned white hot when she realized that just that morning Jackson had been inside her body, inside her head. They'd been playful and intense, momentarily allowing her to pretend it wouldn't all be over soon. That it might all work out.

But then he was spouting off crap to her ex and beating the hell out of him. In a bar.

What a jerk. He'd promised no more fighting in her honor.

Her third and most lethal thought was that Dallas the girl-hitting ex-boyfriend from hell had shared her most private secret with nearly everyone there. She rubbed her chest, where the sick feeling coursing through her body pressed in and grew stronger.

Jackson knew about the baby, and he knew about her accident. And he'd beaten the crap out of the guy responsible for both. Well, if she was honest with herself, which wasn't something she really thrived on, she could admit the crash had been her fault. Of course, the tears she couldn't see through and the swelling welt on the back of her head were on him, and they had definitely contributed to her collision with that stupid tree. Which was exactly why she stayed away from men with sexy smirks and lazy swaggers. They were dangerous liars.

Except for Jackson. She kept coming back to him. And he kept coming back to her.

Jami pulled her favorite quilt up over her legs and looked down into the teacup warming her cold hands now as if looking for the answers in the grounds. But answers to exactly which questions she wasn't quite sure.

Questions like why a woman like her, one who abhorred violence and actually helped to rescue women from their violent lives, felt a rush of purely female satisfaction when she watched Jackson's big steely fists connect with Dallas's smug square jaw and bloated gut. Questions like why she had wanted him to slug Dallas a couple more times before Mason and the bouncers had pulled him off. Questions like why she hadn't decided to walk out of the bar without Jackson until she got a full look at Dallas's bloodied and swelling face.

Sipping the warm tea, she let the chamomile warm her parched throat. The delicate hints of honey and lemon soothed her tattered nerves along with the ache in her chest.

What had he said to her? He'd babbled about her being hurt…that Dallas had hurt her. Was that why he mangled her ex's face?

The truth didn't dawn slowly over Jami. Instead it punched her right in the gut. *Bam*. She was angry at Jackson for breaking his promise, not for protecting her honor. Because, in his mind, that's what he was doing. The promise had probably fled his mind the second Dallas impugned her honor.

She didn't want to be the kind of woman who let her past dictate her present, but she avoided relationships because the one with Dallas had nearly killed her physically. Although the emotional pain from Jackson's abandonment had been more painful and damaging. Both times, she'd been forced to seek refuge at home, with her parents. Both times, they'd taken the opportunity to remind her what a foolish little girl she was. Didn't she care about how her antics looked to everyone? Wasn't it bad enough Mason had become such a disappointment when he left Harvard and chose to throw away his future?

She had wanted so badly for them to love her, to be proud of her. But, somehow, that didn't seem to matter so much anymore.

"It's not up to us to make them happy, Jami." Her head snapped up to see her brother sitting across from her in her worn leather library chair, the one she'd bought at an estate sale after she'd graduated from college. She hadn't heard him come in. She hadn't even heard him at the door. Kevan must have let him in. "The best we can do is make ourselves happy." His low voice was more soothing than the tea she'd been sipping.

She must have been thinking aloud.

"This isn't about them anymore."

"Isn't it?" He got up and moved to sit next to her on the couch. "Isn't that what it's always been about?"

"Dallas Gale, *my ex-boyfriend*, the boy I thought loved me at one time, told that whole bar what an idiot I am. And my current…uh, friend, beat the hell out of him. Jackson promised he wouldn't be beating on anyone in my name."

"No one heard what Dallas said, and there's no shame for you in what happened. And that dickfuck deserved to have his ass kicked. I'm sorry it wasn't me." The dark smirk dominating her brother's face was disconcerting. She'd had no idea he'd still harbored such hatred for Dallas. Other than right after the accident, they'd never really talked about what had happened to her in the years since. Her parents had swept it under the secrets rug and only dragged it out to keep Jami in line. "He couldn't *not* do something."

"But Jackson heard." She stared down into her empty cup. Perhaps that was what really bothered her. Not the violence, because that might be the only language Dallas understood. But the fact that Jackson now knew of her shameful past. Her dirtiest, saddest secrets. The whole of it.

Her brother wrapped his strong arms around her, pulling her into his side, where she could lay her head on his shoulder.

"Darlin'. Yeah. All he heard was what the asshole did to you. It's when he basically jumped on him and beat the holy fuck out of him." A cold smile covered his rugged face.

They sat in silence for a moment, letting the words sink in. Jax had been angry about Dallas and how he'd treated her. Fingers of shame that had crawled up her spine retreated slightly. She was starting to wonder if maybe she was angry because her belief system prevented her from cheering Jackson on. Or, even worse, kept her from retaliating against Dallas herself. Maybe she was angry because she was realizing that everything that happened to her was tragic, and she'd never allowed herself the chance to truly grieve the loss of her baby.

Her brother's big hand covered hers. "What's really going on with you and Jax? You can tell me. I won't judge. I promise."

She looked at him skeptically, and her big bad brother rolled his eyes and laughed. "I love you, Jami. I promise I'll never let you down again by ignoring what's happening in your life."

"I think I love him, Mason." Her voice was a whisper in the quiet room.

"That's good, right?"

"No. Not good. He has the band. And they're going

to be huge. Really huge. I can't hold him back from his dreams." The stab to her heart was quick, sharp. Saying it aloud made it so much more real.

"Why can't he be part of your dreams and you his?" her brother asked softly.

If only she could. "No matter how much I love him, he needs to be free to pursue his music. And I can't be left behind again. I think it would kill me this time."

Their conversation came to a halt when she reached down and answered a call from her mother. Before Jami could speak, her mother spoke. Five minutes was all it took for Jami to learn the rest of Jackson's story and exactly why they could never be together. And it had nothing to do with Dallas Gale.

Chapter 20

JAX SHUFFLED HIS FEET UNDER THE TABLE. HE CROSSED his legs, placing one ankle on the other knee, then shifted and uncrossed them. Then changed legs. He tapped his fingers on the conference table. His restless gaze flicked to the door and everyone filing back into the room. He was as agitated as a coked-up lemur.

Dammit. He shouldn't just sit there. He should be chasing down Jami, convincing her to forgive him for beating Dallas' ass, for breaking his promise. Finally try and talk to her about the money her parents had offered him to leave. Instead, he was sitting at Joe's conference table making plans for the tour starting in three months. The thought of hitting the road made his mouth dry and his gut churn like a damn volcano. The hollow feeling he'd had since watching Jami leave the bar—leave him—over two weeks before seeped from his chest and into his limbs with an icy chill.

At Mason's request, Jax had given Jami a little time to process the fight at the bar. He'd texted her a hundred thousand times, but he'd refrained from calling her. Barely. He wanted to give her the space she needed, but if he gave her too much he might lose her forever. Then again, he might have lost her already. And, if he hadn't yet, he would when she learned the full truth.

That thought made his stomach churn harder.

As his bandmates gathered back at the table after the

quick break, he spread out his hands on the table, the bruises still dark and the scrapes an angry red. They didn't hurt any longer. A couple ibuprofen tablets and icing his hands after a brawl were part of the routine. As an artist and musician he knew how to care for his moneymakers. Lots and lots of ice.

Over and over, the fight had rolled around in his head. At first the memory was marble-smooth and clear. Pretty quickly it grew to a full-sized boulder: rough, unpredictable, overwhelming. But each time he analyzed his feelings and each time he came to the same conclusion.

Respect. Rage. Regret.

He didn't want to admit it, wished he could feel worse about smashing that asshat in the face, but Jax had grown two feet taller and his chest had expanded to fill the room when he'd landed that first punch on Gale's ugly mug. After that it was game on. He put everything he had into beating that fucker and making him pay for his callous disregard for someone as precious as Jami.

Still, he couldn't understand how a man could treat a woman like that under any circumstances. The thought made his whole body seethe with molten rage, heating his frozen blood, burning him from the inside out. He could see it…could see a younger Jami tracking down Dallas at a party. Her nervous excitement to tell him her unexpected news, her disappointment at seeing him with another woman. What he couldn't stop seeing was Dallas hitting her in the belly and tossing her against the wall. Jami was tiny. Fierce, yes, but so small. Dallas wasn't as tall as Jax, but he was a whole head taller than Jami and twice as wide. Not to mention a football player.

What kind of monster did that?

Apparently a lot of men did, or Quirk and other places like it wouldn't exist. Kids like Calvin and his mom wouldn't bear the scars on their faces and in their souls if men could control themselves, their need to hurt, to conquer, to control at all costs.

Glancing down at his phone, he hoped to see a text or missed call from Jami, but knew there'd be nothing. Not because he hadn't felt his phone buzz in his pocket, but because he knew Jami well enough to understand where she was. She was in a very dark, very lonely place, one that wouldn't allow her to call him.

"Okay." Joe sat at the head of the table and clapped his hands together once, the sound a sharp gunshot bouncing off the glass wall and startling Jax out of his pity party. "Now that the first tour and merchandising contracts have been handled by Jami, as well as the negotiations for the recording contract, and we've covered the tour dates and travel logistics, we should probably finish up with our first show next weekend."

Jami. Hearing her name twisted his insides and hurt his head. He felt scraped raw.

"Oh, and here she is with our copies of the contracts."

Jax's breath stuttered. She who? Not Jami. Here?

He swung his head back toward the door and there she stood, gorgeous in a pink suit, every button on her white blouse buttoned tightly. Her hair was pulled back in a snug, smooth ponytail, not her usual French twist, her blond hair bright and shiny under the office lights. She looked beautiful, but he could see the dark circles shadowing her eyes and grim set of her lips. Her eyes flicked to his as she clutched the thick folders to her belly, but she quickly looked back toward Joe.

"I'm sorry. I didn't mean to interrupt. I hadn't realized you were meeting. I came by to drop the contracts off." Her voice was wobbly and her eyes darted from person to person.

"We were just wrapping up. Do you have a minute?"

She nodded, and Joe waved her over next to him. "Come sit for a few minutes. We were getting ready to discuss the benefit show next weekend."

She smiled with a politeness that didn't reach her eyes and moved to the chair Joe indicated. As she passed, her back rigid as a pole, she didn't look over at Jax. No matter how hard he willed her to, she wouldn't do it. She shifted her head to the side like the wall was suddenly fascinating instead of boring and beige. But her ignoring him didn't prevent him from watching her. Or smelling the veritable fucking flower garden she exuded when she strode by.

God, he'd missed her. After two weeks without her, watching her fiddle with her pearl choker made his insides ache and his skin tight like a shirt that was left too long in the dryer. He needed to fix this thing with her, because he wasn't quite sure he could survive losing her again. The life he'd been living so far was a shadow of what he felt when he was with her. He didn't want to go back to that. Somehow he had to reach her, get past her walls.

"Okay, folks, I'm passing down the outline Jolt sent over for the show." Joe turned to face Jami on his right. "Both the venue and the band have agreed to donate ticket returns and forty percent of all food and booze to the center. Also, since it's an all-ages show, we got some special tickets for you to hand out to Quirk families and volunteers." He passed down the stack of colorful printed tickets.

"Joe…you guys, I'm so grateful for everything you're doing. I don't know how to thank you." Jami's voice lost its strength and her hands shook as Mandi handed her the tickets. He loved how his rough-around-the-edges sister held Jami's hand a little longer than necessary and gave her a reassuring smile. His heart grew a little more, taking up a little more space in his hollow chest. He loved those two women more than he'd ever thought possible. But the way Jami avoided his gaze was troubling.

They weren't done. Not by a long shot. He needed to apologize for losing it at the bar. Tell her the rest of the story. He had to make her see that he loved her.

Before he realized it, the meeting was over and everyone was preparing to leave. His head snapped back and forth. Where was Jami? His pulse quickened and his heart began to race.

Jax lurched to his feet and ran from the conference, slamming into Marco's shoulder. "Whoa, dude. Take it easy. She's got those little tiny legs." He scissored his massive fingers like a running stick figure. "And you're a runner. You'll catch her," he said before Jax turned and kept running. As he hit the front door, he thought he heard Joe mutter something about men always chasing women out of his office.

"Jami, stop!" His voice sent goose bumps down her arms, like it always did.

Even before he called out, Jami knew he'd follow her into the parking lot. Damn man would probably follow her home if she didn't confront him right then. He couldn't help it. She'd tried to sneak out and get a head start on him, but this was probably for the best. It was time for all of this to come to end.

She turned on her heel as he rushed up to her. Reaching back to steady herself on her car, she tried to keep her face a mask of indifference. It was now or never. If he got her alone, she knew without a doubt she'd surrender to her true feelings and give in to him. Despite everything. Despite his betrayal. Despite the fact that he was leaving and would keep leaving.

"I'm sorry," Jackson said. "I can't say it enough. If you need me to I'll tattoo it on my body so you see it every time you look at me. I lost it with Gale. I broke my promise, but I won't ever do it again. I need you to believe that." His eyes were fierce, staring into her eyes, right to her soul. This was going to be harder and more painful than she thought.

"It's not about Dallas. It's not even about the fight. It's what I realized, what I've known all along. We come from different worlds, Jackson. We don't belong together," she cried, hating the shake in her voice.

"You're wrong."

"I'm not." Why couldn't he let her go? He just had to be so stubborn.

"I can tell by the look on your face what you're gonna say next. That's how well I know you." A lock of his dark hair fell forward over one eye, giving him an almost piratical look.

Time to rip the bandage off. Quick and sharp, but

then he'd get over it. And maybe so would she. "You don't know me. You think you do, but you don't."

"Bullshit. I do. And you know it. That's what really scares you, isn't it?" If his beautiful face and long, lean body didn't break her heart, the dark pain in his eyes surely would.

"I can't…" *Too much. Don't slip. Stay strong. Let him go. He broke his promise. And he lied about why he left.*

"Can't what, Jami? Tell me you love me? You don't have to. I already know you do."

She would never be able to tell him. Once she told him the truth, the real truth of how deeply she loved him and how much he'd anchored her, then he'd never let her go.

"What then? Is it my job? Is it your job?" he asked raising his voice. "We can fix all that shit."

"No, Jackson, we can't. We can't fix the fact that you took money from my parents to leave me. Now I know what you were keeping from me, and I'm not talking about the money they gave your dad." Her eyes began to water, and her chest hurt like little pieces of her broken heart still floated around inside, stabbing her insides. "One of things I adored most about you was your integrity. You didn't take shit from anyone, my parents, your dad, no one. But now…"

He placed his hands on her shoulders, and she resisted the impulse to lean into his body.

"Sunshine, I'm sorry I didn't tell you. I wanted to, but I didn't want to scare you away. When your parents confronted me and told me I was trash, I was hurt and angry. Later, I tried to return the check, but they sent it back every time."

She rolled her eyes. "How convenient for you."

"I donated it to Quirk, Jami. As soon as you told me about the work you do there. The entire $15,000. I only took it in the first place to try and stick it to them. It was an impulse. An impulse that ruined everything."

The anonymous donation. It had been Jackson. Her chest tightened again.

"What a convenient way to assuage your guilt, Jackson. It doesn't matter anyway. It's too late," she nearly spat. It was time to end this.

"No, babe. It's never too late. I am only me when I have you in my life. When you're with me, everything makes sense."

"I have my life and you have yours. And they're not compatible. Go be a rock star. Quit screwing with my life. I'm not for sale anymore, Jackson. I'll be fine. This was fun. To catch up and everything—"

Despite the angry fire in his eyes, his face suddenly looked tired. Sad. Her lips began to quiver, and tears threatened at the back of her eyes. God, this was worse pain than she'd ever felt. Worse than losing her unborn baby. Worse than Jackson leaving her.

"Fun!?" He was yelling now. "*Fun*. I love you, Jami. You're it for me. I know we can make it work." He lowered his voice and looked around the still-empty lot. "All your reasons are excuses! What's this really about? Their dirty money? They didn't buy me off. I regretted the money the second I took it. Is this about me knowing your secret, babe? Because if it is, all I feel is hurt for you and what you went through. Alone." He hugged her close and she let him. Just one more time in his arms. "But you're not alone anymore, sunshine. I love you.

And I hope," he said softly, "that one day you'll want to have a dozen beautiful little babies together, Jami. If you don't, then we'll deal with that, too. I love you. I will do whatever it takes to make this work. I can't let you go again."

Her courage wavered for a moment. What if they could? What if they could fix it all—the past, her fear, his touring and fame, her shitty job, her crappy family? And what would it be like to have a family with a man like him? He would make an insanely amazing father. So calm and cool. So sweet and protective.

She shook her head again. Harder. Hard enough to shake loose her silly fantasies about making a life with Jackson.

"Tell me it's over then," he challenged, his jaw rigid except for the twitch of muscle near his mouth.

She needed to put an end to this torture. Then she ripped her heart from her chest and held it in her hand. "It's over," she whispered.

"You can say it, but I love you just the same. It doesn't change a motherfucking thing, sunshine. We are meant to be together, and you're fucking with fate."

But it did. It changed everything. She'd thought all along that he was the bad boy, the broken rebel. But it had been her, hadn't it? She was the one doomed. She was the one undeserving of his light and his love. She wasn't selfish enough to take it from him. He deserved his dreams—his art, his music. She would be stuck in her fear and pain forever. He didn't deserve any of that.

"Jackson." Her voice cracked, matching her shattered heart. "I can't do this anymore. Go be the rock-star artist you were meant to be."

"Fuck that. It doesn't mean anything without you. What the hell are you doing, Jami? Stop living your life for everyone else. Your past doesn't own you. Your parents are assholes. They don't see the real you and maybe they never will. And Dallas Gale never really had you, did he?" He grabbed her chin, forcing her to look directly into his beautiful gold-flecked eyes. Overwhelmed by the emotion there, she let her lids drop and felt the tears finally slide down her cheeks.

"Open your eyes and look at me. Can't you see how much I love you? How much I've always loved you?"

Her phone started to buzz and she tugged her chin free from his grip to reach for her bag.

"I don't love you, Jackson," she said, metaphorically tossing her sputtering heart against the wall. "I don't want to have kids. Not with you. Not with anyone." She ripped her gaze from his as she pulled her phone to her ear and turned her back.

"Don't." He said it so softly, pleading as she walked away. "Please don't answer that."

"Dillon."

She was only half listening to her boss when she climbed into her car, slammed the door shut, turned it on, and drove away from the only man she would ever love.

Chapter 21

JAMI DIDN'T LOVE HIM. HE LOVED HER WITH ALL HIS heart, and she didn't love him. She didn't fucking love him. Jax stared at the ceiling over his bed as a wave of nausea churned in his gut.

His sister pounded on the door. He knew it was Mandi because she'd been pounding on his door every night since Jami had walked away from him the week before. "Go away, Amanda. I'm fine." He flung his forearm over his eyes.

He wasn't fine. He was so far from fine he might as well be walking on the damn sun.

"Open the door, loser!" Bowen called out. "Quit feeling sorry for yourself."

He pulled his raggedy ass out of bed and yanked the door open, flooding the room with light. Bowen swore and followed him back into the room. "Dude, you fucking reek. When's the last time you showered? You haven't been to work. You haven't been to practice. What the fuck is going on with you?"

Jax lifted his arm and smelled himself. Bowen was right, he was riper than a brown banana. He flopped back down on his bed and groaned. He avoided looking at his friend, feeling like it was his own turn in the intervention hot seat.

Might as well lay it all out there. "She'll never forgive me. She doesn't love me. And I'm so fucking in love with her I can't see straight, okay? I blew it when I left her five years ago. And then completely obliterated it when I pummeled Gale."

"You're kind of pathetic right now, Jax." Bowen punched his arm, but Jax didn't flinch. Maybe the physical pain would distract him from the existential trough of motherfucking doom he was wallowing in.

"I know. I'll get over it. Right now I can't think about anything else but her standing there saying she didn't love me and turning her back on me." He groaned and rolled over toward the wall.

"That's not how I heard it. Kevan said she does love you. Jami cried all night in her arms while she drank herself stupid."

What? Jami was crying? That must mean something, right?

Jax sat up and glared at his friend, who looked really uncomfortable talking about women in relation to love and not banging. "What did she say?"

"That's not my story to tell."

And what did it really matter anyway? She'd said the words, she might as well have meant them. He couldn't keep doing this. The back and forth. The push and pull.

He'd told her flat-out that at some point he'd stop chasing her and she'd have to come for him. Until she did that, he'd never really know where she stood. She could don her armor at any moment and run back to the safety of the Dillon security blanket or her goddamn "plan."

"It's too late. We're done. I'm going on tour, and she's moving on."

"Never realized you were such a pussy," Bowen said, moving toward the door.

"What the hell am I supposed to do?" Jax yelled, throwing a pillow at his friend and missing by a foot.

"You can start with a shower. Then get yourself to practice before your show tomorrow night."

"What about Jami?" Jax hated how whiny he sounded, but Bowen had fed him a little morsel of hope, and he was starting to feel hungry for more.

"Well, I have some ideas about that." And Bowen began to explain a plan that might work. If only Jami would meet him halfway. If only she would fight for them.

☆☆☆

Jami looked at her nearly barren office, feeling far emptier than the moving box in front of her. Two years at the firm, and she had almost nothing to show for it. Her diplomas, a handful of notebooks, a mousepad, and a torn note with Jackson's phone number on it. Sad and pathetic. No personal pictures. No emotional going-away party. Not even an email from her parents telling her what a huge disappointment she was. Nope. Nothing.

She sniffed and blew her sore nose on a tissue. She was definitely a big snotty mess. Crying all night really took a toll on a woman. She didn't need to look in the mirror to know she looked like shit. Felt like it, too. Shoving the note in the old hoodie she wore that still smelled of Jackson, she felt that old emptiness expand in her chest. But she also felt something else. Something that felt a lot like relief. And hope.

After their confrontation in Joe's parking lot, she'd driven straight home and drunk an entire bottle of wine. She'd called Kevan, of all people, who came over immediately and spent the night holding her, rocking her and telling her everything would be okay because love always wins. But only if Jami put on her big-girl panties and quit fucking around. So that's what she'd done. Starkly sober the next morning, she'd thrown on the only pair of jeans she owned and a T-shirt and driven straight to her parents' house.

They'd been smugly happy to see her before she told them they were no longer invited to control her emotions or her life. She was drawing the line. Her life, her rules. They'd told her to leave. So she had, finally free of their oppressive manipulations and emotional blackmail.

The following day, she went to see Karen about the director position and then quit her job. That had been kind of fun. For once, she was taking real control, not just pretending. Quitting was the first step of many, she hoped, in the right direction.

Maybe back toward Jackson, if he'd have her. Toward the future. Toward home. Because that's what Jackson was to her: home. His calm, protective manner was enough to quell her storm, her chaos. The really amazing thing was that Jackson didn't see it as chaos. He saw her the way she was. He loved her rules as much as he loved the wildness bubbling below the surface of her carefully fabricated exterior. But had she pushed him too far away this time?

"You all packed up?"

She looked up to see Suzanne standing at the door-way, impeccable in a red pencil skirt and matching fitted jacket. She was twisting her hands in front of her, showing a nervousness that Jami had never seen before. "Ready to move on?"

"Yep. Thank you for the opportunity, Suzanne. I'm sorry it didn't work out, but I'm sure you'll find someone to replace me pretty easily." She smiled. Frankly, she couldn't care less whether or not they replaced her quickly. She couldn't care less what any of them did. Yes, they'd given her a job fresh out of school, but they'd never utilized her skills.

Fuck her. Fuck them.

Jami snorted, not caring whether or not it was appropriate or what Suzanne might think. Jackson had been right. She needed to figure out who she really was and to stop living her life for everyone else. After throwing the last few items from her desk into the box, she stood. Turning, she was surprised to see Suzanne still standing there.

"What do you want, Suzanne? I signed all the paperwork, turned in my files and keys. What more could you possibly need from me?"

Suzanne sighed, long and hard. "An apology."

What the hell? Seriously? What could Jami possibly have to apologize to any of the Horndeckers for? She was seconds away from shoving Suzanne out of the way and storming out. Either that or throwing her box down and handling it Jackson's way. She smiled to herself. Actually, Jackson only threw down for her when he felt she was hurt. And she hurt right now, but this she could take care of her own.

Suzanne held up hands. "Whoa. It's not what you think," she said the words quickly. "I mean I owe you an apology."

Jami shifted the box to her side, settling it on to her hip. "Go on."

"Carl called your dad after you interviewed here. They made a deal. Carl would hire you but make you feel useless. And keep an eye on you."

"Why?" It sounded like something her father would do. Carl had always been so solicitous when it came to her father, but Jami had never understood his motivation.

"Carl wanted to be buddies with your dad. He's a powerful guy." Suzanne shrugged her narrow shoulders. "And your dad wanted you to be miserable enough to go work for his firm." They used her to make political patty-cake with her father without ever letting her actually practice law.

They stood there silently for a moment staring at each other. "So I'm sorry, Jami. I'm sorry I was a bitch. I'm sorry I went along with Carl and your dad, and I'm sorry we didn't make you happier here. You really are brilliant, and you're going to be a phenomenal attorney wherever you're going." She pursed her lips, smooshing them from side to side. "Can I ask where you're going?"

Jami felt the smile start in her toes and move through her body until it finally reached her mouth. "I've accepted a position as the codirector of the Portland Community Women's Resource Center."

"Really?" Suzanne squeaked, looking as if she were somewhere else. "I always wanted to do something like that. Make the world better. That's awesome you're actually doing it."

Jami walked to the door and Suzanne stepped aside so she could pass. "You should live your own life, Suzanne. I spent way too long pretending I was someone else to make other people happy. But I was miserable.

I choose to be happy. I choose to be me…whoever that turns out to be."

She left Suzanne staring after her as she walked to the lobby and waited for the elevator. When one of the paralegals asked her where she was going, she smiled and said, "I'm going to get my rock star."

Chapter 22

JAMI HAD BEEN WATCHING THE ENTRANCE OF THE Crystal Rose Grill for the last hour, waiting for Jackson and his long legs to walk through the door. She knew he'd be there. No matter how upset or angry he was with her, there was no way Jackson Paige would disappoint the kids and fans. Wouldn't happen.

What she didn't know and what she was terrified to even consider, was whether or not Jackson would take her back. The real her. The ugly, not perfect, not always prim-and-proper Jami. Or was it too late? Had she damaged their connection forever when she'd sliced it through with her words?

Before too long, she was dragged off by Joe and various sponsors. Shaking hands, introducing families and donors, fans and bands. There wasn't any time for her to stare morosely at the door and long for her lost love. She had a benefit to put on, and the show must go on.

When Kevan strutted up dressed in a deep maroon dress—something Marilyn Monroe herself would've worn—and black sky-high peep-toe heels, Jami felt relief flood her system. Somehow the crazy pinup businesswoman had become someone she truly trusted and made her feel anchored, loved. Kevan hip-checked her, which turned into more of a side check because of their height difference.

"He'll be here, you know," she yelled over Bowen and Nathan's band, Toast, starting the last song of their set.

Jami nodded. "I hope so. I don't know if I've screwed it up too badly. If it's too late."

"Do you love him?"

"Yes. Very much. I think I always have."

Kevan nudged her with her elbow and pointed to the door. "Then go tell him."

She saw him before he saw her. He sauntered in, all long limbs and broad shoulders, wearing those damn leather pants and a Jack White tour T-shirt. His hair was styled back and he had a pretty substantial beard growing in. She marveled again that such a beautiful man loved her. Or he had, anyway, until she had gone and messed it up by lying to him.

His gaze caught hers, and his face lit with a smile for a moment, before it slid away and fell into a more neutral expression. When two women and a man greeted him, she lost sight of him in the crowded venue. As she started across the room, the lights went up and Karen's voice boomed over the sound system.

"Let's give it up for local favorites, Toast." And the crowd went berserk, yelling and screaming.

Damn. She had work to do.

"Now before we bring on the big show, our local heavy-metal heroes, Manix Curse…" She paused until the clapping and hollering stopped. "I'd like to introduce the two new directors for the Portland Community Women's Resource Center. Ella and Jami, please come up here."

The next few minutes were a blur as both Ella and

Jami took turns talking about Quirk and thanking every-one involved in the fundraiser. Although she couldn't see him with the bright lights shining, she could feel his eyes burning through whatever barriers she had left. They were all gone. She was cracked wide open for him to see everything. For everyone to see it all.

As Karen was introducing Manix Curse, Jami made her way down the steps backstage. Suddenly she felt a familiar set of hands wrap around her shoulders from behind.

She smiled to herself, relief making her legs almost buckle. "What's this all about, sunshine?" She loved the feeling of his hands on her body and the way he pressed into her, surrounding her in his strength—strength she was going to need.

Turning with his hands still on her shoulders, she smiled up at him. "This is me coming after you." The surprise in his eyes sent ribbons of shame through her, but she swallowed and continued. "I choose you, Jackson Paige. I will always fight for us."

Before he could respond, Marco and Conner ran by, each grabbed one of his arms and dragged him up onto the stage. "This isn't over, sunshine," he yelled over his shoulder.

She hoped that was true. Hoped he meant their life together and not only the conversation. She was going to move forward no matter what happened, but being with Jackson and then not being with him was akin to being awake and then being asleep. Night and day.

She took a deep breath, letting the air fill all her dark hollow places, and then exhaled slowly. Closing her eyes and leaning against the wall backstage, she heard Jackson yell and start pounding his drum kit. She could feel the thumping through the wall, feel his power, his passion, and his pain. Soon the others joined him and the party was on.

When she opened her eyes, Jami smiled and walked down the hall and back out to the front area where Kevan and Mason had saved a seat for her. She loved seeing her big bad brother go to mush for Kevan. Jami didn't believe there was one single thing Mason wouldn't do for her, and vice versa. Their love was real and true and heartbreakingly beautiful.

She plopped down next to them in the empty chair to enjoy the show and wondered if she and Jackson had a chance at something as precious as what Mason and Kevan had found.

Or if they'd missed their chance altogether.

Two hours later, he finally pulled up to her house in his truck. After the show, he'd been surprised when Mason handed him a note from Jami. His heart had sunk. She was ending it for good. Forever. But then he opened and read it.

> J—
>
> *If you'd like to finish our conversation, please meet me at my house after the show.*
>
> —J

Not a lot to go on there. They did need to talk. But where was her head? The announcement about her and Ella heading up Quirk had flipped everything on its head. He'd gone to the show thinking there would be no joy, no future with the woman he loved. In fact, he'd been prepared to beg her to back to him or serenade her or something. Instead it was exactly the opposite. Maybe she had forgiven him. Could she let go of their past so they could have a future?

After saying good-bye to everyone, he'd driven home to take a quick shower and put on a fresh set of clothes. Less than twenty minutes later, he was out the door and on the way to her part of town.

When he finally knocked on the door, he had to force himself not to pound it down. He'd spent nearly three weeks without her. A fucking long, miserable twenty-one days of hell. He wanted to hold her in his arms, touch her face, run her hair through his fingers. Placing his hand on her shoulders before Manix's set had relit the fire in his veins. And his dick. One platonic touch of Jami's skin and—instaboner.

She swung the door open and tentatively moved forward as if to hug him, but then stepped back to let him in.

But he didn't move. "What am I doing here, Jami?" The hurt on her face tightened around his heart, filling him with guilt.

She closed her eyes for a moment and took a deep breath. He noticed she'd changed from the short, sparkly silver getup she'd been wearing earlier into a thigh-length pink plaid robe. *Fuck*. He could see her creamy thighs beneath the silky material. He was a goner if he didn't keep his focus elsewhere.

He looked up to see her staring at him. "We need to talk."

No more games. No more avoiding the real stuff.

This was it and he was going for it. "What are we talking about?"

"Us, Jackson. What happened…you know…everything. Please come in."

He walked past, trying to ignore the scent of flowers that permeated his nose. God, she smelled so fucking good. How the hell was he supposed to concentrate with her thighs on display and her smelling like goddamn roses?

He stopped abruptly. The house was dark except for the ethereal glow of candles everywhere. Soft music played in the background. Paolo Nutini. Sexy. Perfect. She had set the scene for seduction, for love. This was not a break-up-and-get-on-with-your-life discussion. This was a conversation with great potential. Suddenly his mood shifted like the sun had come out after weeks of Portland rain. His own sunshine.

He sat on the couch and she handed him a beer before settling across from him, a glass of wine sitting on the table in front of her.

She tucked her knees under her and pulled a small quilt over legs. "Where do I start?"

"Start with how you love me, but you're too much of a fucking coward to say it."

"I'm not a coward." He could see her cheeks blush in the candlelight.

"Liar."

"I'm a coward and a liar? Wow. Don't pull any punches, Jackson."

"Yep. A coward and a liar."

"Fuck you." Her voice was a coarse whisper. Good. Finally something.

"No, fuck you, Jami. I love you. I'm not afraid to say it. I'm not afraid to yell it." He leaned forward and grabbed her shoulder with one hand and tipped her chin up so he could see her face. "But I'm done living a lie. I. Love. You." He dropped his hands and shrugged, looking away toward the fireplace. Her hand grabbed his. He didn't turn to face her, but heard her sob.

"Look at me, please," she pleaded.

He turned and saw the fear in her eyes, but he also saw the set of her shoulders. Determined. "I'm so afraid, Jackson. I can't hand you my heart and have you trample and toss it again." Her voice sounded so quiet, but solid, strong. Full of resolution.

"I won't, Jami." And he meant it. He was never giving her up again. Never.

She stood and tugged his hand. He stood slowly and took a half step toward her. Her chest pushed against him, and she stared up into his eyes. For the first time, it felt as if she was allowing him to see the real her, and it made him gasp.

"Hello, Jami," he whispered and caressed her cheek with his thumb, outlining her jaw, her lips.

"Hello, Jackson." She smiled. Sweet and dark and full of love.

"Was there something you wanted to tell me?"

She nodded. "Yes."

"Well…"

"Well…my feelings for you run so deep and are so strong it took me a while to realize that it was only love. Hey, don't frown. Hear me out." She wrapped her arms around his waist and laid her head on his chest. "What I feel for you seems so crucial, so important, it was almost overwhelming. It didn't seem normal. I mean, how could something so powerful be plain old love?" She pulled back and looked pleadingly into his eyes.

"I think I let my parents' bullshit cloud my self-worth, but also my definitions. I mean, is it even healthy how much I love you? I feel like I'm missing something of myself when you're gone. Did that make me codependent and sick like some of the men that I see at the center chasing after their broken relationships, saying they love their girlfriends and wives, when really it's something so much darker, uglier?

"But then I realized you actually make me better. You encourage me to be who I really am and not because it benefits you. Why do you do that, Jackson? Why do you push me to do things that might actually keep me from being with you? Tell me." Her last words were delivered on a sob and tears began to slide down her cheeks.

"You know why, sunshine."

She shook her head. "I need you to tell me."

"It's for the same twisted reason you thought you had to break up with me and told me to go on tour. I do it because I love you. I genuinely fucking love you. And your happiness matters more to me than anything else."

She smiled. That gorgeous I-will-conquer-the-world-for-you smile. And Jax knew then that any of the remaining reservations she had had taken a hike because the woman in his arms was his. All his.

"I took the job at Quirk," she said against his chest and he tightened his arms around her.

"And I'm so fucking proud of you."

"I forgive you for everything. For taking the money.

For staying with your sister. I probably wasn't ready for you back then anyway."

He took a deep breath, one filled with hope and love and the future. "Thank you, baby."

"And I'll be here waiting for you when you get back from your tours. I will always be here waiting for you to come home. Back to me."

"I know you will. But I've had my contract amended."

She pulled back and looked at him. "What?"

"Don't worry, counselor. I did it for you. For us. A surprise." When she didn't say anything, he smiled. He liked ruffling his girl's feathers. "My new tour amendment stipulates that I will be on tour one month on and one month off, or week on, week off. It depends."

"I don't understand." The sweet smile and her scrunched forehead gave her an almost childish look. He kissed her nose and sat down, pulling her down on the couch next to him.

"Declan, Toast's drummer, is going to sit in for me on tour. I'll only be on the road for half the tour, like four weeks at a time with a four-week break in between. That way I can help Tony and Nathan keep the shop going when the band's on tour, since it's basically all of Tatuaggio. It also means I can help run the art program at the center."

Tears continued to slide down her face. But then she grinned. A smile that made the whole room blindingly bright.

"Before you say anything. I need you to know I did it for you *and* I did it for me. I need this." He waved his hand between them. "I've never been happier than I am with you. I've always loved you. Maybe that's why I ran away the first time. I was terrified that you were the one and that I was going to fuck it up like my dad."

"But you're not your dad."

"No. I'm not. And you have brought me back to life. I want whatever life we can make together. We have a second chance." He kissed her gently, brushing his mouth against hers, but she bit her sharp teeth into his bottom lip and tugged.

"I missed you, Jackson." She reached around and unpeeled his hand from her back, tucked it into the front of her robe where—lo and be-fucking-hold—Jami was naked. Her nipples were already hard as he cupped her breast and flicked his thumb over the tight bud. Jax pulled free and grabbed her by the hips, yanking her over his body so she straddled his thighs, and she ground her pussy against his thickening cock.

"Tell me what you want." He pulled her down tight against him and kissed her with fierce determination, telling her with his mouth and his hands that she would always be his. And he hers.

"You. I want you. All of you. I want to feel you push into me. I want to come apart under your hands. Your mouth." Her words created a tornado inside his chest that quickly wiped out any rational thought as it whipped through his body and went straight to his cock. "I want to smell you all over me, know that you're mine."

He growled. She was testing his limits, threatening his steely control as he wrapped his fingers around her ass cheeks and squeezed. She arched into his body and cried out. Her hands dug under his shirt and she pulled at it, forcing him to let go of his prize and raise his arms over his head as she ripped it off. He toed his shoes off and she unbuttoned his jeans. Tugging her robe down and letting it drop to the floor, she stood naked in front of him. Her curvaceous body glowed in the candlelight. Angelic. Resplendent. Gorgeous.

"You're so fucking beautiful," he said as he ditched his pants and boxers in time for her to drop to her knees and look up through her light lashes. Her eyes locked with his as she dipped her head and took him deep into her mouth. His woman wasn't fucking around.

She wrapped her hand around his cock and began to stroke as she moved up and down, slowly. He pulled her hair to the side so he could see her stunning face and her pink glossy lips moving up and down on him. Feeling overwhelmed and not wanting to let their sexual reunion be over too quickly, he pulled her up and held her over his cock. She reached down and lined him up with her opening, moving slowly down with a twist of her hips.

Her gasp and wide eyes did something to his insides. That thing that had been growing, unfolding in his chest busted wide open. There was no longer the achy loneliness, not even a trace of it. This woman's sunshine took away all his darkness and filled it with life, with light.

He let her move up and down on him, letting her set the pace and take what she needed. But the look in her eyes and the tilt of her lips had him reaching up to cup her face.

"I love you. I fucking love you. We need to get married."

She laughed. "Really, rock star, that's your proposal?"

"Yep. And I'll keep asking every day until you say yes."

She swiveled her hips and he reached down to pinch her clit. She screamed his name. And the one word he really needed to hear: "Yes." Then her walls began to quiver and he felt the lightning in the soles of his feet before he exploded inside her, pouring his seed into her body as she shook and cried out.

Afterward, as they lay in her bed and listened to the song of rain echoing on her roof, he held her snug to his side. Where she fit perfectly. She was tracing circles on his hand when she stopped and squeezed his hand three times.

"Does that mean something?"

"Hmmm. It's a secret code between Mason and me. It means 'I love you.'"

He smiled and leaned over to kiss her. "I knew you loved me. You did that before. That day at practice. Did you know then?"

"Probably. Oh shit," she muttered and sat up.

"What's wrong?"

"We didn't use a condom and I'm not on the pill." Her face paled. He grabbed her hand and squeezed three times, and her expression softened.

"And you don't want kids."

She flushed. "No. I do. I lied. I mean, I'm afraid of having them. But I want them."

"With me?"

"Only you." She smiled, weak and watery. "Do you want kids?"

He nodded and pulled her underneath him where he proceeded to make love to her again.

Later that night, after they'd eaten a post-concert, post-sex meal of cookies and root beer, she kissed his chest.

"I love you, Jackson Paige. Now go to sleep."

He pinched her nipple with a playful tweak. "Why? Got plans tomorrow?"

"Yep. And so do you."

He groaned, not looking forward to an early morning on little sleep. Maybe he could convince her to sleep in. "Oh yeah, what's that?"

"We have an art and music program to get off the ground tomorrow."

"And the adventure begins."

And so the adventure began.

Epilogue

JAMI WALKED INTO TATUAGGIO WITH HER ARMS FULL of paper bags to find Mason and Kevan's party already in full swing. Because her new group of friends—the one her brother had discovered and Jackson had pulled her kicking and screaming into—had their combined bachelor-bachelorette party at a tattoo parlor. Free tattoos for everyone. She laughed to herself. If this wasn't irony, she didn't know what the hell was.

All the usual suspects where there. Some were under the gun—the tattoo machine—and others had started on the keg of beer from the brewpub around the corner. Marco was talking with Ella and Mandi on the couches. Nathan was having a heated discussion with Tony's daughter, Isabella. Conner was working on Bowen's wrist. Joe and Tony were having beers at his counter. And Kevan and Quinley, the shop's newest employee, were looking at something on the front desk's computer screen while Mason leaned against the wall, purveying the scene. Electronica music blared over the speakers, and the partiers yelled over the music. Just another day with this crazy nutball group of people. Her family. And she loved them.

"Food's here," she called out to the group as she went about setting up the appetizers on the table in the front lobby.

"Hey, sunshine," Jackson, who was still drinking

soda and working on an ankle piece for Gabby, called out. She walked over to him, taking in his long, tall body, his elegant hands creating art on her friend. He was beautiful. Art creating art. She sighed. And he was hers.

"I was telling Gabby about the first time you came in here. Apparently you ran to her and Ella and told them all about me." He smirked, but kept working on the purple scrolls and swirls on Gabby's foot. "I knew it then, you know. I knew I would get you back."

She felt the blush start on her neck and move up to her cheeks. His honesty and openness nearly brought her to her knees every day. She stood by her brother and nibbled on a cracker while Jackson cleaned up Gabby's ankle and then sanitized his station. Finally, he snapped off his gloves and tossed them in the garbage before walking over to her with a mischievous look in eyes. Frankly, that was an everyday occurrence, since the word personified her boyfriend, but he looked particularly impish—if that were even possible—at that moment.

When he reached her he held out his hands and she took them in hers, instantly warmed by his grip and the hold he had on her. She went to move into him, but he did something completely unexpected and dropped to a knee, still holding her hands. He laughed and his smile reached the stars. "You should see your face right now, sunshine. Fucking radiant."

"What are you doing, Jackson?" she gasped. Someone was sniffling behind her and someone else was all-out crying. He pulled a blue velvet box from his pocket and flipped it open. Nestled in the velvet box was a stunning art deco ring with a large pink diamond in the center.

"I'm proposing, my love. From the very first day I met you, I think I knew you were the one for me. But I was a coward and I ran away. I'm never running away again. I love you, and I want to have a million prissy little babies with you. Will you marry me?"

"You never gave up on me. Even when I was running scared."

"Never give up. Never surrender," he said, and slipped the ring on her finger.

She stared at him, eyes wide and lips pinched together, and then down at the ring. And then she burst out laughing. "You did not just propose to me, Jackson Paige, and then quote *Galaxy Quest*."

He stood and leaned forward. She loved the way his body curved around her smaller one, how she fit so perfectly with him. In everything. "I did, sunshine," he whispered into her ear, and his tongue traced the round of her earlobe. He chuckled when she gasped softly. "Meant it, too. I will never give up on you. On us."

Unshed tears pooled in her eyes, and she smiled, because he was everything good and wonderful. "God, I love you. So much."

He reached around and squeezed her butt. She laughed, loving the way it fit in his palms. "It's because I'm rad in bed, right?"

"Yes, Jackson, I'm marrying you because you're rad in bed."

"Soooo, that's a yes then?"

"Definitely a yes."

Jami untangled herself from Jackson's arms and sat down on the table at his station. Taking a deep breath, she held out her wrist. "I'm ready."

A huge smile spread across his handsome face. "Yeah?"

She nodded. As he set out the ink cups and prepared the area for her first tattoo, she was struck again by how much her life had changed in such a short time. By how much gratitude she felt to have such loving, kind people. By Jackson. He wrapped his gloved fingers around her wrist to hold it still while he quickly sketched out the small heart on her wrist with a skin marker. Even that professional action sent little fissures of desire through her body.

Leaning forward, with her arm flat on the padded arm of the table, she took in the beautiful man—her man— across from her before she closed her eyes. She felt the sharp pricks of the needles as they began to trace the simple heart he'd designed for her.

Jami was finally free. Free from her own self-imposed prison of the past, free from the suffocating expectations of her parents, free from the hollow loneliness that had become her normal.

BEAUTIFUL MESS PLAYLIST

In times of joy and in times of grief, I almost always turn to music. It acts as a salve to my battered soul, and gives voice to the feelings I cannot. Below is a partial playlist of some of the music that helped me cope during this past year. For complete Spotify and Google Play Music playlists, please visit my website at www.kaseylane.com.

"Come Over" by Sam Hunt
"Under the Influence" by Elle King
"Powerful" by Major Lazer (featuring Ellie Goulding)
"Iron Sky" by Paolo Nutini
"For Whom the Bell Tolls" by Metallica
"Trees" by Twenty One Pilots
"Never Be Like You" by Flume (featuring Kai)
"Buried Alive" by Avenged Sevenfold
"Shy Boy" by JD McPherson
"Forget It" by Getter (featuring Oliver Tree)
"Say My Name" by Scott Bradlee's Postmodern
    Jukebox
"Falling in Love with You Again" by Imelda May
"Fell in Love with a Girl" by The White Stripes
"The End" by In Flames
"A Different World" by Korn (featuring Corey Taylor)
"I Walk the Line" by Halsey
"Summertime" by Parov Stelar (featuring Maya
    Bensalem)

✯ ✯ ✯

ACKNOWLEDGMENTS

As always, it starts with my husband. His love, his encouragement, and his tenacity keep me moving forward when I get frustrated and dramatic about deadlines. Love can't fix all things, but writing love stories helps me cope and create and remember. It gives me hope and provides a place for me to run away to. I hope that romance books do the same for readers...help them remember what is good and beautiful in our very complicated world.

This book was initially for my agent, Cate Hart, because Jax is her true book boyfriend, but I was in the middle of writing this story when the unthinkable happened and my family and loved ones were plummeted into a world of grief. It's hard to write about conflict, and even love, when your whole worldview has changed and everyone around you is in pain. The second half of Jax's story was written on the road as I traveled back and forth between my family and my friend's family. Without the support of the Rustigans, my husband and children, my aunt, and my parents (thanks, Mom, for reading everything I write, and Dad for acting like I'm a rock star), I would never have found the strength to finish this book. I would not have been able to face all those blank pages without the patience of my editor, Cat Clyne, and all the amazing folks at Sourcebooks, and the talent and love of my CPs/writer tribe, Kaylie Newell and RJ Garside, as well as the friendship and support of Adriana Anders, Amanda Bouchet, and Heather Van Fleet. The support of my local writer friends was amazing. They sat next to me at the coffee shop every week while I cried and ranted for months. I love you guys.

If you're suffering or someone you love is struggling, please reach out and ask for help. If you are a survivor, please don't grieve alone. Contact the American Foundation for Suicide Prevention or call the National Suicide Prevention Lifeline at 1-800-273-TALK (8255). ♥♥♥

✯ ✯ ✯

ABOUT THE AUTHOR

Award-winning debut author Kasey Lane writes sexy romances featuring music, hot guys with ink, kick-ass women, and always a happily-ever-after. A California transplant, she lives with her high-school crush turned husband, two smart but devilish kids, two papillons, three cats, and several chickens in the lush Oregon forest. Visit her at www.kaseylane.com.

UNDER HER SKIN

First in an exciting dark contemporary series from debut author Adriana Anders

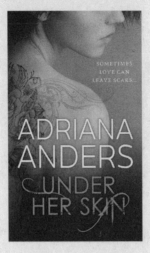

A dark relationship left Uma alone and on the run. Beneath her clothing, she hides a terrible secret—proof of her abuse, tattooed on her skin in a lurid reminder of everything she's survived.

Caught between a brutal past and an uncertain future, Uma is reluctant to bare herself to anyone, much less a rough ex-con whose rage drives him in ways she doesn't understand. But beneath his frightening exterior, Ivan is gentle. Warm. Compassionate. And just as determined to heal Uma's broken heart as he is to destroy the monster who left his mark scrawled across her delicate skin.

For more Adriana Anders, visit:
www.sourcebooks.com

RECKLESS HEARTS

It's three alpha men and a baby in this steamy
contemporary romance series

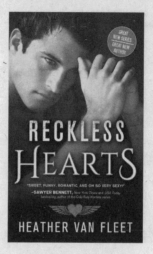

Addison Booker needs a job desperately. She shows up to
interview for a nanny position only to find the sexy, cocky
man she can't get out of her head. Collin Montgomery
knows hiring her is a bad idea—she's the hottest, smartest
woman he's ever met and they disagree about almost
everything—but Addison is so good with little Chloe. And
there's no substitute for chemistry, right?

*"An emotional, heartfelt, and absolutely beautiful
story. I wanted each character to be my best friend."*

**—Jennifer Blackwood, *USA Today*
bestselling author**

For more Heather Van Fleet, visit:
www.sourcebooks.com

BEAUTIFUL CRAZY

First in the Rock-N-Ink series from author Kasey Lane

Kevan Landry has one shot to sign the metal band Manix Curse and get her fledging PR firm off the ground. If she doesn't succeed, she'll lose more than her company.

Mason Dillon heads the most successful music PR firm in Portland and has been commissioned with signing Manix Curse. But after going head-to-head with Kevan over the band, work is the last thing on his mind.

Forced to prove their marketing skills, the pair wages a battle for the band. If they can set aside their differences, they may find together they're the right mix of sexy savvy to conquer the bedroom and the boardroom.

"Kasey Lane gives readers a rockin' romance that sings!"

—**Marie Harte, *New York Times* and *USA Today* bestselling author**

For more Kasey Lane, visit:
www.sourcebooks.com